Praise for Anne Perry
and her
CHARLOTTE AND THOMAS PITT NOVELS

THE CATER STREET HANGMAN

"Pitt's compassion and Charlotte's cleverness make them compatible sleuths as well as extremely congenial characters. . . . Perry has the great gift of making it all seem immediate and very much alive."

—*The Philadelphia Inquirer*

TRAITOR'S GATE

"Perry's infallible feeling for historical moment yields animated political views of Victorian society at play and tantalizing glimpses of a confident, assertive creature known as 'the new woman.' "

—*The New York Times Book Review*

BLUEGATE FIELDS

"For readers longing to be in 1890s London, Perry's tales are just the ticket."

—*Chicago Tribune*

FARRIERS' LANE

"Gripping and intense . . . [Anne Perry's] characters are authentically and appealingly drawn, and her plot is sinister."

—*Booklist*

By Anne Perry

Featuring William Monk

The Face of a Stranger
A Dangerous Mourning
Defend and Betray
A Sudden, Fearful Death
The Sins of the Wolf
Cain His Brother
Weighed in the Balance
The Silent Cry
A Breach of Promise
The Twisted Root
Slaves of Obsession
Funeral in Blue
Death of a Stranger
The Shifting Tide
Dark Assassin
Execution Dock
Acceptable Loss
A Sunless Sea
Blind Justice
Blood on the Water
Corridors of the Night
Revenge in a Cold River
An Echo of Murder

Featuring Charlotte and Thomas Pitt

The Cater Street Hangman
Callander Square
Paragon Walk
Resurrection Row
Bluegate Fields
Rutland Place
Death in the Devil's Acre
Cardington Crescent
Silence in the Hanover Close
Bethlehem Road
Highgate Rise
Belgrave Square
Farriers' Lane
The Hyde Park Headsman
Traitor's Gate
Pentecost Alley
Ashworth Hall
Brunswick Gardens
Bedford Square
Half Moon Street
The Whitechapel Conspiracy
Southampton Row
Seven Dials
Long Spoon Lane
Buckingham Palace Gardens
Treason at Lisson Grove
Dorchester Terrace
Midnight at Marble Arch
Death on Blackheath
The Angel Court Affair
Treachery at Lancaster Gate
Murder on the Serpentine

ASHWORTH HALL

A CHARLOTTE AND THOMAS PITT NOVEL

Anne Perry

Ballantine Books Trade Paperbacks
New York

2011 Ballantine Books Trade Paperback Edition

Published in the United States by Ballantine Books,
an imprint of The Random House Publishing Group,
a division of Random House, Inc., New York.

Originally published in hardcover in the United States by Fawcett Books,
an imprint of The Random House Publishing Group,
a division of Random House, Inc., in 1997.

Library of Congress Cataloging-in-Publication Data

Perry, Anne.
Ashworth Hall / Anne Perry.
p. cm.
ISBN 978-0-345-51421-9
ISBN 978-0-307-76767-7 (ebook)
I. Title.
PR6066.E693A9 1997
823'.914—dc21 96-47716

Printed in the United States of America

www.ballantinebooks.com

Book design by Holly Johnson

To my mother, for her courage and belief,
and to Meg MacDonald for her friendship,
her good ideas, and her untiring constructive comments

ASHWORTH HALL

CHAPTER ONE

Pitt stared down at the body of the man lying on the stones of the alley. It was a gray October dusk. A few yards away on Oxford Street the carriages and hansoms were whirling by, wheels hissing on the wet road, horses' hooves clattering. The lamps were already lit, pale moons in the gathering darkness.

The constable shone his lantern on the dead face.

" 'E's one o' ours, sir," he said with tight anger straining his voice. "Least 'e used ter be. I know'd 'im. That's why I sent for you personal, Mr. Pitt. 'E went orff ter summink special. Dunno wot. But 'e were a good man, Denbigh were. I'd swear ter that."

Pitt bent down to look more closely. The dead man—his name was Denbigh, according to the constable—looked to be about thirty and was fair skinned, dark haired. Death had not marred his features. He looked only slightly surprised.

Pitt took the lantern and shone it slowly over the rest of him. He was dressed in very ordinary cheap fabric trousers, plain cotton collarless shirt and poorly cut jacket. He could have been a laborer or factory worker, or even a young man come in from the country looking for employment. He was a little thin, but his hands were clean, his nails well cut.

Pitt wondered if he had a wife and children, parents, someone who was going to grieve for him with the deep, hurting pain of love, more than the respect this constable beside him felt.

"What station was he from?" he asked.

"Battersea, sir. That's w'ere I knew 'im. 'E weren't never in Bow Street, which is w'y you don't know 'im, sir. But this in't no ordinary murder. 'E's bin shot, an' street robbers don' carry guns. They uses knives or a garrote."

"Yes, I know that." Pitt looked through the dead man's pockets gently, his fingers searching. He found only a handkerchief, clean and mended carefully on one corner, and two shillings and ninepence ha'penny in change. There were no letters or papers to identify the body.

"You're sure this is Denbigh?"

"Yes sir, I'm sure. I know 'im quite well. Only for a short time, but I remember that mark wot 'e got on one ear. Unusual, that is. I remember people's ears. Yer can make a lot of things look different, if yer wants ter pass unnoticed, but almost everyone forgets their ears stays the same. Only thing yer can do is get 'air wot ides 'em. I wish as I could say as it wasn't, but that's Denbigh, poor soul."

Pitt straightened up. "Then you were right to call me, Constable. The murder of a policeman, even one off duty, is a very serious thing. We'll start as soon as the surgeon comes and takes the body. I doubt you'll find any witnesses, but try everyone. Try again tomorrow at the same time. People may pass regularly on their way home. Try the street traders, cab drivers, try the nearest public houses, and of course all the buildings around with a window onto the alley, any part of it."

"Yes sir!"

"And you've no idea who Denbigh was working for now?"

"No sir, but I reckon as it were still some department o' the police, or the gov'ment."

"Then I think I had better find out." Pitt rammed his hands into his pockets. He was cold standing still. The chill of the place, islanded in death as it was, only yards from the rattle and bustle of traffic, seeped into his bones.

The mortuary wagon pulled up at the end of the alley and turned awkwardly to come down, the horses whinnying and swinging shy at the smell of blood and fear in the air.

"And you'd better search the alley for anything that might be of meaning," Pitt added. "I don't suppose the gun is here, but it's possible. Did the bullet go right through him?"

"Yes sir, looks like it."

"Then look and see if you can find it. Then at least we'd know if he was shot here or brought here after he was dead."

"Yes sir. Immediately, sir." The constable's voice was still harsh with anger and hurt. It was all too close, too very real.

"Denbigh." Assistant Commissioner Cornwallis looked very unhappy. His strong features made him appear particularly bleak with his overlong nose and wide mouth. "Yes, he was still on the force. I can't tell you precisely what he was doing, because I don't know, but he was involved with the Irish Problem. As you know, there are a great many organizations fighting for Irish independence. The Fenians are only one of them, perhaps the most infamous. Many of them are violent. Denbigh was an Irishman. He'd worked his way into one of the most secret of these brotherhoods, but he was killed before he could tell us what he'd learned, at least more than the sort of thing we already know or take for granted."

Pitt said nothing.

Cornwallis's mouth tightened. "This is more than an ordinary murder, Pitt. Work on this one yourself, and use your best men. I would dearly like to find whoever did this. He was a good man, and a brave one."

"Yes sir, of course I will."

But four days later, with the investigation progressing only slowly, Pitt was visited in his office by Cornwallis again. He brought with him Ainsley Greville, a minister from the Home Office.

"You see, Inspector Pitt, it is of the utmost importance it should have every appearance of being a perfectly ordinary late-autumn country house party. Nothing that can be helped should detract from that, which is why we have come especially to you." Ainsley Greville smiled with considerable charm. He was not a handsome man, but he had great distinction. He was tall with slightly receding, wavy hair, and a long, rather narrow face and regular features. It was his bearing and the intelligence in his eyes which made him unusual.

Pitt stared back at him, still without understanding.

Cornwallis leaned forward in his chair, his face grave. He had been in the position only a short time, but Pitt knew him well enough to realize he was uncomfortable in the role he was being required to play. He was an ex-naval captain, and the reasonings of politics were strange to him. He preferred ways far more direct, but he, like Greville, was answerable to the Home Office, and he had been given no alternative.

"There really is hope of some degree of success," he said earnestly. "We must do everything we can to assist. And you are in the ideal position."

"I am fully involved with the Denbigh case," Pitt replied. He had no intention of handing it over to anyone else, regardless of this new issue.

Greville smiled. "I personally would appreciate your assistance, Superintendent, for reasons which I shall explain." He pursed his lips slightly. "And which I regret profoundly. But if we can move even a single step forward in this matter, the whole of Her Majesty's government will be in your debt."

Pitt thought he was overstating the case.

As if he had read Pitt's thoughts, Greville shook his head slightly. "The conference is to sound out opinions on certain reforms in legislation concerning land laws in Ireland, a further Catholic emancipation. Now perhaps you perceive both the importance of what we hope to achieve and the necessity for secrecy?"

Pitt did. It was most unpleasantly clear. The Irish Question, as it had been known, had plagued successive governments since the time of Elizabeth I. It had brought down more than one. The great William Ewart Gladstone himself had fallen on the issue of Home Rule only four years before, in 1886. Still, the murder of Denbigh was of more urgency to him, and certainly more suited to his skills.

"Yes. I see," he replied with a chill. "But—"

"Not entirely," Greville cut across him. "No doubt you appreciate that every effort to struggle with our most intractable domestic problem should be made discreetly. We don't wish to trumpet our failure abroad. Let us wait and see if it succeeds, and to what degree, before we choose what to tell the world." His face darkened a little, a shadow of anxiety in his eyes which he could not conceal. "There is another reason, Superintendent. Obviously the Irish are aware of the conference. It would hardly be of any purpose if they did not attend, and I shall personally inform you of all I know which is relevant regarding those who will be present. But we are not certain how far the information has gone. There are circles beyond circles, betrayals, secret loyalties—the whole society is riddled with them. We have done the best we can, but we still cannot trust entirely."

His expression became even bleaker, and his mouth pulled tight at the corners. "We had placed a man within one of the secret societies, hoping to learn the source of their information." He let out his breath slowly. "He was murdered."

Pitt felt the coldness settle inside him.

"I believe you are investigating the case." Greville looked very steadily in Pitt's eyes. "James Denbigh. A good man."

Pitt said nothing.

"And I have also received threats to my life, and one attempt, some three weeks ago now, but nonetheless most unpleasant," Greville continued. He spoke quite lightly, but Pitt could see the tension in his body. His long, lean hands were stiff where they lay, one on his knee, the other on the arm of his chair. He concealed it well, but Pitt understood fear.

"I see." This time he did. "So you wish a discreet police presence."

"Very discreet," Greville agreed. "The conference is to be held at

Ashworth Hall. . . ." He saw Pitt stiffen. "Precisely," he said with a flicker of appreciation. "The country home of your wife's sister, sometime Viscountess Ashworth, now Mrs. Jack Radley. Mr. Radley is one of our brighter young members of Parliament and will be a most excellent asset in the discussions. And Mrs. Radley, of course, will be the ideal hostess. It will not be unnatural for you and your wife to attend also, being family members."

It would be most unnatural. Emily Ellison had married well above herself in Lord Ashworth. Her sister, Charlotte, had horrified genteel society by marrying as far below. Young ladies in good families did not marry policemen. Pitt spoke well. He was the son of a gamekeeper on a large country estate, and Sir Arthur Desmond, the owner of the estate, had seen fit to educate him with his own son, to give Matthew a companion and someone against whom to measure himself. But Pitt was not a gentleman. Greville must know that, in spite of Pitt's promotion . . . surely?

Pitt must not allow himself to imagine Greville mistook him for one of his own station just because he sat behind this elegant desk with its green leather inlay. His predecessor, Micah Drummond, had been a gentleman, ex-army. Cornwallis most certainly was also, if perhaps of a lesser standing. He had risen through merit on active service. Did Greville think Pitt of the same mold? It was a flattering thought . . . but a delusion. He wanted Pitt in order to protect his conference without it being apparent.

"And you believe this threat to you is in connection with your work with the Irish Conference?" Pitt said aloud.

"I know it," Greville replied, watching Pitt closely. "There are many factors and individuals who would not wish us to succeed. That is surely clear enough in Denbigh's murder?"

"You are threatened by letter?" Pitt asked.

"Yes, from time to time." Greville shrugged very slightly, a gesture of dismissal. Giving it words seemed to have left him less isolated. He relaxed a little. "One expects a certain amount of opposition, even threats. Usually they are of no consequence at all. Had there not been an actual attempt, I should have ignored them as someone simply airing their feelings in a particularly distasteful manner, if not uncommon. The Irish Problem, as you must know, is one of a violent nature."

That was an understatement of phenomenal proportions. It was impossible to estimate the number of people who had died in battles, riots, famine and murder in a greater or lesser way connected with the problem of Irish history. Pitt was fairly familiar with the Murphy riots in the north of England, where a rabid Protestant had traveled around the countryside stirring up fanatical anti-Catholic feeling which had ended in looting, fires, the destruction of whole streets of houses, and several deaths.

"You had better take someone thoroughly reliable with you," Cornwallis said gravely. "Naturally we will have men around the hall and the village, posing as gamekeepers or farm laborers and so on. But you should have someone inside also."

"Another guest?" Pitt said in surprise.

Cornwallis smiled bleakly. "A servant. It is quite usual when going to a country house party to take two or three of your own servants. We shall simply send one of our best men as your valet. Who would you suggest—Tellman? I know you do not particularly like him, but he is intelligent, observant and not without physical courage, if it should be needed. Please God, it will not."

Pitt would have preferred someone else be sent to Ashworth Hall, but he realized that by virtue of his relationship to the Radleys he was uniquely suited. However, he could at least leave Tellman, his best man, in charge of the Denbigh investigation. He did not actually dislike Tellman, not now that he knew him rather better, but he thought Tellman still disliked him. Tellman had made no secret of the fact that he resented Pitt's promotion. Pitt was from the ranks, no better than the others. He should not aspire to ape his superiors, let alone try to be one. Positions like that previously held by

Micah Drummond were for gentlemen. Rank was the only acceptable qualification for authority. Ambition was not, and Tellman thought that Pitt was ambitious.

He was mistaken. Pitt would have remained where he was and been perfectly happy had he not a family who deserved of him the best he could provide. But that was none of Tellman's concern.

"I cannot imagine Tellman acquiescing to being a valet," he said to Cornwallis. "Even for a week! Least of all to me . . . Can I tell him about Denbigh?"

A very powerful humor flashed in Cornwallis's dark eyes, but he kept it from his mouth.

"Not yet. I am sure when Mr. Greville explains to him the importance of your mission he will be happy to do it to the best of his ability. You will have to have patience with his inexperience as a valet."

Pitt forbore from replying.

"Who are the guests to be?" he asked instead.

Greville leaned back in his chair again and crossed his legs. He did not need to ask if Pitt had accepted the task. Pitt had no choice.

"In order to keep the appearance of a perfectly ordinary weekend, my wife will accompany me, as would be natural on a social occasion," he began. "As perhaps you are aware, the factions in Irish politics are not simply Catholic and Protestant, although those are the two principal divisions. There are always class divisions also, between those who own land and those who do not."

He moved very slightly in a gesture of resignation and regret. "That used to be directly according to religion. For decades all Catholics were banned from owning property; they could only rent, and as you may be aware, some of the landlords exercised their power in the most brutal fashion. Others, of course, were the very opposite. Many bankrupted themselves trying to take care of their dependents during the potato famine in the forties. But memory is subject to great distortion, even without the added twists of Nationalist propaganda and folklore perpetuated in story and song."

Pitt was on the edge of interrupting. He only wished to know who was expected, how many people he would have to consider.

But Greville did not permit anyone to override him when he was in command of the situation.

"And all points of view have their moderates and their radicals who at times can hate each other even more than they hate the opposition," he went on. "And those whose families have been part of the Protestant Ascendancy for generations, and have convinced themselves it is the will of God, can be harder to move in their opinions than any old-fashioned martyr, believe me. I think some of them would welcome a den of lions, and even a good stake to be burned at."

Pitt could hear the exasperation in his voice, and caught a momentary glimpse of the years of frustration of the would-be peacemaker. He felt a surge of sympathy towards Greville which surprised him.

"There are four principal negotiators," Greville continued. "Two Catholic and two Protestant. Their particular points of view do not need to interest you, at least at this juncture, and I think not at all. There is the very moderate Catholic Padraig Doyle. He has fought in the cause of Catholic emancipation and land reform for many years. But he is a respected figure; not, so far as we know, associated with any form of violence. He is my brother-in-law, in fact. But I would prefer that the other participants did not know that at this stage. They might consider me unduly partisan, which I am not."

Pitt waited without interruption.

Cornwallis made his fingers into a steeple and listened attentively, although presumably he was already aware of all that Greville was saying.

"He will come alone," Greville resumed. "The other Catholic representative is Lorcan McGinley, a younger and very different kind of man. He can be charming when he chooses, but lives in a state of permanent anger. He lost family in the potato famine, and land to the Protestant Ascendancy. He is quite openly an admirer of people like Wolfe Tone and Daniel O'Connell. He is for a free and independent

Ireland under Catholic rule, and God knows what would happen to the Protestants then."

He shrugged. "I don't know myself how close his ties are to Rome. The dangers of reciprocal persecution of Protestants might be very real indeed, or equally it might be a great deal more extreme in talk than in fact. This is one of the things we need to find out in this conference. The last thing we want is civil war, and I assure you, Superintendent, it is not an impossibility."

Pitt was chilled. He had enough schoolroom memory of what the English civil war was accounted to have been, the death and bitterness which took generations to heal. Ideological war had a brutality unlike any other.

"McGinley will bring his wife," Greville went on. "I know very little about her, except that she is apparently a Nationalist poet. Therefore we may presume a romantic, one of those highly dangerous people who create stories of love and betrayal, heroic battles and splendid deaths that never happened, but they do it so well, and set it to music, that it becomes legend and people believe it."

His face pinched with anger and distaste—and a shadow of frustration. "I've seen a whole roomful of grown men weeping over the death of a man who never lived and leaving the place swearing vengeance on his killers. Try to tell them the whole thing is an invention and they'd lynch you for blasphemy. You'd be trying to deny Ireland its history!" There was bitterness in his voice and a sharp downward curl to his lips.

"Then Mrs. McGinley is a dangerous woman," Pitt agreed.

"Iona O'Leary," Greville said quietly. "Oh yes, indeed. And her husband's passion stems from just such stories as those she creates, although I'm not sure if either of them knows the truth anymore. There's so much emotion twined through it I'm not sure that anyone does, and so much tragedy and very real injustices."

"And McGinley has no prejudice against violence?" Cornwallis asked.

"None at all," Greville agreed. "Except its possible failure. He is willing to live or die for his principles, as long as they provide the freedom he wants. I have no idea if he knows what sort of a country they will produce. I doubt he has thought so far."

"The Protestants?" Pitt asked.

"Fergal Moynihan," Greville answered. "Just as extreme. His father was one of the hellfire Protestant preachers, and Fergal has inherited the old man's conviction that Catholicism is the work of the devil and priests are all leeches and seducers, if not actual cannibals as well."

"Another Murphy," Pitt said dryly.

"Of the same breed." Greville nodded. "A little more sophisticated, at least outwardly, but the hatred is the same, and the unshifting belief."

"Is he coming alone?" Pitt enquired.

"No, he is bringing his sister, Miss Kezia Moynihan."

"So possibly she is of the same persuasion?"

"Very much so. I have never met her, but I am told, by men whose opinions I trust, that she is a very competent politician, in her own way. Had she been a man, she might have served her people most effectively. As it is, it is unfortunate she is not married, or she might be the intelligence behind some useful man. But she is close to her brother, and might well be a practical influence on him."

"Hopeful," Cornwallis observed, but his voice had no lift to it, and his face, with its long nose and wide mouth, held little light. He was a man of average height, of slender build but with broad, square shoulders. He was prematurely completely bald, but it suited him so naturally one realized it only with surprise.

Greville did not reply.

"The last representative is Carson O'Day," he finished. "He is from a very distinguished Protestant landowning family and probably the most liberal and reasonable of them all. I think if Padraig Doyle and O'Day can reach some compromise, the others may be able to be persuaded at least to listen."

"Four men and two women, apart from yourself and Mrs. Greville and Mr. and Mrs. Radley," Pitt said thoughtfully.

"And yourself and your wife, Mr. Pitt," Greville added. Of course Charlotte would go. There could never have been any question about it. Still, Pitt felt a lightning bolt of alarm at the thought of what danger, or sheer chaos, Charlotte could get herself into. The trouble she might cause with Emily to assist her brought a word of protest to his lips.

"And of course everyone's servants," Greville went on inexorably, ignoring him. "I imagine each person will bring at least one indoor servant—possibly more—and a coachman, groom or footman."

Pitt could see it assuming nightmare proportions.

"That would be a small army!" he exclaimed. "You will have to make arrangements for them to come by train, and have them met by Mr. Radley's carriage at the station. A valet for each man and a maid for each woman will be the maximum we can watch or protect."

Greville hesitated, but the reasoning was overwhelming.

"Very well. I will arrange it. But you will come, with your own 'valet'?"

There was no point in hesitation. He had no choice.

"Yes, Mr. Greville. But if I am to be of any service to you, I must ask you to take any advice I may give you regarding your safety."

Greville smiled, a trifle tight-lipped.

"Within the bounds of fulfilling my duty, Mr. Pitt. I could remain at home with a constable at my entrance and be perfectly safe, and accomplish nothing at all. I shall weigh the danger against the advantage, and act accordingly."

"You mentioned an attempt on your life, sir," Pitt said quickly, seeing Greville about to rise. "What happened?"

"I was driving from my home to the railway station," Greville recounted, keeping his voice deliberately very level, as though the matter were of no more than casual importance. "The road was through open countryside for the first mile, then a wooded stretch of about two miles before another similar distance through farmland to the village. It was during the drive where the road is concealed by trees that another very much heavier coach came out of a side turning and drew behind me at close to a gallop. I told my coachman to hasten to a place where he could get off the road safely to let it pass, but it quite quickly became apparent that the other driver had no intention of slowing down, let alone remaining behind me."

Pitt noticed that Greville was sitting more rigidly as he recalled the event. In spite of his effort at calm, his shoulders had stiffened and his hand was no longer at ease on his knee. Pitt remembered the body of Denbigh in the London alley, and knew Greville had every cause to be afraid.

"My driver had moved to the left of the road," Greville went on, "at some danger, since it was heavily rutted from recent bad weather, and reined in the horses to little more than a walk. However, the other vehicle came by still at a hectic pace, but instead of swerving to avoid us and swinging wide, the driver quite deliberately steered so that he crashed into the side of us and all but tipped us over. We broke a wheel, and one of the horses was injured, fortunately not critically. A neighbor passed by a few moments afterwards and took me to the village, while my coachman cared for the injured animal and I sent assistance back to him."

He swallowed with slight difficulty, as if his mouth were dry.

"But had no other vehicle chanced to pass that way at that precise time, I do not know what would have happened. The other coach simply kept going, increasing speed again and disappearing."

"Did you discover who they were?" Pitt asked.

"No," Greville said flatly, a frown between his brows. "I had enquiries made, naturally, but no one else saw the men. They did not go on to the village. They must have turned off somewhere within the wood. I saw the driver's face as he passed. He turned towards me. He had his animals under perfect control. He intended to push us off the road. I shall not forget the look in his eyes easily."

"And no one else saw this coach before or afterwards, to assist in identifying it?" Pitt pressed, although he had no hope it would be of use. It was simply a matter of showing Greville he took him seriously. "It was not hired from a local stable, or even stolen from someone nearby, a farm or a large house?"

"No," Greville answered. "We were unable to learn anything of use. Tinkers and traders of one sort or another come and go along the roads. One coach without a coat of arms looks much like another."

"Would not a tinker or trader have a cart?" Pitt asked.

"Yes, I suppose so."

"But this was a coach, closed in, with a driver on a box?"

"Yes . . . yes, it was."

"Anyone inside?"

"Not that I saw."

"And the horses were at a gallop?"

"Yes."

"Then they were good horses, and fresh?"

"Yes," Greville said, his eyes on Pitt's face. "I see what you mean. They had not come far. We should have pursued the matter further. We might have found out whose they were, and who owned or bred them for that occasion." His lips tightened. "It is too late now. But if anything further should happen, it will be in your hands, Superintendent." He rose to his feet. "Thank you, Commissioner. I am much in your debt also. I realize I have given you little notice, and you have accommodated me excellently."

Pitt and Cornwallis both rose also and watched as Greville inclined his head, walked straight-backed to the door and left.

Cornwallis turned to Pitt.

"I'm sorry," he said before Pitt could speak. "I only heard this morning myself. And I am sorry you will have to hand over the Denbigh case to someone else, but there is no help for it. You are obviously the only person who can go to Ashworth Hall."

"I could leave it with Tellman," Pitt said quickly. "Take someone else as 'valet.' There could hardly be anyone worse!"

A shadow of a smile crossed Cornwallis's face.

"There could hardly be anyone who would dislike it more," he corrected Pitt. "But he will make an excellent job of it. You need your best man there, someone you know well and who can think for himself in a new situation, adapt, have the personal courage if there should be another threat to Greville's life. Leave Byrne in charge here. He's a good, steady man. He won't let it go."

"But . . ." Pitt began again.

"There isn't time to bring in anyone else," Cornwallis said gravely. "For political reasons they have conducted it this way. This is a highly delicate time for the Irish situation altogether." He looked at Pitt steadily to see if he understood. He must have realized that he did not, because he went on after only a moment's hesitation. "You are aware that Charles Stewart Parnell is the most powerful and unifying leader the Irish have had for many years. He commands respect from almost all sides. There are many who believe that if there can be any lasting peace effected, he is the one man all Ireland will accept as leader."

Pitt nodded slowly, although already he knew what Cornwallis was going to say. Memory came back like a tide.

Cornwallis looked tight-faced and a trifle confused. Moral matters of a personal nature were subjects he did not enjoy addressing. He was a very private man, not at ease with women because his long years at sea had deprived him of their company. He held women in a greater respect than most warranted, judging them to be both nobler and more innocent than they were, and a great deal less effectual. He believed, as did many men of his age and station, that women were emotionally fragile and free from the appetites that both fired and, at times, degraded men.

Pitt smiled. "The Parnell-O'Shea divorce," he said for him. "I suppose that is going to be heard after all. That is what you are referring to?"

"Indeed," Cornwallis agreed with relief. "It is all most distasteful, but apparently they are bent on pursuing it."

"You mean Captain O'Shea is, I presume?" Pitt said. Captain O'Shea was not a very attractive character. According to the account which was more or less public, he seemed to have connived at his wife's adultery with Parnell—indeed, to have put her in his way—for O'Shea's own advancement. Then when Katie O'Shea had left him entirely for Parnell, he had made an open scandal of it by suing for divorce. The matter was to be heard any day now. The effect it would have on Parnell's parliamentary and political career could only be guessed at.

What it would do to his support in Ireland was also problematical. He was of Anglo-Irish Protestant landowning descent. Mrs. O'Shea was born and raised in England, from a highly cultured family. Her mother had written and published several three-volume novels. She too was Protestant. But Captain William O'Shea, looking and sounding like an Englishman, was Irish by lineage and an unostentatious Catholic. The possibilities of passion, betrayal and revenge were endless. The stuff of legend was in the making.

Cornwallis was embarrassed by it. It was something he could not ignore, but it was full of elements of personal weakness and shame which should have been kept decently private. If a man behaved badly in his personal life, he might be ostracized by his peers; one might cease even to recognize him in the street. He might be asked to resign from his clubs, and if he had a whit of decency left he would preempt that necessity by doing it beforehand. But he should not display his weakness to the public gaze.

"Does the O'Shea case have any bearing on the meeting at Ashworth Hall?" Pitt asked, returning them to the purpose at hand.

"Naturally," Cornwallis replied with a frown of concentration. "If Parnell is publicly vilified and details of his affair with Mrs. O'Shea are disclosed which put him in an unsympathetic light, a betrayer of his host's hospitality, rather than a hero who fell in love with an unhappy and ill-used wife, then the leadership of the only viable Irish political party will be open to anyone's ambition. I gather from Greville that both Moynihan and O'Day would not be averse to grasping for it. Actually, O'Day at least is loyal to Parnell. Moynihan is far more intransigent."

"And the Catholic Nationalists?" Pitt was confused. "Isn't Parnell a Nationalist too?"

"Yes, of course. No one could lead an Irish majority if he were not. But he is still Protestant. The Catholics are for nationalism, but under different terms, far closer to Rome. That is a great deal of the issue: the dependence upon Rome; the religious freedom; old enmities dating back to William of Orange and the Battle of the Boyne, and God knows what else; unjust land laws; the potato famine and mass emigration. I am not honestly sure how much of it is just remembered hate. According to Greville, another major bone of contention is the Catholic demand for state-funded separate education for Catholic children, as compared to one school for all. I readily admit, I do not understand it. But I accept that the threat of violence is real. Unfortunately, history bears too excellent a record of it in the past."

Pitt thought again of Denbigh. He would far rather have remained in London to find whoever had killed him than guard politicians at Ashworth Hall.

Cornwallis smiled with ironic appreciation. "There may be no more attempts made," he said dryly. "I would imagine the danger to the representatives would be greater before they arrive, or after they leave. They are less vulnerable while actually at Ashworth Hall. So is Greville, for that matter. And we will have at least a dozen other men in the village and around the grounds of the hall. But I must oblige Greville, if he feels he is in any danger. If there were to be a political assassination of one of the Irish representatives while at Ashworth Hall because we do not take the matter seriously, then surely I do not need to explain to you the damage it could do? It could set back peace in Ireland by fifty years!"

"Yes sir," Pitt conceded. "Of course I understand."

Cornwallis smiled, for the first time real humor lighting his eyes. "Then you had better go and inform Tellman of his new duties. They are to begin this weekend."

"This weekend!" Pitt was staggered.

"Yes. I'm sorry. I told you it was short notice. But I am sure you will manage."

Tellman was a dour man who had grown up in bitter poverty and still expected life to deal him further blows. He was hardworking, aggressive, and would accept nothing he had not worked for. As soon as he saw the look on Pitt's face he regarded him suspiciously.

"Yes, Mr. Pitt?" He never used "sir" if he could avoid it. It smacked of respect and inferiority.

"Good morning, Tellman," Pitt replied. He had found Tellman in one corner of the charge room and they were sufficiently private for the confidentiality of what he had to say. There was only one sergeant present and he was concentrating on writing in the ledger. "Mr. Cornwallis has been in. There is a job for you. We are needed for this coming weekend. In the country."

Tellman raised his eyes. He had a lugubrious face, aquiline-nosed, lantern-jawed, not undistinguished in his own fashion.

"Yes?" he said doubtfully. He knew Pitt far too well to be duped by courtesy. He read the eyes.

"We are to guard the welfare of a politician at a country house party," Pitt continued.

"Oh yes?" Tellman was on the defensive already. Pitt knew his mind was conjuring pictures of rich men and women living idly on the fat of the land, waited on by people every bit as good as they but placed by society in a dependent position—and kept there by greed. "Politician being got at, is 'e?"

"He's been threatened," Pitt agreed quietly. "And there has been at least one attempt."

Tellman was unimpressed. "Did more than 'attempt' to poor Denbigh, didn't they? Or don't that matter anymore?"

The room was so quiet Pitt could hear the scribbling of the sergeant's quill on the paper. It was cold, so the windows were closed against the noises of the street. Beyond the door two men were talking in the passageway, their words inaudible, only the murmur of voices coming through the heavy wood. "This is the same case, only the other end of it," he said grimly. "The politician concerned is involved in the Irish Problem, and this weekend is an attempt at least to begin a solution. It is extremely important that there be no violence." He smiled at Tellman's challenging eyes. "Whatever you think of him personally, if he can bring Ireland a single step closer to peace, he's worth the effort to preserve."

The ghost of a smile flickered over Tellman's face.

"I suppose so," he said grudgingly. "Why us? Why not local police? They'd be far better at it. Know the area, know the locals. Spot a stranger where we wouldn't. I'm good at solving murders once they've happened, and I want to catch the bastard who killed Denbigh. I dunno a thing about preventing one at political parties. And with respect, Mr. Pitt, neither do you!" He put the "with respect" into his words, but there was not a shred of it in his voice. His next question betrayed his thoughts. "I suppose you agreed to it? Didn't ask for it, did you?"

"No, I didn't. And it was an order," Pitt replied with a smile which was at least half a baring of the teeth. "I have no choice but to obey orders given me by a superior, just as you have now, Tellman."

This time Tellman's amusement was real.

"Run out on Denbigh, are we, and going to skulk around some lordship's house instead, keeping an eye on peddlers and footpads and strangers lurking in the flower beds? A bit beneath the superintendent o' Bow Street Station, isn't it . . . sir?"

"Actually," Pitt replied, "the party is to be held at my sister-in-law's country house, Ashworth Hall. I shall be going as a guest. That is why it has to be me. Otherwise I should stay here on the Denbigh case and send someone else."

Very slowly Tellman looked up and down Pitt's lanky, untidy figure, his well-tailored jacket pulled out of shape by the number of odd articles stuffed into his pockets, his clean white shirt with tie slightly askew, and his hair curling and overlong.

His face was almost expressionless. "Oh, yes?"

"And you will be going as my valet," Pitt added.

"What?"

The sergeant dropped his pen and splurted ink all over the page.

"You will be going as my valet," Pitt repeated, keeping all emotion from his voice.

For an instant Tellman thought he was joking, exercising his rather unreliable sense of humor.

"Don't you think I need one?" Pitt smiled.

"You need a damn sight more than a valet!" Tellman snapped back, reading his eyes and realizing suddenly that he meant it. "You need a bleedin' magician!"

Pitt straightened up, squared his shoulders and pulled his lapels roughly level with each other.

"Unfortunately, I shall have to make do with you, which will be a grave social disadvantage. But you might be more use to the politician concerned—at least in saving his life, if not his sartorial standards."

Tellman glared at him.

Pitt smiled cheerfully. "You will report to my home by seven o'clock on Thursday morning in a plain dark suit." He glanced down at Tellman's feet. "And new boots, if those you are wearing are all you have. Bring with you clean linen for six days."

Tellman stuck out his lean jaw.

"Is that an order?"

Pitt raised his eyebrows very high. "Good heavens, do you think I'd be taking you if it weren't?"

"When?" Charlotte Pitt said in incredulity when she was told. "When did you say?"

"This coming weekend," Pitt repeated, looking very slightly abashed.

"That's impossible!"

They were standing in the parlor of their house in Keppel Street, Bloomsbury, where they had moved after Pitt's recent promotion. Until this moment, for Charlotte at least, it had been a very ordinary day. This news was astounding. Had he no conception of the amount of preparation necessary for such a weekend? The answer to that was simple. No, of course he hadn't. Growing up on a country estate had made him familiar with such houses, probably with the number and duties of the staff, and perhaps with the daily routine when there were guests. But it had not given him any knowledge of the number and type of clothes those guests were expected to bring. A lady might wear half a dozen dresses on any given day, and certainly not recognizably the same gown for dinner every evening.

"Who else will be there?" she demanded, staring at him in dismay.

The expression in his face made it obvious he still did not grasp what he was expecting of her.

"Ainsley Greville's wife, Moynihan's sister and McGinley's wife," he replied. "But Emily is the hostess. All the duties will fall on her. You haven't any need to worry. You will be there simply to lend me credibility, because you are Emily's sister, so it will seem natural for us to attend."

Frustration boiled up inside her. "Oh!" She let out a cry of exasperation. "Thomas! What do you suppose I am going to wear? I have about eight autumn or winter dresses to my name! And most of those are rather practical. How on earth can I beg or borrow ten more between now and Thursday?" Not to mention jewelry, shoes, boots, an evening reticule, a shawl, a hat for walking, dozens of things which, if she did not have them, would instantly make her conspicuously not a guest but a poor relation. Cornwallis's idea of making the party appear like any other would be defeated before it began.

Then she saw his concern, and his doubt, and instantly she wished she had bitten her tongue before she had spoken. She hated the thought that her blurted words had made him feel as if he should have provided better for her, to keep up with Emily. Occasionally she had longed for the same pretty things, the glamour, the luxury, but at that moment, nothing had been further from her mind.

"I'll find them!" she said quickly. "I'll call Great-Aunt Vespasia, and I daresay Emily herself can lend me something. And I'll visit Mama tomorrow. How many days did you say it was for? Shall I take Gracie? Or shall we have to leave her here to care for Daniel and Jemima? We are not taking the children, are we? Is there any real danger, do you think?"

He still looked a trifle mystified, but the anxiety was clearing from his eyes.

"We need to take Gracie as your maid. Is your mother at home at present?"

Caroline had fairly recently remarried, most unsuitably—to an actor seventeen years her junior. She was extremely happy though she had lost several of her previous friends. She had made numerous new ones and traveled a great deal since Joshua's profession took him out of London at times.

"Yes," Charlotte said quickly, and then realized she had not actually spoken to her mother for over a fortnight. "I think so."

"I don't think there is any danger," he said seriously. "But I am not sure. Certainly we shall not take Daniel and Jemima. If your mother cannot care for them, we shall leave them with Emily's children in her town house. But you can call Aunt Vespasia tonight."

Lady Vespasia Cumming-Gould was Emily's great-aunt by her first marriage, but she had become ever closer in friendship to both sisters—and also to Pitt, frequently involving herself in those cases which concerned high society, or social issues in which she had a crusading interest. In her youth she had been one of the outstanding beauties of her generation. Now in age she still preserved a timeless elegance and the bearing and dignity of one of England's great ladies. She also had a tongue she no longer felt the need to curb, because her reputation was beyond damaging, and her spirit accepted no artificial bounds.

"I shall," Charlotte agreed. "Right away. How many days did you say?"

"You had better prepare for five or six."

She swept out, her head already whirling with ideas, problems, domestic details, plans and difficulties.

She picked up the telephone and had little trouble in establishing a connection with Vespasia's house in London. Within three minutes she was talking to Vespasia herself.

"Good evening, Charlotte," Vespasia said warmly. "How are you? Is all well?"

"Oh yes, thank you, Aunt Vespasia, everything is very well. How are you?"

"Curious," Vespasia replied, and Charlotte could hear the smile in her voice. She had intended to be tactful and approach her request obliquely. She should have known better. Vespasia read her too well. "About what?" she said airily.

"I don't know," Vespasia replied. "But once we have dispensed with the trivia of courtesy, no doubt you will tell me."

Charlotte hesitated only a moment. "Thomas has a case," she admitted, "which requires that we both spend several days in a country house." She did not specify which one, not because she did not trust Vespasia absolutely, but she was never totally sure if the telephone operator could overhear any of the conversation.

"I see," Vespasia replied. "And you would like a little counsel on your wardrobe?"

"I am afraid I would like a great deal!"

"Very well, my dear. I shall consider the matter carefully, and you may call upon me tomorrow morning at eleven."

"Thank you, Aunt Vespasia," Charlotte said sincerely.

"Not at all. I am finding society very tedious at the moment. Everything seems to be repeating itself. People are making the same disastrous alliances they always have, and observers are making the same pointless and unhelpful observations about it. I should welcome a diversion."

"I shall be there," Charlotte promised cheerfully.

Charlotte then telephoned her mother, who was delighted to

have the children. She hung up the receiver and went upstairs briskly to start sorting out petticoats, stockings, camisoles—and of course there was the whole matter of what Pitt would take. He must look appropriate as well. That was most important.

"Gracie!" she called as soon as she reached the landing. "Gracie!" She would have to explain at least the travel plans to Gracie, and what would be expected of her, if not yet anything of the reason. There were hundreds of things to be done. The children's clothes must be packed, and the house be made ready to leave.

"Yes, ma'am?" Gracie appeared from the playroom, where she had been tidying up after the children had gone to bed. She was twenty now, but still looked like a child herself. She was so small Charlotte had to take up her dresses, but at least she had filled out a little bit and did not look so much like the waif she had been when she first came to them at thirteen. But the biggest change in her was her self-assurance. She could now read and write, and she had actually been of marked and specific assistance in more than one case. She had the most interesting master and mistress on Keppel Street, possibly in Bloomsbury, and she was satisfyingly aware of it.

"Gracie, we are all going away this coming weekend. Daniel and Jemima will go to my mother's in Cater Street. Mrs. Standish will feed the cats. The rest of us are going to the country. You are coming with me as my maid."

Gracie's eyes widened. This was a role she was untrained for. It was socially several stations above household, and she had begun life as a maid of all work. She had never lacked courage, but this was daunting, to say the least.

"I shall tell you what to do," Charlotte assured her. Then, seeing the alarm in her eyes, "It is one of the master's cases," she added.

"Oh." Gracie stood quite still. "I see. Then we in't got no choice, 'as we!" She lifted her chin a trifle. "We'd best be gettin' ready, then."

CHAPTER TWO

The carriage, which like the clothes had been borrowed from Aunt Vespasia for the occasion, arrived at Ashworth Hall late on Thursday morning. Charlotte and Pitt had sat in the back, facing forward. Gracie and the policeman, Tellman, had sat in the front, facing the way they had come.

Gracie had never ridden in a carriage before. Normally she used the public omnibus if she needed to travel at all, and that was extremely rarely. She had never been at such a speed before, except once when she had, to her terror and amazement, ridden in the underground train. That was an experience never to be forgotten, and if she had any say in the matter, never to be repeated either. And it did not count, because it was through a black tunnel, and you could not see where you were going. To sit in a comfortably upholstered seat, with springs, in a carriage with four perfectly matched horses, and fly along the roads into the countryside was quite marvelous.

She did not look at Tellman, but she was acutely conscious of him sitting bolt upright beside her, exuding disapproval. She had never seen such a sour face on anybody before. From the look of him you would have thought he was in a house with bad drains. He never said a word from one milestone to the next.

They swept up the long, curving drive under the elm trees and stopped in front of the great entrance with its magnificent front door, the smooth, classical pillars and the flight of steps. The footman jumped down and opened the door, and another footman appeared from the house to assist.

Even Gracie, a servant, was given an arm to balance her as she alighted. Perhaps they thought she would be likely to fall without it, and they might be right. She had forgotten how far down it was to the ground.

"Thank you," she said primly, and straightened her dress. She was a lady's maid now, and should be treated as such. She should accept such courtesies as her due . . . for the weekend.

Tellman grunted as he got out, regarding the liveried footman with conceded disgust. However, Gracie noticed he could not help looking up at the house, and in spite of his best intentions, there was admiration in his eyes for the sheer magnificence of the Georgian windows, row upon row, and the smooth ashlar stone broken by the scarlet creeper which climbed it.

Charlotte and Pitt were welcomed inside.

Tellman went as if to follow Pitt.

"Servant's entrance, Mr. Tellman," Gracie whispered.

Tellman froze. A tide of color swept up his cheeks. At first Gracie thought it was embarrassment, then she realized from his rigid shoulders and clenched fists that it was rage.

"Don't show up the master by making a fool o' yerself, goin' w'ere it in't your place!" she said under her breath.

"He isn't my master!" Tellman retorted. "He's a policeman, just like any of us." But he turned on his heel and followed Gracie, who was walking behind the footman as he showed them around to the side—a considerable way in a house the size of this one.

The footman took them in through the smaller entrance, along a wide passage, and stopped at a doorway where he knocked. A woman's voice answered and he opened the door and showed them in.

"Tellman and Phipps, Mr. and Mrs. Pitt's personal servants, Mrs.

Hunnaker," he said, then withdrew, closed the door behind him and left them alone in a neat, well-furnished parlor with easy chairs, a pleasant piece of carpeting, two pictures on the walls and clean antimacassars on the chair backs. Embroidered samplers hung above the mantelpiece, and there was a brisk fire burning in the wrought-iron grate surrounded by painted tiles.

Mrs. Hunnaker was in her fifties with a long, straight nose and thick gray hair which was extremely handsome, lending her face a certain charm. She looked like a well-bred governess.

"I expect you'll find it strange," she said, regarding them closely. "But we'll make you welcome. Danny'll show you your rooms. Men servants use the back stairs, women the front. Don't forget that." She looked particularly at Tellman. "Mealtimes are breakfast in the servants' hall at eight o'clock. Porridge and toast. You will eat with the servants, naturally. Dinner is between twelve and one, and supper will be before the guests'. If your lady and gentleman want you at these times, Cook'll keep you something. Ask, never take. Likewise, if your lady and gentleman wants a cup of tea, or a little something to eat, ask Cook if you can prepare it. We can't have every servant in the house coming and going willy-nilly or we'll never get a decent meal served. Laundry maids'll wash for you, but expect you to do your own lady's ironing." She looked at Gracie.

"Yes, ma'am," Gracie said obediently.

"Doubtless you've got all your own needles and threads, brushes and the like." That was a statement, not a question. "If you need anything from the cellar or the pantry, ask Mr. Dilkes, he's the butler. Don't go outside unless someone sends you. As far as the other guests are concerned, speak when you are spoken to, but don't let anyone put on you. If you can't find anything as you want, ask someone. It's a big house and folks can easy get lost. I hope you'll be very comfortable here."

"Thank you, ma'am." Gracie bobbed a half curtsy.

Tellman said nothing.

Gracie kicked him unobtrusively, but hard.

He drew in his breath with a hiss.

"Thank you," he said tersely.

Mrs. Hunnaker pulled on a bell cord, and a maid answered almost immediately.

"These are Mr. and Mrs. Pitt's servants, Jenny. Show them the laundry, the stillroom, Mr. Dilkes's pantry and the servants' hall. Then take Phipps to her room, and have one of the footmen take Tellman to his."

"Yes, ma'am." Jenny bobbed a curtsy obediently and turned to lead them.

Gracie had never before been addressed by her surname, but she realized it was probably the way in a large house. Charlotte had warned her that visiting valets and ladies' maids were sometimes known by the names of their employers. If "Pitt!" were called out by any of the senior servants, it would be she, or Tellman, who was wanted. It would all take a lot of getting used to. But it was a wonderful adventure, and she was always eager for new experiences.

Tellman, on the other hand, still looked as if he had sucked on a lemon.

The room she was shown was very pleasant, if somewhat smaller than her own in Keppel Street, and certainly not nearly as cozy. There was nothing of a personal nature in it. But then it was probably not occupied very often, and never by one person for more than a week or two at a time.

She set her bags down, opened one up, then remembered that of course she would have to go downstairs and unpack all Charlotte's things first, hang them up and make sure all was well. That was what ladies' maids were for. She wondered if Tellman had remembered that was what he was supposed to do too. There was no way she could help him, because she had no idea where his room was.

She found Charlotte and Pitt's suite of rooms in the main house after asking one of the upstairs maids. She knocked and went in.

There was a large bedroom with a rose-colored carpet. Huge windows overlooked a large lawn with towering blue fir trees, and to the left was a flat-topped cedar which was the loveliest thing she had ever seen. It spread wide and delicate, almost black-green against a windy sky. The curtains were splashed with roses and had wonderful swags and drapes and cords in crimson.

"Oh blimey!" she said in a gasp, then caught herself just in time. There was someone in the dressing room. She went past the round table with a bowl of chrysanthemums on it and tiptoed to the door. She was about to knock when she saw Tellman, standing and watching as Pitt unpacked his own cases and hung up his clothes. Of course, Tellman had probably never even seen a gentleman's evening clothes like these before, let alone learned how to care for them. Still, it was shocking that in a house like this Pitt should be doing it himself. What would people think?

"I'll help wi' that, sir," she said briskly, pushing the door open. "You should be downstairs meeting all them people wot you're 'ere to look after." She gave Tellman a meaningful glance, in case he imagined that was a leave for him to go as well.

Pitt turned around, hesitated a moment, glanced at Tellman, then back at Gracie.

"Thank you," he accepted with a wry smile, and with a nod at Tellman, he left.

Gracie turned to Charlotte's three large trunks and opened the first. On the top was a magnificent evening gown in oyster-colored satin, stitched with pearl beads and draped with silk chiffon. A glance at the side seam of the bodice told her it had been very rapidly and very skillfully let out at the back. No doubt it belonged to Lady Vespasia Cumming-Gould. Gracie knew every one of Charlotte's few dresses, and this certainly was not among them. She lifted it up very carefully, a warm rush of gratitude filling her that Lady Vespasia should be so generous to save Charlotte's self-esteem in this company—most especially before her sister, who had married so well. As far as money was concerned, that is. No one could match the master for being a person that really mattered in the world.

She found a hanger and arranged the gown so it lay properly and turned to put it in the wardrobe.

Tellman was staring at her, mesmerized.

"What's the matter wi' you?" she said briskly. "In't yer never seen a lady's gown afore? Get on 'anging up them suits an' then you can go an' find out where the irons are, and the upstairs stove for makin' tea, an' the bathroom an' like. I don' suppose yer know 'ow ter draw a bath?" She sniffed. "Don't suppose yer got a bath? An' 'ot water for the mornin's? An' polish for the master's boots? They'll 'ave ter be done every night." She looked at the disgust in his face. "Not that yer've got much ter do, not like as I 'ave! Gentlemen only changes once or twice a day. Ladies change up ter five times. But yer'll 'ave ter make sure shirts is clean . . . always! I'll give yer 'ell ter pay if yer let the master down by sending 'im out wi' a shirt wot in't perfick."

"He's not my master," Tellman said between his teeth. "And I'm not a bleedin' nursemaid!"

"You're not any bleedin' use!" she snapped back at him. "And we'll 'ave no language in 'ere, Mr. Tellman. It in't done. D'you 'ear me?"

He stood still, glaring at her.

"If yer too proud ter do yer job proper, then yer a fool," she said tartly, turning back to the trunk and taking out the next gown, one in autumn gold taffeta. This was plainer, one of Charlotte's own, but very becoming to her auburn coloring. "Pass me one o' them 'angers," she instructed.

He passed it grudgingly.

"Look, Mr. Tellman," she said, putting the dress on the hanger carefully, then handing it to him to hang in the wardrobe and moving to the next garment, a day dress in deep blue gabardine. Below that was a morning dress, and another, and another. There were three more dinner dresses and several morning and day dresses in the other trunk, plus blouses, camisoles and other underwear, and of course plenty of petticoats. But she would not take them out until Tellman had gone. It was none of his affair what a lady wore beneath her gowns. "Look," she started again, "you an' me is 'ere ter 'elp the master do 'is job an' protect whoever it is wot's in danger. To do that right, we got ter look like we come ter this kind of 'ouse reg'lar an' knows wot we're doin'."

She handed him the next gown and fixed him with a strict stare.

"You may think it's terrible beneath yer ter be a servant, an' by the curl o' yer lips yer do. . . ."

"I don't believe in one man being servant to another," he said stiffly. "I don't wish to insult you, because it isn't your fault you were born poor, any more than it's mine I was. But you don't have to accept it as if you deserved it, or treat other people as if they were better just 'cos they have money. All this bowing and doffing turns my stomach. I'm surprised to see you do it like it comes natural."

"Think too much o' yerself, you do," she said philosophically. "Got more prickles than one o' them little beasts wot live in 'edges. Seems ter me yer got two choices. You can be a good servant and make a fair job of it, or yer can be a bad one an' make a mess of it. I think enough o' meself ter make the best of it I can." She grunted, then went back to the second trunk and began to take the dresses out of it and lay them carefully on the bed before looking for more hangers.

Tellman thought about it for a few more moments, then apparently appreciated that, at least for now, he had little choice in the matter. Dutifully, he hung up the rest of Pitt's clothes, then set out his brush, shirt studs, collar studs and cuff links, then his shaving soap, brush, razor and strop.

"I'm going to look around the house," he told her stiffly when he had finished. "I'd better do my proper job as well. That's what Mr. Cornwallis sent me here for." He looked very slightly down at her, which, since he was the best part of a foot taller, was not difficult. He was also fourteen years older, and was not going to let some twenty-year-old slip of a girl take liberties just because she knew how to unpack a trunk.

"Good idea," she said crisply. "Now yer done that"—she nodded towards Pitt's empty case—"you in't no use 'ere. These things in't your place ter see. But you can come back an' put these cases in the boxroom later on. An' yer better not go around givin' yerself no airs," she added as he reached the door. "Yer don' want them thinking as yer more'n a valet, although a valet is very superior as servants go. An' don't forget that neither, an' go mixin' familiar wi' the like o' footmen an' bootboys."

"And how do you know all that?" he asked, his eyebrows raised high. "Seeing as you only just arrived, same as I did."

"I bin in service for years," she said expansively. It was none of his business that all of it had been with Charlotte, and she had her ideas of a house like this from bits and pieces she had overheard and the very occasional visit, and to be honest, more than a little guesswork. She gave him a level stare. " 'Ow long are yer goin' ter stand there then, like one o' them things gentlemen puts their umbrellas on?"

"Service," he said grimly, then turned and marched out.

"In't nothin' wrong in service," she said to his retreating back. "I'm warm and comfortable every night an' I eat every day, an' that's mor'n a lot can say! An' I keep company wi' decent folks, not like wot you do!"

He did not reply.

Gracie finished the rest of Charlotte's unpacking, enjoying the touch and the luxurious colors of the borrowed gowns, hanging them carefully, smoothing the skirts to stay without creasing, touching her fingers to the beading and the lace and the silk chiffon so fine one could read a book through it.

She was very nearly at the end of the undergarments when there was a knock at the door. She was all ready to face Tellman again and give him another piece of her mind if he was still so contrary, but when she answered, it was not Tellman who came in but a dark-haired rather handsome woman of about thirty, in a maid's dress, but with the bearing of one who is very sure of herself. Gracie guessed immediately it must be another lady's maid. Only a lady's maid or a governess would behave with such superiority, and there were no governesses here.

"Morning," the woman said cautiously. "I'm Gwen, Mrs. Radley's maid. Welcome to Ashworth Hall."

"Good morning," Gracie replied with a hesitant smile. This woman had achieved what Gracie would most like to be. She would need her help, and example, if she were not to let Charlotte down. "Thank you very much."

"Mrs. Radley said there might be some things Mrs. Pitt would care to borrow, for the occasion. If you'd like to come with me, I'll show you and let you hang them in here."

"Thank you. That would be very good," Gracie accepted. She thought of making some remark as to why Charlotte needed to borrow gowns, then changed her mind. Gwen probably knew perfectly well the reason. Few people had any secrets from ladies' maids. She followed obediently and was shown half a dozen gowns, morning dresses, afternoon dresses and an evening dress of rich wines and rose, which in her private opinion would not have suited Mrs. Radley's delicate fair coloring at all. Either she had made a very bad purchase or she had got it with the intention of giving it to Charlotte at some time.

"Very handsome," she said, trying to hide at least some of her awe. She did not want to appear ignorant.

"I'm sure it will become Mrs. Pitt very well," Gwen said generously. "Then if you like, I'll show you around the upstairs and have you meet the other ladies' maids."

"Thank you very much," Gracie accepted. It was most important she learn everything she could. One never knew when it might be needed. And if there really were danger, even a crime in the offing, she must know the house, the people, their natures and loyalties. "I'd like that," she added with a smile.

Gwen proved most agreeable. Perhaps Mrs. Radley had confided in her something of the true nature of the weekend. Gracie found herself liking her—and the task of becoming familiar with the upstairs of the house, the staircases, the quickest way to the kitchens or the laundry room, the ironing room and the stillroom, and how to avoid the footmen, the bootboys and the butler, whose authority was absolute and whose temper was uncertain.

Charlotte had told her something of the guests who were expected, and she met Miss Moynihan's maid, who was a pleasantly spoken French girl with a nice sense of humor. Mrs. McGinley's maid was an older woman with a habit of shaking her head as if in premonition of some disaster, and Doll, a very handsome girl in her mid-twenties, was Mrs. Greville's maid. She was tall, a good six inches taller than Gracie, and with a fine figure. She reminded Gracie of what a really excellent parlor maid should look like, except for a certain sadness in her, or perhaps it was aloofness. Gracie would have to know her better to decide.

She was on her way upstairs, having parted from Gwen, when she saw a young man starting down. Her first thought was what a charming face he had. His hair was very dark, black in the inside light, and his mouth was gentle, as if his mind might be full of dreams.

Then her second thought was that she must have mistaken the stairs and be on the wrong flight. She stopped, feeling the blood rush up her face. She would have to meet such a person when she had made such a foolish error. And yet looking up at the landing above, it was exactly like the one she had come down from. The small table had white chrysanthemums on it in a green vase, against pale green-and-white wallpaper. There was even a gas bracket with a frosted-glass mantle exactly like the one she had seen on the way down. How confusing to have two stairs so much the same.

He had stopped also.

"Beggin' your pardon," he said in a soft Irish accent, quite different from that of Miss Moynihan's maid. He must be from another part of the country. He stood aside for her to pass, smiling and meeting her eyes. His were very dark, the darkest she had ever seen.

"I . . . I think I'm on the wrong stair," she stammered. "I'm sorry."

"The wrong stair?" he asked.

"I . . . I must be on the menservants' stairs, not the women's," she said, feeling the heat burning in her cheeks.

"No," he said quickly. "No, I'm sure it's me on the wrong one. Sure I didn't even think of it. You must be visiting here, like me, or you'd know for certain."

"Yes. Yes, I belong to Mrs. Pitt. I'm her lady's maid."

He smiled at her again. "I'm Mr. McGinley's valet. My name's Finn Hennessey. I come from County Down."

She smiled back at him. "I'm Gracie Phipps." She came from the back streets of Clerkenwell, but she wasn't going to say so. "I'm from Bloomsbury." That was where she lived now, so it was true enough.

"How do you do, Gracie Phipps." He inclined his head in a very slight bow. "I think there is going to be a rare party this weekend, especially if this fine weather holds. I've never seen such a garden, so many great trees. It's a lovely land." He sounded vaguely surprised.

"Have you never been to England before?" she asked.

"No, I never have. It's not much like I expected."

"What did you think it'd be, then?"

"Different," he said thoughtfully.

"Different how?" she pressed.

"I don't think as I know," he confessed. "Different from Ireland, I suppose. And at least for this one bit of it, it could be Ireland, with all those trees, and the grass, and flowers."

"Is Ireland very beautiful?"

His face softened and his whole body seemed to ease, till instead of standing to attention there was a grace in him as he leaned against the rail, his eyes bright.

"It's a sad country, Gracie Phipps, but it's the most beautiful God ever made. There's a wildness to it, a richness of color, a sweetness on the wind you couldn't know unless you'd smelled it. It's a very old land, where once heroes and saints and scholars lived, and now the memory of those days aches in the color of the earth, the standing stones, the trees against the sky, the sound of a storm. But there's no peace in it now. Its children go cold and hungry, and the land belongs to strangers."

"That's terrible," she said softly. She did not know what he was talking about that was different from the harshness and the poverty there was anywhere, but the pain in his voice moved her to a swift compassion, and his words conjured a vision of something precious and lost. Injustice always angered her, more since she had worked for Pitt, because she had seen him fight it.

"Of course it is." He smiled at her with a little shake of his head. "But maybe we'll do something about it this time. We'll win one day, that I promise you."

She was prevented from replying by Mrs. Moynihan's lady's maid coming along the top corridor and reaching the head of the stairs.

"Sure I'm in the wrong place," Finn Hennessey apologized to her. "It's that easy to get lost in a house this size. I'm sorry, ma'am." After a quick look at Gracie, he went back up and disappeared. Gracie continued on her way, but her head was whirling, and five minutes later she had taken a wrong turning and did not know where she was either.

Upon arriving Pitt had gone almost immediately to talk to Jack Radley about the situation which faced them, and to inform Ainsley Greville that he was there, as was Tellman. He must also learn what other provisions had been made by the local police, and by Ashworth Hall's own menservants, and what Greville had told them of the situation and its dangers.

Charlotte went straight to see Emily, who was in the upstairs boudoir, having expected her arrival and longing to talk to her.

"I'm so glad you came!" she said, throwing her arms around her and hugging her tightly. "This is my first really important political weekend, and it's going to be absolutely fearful. In fact, it already is." She stood back, pulling her face into an expression of acute anxiety. "You should feel the tension. If these people are typical of the rest of the Irish, I can't imagine how anyone thinks they are going to find peace between them. Even the women dislike each other."

"Well, they are Irish as much as the men," Charlotte pointed out with a smile. "And possibly they are Catholic or Protestant as much, or just as dispossessed, or just as frightened of losing what they have and have worked for."

Emily looked surprised. "Do you know something about it?" She was wearing a morning dress of pale green, a color which suited her fair hair and complexion extraordinarily well, and she looked quite lovely in spite of her agitation.

"Only what Thomas told me," Charlotte replied. "Which was not a great deal. Naturally he had to explain why we were here."

"Why are you?" Emily sat down in one of the large, floral-covered chairs and pointed to another for Charlotte. "Of course you are most welcome, I don't mean to sound ungracious. But I should like to know why anyone thinks the police should be here. They are hardly going to come to blows, are they?" She looked at Charlotte with a half smile, but there was a note of genuine alarm in her voice.

"I doubt it," Charlotte replied candidly. "I think there is probably no danger at all, but there have been threats on Mr. Greville's life, so they have to take every precaution."

"Not from one of the guests here!" Emily said with horror.

"I shouldn't think so, but naturally they were anonymous. No, I expect it's just a matter of being careful."

"Anyway, I am very glad you are here." Emily relaxed a little. "It is going to be a most testing weekend, and it will be far easier with you to help than trying to do it alone. I've often had visitors here before, of course, but of my own choosing, and people who like each other. For goodness sake, do try to be tactful, won't you?"

"Do you think it will make any difference?" Charlotte said with a grin.

"Yes! Don't talk about religion, or parliamentary franchise or reform, or education . . . or landowning, or rents, or potatoes . . . or divorce. . . ."

"Potatoes or divorce!" Charlotte said incredulously. "Why in heaven's name should I talk about potatoes or divorce?"

"I don't know. Just don't!"

"What can I talk about?"

"Anything else. Fashion . . . except I suppose you don't know about it. Theater—but you don't go to the theater, except with Mama, to watch Joshua—and you better not mention that our mother has married an actor, and a Jewish one at that. Mind, I think the Catholics are too busy hating Protestants, and the Protestants hating Catholics, to care about Jews one way or the other. But they probably all think anyone on the stage is wicked. Talk about the weather and the garden."

"They'll think I'm a simpleton!"

"Please!"

Charlotte sighed. "Yes," she agreed. "It is going to be a difficult weekend, isn't it?"

Luncheon fulfilled her prophecy. They met in the large dining room around a table long enough to seat twenty but set for twelve. Jack Radley welcomed Charlotte, and then introduced her, and of course Pitt, to the rest of the company, and they all took their places. The first course was served.

Charlotte had been placed between Fergal Moynihan on her left and Carson O'Day on her right. Fergal was a striking-looking man of slightly above average height and refined aquiline features, but she thought there seemed little humor in his face. She was not immediately drawn to him, although perhaps it was her image of an intransigent Protestant which unfairly prejudiced her.

Carson O'Day was a smaller man, far grayer, and at least fifteen or twenty years older, but there was a strength in him it did not take more than a glance to see. His manner was benign and courteous, although beneath the niceties of the social situation it was easy to see his gravity and the fact that he never for an instant forgot the reason they were met.

Opposite her was Padraig Doyle, also an older man, perhaps in his middle fifties, with a genial expression and the kind of features which could not honestly be described as handsome, being too uneven, his nose too long and slightly crooked, but there was laughter and imagination in him, and Charlotte felt even before he spoke that he might be most entertaining company.

Although Emily was the hostess, once she had seen that everyone was seated and served she made no demur about Ainsley Greville assuming a natural leadership of the occasion. His wife, Eudora, was a remarkably handsome woman, looking to be several years younger than he, with very fine, rich, auburn coloring; wide, brown eyes; high cheekbones, and a lovely mouth. She was modest of manner, and it only added to her charm.

The other two women at the table were less easy for Charlotte to see, but as soon as the opportunity offered itself, she studied them discreetly. Kezia Moynihan bore a superficial resemblance to her brother. Her coloring was also fair, with very clear, almost aqua, eyes and thick hair which looked enviably easy to dress. But unlike Fergal, there was a quickness in her expression, as if humor came to her naturally, although perhaps temper also. Charlotte found it an easier face to like.

Iona McGinley was a dramatic opposite. Her slender hands moved nervously on the white tablecloth. Her hair was almost black, and her dark blue eyes were wide, vulnerable, full of dreams and inward thoughts. She spoke very little, and when she did her voice was soft with a southern lilt almost like music itself.

The only other person present was Lorcan McGinley, fair haired with a long, narrow face, wide mouth and very blue eyes which were startling, almost sky blue, disconcertingly direct.

The conversation began with a few remarks which seemed

harmless to the degree they were almost banal, especially among people who had all been present since the previous afternoon, therefore had shared at least two meals before.

"Very mild," Kezia said with a smile. "I notice there are still a great many roses in bloom."

"We sometimes get them right up until Christmas," Emily replied.

"Does the rain not rot them?" Iona asked. "We find at home it tends to."

"We are not so wet further east," Carson O'Day put in.

There was a sudden silence, as if the remark had been critical.

Emily looked from one to the other of them.

"Yes it does, occasionally," she said to no one in particular. "I think it is a matter of luck. There seem to be a lot of berries on the hawthorns this year."

"Some say it means a cold winter," Lorcan observed without looking up from his plate.

"That's an old wives' tale," Kezia replied.

"Old wives are sometimes right," her brother pointed out without a smile. He looked at Iona, and then away again quickly, but not before their eyes had met. He continued with his soup.

Emily tried again with a different subject. This time she addressed Eudora Greville.

"I hear Lady Crombie is planning to visit Greece this winter. Have you ever been?"

"About ten years ago, but in the spring," Eudora replied, taking up the opportunity to assist. "It was very beautiful indeed." And she proceeded to describe it. No one was really listening, and perhaps she did not care whether they were or not. It was a safe subject, and the tension eased.

Charlotte would have liked to help as well, but all she could think of was politics, divorce or potatoes. Everything seemed to lead back to these, one way or another.

She was happy to look agreeable and affect a great interest in travel, asking questions every time it seemed the discussion might flag. It looked as though it would be a very long weekend indeed. Five or six days of this, with at least three meals every day, not counting afternoon tea, would seem like the best part of a year.

She watched the others around the table as one course was removed and the next served. Ainsley Greville appeared very much at ease, but looking more closely at his hands, she saw that when he had no food they did not lie loosely on the cloth beside his place, but one finger drummed silently, and now and then the smile on his face became fixed, as if there by effort not instinct. The responsibility for this conference must lie heavily upon him. For all his experience, and no doubt the rewards, she felt a moment's pity for him.

Eudora, on the other hand, seemed quite comfortable. Was she a far better actress? Or had she little idea of the true nature of the weekend?

Padraig Doyle also seemed to find genuine satisfaction in his meal and ate it with enjoyment, giving sincere compliments to the cook, through Emily. But since he was the representative of a major cause, he must be aware of the task which faced them and the difficulties of finding any semblance of a solution. He was simply a very fine actor. Regarding him while the main course was removed and dessert was served, Charlotte thought she saw in his face the quick emotions of an artist, the wit of a raconteur. He certainly told a very lively tale of his own travels in Turkey, mimicking various people he had met and describing their clothes and general appearance with poetic detail. Several times he set them laughing.

Charlotte noticed he spoke to Eudora very easily, as if he had known her for some length of time.

She was also aware of the brittleness between Lorcan McGinley and Fergal Moynihan, as if they could barely bring themselves to agree even upon complete irrelevances, such as the exorbitant price of decent accommodation abroad or the discomforts of travel in bad weather.

Kezia seemed very close to her brother, supporting whatever view he offered, while she never directly agreed with or contradicted O'Day.

Iona McGinley, on the other hand, seemed self-conscious when she spoke either directly to Fergal Moynihan or gave an opinion on something he had said.

Several times Charlotte caught Pitt's eye and saw the flicker of anxiety in his gaze as he too studied the guests. And she saw Jack and Emily look at one another more than once in silent understanding and sympathy.

The meal was drawing to a grateful close when one of the footmen came to Jack's side and announced that there was a Mr. Piers Greville arrived, and should he show him in.

Jack hesitated only a moment. "Yes, of course." He looked across at Ainsley, then at Eudora, and saw the complete surprise in their eyes.

"I don't know," Eudora said simply. "I thought he was still up at Cambridge. I do hope nothing is wrong!"

"Of course not, my dear," Ainsley assured her, although his expression belied his words. "I daresay he went home, which is only about eleven miles away, after all, and when he was told we were here, he decided to come and see us. He could have no idea it would be unsuitable." He turned to Emily. "I'm sorry, Mrs. Radley. I hope it does not inconvenience you?"

"Of course not. He is most welcome." Emily said the only thing she possibly could. In high society people frequently turned up at country house parties uninvited. Hospitality was always given, and could be equally reciprocated when the host should return the visit at some other time. People came and went as suited them, although less so now that train travel stretched easily and conveniently all over the country. In earlier days one might be obliged to stay for a month or two at a time, simply because of the physical trial of moving, especially on appalling roads, heavily rutted by rain and sometimes unpassable in winter. "It will be charming to meet him," she added.

Charlotte looked across the table to Pitt. He smiled back at her ruefully. It was just one of the many unexpected possibilities that could arise. No one had asked him, but then to do so would have betrayed his importance, which would immediately rob him of the only advantage he had.

The footman bowed and retreated to obey.

Piers Greville came in a moment later. He was not quite as tall as his father but he had the same coloring, and a regularity and charm of feature which were more like that of his mother. On this occasion his whole being was alight with excitement and anticipation. There was a flush in his cheeks and his gray-blue eyes were bright. He spoke first to Emily.

"Mrs. Radley, how do you do? It really is very generous of you to allow me to burst in on you like this. I appreciate it enormously. I shall try to be the least possible inconvenience, I promise." He turned to Jack, still smiling. "And to you too, sir. In advance, I thank you profoundly." He looked swiftly around the table, acknowledging each of them although he could have no idea who they were.

Everyone smiled back, some with genuine warmth, like Kezia Moynihan, others gradually, without more than courtesy, like her brother and Lorcan McGinley.

Piers turned to his father.

"Papa, I had to come because this week is the only opportunity I have within the next two months, and I felt the news could not wait." He swiveled around to his mother. "Mama . . ."

"What news?" Ainsley asked, his voice very level, noncommittal.

Eudora looked puzzled. Obviously, whatever Piers had to say was not expected. Presumably it could not concern his studies or any examinations he was to take.

"Well?" Ainsley asked, his eyebrows raised.

"I am betrothed to be married!" Piers said with happiness filling his face and ringing in his voice. "She is the most unique and marvelous person I have ever known. She is quite beautiful and you will love her."

"I didn't even know you had met anyone," Eudora said with a mixture of surprise and anxiety. She made herself smile, but there was a flicker of pain behind it. Watching her, Charlotte thought for a flying moment of her own son, Daniel, and wondered if she too would be caught unaware when he fell in love, if she would not be close enough to him for him to have confided in her long before asking a woman to marry him. It gave her a sharp feeling of fear for the loss.

Ainsley was more practical.

"Indeed. Then I imagine congratulations would be appropriate. We shall discuss the arrangements at a more suitable time, and of course we shall wish to meet her and her parents. Your mother will no doubt have much to ask her mother, and to tell her."

A shadow passed over Piers's face. He looked very young, and suddenly also vulnerable.

"She has no parents, Papa. They died of fever when she was a child. She was brought up by grandparents, who are unfortunately also dead now."

"Oh dear!" Eudora looked startled.

"As you say, unfortunate," Ainsley agreed. "But obviously it cannot be helped. And there is plenty of time. You cannot consider marriage until you are qualified and have purchased a practice, and possibly not for the first year or two after that."

Piers's expression tightened and some of the light faded from his eyes. The thought of waiting so long would be hard for any young man in love, as he so clearly was.

"When may we meet her?" Eudora asked. "Is she in Cambridge? I imagine she is."

"No . . . no, she is in London," Piers said quickly. "But she is coming here tomorrow." He swung around to Emily. "If I have your permission, Mrs. Radley? I realize it is a fearful impertinence, but I do so badly want her to meet my family, and for them to meet her, and this is the only chance for at least another two months."

Emily swallowed. "Of course." Again she made the only

answer she could. "She will be most welcome. Congratulations, Mr. Greville."

He beamed. "Thank you, Mrs. Radley. You are terribly generous."

After the meal was over the men adjourned to begin their discussions, and Emily went to inform the housekeeper that there was an extra guest and require that a room be prepared for him, and one for the following day for the young lady who was expected.

After that she joined the other women in a gentle stroll around the gardens in the late sunshine, showing them the maze, the orangery, the long lawn with its herbaceous borders, now full of chrysanthemums and late asters, the water lily pools and the woodland walk with its ferns, wild white foxgloves, and then back through the beech walk and ending in the rose garden.

Afternoon tea in the green room offered the first opportunity, and necessity, for conversation. Until then, comments on flowers and trees had been sufficient. Emily had walked with Eudora and Iona, Charlotte had followed a step or two behind with Kezia. It had all seemed very agreeable.

Now, in the green room, with its French windows onto the terrace and the grass sloping down to the rose garden, the fire crackling brightly and the silver tray of hot crumpets and butter, delicate sandwiches and small iced cakes, it was impossible to avoid speaking to each other.

The maid had passed the teacups and withdrawn. After the exercise Charlotte was hungry and found the crumpets delicious. It was not easy to eat them in a ladylike fashion and not drip hot butter onto the bosom of her dress. It required a degree of concentration.

Kezia looked at Emily gravely. "Mrs. Radley, do you think it will be possible to purchase a newspaper in the village tomorrow—if I sent one of the footmen for it, if you wouldn't mind?"

"The *Times* is delivered here every day," Emily replied. "I expect we have already arranged to have several copies sent, but I will make sure that it is so."

Kezia smiled dazzlingly. "Thank you very much. That is most generous."

"I don't imagine there will be much news of Ireland in it," Iona observed, her eyes wide. "It will be all English affairs, English social news and theaters and financial dealings, and of course a certain amount of what is happening abroad."

Kezia returned her stare. "The English Parliament governs Ireland, or had you forgotten that?"

"I remember that even in my sleep," Iona replied. "Every true Irish man or woman does. It's only you who want to remain in the English pockets who let yourselves forget what it means, the shame and the grief of it, the hunger, the poverty and the injustice."

"Yes, the whole of England is riding on Ireland's back, I know that," Kezia said sarcastically. "So small as Catholic Ireland is, it's no wonder it finds the weight too much! You must work like galley slaves to keep us all going."

Emily leaned forward to say something, but Eudora spoke first.

"The hunger was to do with the potato blight," she said firmly. "And that was neither Catholic nor Protestant. It was an act of God."

"Who is neither Catholic nor Protestant . . ." Emily added in.

" 'A plague on both your houses!' " Charlotte quoted, then wished she had bitten her tongue.

They all turned to stare at her, eyes wide.

"Are you an atheist, Mrs. Pitt?" Eudora asked incredulously. "You don't follow Mr. Darwin, do you?"

"No, I'm not an atheist," Charlotte said hastily, the color burning up her cheeks. "I just think to watch two supposedly Christian peoples hating each other over the nature of their beliefs must make God absolutely furious and exasperated with us all. It's ridiculous!"

"You wouldn't say that, you couldn't, if you had any understanding of what the real differences are!" Kezia leaned forward, her face filled with emotion, her hands clenched on her deep-wine colored skirts. "Great evils are taught: intolerance, pride, irresponsibility, immorality of all sorts, and the great and beautiful truths of God, of purity, diligence and faith are denied! Can there be a greater evil than that? Can there be anything more worth fighting against? If you care about anything at all, Mrs. Pitt, you surely must care about that? What else on the face of the earth can be as important, as precious, and worth living or laboring for? And if you lose that, what else is left that is of any value at all?"

"Faith and honor, loyalty to one's own," Iona answered, her voice thick with emotion. "Pity for the poor of the earth, and the power to forgive, and the love of the true Church. All things which you wouldn't understand, with your hard heart and your self-satisfied quickness to judge others. If you were to find a man who'll watch the poor starve and tell them it's their own fault, go look for a Protestant, preferably a Protestant preacher. He'll talk about hellfire and light the coals while he's speaking. There's nothing pleases him so much, while he's at his Sunday dinner, as to think some Catholic child's starvin', or makes him sleep so sweet as to believe we'll all be freezin' in a ditch when he's driven us out of our homes and repossessed the land that was ours from birth, and our fathers' fathers' before that back to the beginnin' o' time."

"That's a load o' romantic nonsense, and you know it!" Kezia said, her pale eyes brilliant, almost turquoise in the light. "There's many a Protestant landlord went bankrupt tryin' to feed his Catholic tenants during the famine. I know that, my grandfather was one of them. Not a ha'penny did he have left when it was over. The famine was half a century ago. That's the trouble with you, you all live in the past. You nurture old pains like you're frightened to let them go. You carry around your griefs as if they were your children! Catholic emancipation's a fact."

"Ireland is still ruled by a Protestant Parliament in London!" Iona spoke only to Kezia; there might not have been anyone else in the room.

"And what is it you want?" Kezia shot back at her. "A Catholic Curia in Rome? That is what you want, isn't it? That we all have to answer to the Pope? You want papist doctrine to be the law of the land, not just for those that believe in it but for everyone. That's it!

That's the core of it! Well, I'd sooner die than give up my right to freedom of religion."

Iona's eyes burned with derision. "So you're afraid that if we get power, we'll persecute you—just the way you persecuted us. Then you'll have to fight for a Protestant emancipation, so you can own your own land instead of centuries of being at the mercy of landlords, so you can vote on the laws of your own land, or practice in the professions like any other man. That's what frightens you, isn't it? We've learned what oppression is, God knows, we had good enough teachers!"

Eudora intervened, her face pale, her voice tight in her throat. "Do you want to live in the past forever? Do you want to spoil the chance we have now of ending the hatred and the bloodshed and creating a decent country, under Home Rule at last?"

"Under Parnell?" Kezia said harshly. "Do you think he'll survive this? Katie O'Shea put an end to that!"

"Don't be such a hypocrite," Iona retorted. "Sure he's as guilty as she is. It's Captain O'Shea who is the only innocent one."

"The way I read it," Charlotte interrupted, "Captain O'Shea threw them together for his own political advancement. Which makes him as guilty as anyone, and for a less honorable reason."

"He didn't commit adultery," Kezia lashed out, her face flushed with anger and indignation. "That is a sin next to murder."

"And manipulating another man to fall in love with your wife, and then selling her to him for your profit, and when it doesn't work, pillorying her in public is all right?" Charlotte asked incredulously.

Emily let out a long groan.

Eudora looked around the room frantically.

Suddenly Charlotte wanted to laugh. The whole scene was absurd. But if she did, they would all think she had taken leave of her senses. Perhaps that would not be a bad thing. Anything might be better than this.

"Have another crumpet?" she offered Kezia. "They really are delicious. This conversation is appalling. We have all been unpardonably rude and placed ourselves in positions from which we have no way of retreating with any dignity at all."

They stared at her as if she had spoken in tongues.

She took a deep breath. "The only way would be to pretend none of it happened and start again. Tell me, Mrs. Moynihan, if you had a considerable sum of money, and the time to indulge yourself, where would you most like to travel, and why?"

She heard Emily gulp.

Kezia hesitated.

The fire sank with a shower of sparks. In a minute or two Emily would have to ring for the footman to come and stoke it up again.

"Egypt," Kezia replied at last. "I should like to sail up the Nile and visit the Great Pyramids and the temples at Luxor and Karnak. Where would you like to go, Mrs. Pitt?"

"Venice," Charlotte said without thinking. "Or . . ." She had been going to say "Rome," and then bit her tongue. "Or Florence," she said instead. She could feel hysteria rising in her. "Yes, Florence would be marvelous."

Emily relaxed and rang the bell for the footman.

Gracie had a very busy afternoon. She found Gwen continuously helpful, but it was Doll, Eudora Greville's maid, who taught her how to make silk stockings look flesh colored by adding to the washing a little rose-pink and thin soap, then rubbing them with a clean flannel and mangling them nearly dry. The result was excellent.

"Thank you very much," she said enthusiastically.

Doll smiled. "Oh, there's a few tricks as are worth knowing. Got plenty of blue paper, have you? Or blue cloth will do as well."

"No. What for?"

"Always put white clothes away in a box or drawer lined with blue. That way they won't go all yellow. Nothing looks worse than whites as 'ave gone yellow. Come to that, I s'pose you know how to care for pearls?" She saw from Gracie's face that she didn't. "It's easy when you know how, but make a mistake an' you could ruin 'em—or worse, lose 'em altogether. Like in vinegar!" She gave a wry little laugh. "You boil bran in water, then strain it, add a little tartar and alum, hot as you can stand. Then rub the pearls in your 'ands till they're white again. Then rinse 'em in lukewarm water and set 'em on white paper and leave 'em in a dark drawer to cool off. Works a treat."

Gracie was very impressed. A few days at Ashworth Hall, paying attention, and she was going to be on the way to becoming a real lady's maid. And she could read and write as well.

"Thank you," she said again, lifting her chin a little higher. "That's very gracious of you."

Doll smiled, and something of the guardedness in her relaxed.

Gracie would like to have stayed and talked longer with her, learned more, but in displaying her own lack of experience she was inviting speculation as to why Charlotte should have such an ignorant maid.

"I'll make a note o' that, for if any of our pearls should get dull or lose their color," she said with aplomb. Then she excused herself and returned upstairs.

However, she very quickly became bored, as there was nothing for her to do, so she decided to explore the rest of the servants' parts of the hall. In the laundry wing, she found the maids relaxing and giggling together after a hard morning's toil with steamy sheets and towels. One of the housemaids was ironing. The others, she was told, were carrying coals up to the dressing rooms to light the fires in time for changing for dinner.

She saw Tellman walking across the yard back from the stable, looking grim. She felt sorry for him. He was out of his depth. He probably had not the least idea how to do his job; all the well-trained valets of the other gentlemen would be bound to notice it. She really ought to offer him a little help. At the moment he looked like a spoilt child about to throw a tantrum. She had found with Charlotte's children, once they were out of the three-year-old frustration tempers, such incidents usually occurred because they felt somehow overlooked or unimportant.

"Beginning to find your way around, Mr. Tellman?" she said cheerfully. "I never bin in such a big place before, an' I don't even 'ave ter bother wi' outside."

"Well I do," he said tartly, looking sour. "If we do get any trouble it won't be blacking boots an' carrying coals they'll be thanking me for!"

"You shouldn't be carrying coals," she said quickly. "You're an upper servant, not a lower one. In fact, you are one of the top ten, so don't let anyone take advantage of you."

His face twisted with disgust. "One of the top ten! Don't be ridiculous. If you spend your time waiting on other folk and taking orders, you're a servant, and that's all there is to it."

"It most certainly is not!" she said indignantly. "That's like saying if you're a policeman it's all the same whether you're a senior detective wi' knowledge and cleverness or a rozzer wot walks the beat carryin' a lantern an' don't know a robber from a priest less someone shouts 'Stop thief!' "

"But you're at other people's beck and call," he said.

"An' you in't?"

He started to deny it, then met her blunt, candid gaze and changed his mind.

"An' if yer don't know wot ter do, I'll find out for yer," she said generously. "You don't want ter look like yer don't know yer job. I'll show yer 'ow ter brush a gentleman's coat proper, an' 'ow ter take orff spots. Do yer know 'ow ter get grease orff?"

"No," he said grudgingly.

"An 'ot iron an' thick brown paper, but not too 'ot. Lay it on a piece o' white paper first, an if it don't scorch, it's a' right. If that don't 'move it all, a little bit o' clean cloth an' spirit o' wine. If'n yer get stuck, come an' ask me. Don't let 'em see as yer don' know. I'll find out for yer."

She could see from his face that he resented it profoundly, yet he could appreciate the point of her argument.

"Thank you," he said between his teeth, then turned and walked into the house without looking back.

She shook her head and went on with her explorations.

She was in the stillroom when she saw Finn Hennessey again, his dark head and slender shoulders unmistakable. He stood with a grace unlike anyone else's.

He turned the moment he heard her step, and his face lit up with pleasure when he saw her.

"Hello, Gracie Phipps. Looking for someone?"

"No, just discoverin' the 'ouse, so I know where ter find things," she replied, delighted to have encountered him, and yet now tongue-tied for something sensible to say.

"Very wise," he agreed. "So am I. Funny isn't it, how we work so hard for days preparing to come, and when we're here, at least today, there's almost nothing to do until dinner."

"Well, at 'ome I 'ave children ter care for as well," she said, then realized that categorized her as a maid of all work, and wished she had kept silence.

"Do you like that?" he asked with interest.

"Oh yeah. They're pretty much obedient, an' ever so bright."

"And healthy?"

"Yeah," she said with surprise. She saw the shadow in his face. "Isn't children 'ealthy where you come from?"

"Where I come from?" he repeated. "The village my mother lived in, and her mother before her, is a ruin now. It was abandoned after the famine. There used to be close to a hundred people there, men, women and children. Now it looks like the tombs of a departed race crumbling back into the earth."

She was genuinely shocked. "That's terrible. Yer ma married an' moved then? Din' she 'ave no brothers wot stayed there?"

"She had three. Two of them were evicted when the land was sold and the new landlords put it to grazing. The third, the youngest, was hanged by the British because they thought he was a Fenian."

She heard the pain in him, but she did not understand the story. She was perfectly familiar with poverty. The London streets in some areas could equal anything Ireland could offer. She had seen children starved, or frozen to death. She had been cold and sick often enough herself before she had been taken into service by Pitt.

"Was a wot?" she said quietly.

"A Fenian," he explained. "A secret brotherhood of Irishmen who want freedom for Ireland, to rule themselves and follow our own ways—those of us that are left. God knows how many that is. We've been driven from the land by greedy landlords till there are only ghost villages left in the west and the south."

"Driven where to?" She tried to imagine it. It was the only part of his story which was outside her own experience.

"America, Canada, anywhere as'll have us, where we can find honest work, and food and shelter at the end of it."

She could think of nothing to say. It was tragic and unjust. She could understand his anger.

He saw the compassion in her face.

"Can you imagine it, Gracie?" he said softly, his voice little more than a whisper. "Whole villages dispossessed of the land and the homes where they were born and where they'd labored and built, driven out with nowhere to go, even in winter. Old men and women with babies in arms, children at their skirts, sent out into the wind and the rain to fend for themselves any way they could. What kind of a person would do that to another creature?"

"I dunno," she answered solemnly. "I in't never met no one as'd do nothing like that. I only know landlords wot throw out a family 'ere or there. It in't 'uman."

"You're right about that, Gracie. Believe me, if I were to tell you all Ireland's ills, we would still be here long after this weekend party is over and the politicians have gone back to London or Dublin or Belfast. And that would be barely the beginning of it. Poverty's everywhere, I know that. But this is the slow murder of a nation. No wonder it rains in Ireland till the very earth shimmers green. It must be the angels of God weeping at the suffering and the pity of it."

She was still picturing it in her mind and trying to work her way through the sadness when they were interrupted by Gwen coming in to find some of the ingredients for making "Lady Conyngham's lip honey."

"How do you do that?" Gracie asked, ever eager to learn.

"Take two ounces of honey, one of purified wax, half an ounce of silver litharge and the same of myrrh," Gwen answered obligingly, happy to share her knowledge. "Mix this over a slow fire, and add any perfume you care for. I'm going to use milk of roses. It should be up on that shelf." She nodded to a point just above Gracie's head. She smiled at Finn Hennessey, and quickly he opened the cupboard and passed the container down to her.

She flashed him a warm glance and looked disposed to remain a few moments longer. Gracie considered standing her ground, then decided it would look childish. She excused herself and went off, but wondering if he was watching her or if he had already lost himself in conversation with Gwen.

At the corner of the corridor she could not resist turning her head, and felt a soaring of her heart to meet his eyes and know that his mind was still upon her.

Dinner was a very stilted affair to begin with. None of the women had forgotten the bitterness of the conversation over afternoon tea, and both Charlotte and Emily were dreading a similar scene.

Fergal Moynihan arrived looking grim, but maintained a very formal courtesy with absolute, almost studied equality towards everyone.

Iona McGinley looked beautiful in an intense way. She had chosen a very dramatic gown of blue, almost purple, and it made the skin of her neck and shoulders look very white and fragile. Charlotte had been told Iona was a poetess, and looking at her now she could well believe it. She seemed a figment of some romantic dream herself, and a curious, faraway smile played about her lips as though she were more often dreaming than thinking of the mundane politeness of a dinner party.

Piers Greville sat in his own little island of happiness. His parents were both fully occupied trying to behave as if the company were at ease and making small talk about innocuous matters.

Kezia also looked very fine in an utterly different manner. It would have been difficult to find two women more wildly in contrast than she and Iona McGinley. She wore a shimmering aquamarine gown with delicate embroidery asymmetrically down one side. Her shoulders were rich and milky smooth, her bosom very handsome. Her fair hair caught the light, and she seemed almost to glow with the richness of her coloring. Charlotte saw a flicker of appreciation on Ainsley Greville's face, and on Padraig Doyle's, and was not surprised.

Charlotte had dressed with Gracie's help. She wore one of Aunt Vespasia's gowns, not the oyster satin—she was keeping that for the most important occasion—but one in a deep forest green, very severely cut, which was a great deal more flattering than she would have supposed. It all lay in the cut of the bosom, the waist, and the way the skirt draped over the hips and under the tiny bustle, most fashionably reduced from previous years. She saw a flash of admiration in the eyes of more than one of the men, but more satisfying than that, a swift glance of envy from the women.

Fergal spoke to Iona, some trivial politeness, then Lorcan interrupted. Padraig Doyle smoothed over the situation with an anecdote about an adventure on the western frontiers of America and set everyone laughing, if somewhat nervously.

The next course was served.

Emily introduced some harmless subject, but she was obliged to work very hard to keep it so. Charlotte did all she could to help.

After the last course was completed the ladies adjourned to the withdrawing room, but were very soon followed by the gentlemen, and someone suggested a little music. Possibly it was intended to flatter Iona.

She did indeed sing beautifully. She had a haunting voice, far deeper than one might have expected from such a fragile figure. Eudora played the piano for her, with a surprisingly lyrical touch, and seeming at ease even with old Irish folk tunes which fell in unusual cadences, quite different from English music.

At first Charlotte enjoyed it very much, and after half an hour began to find herself relaxing. She looked across at Pitt and caught his eye. He smiled back at her, but she saw he was still sitting upright and every now and again his eyes would wander around the room from face to face, as if he expected some unpleasantness.

It came from the one quarter she had not foreseen. Iona's songs became more emotional, more filled with the tragedy of Ireland, the lost peace, the lovers parted by betrayal and death, the fallen heroes of battle.

Ainsley shifted uncomfortably, his jaw tightening.

Kezia was growing more flushed in the face, her mouth set in a thinning line.

Fergal never took his eyes from Iona, as if the music's beauty had entered his soul and both the pain of it and the accusations against his own people were inextricably mixed, paralyzing his protest.

Then Emily moved as though to speak, but Eudora kept on playing, and Lorcan McGinley stood between her and Iona, his fair face transfixed with the old stories of love betrayed and death at British hands.

It was Padraig Doyle who intervened.

"Sure an' that's a lovely sad song," he said with a smile. "All about a relative o' mine too. The heroine, Neassa Doyle, was an aunt o' mine, on my mother's side." He looked across at Carson O'Day, who so far had said nothing, his expression impossible to read. "And the hero, poor man, could be a relative o' yours, I'll swear?"

"Drystan O'Day," Carson agreed bleakly. "One tragedy among many, but this one immortalized in music and poetry."

"And very beautiful it is too," Padraig agreed. "But how about we exercise the good manners we're famous for and sing some of our host's songs as well, eh? What do you say to a few happier love songs? We'll not send you to bed in tears, shall we? Self-pity never was a handsome thing."

"You think Ireland's woes are self-pity?" Lorcan said dangerously.

Padraig smiled. "Our woes are real enough, man. God and the world know that. But courage sings a gay song, as well as a sad one. How about 'Take a Pair of Sparkling Eyes'? Is that not a fine song?" He turned to Eudora. "I've heard you play that one from memory. Let's be hearing it now."

Obediently she moved into its lovely, soaring melody, and he began to sing in a lyrical Irish tenor, sweet and true, filled with joy. Without meaning to, Emily began to hum along with him, and he heard her and beckoned with his hands to encourage her.

Within ten minutes they were all singing from Gilbert and Sullivan, happy, dancing music, and all the room was obliged to let go of anger and tragedy, at least for an hour.

Charlotte slept in emotional exhaustion, but her sleep was not restful. She was disturbed by dreams of anxiety, and for seconds it only seemed like a continuation when she heard the screaming.

She was emerging from the webs of sleep when Pitt was already out of bed and striding towards the door.

The screaming went on, high and shrill with rage. There was no terror in it, only uncontrollable, hysterical fury.

Charlotte almost fell out of bed, tripping over the full skirts of her nightgown, her hair in a loose braid and half undone.

Pitt was on the landing, staring at the doorway of the room opposite, where Kezia Moynihan stood, her eyes wide, blazing, her face white but for two spots of hectic color in her cheeks.

Emily was coming from the west wing, her hair loose, her nightgown covered by a pale green robe, her face ashen. Jack had obviously risen earlier and was running up the stairs from below.

Padraig Doyle emerged from a door further down, and then a second after, Lorcan McGinley.

"What in God's name has happened?" Jack demanded, looking from one to another of them.

Charlotte stared beyond Pitt in through the open door, still held wide by Kezia. She saw a huge brass-ended bed, its cover rumpled, and half sitting up, her black hair falling over her shoulders, Iona McGinley. Beside her, his striped nightshirt askew, was Fergal Moynihan. Iona made a halfhearted attempt to shuffle under the bedclothes.

The scene admitted no explanation.

CHAPTER THREE

Emily was the first to move. There was no conceivable denial to make. There was only one interpretation possible. She moved forward and took Kezia's hand, pulling her quite sharply out of the doorway, and reaching for the handle, jerked it shut.

Charlotte unfroze and turned to face everyone else, now gathering on the landing.

"What's happened?" Carson O'Day asked, his face filled with anxiety bordering on fear.

Charlotte felt a surge of wild laughter inside herself. She knew he had imagined an attack, the violence that had surely been at the back of everyone's minds, the reason Pitt was here. She could see it mirrored in his eyes. And this was so utterly different, almost banal, the sort of domestic tragedy or farce that happened anywhere.

"Everyone is perfectly safe," she said clearly and a little loudly. "No one is injured." Then she saw Lorcan McGinley's white face and regretted she had chosen precisely those words, but to apologize would only make it worse.

Emily had her arm around Kezia and was trying, unsuccessfully, to steer her away and back to her own bedroom.

Pitt saw her difficulty and went to Kezia's other side.

"Come," he said firmly, taking her arm and putting his weight behind his movement. "You'll catch a chill out here." It was a meaningless statement. She had a robe over her nightgown and the house was not cold, but it had the desired effect, for an instant breaking the spell of her rage. He and Emily, one on either side, led her away.

This left Charlotte alone to think of something to say to everyone else. Jack was at the top of the stairs now, but he had no idea what had happened.

"I'm very sorry for the disturbance," she said as calmly as she could. "Something has occurred which has distressed Miss Moynihan very much, and no doubt others among us as well. But there is nothing to be done for the moment. I think it would be best if we all returned to our own bedrooms and dressed. We cannot help here, and we shall only catch cold."

That was true; Eudora Greville had picked up a robe before responding to Kezia's screams. Everyone else had only nightgowns or nightshirts on.

"Thank you, Mrs. Pitt," Ainsley said with a sigh of relief. "That is very wise advice. I suggest we all take it." And with a bleak smile, pale-faced, he turned around and walked back towards his bedroom. After a second's confused hesitation, Eudora followed behind him.

Padraig Doyle looked at Charlotte in concern, then realized that the situation, whatever it was, was one which was best left alone, and he too went. The others followed, leaving only Lorcan standing facing Charlotte.

"I'm sorry, Mr. McGinley," she said very quietly, and she meant it with a depth which surprised her. He had not been a man she liked instinctively, but now her hurt for him was real. There was nothing in his face to indicate whether he had had the slightest idea that his wife was having an affair. The shock in it now, the pallor and hollow eyes, could have been disbelief, and then the stunning realization, or simply the agonizing embarrassment and shame of having it exposed in front of the other guests in the house.

Whatever it was, there was nothing else to say which would not make it even worse.

He did not reply, and she was frightened of the look in his eyes.

Breakfast was appalling. Emily was at her wits' end to know what to say or do to maintain even a veneer of civilized behavior. Of course it was not the first country house party where adultery had taken place. In fact, it probably happened as often as not. The differences were two: most people were discreet enough, and careful enough, not to be discovered, and if anyone did chance to interrupt something unfortunate, they kept their own counsel about it and looked the other way. Certainly they did not scream themselves hoarse and wake the entire household. And normally one took great care not to invite people who were at odds with each other. It was a principal part of a hostess's skill to know who cared for whom, and who did not.

When Jack first ran for Parliament she had had no conception of the difficulties she might face in entertaining. She was perfectly aware of the usual social pitfalls, the problems of obtaining and keeping a good cook and good servants in general, of wearing exactly the right clothes, of learning the orders of precedence of all the various titles of aristocracy, of devising menus which were imaginative but not eccentric and entertainments which could not go wrong and yet were still interesting.

Religious and national hatreds were new to her. Even the idea of hating someone because of his or her beliefs was beyond her thoughts. Yesterday had teetered on the edge of disaster once or twice. Today seemed irredeemable. She sat at the foot of the breakfast table as people came in one by one, passing the sideboard with its chafing dishes of kedgeree, deviled kidneys, scrambled eggs, poached eggs, bacon, sausages, smoked finnan haddock, kippers, and grilled mushrooms.

Padraig Doyle helped himself generously. She had judged him

aright as a man who enjoyed his physical well-being and who guarded his energy with care.

Ainsley Greville similarly did not ignore his meal, although he took little relish in it. He was absorbed in his thoughts, his face tense. There was a certain stillness about him.

O'Day ate sparingly. McGinley hardly touched his plate, merely pushing the food around every so often. He looked wretched, and excused himself after less than ten minutes. He had spoken to no one.

Fergal Moynihan was profoundly unhappy, but he remained at the table, although he spoke barely a word. Iona sipped tea and ate nothing, but she seemed less distraught than he, as if she had a kind of inner conviction which sustained her.

Piers, who had no idea what had happened, tried to make some sort of conversation, and Emily found herself delighted to ask him about his studies at Cambridge and learn that he was in his final year of medicine and hoped shortly to graduate well. Of course, it would be some time after that before he could obtain a practice of his own, but he was looking forward to it with enthusiasm.

Now and again she saw Eudora look faintly surprised, as if she had not realized the depth of his feelings. Perhaps he did not speak so fully at home, assuming she already understood.

The rest of the company struggled on in jerky conversation about trivia. Kezia did not come down at all, and after about half an hour Charlotte glanced at Emily, then arose, excused herself and disappeared. Emily was almost certain she had gone in search of Kezia. She wondered if it was wise, but perhaps it had to be done, and she shot her a smile of gratitude.

She was correct. Charlotte went partly out of concern for Kezia, whom she had liked, but more out of care for Emily and Pitt. If no one made any effort to comfort her and at least calm her mounting hysteria, if she felt totally alone, she might lose all control and behave with an even more damaging effect. She was obviously shocked.

At the top of the stairs Charlotte saw a very handsome girl with thick, honey-fair hair and a very fine figure. She looked like a parlor maid because of her beauty—and that was not too strong a word—but she wore no cap, and a parlor maid would not be upstairs. She must be someone's lady's maid.

"Excuse me," Charlotte asked her. "Can you tell me which is Miss Moynihan's room?"

"Yes ma'am," the girl replied obediently. Her expression was pleasant, but there was a gravity, almost a sadness, in her eyes and mouth, as if she rarely smiled. "It's the second door on the left, 'round the corner past the bowl of ivy." She hesitated. "I'll show you."

"Thank you," Charlotte accepted. "You are not her maid, are you?"

"No ma'am, I'm Mrs. Greville's maid." She led the way and Charlotte followed her.

"Do you know where Miss Moynihan's maid is? It might be quite a good idea to have her help. She is bound to know her mistress well."

"Yes ma'am. I believe she is in the laundry, cooking rice."

"I beg your pardon?" The answer seemed to make no sense at all. "You mean the kitchen?"

"No ma'am, to make congee." A ghost of amusement flickered across her face. She was not unfriendly. "That's rice-water, ma'am, for washing muslin. Gives it body. But you have to make it first. Rice is kept in the laundry for it. Cook wouldn't allow us in the kitchen for that. Leastways, our cook wouldn't."

"No," Charlotte agreed. "No, of course not. Thank you." They were at the bedroom door. She would just have to manage without the maid's assistance.

She knocked.

There was no answer. She had only half expected one. She had already made up her mind what to do. She knocked again, and then, exactly as if she were a maid, she simply opened the door and went in, closing it behind her.

It was a lovely room, decorated in sunny florals, daffodil yellows and apple greens with touches of blue. On the table there was a vase of white chrysanthemums and blue asters, and a pile of papers, and

Charlotte remembered that Kezia was said to be as deeply involved in politics as her brother, and perhaps at least as gifted. It was only that she was a woman, and unmarried, that had kept her from more open influence.

Kezia was standing now in front of the long window and staring out of it. Her hair was loose down her back and she had not yet bothered to dress. Presumably she had deliberately sent her maid away.

She did not even turn as Charlotte came in, although she must have heard the door opening, even if she did not hear footsteps on the soft carpet.

"Miss Moynihan . . ."

Kezia turned very slowly. Her face was puffed, her eyes red. She looked at Charlotte with slight surprise and the beginning of resentment.

Charlotte had expected it; after all, she was an intrusion.

"I need to speak to you," she said with a very slight smile.

Kezia stared at her in disbelief.

Charlotte went on regardless. "I could not simply eat my breakfast as if everything were more or less all right. You must feel dreadful."

Kezia was breathing very deeply, her breast rising and falling. On her face was a mixture of emotions: anger, and a wild desire to laugh, even an ache for physical violence of some sort to release the helpless fury inside, and a fierce contempt for Charlotte's impertinence and utter lack of understanding.

"You haven't the remotest idea," she said harshly.

"No, of course I haven't," Charlotte agreed. She could readily comprehend shock, embarrassment and shame. A certain anger was natural, but not the rage which almost choked Kezia. Even as she stood there in her beautiful white robe with its lace edges, her body was shaking with it.

"How could he do such a thing?" she blazed, her eyes diamond bright and hard. "It is despicable beyond excuse, beyond any kind of pardon." Her voice choked in her throat. "I thought I knew him. All these years we've fought for the same things, shared the same dreams, suffered the same losses. And he does this!" The last word was almost a shriek.

Charlotte could hear her control slipping away again. She must talk, say something, anything, to try to soothe away some of the explosive pain inside her. She should feel she had at least one friend.

"When people fall in love they can do so many foolish things," she began. "Even things which are quite outside their usual character—"

"Fall in love?" Kezia shouted, as if the phrase were meaningless. "People? Fergal is not just 'people'! He is the son of one of the greatest preachers who ever taught the word of God! A just and righteous man who lived all the Commandments and was a light and a hope to all Ulster. He lived his whole life to keep the faith and the freedom of Ireland from the dominion and corruption of popery." She waved her arm almost accusingly. "You live in England. You haven't faced that threat in centuries. Don't you read your history? Don't you know how many men Bloody Mary burned at the stake because they wouldn't forsake the reforms of the Protestant church? Because they wouldn't get rid of superstition and indulgences and the sin that riddled the whole hierarchy from top to bottom?" She did not stop for breath. Her face was bright and ugly with rage. "From an arrogant Pope who thinks he speaks for God, right down through an Inquisition which tortures to death people who want to read the Holy Scriptures for themselves, even through a licentious and idolatrous clinging onto worship of plaster statues and thinking all their sins can be forgiven if they pay money to the church and mumble a few prayers while they count their beads!"

"Kezia . . ." Charlotte began, but Kezia was not listening.

"And Fergal was in bed not only with a Catholic whore . . ." She went on, growing more and more shrill. "Not only an adulteress, but one who tears Ireland apart by writing her poetry full of lies and firing up stupid, ignorant men's imaginations with sentimental and maudlin songs about heroes who never were and battles that didn't happen!"

"Kezia . . ."

"And you want me to understand why he did that, and overlook it? You want me to—" Her voice caught in a sob and she could barely struggle on. "You want me to say that's all right? It's only a human weakness, and we should forgive? Never!" She clenched her fists in front of her, her white hands smooth, the knuckles shining. "Never! It is unpardonable!"

"Isn't anything pardonable, if you repent?" Charlotte said quietly.

"Not betrayal." Kezia jerked her head up haughtily, her voice catching in her throat. "He has betrayed everything! He is the ultimate hypocrite. He is nothing he made me believe he was."

"He's fallible," Charlotte argued. "Of course it's wrong, but surely it is one of the most understandable of sins?"

Kezia's hair was a bright halo around her, with the light shining gold through it.

"Hypocrisy? Cheating? Lying? Betraying all you have stood for, all those who have believed in you? No! No, it is not understandable, nor can it be forgiven. Not by me, anyway." She turned away and stared out of the window again. Her shoulders were stiff, her whole body filled with resistance.

There was no point in arguing further. It would only increase her resolve. Charlotte was beginning to appreciate the depth of hatred in the Irish Problem. It seemed to be in the blood and the nature. There was no yielding, no exception made. It was stronger than family love or even the desire to keep the warmth and the sweetness of one's deepest ties and companionships.

And yet she could remember her own pain of disillusion long ago when she had discovered Dominic's feet of clay, exactly the same sort of thing. He was her elder sister Sarah's husband, and she had adored him, quite unrealistically. For a while the loss of the dream had seemed unbearable. Then she had come to know him more truly, and they had reached a kind of friendship based on affection and forgiveness, and it had been a far cleaner, stronger thing.

"If you'd like to walk alone, I doubt there'd be anyone except perhaps a gardener in the maze," she said aloud.

"Thank you." Kezia did not move even her head, but stood with her robe clasped around her, as if it could protect her and she were afraid someone was going to tear it away.

Charlotte went out and closed the door again.

The ladies spent the morning writing letters, making small talk about various attractive or interesting objects of art in the house, and looking idly at the books of incidentals lying around on tables in the withdrawing room or boudoir. They were collections of designs, paintings, etchings, silhouettes or lace, and other such bits and pieces which formed designs of beauty or interest. It was a common practice for ladies of leisure to create them, and comparing one person's skill or idea with another was a pleasure. Emily had not made it hers. She loathed such things, and took good care to see she had not the time, but she had been given them by various guests and was grateful to have them.

It was at least less difficult with Kezia absent. Had she chosen to come it would have been impossible. The previous day's quarrel would have been little to compare with today's.

The gentlemen resumed their deliberations, smoothly guided by Ainsley. Not surprisingly, the atmosphere was brittle, but O'Day and Padraig Doyle shared a dry laugh as they walked across the hall back to the library. And Jack, following with Fergal Moynihan, seemed to be having an agreeable enough conversation.

Pitt found Tellman trudging through the stable yard and looking grim.

"There are far too many men around here," he said as soon as he was close enough to speak without being overheard by the grooms and coachmen in the vicinity. "Don't know who half of them are. Could be anybody."

"Most of them are longtime servants of the hall," Pitt replied. He was in no mood to indulge Tellman's prejudices. "They've been here for years and have no connection with Irish politics whatever. It's strangers we need to keep a watch for."

"What are you expecting?" Tellman raised his eyebrows sarcastically. "An army of Irish Fenians marching up the drive with guns and explosives? Judging by the atmosphere in the house, they'll be wasting their time. That lot'll kill each other and save them the bother."

"That the servants' gossip, is it?" Pitt enquired.

Tellman shot him a glance that should have withered him on the spot.

"It wouldn't make any sense to attack each other here," Pitt elaborated patiently. "It's far too obvious. They'll only make a martyr of the victim and blacken their own names, not to mention end their lives on the gallows. None of the men here are fanatic enough to want anything so pointless."

"You think not?" Tellman walked with his head down, his hands jammed into his pockets.

Pitt saw a gardener cross the end of the path and go into the maze a hundred feet ahead of them.

"Walk properly," he said quickly. "Take your hands out of your pockets."

"What?" Tellman stared at him.

"You're supposed to be a valet," Pitt repeated tensely. "Walk like one. Take your hands out of your pockets."

Tellman swore under his breath, but he obeyed.

"This is a waste of time," he said bitterly. "We should be back in London finding out who killed poor Denbigh. That's something that really matters. Nobody's ever going to sort this lot out. They hate each other, and always will. Even the bleedin' servants won't talk civilly to each other."

He swiveled to look at Pitt, his brow puckered. "Did you know servants are even more particular about rank and status than their masters?" He let out his breath in a sigh. "Everyone's got their job, and they'd let the whole house grind to a stop sooner than let one man do another man's duty, even if it's as trifling as carrying a coal bucket a few yards. Footmen won't lift a damn thing if it's the housemaid's job. Stand and watch the poor girl struggle with it, they will.

There's so many of them I don't know how they ever keep it all straight." His lean face was tight-lipped with contempt. "We all eat in the servants' hall, but the first ten carry their pudding into the housekeeper's sitting room. I hope you appreciate, Superintendent, that you are considered the lowest-ranking gentleman here, so I have to follow after the other valets, in strict order of precedence." It was said with a mixture of venom and contempt.

"I can see it bothers you." Pitt carefully put his hands in his pockets. "Just remember what we are here for. You may be a poor valet, but what matters is that you are a good policeman."

Tellman swore again.

They were walking around the outside of the building, observing the approaches, the cover afforded by outbuildings and shrubbery.

"Is all that locked at night?" Tellman jerked his head towards the facade with its rows of windows. "Not that it'd make a lot o' difference. A good star-glazier'd cut the glass and be inside in a moment."

"That's why the gamekeeper is around all night with the dogs," Pitt replied. "And we have the local police watching the roads and keeping an eye on the fields as well. The Ashworth Hall staff know their land far better than any outsider will."

"Spoken to the gardeners?" Tellman asked.

"Yes, and the footmen and coachmen, grooms and bootboy, in case anyone shows up at the back door."

"Can't think of anything else to do," Tellman agreed. He looked sideways at Pitt. "D'you think there's any chance they'll agree on anything anyway?"

"I don't know. But I have some respect for Ainsley Greville. He seems to have them talking civilly, which after this morning is a very considerable achievement."

Tellman frowned. "What happened this morning? Your Gracie came downstairs and said there was a terrible screaming going on, but she wouldn't say what it was about. She's a curious one, that." He looked away, studying the gravel they were now walking over, their feet crunching noisily. "One minute as soft as warm butter, the next like you'd stuck your hand in a bed o' nettles, all pride and vinegar. Can't make her out. But she's got spirit, and for a servant, she's quite good."

"Don't mistake Gracie," Pitt said with some asperity, as well as a certain amusement. He knew Tellman's opinion of being in service. "She's very clever indeed, in her own way. Got far more practical sense than you have, and at least as much judgment of people."

"Oh, I don't know about that," Tellman protested. "She says she can read and write, but—"

"So she can!"

"But she's still only a bit of a girl."

Pitt did not bother to argue. He started up a flight of stone-flagged stairs.

"So what was the screaming?" Tellman pursued, catching up.

"Miss Moynihan found her brother in bed with Mrs. McGinley," Pitt replied.

"What?" Tellman missed his footing and all but fell over. "What did you say?"

Pitt repeated it.

Tellman swore yet again.

They ate luncheon of cold poached salmon, pheasant in aspic, game pie or jugged hare, fresh vegetables and young potatoes. The butler came in discreetly and in a low voice announced to Emily that a Miss Justine Baring had arrived, and should he show her in or ask her to wait in the withdrawing room and offer her refreshment there.

"Oh, please ask her to join us here," Emily said quickly, glancing around the table only to make sure that they had all heard.

Piers's face brightened and he rose to his feet.

Eudora stiffened expectantly.

Everyone else turned towards the door out of interest or politeness.

The young woman who came in when the butler returned was of average height and very slender, too much so for many people's taste.

She had none of the luxurious curves that were fashionable, as had Kezia, for example, now sitting at table white-faced and still obviously bitterly angry. In this young woman it was her face which was arresting. She was as dark as Iona, but of a completely different cast of feature. There was nothing of the Celtic romance about her; rather, she looked Mediterranean, exotic. Her brow was smooth, her hairline a perfect arc, her eyes long-lashed and exquisite, her cheekbones high, her lips delicate. It was only when she turned sideways one noticed that her nose was very long and distinctly curved. It was the single feature of her face which was quite wrong, and it made her unique and full of character.

"Welcome to Ashworth Hall, Miss Baring," Emily said warmly. "Would you care to join us for luncheon, or have you already eaten? Dessert perhaps? Or at least a glass of wine?"

Justine smiled, still looking at Emily. "Thank you, Mrs. Radley. I should be delighted, if I am not intruding?"

"Of course not." Emily nodded to the butler, who was already standing beside the serving table and had extra silver in his hand. He came forward and began setting a place for Justine, next to Eudora and opposite Piers.

"May I introduce you?" Emily offered. "I believe you have not yet made the acquaintance of your future parents-in-law, Mr. Ainsley Greville . . ."

Justine turned to Ainsley and her body stiffened under its deep rose-pink wool, highly fashionably cut. She might have no family, but she certainly did not lack money or taste. It was a marvelous gown. She took a deep breath and let it out very slowly, as if controlling herself with an intense effort. There was no color whatever in her cheeks, but her complexion was naturally olive toned, and she may have been tired from traveling. For a girl of no breeding to boast, no social connections at all, meeting her fiancé's parents for the first time must be a testing experience. When they were well-born, wealthy, and he held a high position in government, it must be doubly so. Emily did not envy her. She could still recall her first meeting with George's cousins and aunts, which was bad enough. His parents had been no longer alive. That would have been even more difficult.

"How do you do, Miss Baring," Ainsley said after a long moment's hesitation. He spoke slowly, almost deliberately. "We are delighted to meet you. May I introduce my wife." He touched Eudora lightly on the elbow, still keeping his eyes on Justine.

"How do you do, Mrs. Greville," Justine answered, clearing her throat of a little huskiness.

Eudora smiled. She looked nervous as well. "How do you do, Miss Baring. It is delightful to meet you. I hope you will be able to stay long enough for us to become well acquainted."

"Thank you . . ." Justine accepted.

"That rather depends upon Mrs. Radley, my dear," Ainsley said quickly.

Eudora blushed deep pink.

Emily was angry with Ainsley for causing her embarrassment. It was out of character for the diplomat she had perceived.

"I have already said Miss Baring is most welcome," she cut in firmly. "She will be a charming addition to our party for as long as she wishes and is able to remain." She smiled at Justine. "We are two ladies short as it is—in fact, three. You will be a great asset to us. Now, may I introduce you to the other guests?" And she named them one by one around the table. Fergal was courteous, if cool, and Kezia managed a smile. Padraig was charming. Lorcan inclined his head slightly and bade her welcome. Even Carson O'Day expressed pleasure in meeting her.

Piers, of course, did not attempt to mask his feelings for her, and when she met his eyes her own emotions were as plain to see.

He was already on his feet, and pulled out her chair for her, touching her softly on the shoulder as he assisted her to take her place, then returned to his own.

Everyone, except perhaps Kezia, seemed to make an extra effort to hide their antipathies. Perhaps it was self-protection against someone who appeared to have no idea who they were or why they should be here, other than for the most usual of social reasons, as in any other country house party over a long weekend. If she had noticed an unusual number of Irish names, she gave no sign of it.

"How did you meet?" Emily asked politely.

"Quite by accident," Piers replied, obviously happy to discuss anything to do with Justine. He could not keep from glancing at her, and when he did she colored very faintly and lowered her eyes. Emily had the distinct impression it was not shyness of him, or any ordinary self-consciousness, but a shyness of her prospective parents-in-law, sitting only two or three places away. Such modesty was what was expected, and she was going to do exactly what any young woman would, to the least thing.

Emily would have done the same.

Everyone appeared to be listening.

"I was leaving the theater with a group of friends," Piers continued enthusiastically. "I don't even remember what I saw, something by Pinero, I think, but it went right out of my head the moment I met Justine. She was leaving also, with one of my professors—a brilliant man, lecturer in diseases of the heart in particular, and of the circulation. It was quite appropriate that I should speak with him, and I had to seize the chance to be introduced to Justine."

He smiled a little self-mockingly. "I knew she could not be his wife. He is a fellow of the college. I was afraid she might be a niece and he would not approve of a mere student seeking an acquaintance with her."

Justine glanced up at Ainsley, who was looking at her. He looked down again immediately. She seemed uncomfortable.

"And was she?" Eudora enquired.

"No," Piers said with relief. "She was merely a friend. He said she was the daughter of an old student of his with whom he had kept in touch, until he had unfortunately died young."

"How very sad." Eudora shook her head a little.

"And you did not allow the single introduction to be the end to it?" Emily deduced with a smile.

"Of course he didn't." Padraig looked from one to the other of them. "No young man worth his salt would. If you see the one woman in the world who is right for you, you follow her wherever she goes, through cites and countryside, mountains and high seas, to the ends of the earth, if need be. Isn't that so?" He was addressing the table at large.

Piers grinned. "Of course it is."

Iona kept her eyes on her plate.

"Wherever it takes you," Fergal agreed suddenly, looking up at Padraig, then at Piers. "Grip your courage in both hands, and to the devil with fears."

Kezia ground her fork into the last piece of her game pie.

"Come heaven or hell, honor or dishonor," she said very clearly. "Just go on, take what you want, never count the cost or look to see who pays it."

Piers looked disconcerted. He was one of the few who had no idea what had happened that morning, but he was not so blinded by his own happiness that he missed the pain in her voice—and no one at all could have missed the anger, even not knowing what it was for.

"I didn't mean that, Miss Moynihan," he answered. "Of course, I would not have pursued her had there been anything dishonorable in it, for her or for me. But thank heaven, she was as free as I am, and seems to return my feelings."

"Congratulations, my boy," Padraig said sincerely.

The butler served Justine with a little cold salmon, sliced cucumber and potatoes with herbs, and offered her chilled white wine.

Somebody made a comment about an opera currently playing in London. Someone else said they had seen it in Dublin. Padraig remarked on the difficulty of the soprano role, and O'Day agreed with him.

Emily glanced at Jack, and he smiled back guardedly.

The butler and footmen were waiting to serve the next course, as were one or two of the valets. Finn Hennessey was there. Tellman was not, which was almost certainly a good thing.

The men returned to their political discussions. At least outwardly there appeared very little rancor. If they had even approached argument on anything at all it was not hinted at.

The ladies decided to go for a walk in the woods. It was a bright afternoon with a few light clouds and a mild breeze. It could not be counted upon to last. Even the evening could change and bring rain or a sudden drop in temperature. The next day there could be gales, frost, steady drumming sleet, or it could be as pleasant as today.

The six of them set out across the lawn. Emily led the way with Kezia. She tried a conversation but it very quickly became apparent that Kezia did not wish to speak, and Emily allowed it to lapse into a polite silence.

Eudora took Justine and they followed a few yards behind, a marked contrast to each other: Eudora handsome figured, the light bright in her auburn hair, walking with her head high; Justine very slender, almost thin, her hair black as a crow's wing, her movements peculiarly graceful, and when she turned in profile to speak, the extraordinary nose.

Charlotte was left to walk with Iona. It was not something she wished to do, but social duty required it, and loyalty to Emily made it a necessity. She wished she knew the woods better so that they might furnish some subject to discuss. All she could think of was Emily's warnings not to discuss politics, religion, divorce or potatoes. Almost everything that came to her mind seemed to lead to one or the other of them. It was better to walk in silence than be reduced to making remarks about the weather.

She could see Eudora talking to Justine, apparently asking her questions. It was as if she were hungry to learn of a courtship she knew nothing about. Charlotte wondered why Piers had said nothing to her before.

Some remark about Piers and Justine was on her lips, then she bit it off, realizing romance must now be another forbidden subject. What on earth did one say to a married woman one had surprised in bed with another man only that morning? It was a subject no etiquette manual broached. Presumably, well-bred ladies made sure they never did such a thing. If one should be so unfortunate, or so careless, one pretended it had not happened. But that was not possible when someone was screaming at the top of her lungs.

A magpie flew across their path just as they reached the end of the lawn and started down the rhododendron walk.

"Oh, isn't it beautiful!" Charlotte exclaimed.

"One for sorrow," Iona answered.

"I beg your pardon?"

"It is unlucky to see a single magpie," Iona elaborated. "One should see either a pair or none."

"Why?"

Now Iona looked mystified. "It just . . . is!"

Charlotte kept her tone polite and interested. "Unlucky for whom? Do farmers say so, or bird-watchers?"

"No, for us. It is a . . ."

"A superstition?"

"Yes!"

"Oh, I see. I'm sorry. How silly of me. I thought you were serious."

Iona frowned, but said nothing, and Charlotte realized with a jolt that she had been serious. Perhaps she was as much mystic Celt as modern Christian. There was a romantic bravado about her, a recklessness, as if she could see some reality beyond the physical or social world. Perhaps that was the quality in her which had most captured the rather literal-minded Fergal. She must represent for him a realm of magical possibilities, dreams and ideas that had never crossed his thoughts. In a sense he had come newly alive. Charlotte wondered what he gave Iona. He seemed a trifle unyielding. Perhaps it was the challenge. Or perhaps she imagined in him something that was not there?

She cast about for something else to say. The silence was uncomfortable. She noticed the rich quantities of hips on the wild roses as they entered the woods.

"A hard winter coming," Iona said, then flashed a sudden smile. "General knowledge, not superstition!"

Charlotte laughed, and suddenly they were both easier. "Yes, I've heard that too. I've never remembered what they were like long enough to see it if was true."

"Actually," Iona agreed, "neither have I. Looking at all those berries, I hope it isn't."

They walked under the smooth trunks of the beeches, the wind in the bare branches overhead, their feet crunching on the carpet of rust and bronze fallen leaves.

"There are bluebells here in the spring," Charlotte went on. "They come before the leaves do."

"I know," Iona said quickly. "It's like walking between two skies. . . ."

They accomplished the rest of the journey sharing knowledge of nature, Iona telling her stories from Irish legend about stones and trees, heroes and tragedies of the mystic past.

They returned in different order, except that Eudora still walked with Justine, still asking about Piers. Emily shot Charlotte a look of gratitude and exchanged Kezia for Iona.

They saw bright pheasants picking over the fallen grain at the edge of the fields bordering the woods, and Charlotte remarked on them. Kezia answered, but with only a word.

The sun was low in the west, burning flame and gold. The shadows lengthened across the plowed field to the south, its furrows dark and curving gently over the rise and fall of the land. The wind had increased and the starlings were whirled up like driven leaves against the ragged sky, spreading wide and wheeling back in again.

The sunset grew even brighter, the clear stretches of sky between the clouds almost green.

The thought of hot tea and crumpets by the fire began to seem very pleasant.

Gracie was very preoccupied as she helped Charlotte dress for dinner in the oyster silk gown.

"It looks very beautiful, ma'am," she said sincerely, and the magnitude of her admiration for it was in her eyes. Then the moment after she added, "I learned a bit more about why them folks is 'ere today. I 'ope they really can make peace and give Ireland its freedom. There's bin some terrible wrongs done. I in't proud o' bein' English w'en I hear some o' their stories." She put a final touch to Charlotte's hair, setting the pearl-beaded ornament straight. "Not as I believes 'em all, o' course. But even if any of 'em is true, there's bin some awful cruel men in Ireland."

"On both sides, I expect," Charlotte said carefully, regarding her reflection in the glass, but her mind at least half upon what Gracie had said. She looked at Gracie's small face, pinched now with anxiety and compassion. "They're working as hard as they can," she assured her. "And I think Mr. Greville is very skilled. He won't give up."

" 'E better 'adn't." Gracie stopped all pretense of attending to the shawl she had in her hands. "There's terrible things 'appenin' ter all kinds o' people, old women and children, not just men as can fight. Maybe them Fenians an' the like is wrong, but they wouldn't a bin there if'n it weren't fer us bein' in Ireland when we got no place there in the beginnin'."

"There's no point in going back to the beginning, Gracie," Charlotte said levelly. "We probably shouldn't be here either. Who should? The Normans, the Vikings, the Danes, the Romans? The Scots all came from Ireland in the first place."

"No ma'am, the Scots is in Scotland," Gracie corrected.

Charlotte shook her head. "I know they are now, but before that the Picts were. Then the Scots came across from Ireland and drove the Picts out."

"Where'd they go to, then?"

"I don't know. I think maybe they were almost all killed."

"Well, if the Scots came from Ireland and took over Scotland"—Gracie was thinking hard—"who's all in Ireland? Why don't they get on wi' each other, like we do?"

"Because some of the Scots went back again, and by this time they were Protestant and the rest were Catholic. They'd grown very different in the meantime."

"Then they shouldn't oughta gone back."

"Possibly not, but it's too late now. We can't go forward from anywhere except where we are at the moment."

Gracie thought about that for a long time before she conceded it as Charlotte was about to go out of the door.

Charlotte met Pitt at the bottom of the stairs and was caught by surprise at how pleased she was at the start of admiration in his eyes when he saw her. She felt a heat in her cheeks. He offered his arm, and she took it as she sailed into the withdrawing room.

Dinner was again uncomfortable, but eased in some part by the addition of Piers and Justine, which gave everyone something to talk about other than their own interests, or trivia, which were embarrassingly meaningless.

There were too few of them at the table to separate all those between whom there was friction. It was a hostess's nightmare. There was order of precedence to consider. People might be insulted if one did not. If there was no title or office to dictate, then there was age. And yet one could not sit Fergal either next to or opposite Lorcan McGinley, nor could one sit him close to Iona, for reasons which were excruciatingly clear to some and quite unknown to others. Similarly, one could not sit Kezia near to her brother. The rage still simmered in her only just below the heat of explosion.

Carson O'Day was the savior of the situation. He seemed both able and willing to conduct agreeable conversations with everyone, finding subjects to discuss from areas as diverse and innocuous as designs of Georgian silver and the last eruption of Mount Vesuvius.

Padraig Doyle told amusing anecdotes about an Irish tinker and a parish priest and made everyone laugh, except Kezia, a failure which he ignored.

Piers and Justine had real attention only for each other.

Eudora looked a trifle sad, as if she had just realized the loss of something she had thought she possessed, and Ainsley appeared bored. Every now and then Charlotte observed an expression of anxiety in his eyes, a difficulty swallowing, a moment to steady his hand. He would miss something someone had said to him, as if his mind were elsewhere, and have to ask to have it repeated. It must be an appalling responsibility to be in charge of such a conference as this. The burden of succeeding at the impossible had broken both greater and lesser men than he.

And if he was also afraid, he had good reason. There was still the threat of violence which perhaps only he and Pitt really understood.

No one had mentioned the Parnell-O'Shea divorce. If there had been anything of it in the newspapers, it was not referred to.

They were rather more than halfway through the removes—a shoulder of lamb, stuffed beef in pastry, or cold pickled eel with cucumber and onions—when the quarrel began. It was Kezia who started it. All evening she had been barely suppressing her anger. She spoke civilly enough to everyone else, and she ignored Iona as if she had not been there. Her rage was for her brother.

He made a rather sweeping statement about Protestant ethics.

"There is much of it that is personal," he said, leaning forward a little across the table, speaking to Justine. "It has to do with individual responsibility, direct communication between man and God, rather than always through the intermediary of a priest, who, after all, is only mortal, and fallible like all human beings."

"Some more fallible than others," Kezia said bitterly.

Fergal colored very slightly and ignored her.

"The Protestant preacher is merely the leader of his flock," he went on, fixing his gaze on Justine. "Faith is of the utmost importance, simple and utter faith, but not in miracles and magic, in the redeeming power of Christ to save souls."

"We believe in hard work, obedience and a chaste and honorable life," Kezia said, staring at Justine as if no one else had spoken. "At least that's what they say." She swung around to Fergal. "Isn't it, my dear brother? Chastity is next to godliness. No unclean thing can enter into the kingdom of heaven. We are not like people of the Church of Rome, who can sin from Monday to Saturday as long as they tell the priest all about it on Sunday, when he sits in his dark little room behind a grill, and listens to all your grubby little secrets, and tells you to say so many prayers, and it's all washed away—until next time, when you'll do the same thing all over again. I'll wager he could say it for you, he's heard it so many times—"

"Kezia . . ." Fergal interrupted.

She ignored him, fixing Justine with blazing eyes, high spots of color in her cheeks. Her hands, holding her knife and fork, were shaking.

"We are not like that at all. We don't tell anyone our sins, except God . . . as if He didn't already know! As if He didn't know every dirty little secret of our dirty little hearts! As if He couldn't smell the stink of a hypocrite a thousand miles away!"

There was a hot silence around the table. Padraig cleared his throat, but at the last moment could think of nothing to say.

Eudora gave a little moan.

"Really . . ." Ainsley began.

Justine smiled, looking straight back at Kezia. "It seems to me that the only thing that matters is whether you are sorry or not. Whom you tell is beside the point." Her voice was very soft. "If you see that what you have done is ugly, and you no longer wish to do anything like it, then you have to change, and surely that is what matters?"

Kezia stared at her.

It was Fergal who spoiled it. There was a flush of embarrassment on his fair cheeks, but also of self-defense.

"The idea that you are accountable to someone other than God, that any human being is in a position to judge you, to forgive or condemn—"

Kezia swung around in her seat. "You'd like that, wouldn't you?" She laughed harshly, her voice rising out of control. "Nobody is fit to judge you. For God's sake, who do you think you are? We judge you! I judge you, and I find you guilty, you hypocrite!"

"Kezia, go to your room until you have calmed down," he said between his teeth. "You are hysterical. It is . . ."

His words were lost as she flung back her chair, picked up her half-empty glass and threw the dregs in his face. Then she rose to her feet and ran from the room, almost bumping into a maid, coming in with fresh gravy, who moved out of the way only just in time.

The silence burned with embarrassment.

"I'm sorry," Fergal said unhappily. "She is . . . very . . . nervously disposed at the moment. I'm sure she will be profoundly sorry tomorrow. I apologize for her, Mrs. Radley . . . ladies. . . ."

Charlotte glanced at Emily, then stood up. "I think I should go and see if she is all right. She seemed in a state of some distress."

"Yes, yes, that is a good idea," Emily agreed, and Charlotte caught in her eye a glimpse of envy for her escape.

Charlotte left the dining room and, after a glance at the empty hallway, started up the stairs. The only place Kezia could be sure of privacy would be her bedroom. It was where Charlotte herself would have gone had she just made such a scene. She certainly would not want to risk anyone coming after her in some other public place such as the conservatory or the withdrawing room.

On the landing she saw one of the young tweenies, about the age Gracie had been when she had first come to them.

"Did Miss Moynihan come past here?" she asked the girl.

The girl nodded, eyes wide, hair poking out in wisps from under her lace cap.

"Thank you." Charlotte already knew which was Kezia's room, and as before, she went to it and opened the door without waiting for admittance.

Kezia was lying on the bed, curled over, her shoulders hunched, her skirts billowing around her.

Charlotte closed the door and went over and sat on the end of the bed.

Kezia did not move.

There was nothing Charlotte could say which would alter what Kezia had seen and the only possible meaning anyone could attach to it. All that could be changed was how Kezia would feel about it.

"You are very unhappy indeed, aren't you . . . ?" she began quietly, in a calm, unemotional voice.

For several minutes Kezia did not move, then slowly she turned around and sat up, propping herself against the pillows, and stared at Charlotte with profound contempt.

"I am not 'unhappy' "—she pronounced the word distinctly—"as you so quaintly put it. I don't know what your moral beliefs are, Mrs. Pitt. Perhaps fornicating with someone else's wife is perfectly acceptable in your circle, although I should prefer not to think so." She hunched her shoulders, as if she were cold, although the room was warm. "To me it is abhorrent. To anyone at all, it is a sin. In someone who knows the values my brother does, who was raised in a God-fearing household by one of the most honorable, righteous and courageous preachers of his day, it is unforgivable." Her face was ugly with rage as she said it, her clear eyes, red-rimmed with weeping, blazed her fury.

Charlotte looked at her steadily, trying to think of something to say which would reach through the tide of emotion.

"I don't have a brother," she said, searching for ideas. "But if my sister were to do such a thing, I should be hurt and grieved more than anything. I would want to argue with her, ask her why she threw away so much in return for so very little. I don't think I would refuse to speak to her. But then she is younger than I am. I feel defensive for her. Is Fergal older than you?"

Kezia looked at her as if the question was nonsensical.

"You don't understand." Her patience was wearing thin. "I am trying hard to be reasonably civil to you, but you come into my room uninvited and sit here preaching platitudes to me about what you would do in my place, and you haven't the remotest idea what you are talking about. You are not in my place, or anything like it. You have no political ambition or flair. You don't even know what it is for a woman. You are very comfortably married—with children, I expect. You are obviously very fond of your husband, and he of you. Please go away and leave me alone."

Both the condescension and the assumptions galled Charlotte, but she controlled her tongue with an effort.

"I came because I could not go on happily eating my dinner when you are in such distress," she answered. "I suppose what I would do is irrelevant. I just wanted you to see that by refusing to talk to your brother, you are hurting yourself most of all." She frowned. "If you think about it, what is the result of your withdrawing from him going to be?"

"I don't know what you mean." Kezia leaned back, her eyes narrowed.

"Do you think he is going to stop seeing Mrs. McGinley?" Charlotte asked. "Do you think he will realize how wrong it is, that it is morally against all he has believed throughout his life, and certainly politically unwise if he hopes to represent his people? For heaven's sake, isn't Mr. Parnell's situation evidence enough of that?"

Kezia looked faintly surprised, as if she had not yet even thought of that. And yet she must have been aware of the divorce presently being heard in London where Captain William O'Shea was citing Charles Stewart Parnell, the leader of the Irish Nationalist party as corespondent. Perhaps she had refused to realize what O'Shea's victory would mean.

"It doesn't look like it to me," Charlotte continued. "When people fall in love, madly, obsessively, they frequently do not stop to weigh the cost if they are found out. If all that he stands to lose has not held him back, will your displeasure?"

"No," Kezia said with a harsh laugh, as if the idea were funny in a twisting, hurting fashion. "No, of course not! I'm not doing it because of anything I expect him to feel or to do. I'm just so . . . so furious with him I can't help myself. It's not even the denial of his beliefs, the throwing away of his career, or the betrayal of the people who believe in him. It's the sheer damnable hypocrisy that I can never forgive!"

"Can't you?" Charlotte asked with a slight lift of question. "When people you love fall far below what is even honorable, much less what one knows they could be, it hurts appallingly." Swift memories returned of past pain of her own, discoveries she would much rather not have made, and then of the learning to accept afterwards, the slow forgetting of the worst of it, the gentleness that followed for her own sake, to keep the parts that were precious and good. "One is angry because one feels it didn't have to be. But perhaps it did. Perhaps he has to work his way through his weakness in order to conquer it. Eventually he may be less quick to condemn others. He—"

Kezia let out a bark of disgust. "Oh, for heaven's sake be quiet. You have no idea what you are saying!" She moved around and raised her knees, almost protectively. "You are talking pompous rubbish. I could forgive him easily enough if he were merely weak. God knows, we all are."

Her face, with all its soft, generous lines, was twisted hard with pain and the memory of pain. "But when I fell in love with a Catholic man, loved him with all my heart and soul, just after Papa died, Fergal wouldn't even listen to me. He forbade me from seeing him. He wouldn't even let me tell him myself." Her voice was so harsh with remembered pain the words were indistinct. "He told him! He told Cathal I would never be permitted to marry him. It would be blasphemy against my faith. He told me that, too!

"I was too young to marry without permission. He was my legal guardian, and I couldn't have run away without forfeiting the Church's blessing. I listened to Fergal and obeyed him. I let Cathal go." Her eyes filled with tears that spilled down her cheeks, not in fury this time, but remembered sweetness and the reminding of its loss. "He's dead now. I can't ever find him again."

Charlotte said nothing.

Kezia looked at her. "So you see, I can't forgive Fergal for going and lying with a Catholic woman, and somebody else's wife to add to it. When I put flowers on Cathal's grave, how can I explain that to him?"

"I'm not sure I could forgive that either," Charlotte confessed, not moving from where she sat. "I'm sorry I was so quick to presume."

Kezia shrugged, and searched for a handkerchief.

Charlotte handed her one from the bedside cabinet.

Kezia blew her nose fiercely.

"But what I said is still true," Charlotte added apologetically. "He is your only brother, isn't he? Do you really want to cut the bonds that hold you to each other? Won't that hurt you as much as it does him? He's done a terrible thing. He'll suffer for it, sooner or later, won't he?"

"Divine justice?" Kezia raised her eyebrows. "I'm not sure that I believe in it." She tightened her lips, more in self-knowledge than bitterness. "Anyway, I don't think that I'm prepared to wait for that."

"No, quite ordinary human guilt," Charlotte corrected. "And that doesn't usually take that long to come, even if it is not recognized as such immediately."

Kezia thought in silence.

"Do you really want to create a gulf between you that you cannot cross?" Charlotte asked. "Not for him, for yourself?"

Again it was a long time before Kezia replied.

"No . . ." She said at last, reluctantly. She smiled very slightly. "I suppose you are not quite as pompous as I thought. I apologize for that."

Charlotte smiled back. "Good. Pomposity is such a bore, and so masculine, don't you think?"

This time Kezia did actually laugh.

The rest of the evening was strained. Kezia did not return, which was probably as well, but even so, Lorcan's presence was sufficient to keep the disaster in everyone's minds. The subject of the Parnell-O'Shea divorce was studiously ignored, which meant a great deal of political speculation had also to be avoided. The conversation degenerated into platitudes, and everyone was glad to retire early.

Charlotte sat on the dressing stool in the sanctuary of her bedroom.

"This is ghastly," she said, running a silk scarf over her hair to keep it smooth and make it shine. "With this atmosphere one hardly needs to worry about Fenian dynamiters or assassins from outside."

Pitt was already sitting in bed.

"What did Kezia Moynihan say? Is she going to make scenes all weekend?"

"She has a certain amount of justice on her side." She repeated what Kezia had told her.

"Perhaps I should be protecting him," Pitt said dryly. "From Kezia and from Lorcan McGinley, who has even more justice on his side; from Iona, if they quarrel or he breaks it off or she wants to and he won't . . . or from Carson O'Day, for his jeopardizing the Protestant cause."

"Or Emily," Charlotte added, "for making a bad party into a complete nightmare." She put the scarf down and turned out the gas lamp above the dressing table, leaving no light in the room except the glow from the last embers of the fire. She climbed into bed beside him and snuggled down.

For a second morning in a row they were woken by a shrill, tearing screaming.

Pitt swore and stirred, burying his head in the pillow.

The scream came again, high and terrified.

Reluctantly Pitt got out of bed and stumbled across the floor, grasping for his robe. He opened the door and went out onto the landing. Twenty feet away the handsome maid, Doll, was standing in the open doorway of the Grevilles' bathroom, her face ashen, her hands to her throat as if she could barely breathe.

Pitt strode over, put both hands on her shoulders to move her aside, and looked in.

Ainsley Greville lay in the bath, naked, his chest, shoulders and face under the water. There could be no question whatever that he was dead.

CHAPTER FOUR

Pitt swung around, barring the way with his body. "Take her and look after her," he said to Charlotte, who was now on the landing. It was obvious he was referring to Doll, who still stood swaying a little, gasping for breath. He met Charlotte's eyes. "Greville is dead."

She hesitated only a moment, her face tightening, then she walked forward and took the unresisting Doll and, putting her arm around her, guided her away.

There were now several other people gathered, newly awoken, anxious, but still with yesterday's embarrassment high in their minds.

"What is it now?" Padraig Doyle moved past Piers, who was standing, startled and disheveled, next to the banister. A step behind him, Eudora looked worried but not frightened.

Fergal Moynihan was coming out of his room, opposite Pitt's, blinking, his hair poking in spikes as if he were newly awakened. He left the door wide open, and Iona was plainly not present.

"What is it?" Padraig repeated, looking from Pitt to Charlotte and back again.

"I am afraid there has been an accident," Pitt said quietly. There was no point in supposing it was anything else yet. "There is nothing to be done to help at the moment."

"You mean . . . it is fatal?" Padraig looked only momentarily startled. He was not a man to panic or lose control of his composure. "Ainsley?"

"I am afraid so." As he spoke, Pitt was reaching for the bathroom door to close it.

"I see." Padraig turned to Eudora, a great gentleness in him. He put his arm around her shoulders, and the very tenderness of it alarmed her.

"What is it?" she demanded. "Padraig?" She pulled away, turning to face him.

"Ainsley," he answered, looking at her very directly. "There's nothing you can do. Come away. I'll take you back to your room and sit with you."

"Ainsley?" For a moment it was as if she had not understood.

"Yes. He's dead, sweetheart. You must be strong."

Carson O'Day was coming along the passage from behind them, Iona from the other direction, wearing a beautiful midnight-blue robe. It billowed out behind her with her movement, like clouds of night.

Fergal looked startled, perhaps by Padraig's choice of words.

"Mr. Doyle . . ." Pitt began.

Padraig misunderstood him. "She's my sister," he explained.

"I was going to ask you to help Mrs. Greville to her room"—Pitt shook his head a little—"and ask Mrs. Radley's maid to go to her. I don't think her own maid is in any state to help. And would you ask someone, Tellman, to come up here, please?" He looked around. Emily had arrived, her face harassed as she envisioned some new social breach. Jack was nowhere to be seen. Perhaps he had risen early again.

Emily looked at Pitt, and knew that this time it was no simple love affair. She took a deep breath and deliberately steadied herself.

"I'm sorry, but Ainsley Greville is dead," Pitt said to everyone. "There is nothing that can be done to help him. It would be best if you all returned to your rooms and dressed as usual. We cannot be certain yet exactly what happened or what steps we should take next. Have someone find Mr. Radley and inform him."

Padraig had already gone with Eudora.

"I'll do that," O'Day offered. He looked pale but in command of himself. "It's a tragedy that it should happen now. He was a brilliant man. Our best hope for conciliation." With a sigh he swiveled and went downstairs, tying his robe around his waist, his slippers soundless on the wooden stairs.

Piers came forward. "Can I help?" he offered, his voice husky but almost steady. His eyes were very wide and he shook a little, as if he had not yet fully understood. "I've almost completed my medical studies. It would be a lot quicker and more discreet than sending for someone from the village." He gave a little cough. "Then I would like to go and be with my mother. Padraig's marvelous, but I think I should . . . and Justine. She will feel dreadful when she hears. Perhaps I should be the one to tell her—"

"Later," Pitt cut across him. "Now we need a doctor to look at your father."

Piers was jolted. "Yes," he agreed, his face tightening. "Yes, of course."

Pitt pushed the door open and stepped back for Piers to follow him in. On the landing, people were moving away. Tellman should be there soon.

As soon as Piers was in, Pitt closed the door and watched as the young man walked over to the bath, which was full almost to the brim, and to the naked corpse of his father. He stood close behind him, in case the sight should cause him to feel faint. The strongest will is not always proof against sheer physical shock. However many bodies he had seen in the course of his studies, there would be no other like this.

Piers did sway for a moment or two, but he leaned forward and put his outstretched hands on the bath to steady himself. Slowly he knelt down and touched the dead face, then the arms and hands.

Pitt watched. He had never got used to it either, even when it seemed peaceful like this. He had known Ainsley Greville when he was alive, only hours before. He had been a man of unusual vigor and intelligence, a man of powerful personality. This shell lying half below the bathwater was so familiarly him, and yet not him at all. In a sense it was already no one. The will and intellect were somewhere else.

Pitt looked down at Piers's hands. They were strong and slender. They could become a surgeon's hands. They moved quite professionally, instinctively now, testing movement, temperature, exploring for injury without disturbing the body. How much effort did it cost him to be so composed? Whether he had loved him deeply or not, whether they had been close, the man was still his father, a unique relationship.

Pitt stared at the scene to mark in his memory every line, every aspect and detail of what he saw. There was no discoloration in the water.

Where the devil was Tellman?

"He's been dead since last night," Piers said, rising to his feet. "I suppose that's really rather obvious. The bathwater is cold. I assume it must have been hot when he got into it. It will have delayed the onset of rigor, but I don't suppose that is of any importance." He straightened up and took a step backward. His face was very white and he seemed to be finding it difficult to catch his breath. "It is easy enough to see what must have happened. There is a very bad blow at the back of his head. I can feel the depression in the skull. He must have slipped when he was climbing in the bath, or maybe trying to get out." His eyes deliberately avoided the bath. "Soap perhaps. I don't see a tablet, but there is some dissolved in the water. Maybe you don't need much? He struck his head and lost consciousness. People do drown in baths. It happens too often."

"Thank you." Pitt watched him closely. That calm might hide emotion almost beyond bearing, might give way to shock at any moment.

"You'll have to get someone else for the certificate, of course,"

Piers hurried on. "They wouldn't accept it from me, even if I were not his . . . his son." He swallowed. "I'm . . . I'm not qualified yet."

"I understand." Pitt was about to add more when there was a sharp rap on the door. He opened it and Tellman came in, looked hastily at Piers, then at the body in the bath. He turned back to Pitt.

"May I go to Justine?" Piers asked, frowning slightly at Tellman. He did not understand the intrusion of a manservant.

"Certainly," Pitt answered. "And your mother, of course. Do I understand that Mr. Doyle is her brother?"

"Yes. Why?"

"I imagine he will help you in the arrangements that will need to be made, but I would be obliged if you could let me know before you contact anyone outside Ashworth Hall."

"Why?"

"Your father was a government minister in a sensitive position, especially this weekend. The Home Office should be informed officially before anyone else."

"Oh . . . yes, of course. I didn't think. . . ." If he wondered why Pitt should consider such a thing, he did not say so. Probably his emotions were far too occupied for such trivialities.

As soon as he had gone Tellman bent forward and looked more closely at the body.

"Natural or accident?" he asked, although there was skepticism in his voice. "Odd, isn't it, after all our fears and precautions."

Pitt took the towel off the rail and spread it over the middle of the body in some sort of modesty.

"It looks as if he slipped and knocked himself unconscious on the back of the bath," he said thoughtfully.

"What, then, drowned?" Tellman regarded the body with puckered brow. "I suppose so. Seems odd, first when he was threatened." He walked over to the small window and examined it. It was about two feet square, the opening half that. They were twenty feet above the ground.

Pitt shook his head.

Tellman abandoned the idea. He returned to the bath.

"Any harm if we move him?" he asked.

"We're going to have to," Pitt conceded. "And long before we fetch any doctor from the village. I'll have to call Cornwallis, but I want to know as much as I can before I do."

Tellman snorted. "So we don't have to play games anymore?"

Pitt looked at him with an ironic smile. "Let's be discreet a little longer. Hold him up and I'll have a closer look at the wound at the back of his head."

"Suspicious?" Tellman glanced at him quickly.

"Careful," Pitt replied. "Hold him up. Take his arms and pull him forward a bit, if you can. He's very stiff still. I just want to see the wound."

Tellman obliged, somewhat awkwardly, getting his cuffs wet to his considerable annoyance.

Pitt looked closely, then felt the wet hair very gently with the tips of his fingers. As Piers had said, the indentation of the crushed bone was easy to find, a long ridge at the very base of the skull, rounded, quite wide.

"Right?" Tellman asked.

Pitt felt it again. It was straight, absolutely regular, about the width of the rim of the back of the bath.

"What's the matter?" Tellman said impatiently. "He's very awkward to hold! He's as stiff as a poker, and slipping. There must be soap in this water!"

"There often is in baths," Pitt agreed. "But that suggests Piers was right, and he was about to get out when he slipped rather than getting in."

"What does it matter?" Tellman was getting wetter, and the water was cold.

"It probably doesn't," Pitt conceded. "Just makes it more likely, that's all. The soap, I mean. Slippery."

"Should wash at a basin, like anyone else!" Tellman snapped. "Can't drown yourself in a basin."

"It's not the right shape," Pitt said very quietly.

Tellman was about to make a tart reply, then looked more closely at Pitt's face. "What isn't?"

"This wound. The back edge of the bath curves around. Look at it! The wound is straight."

Tellman stared at him. "What are you saying?"

"I don't think he hit himself on the rim of the bath."

"What then?"

Pitt turned and looked around the room slowly. It was quite large, about ten feet by fourteen feet. The bath was in the center, opposite the door. There were two separate rails for towels, a washstand with basin and beside it a large, blue-and-white china ewer. Another smaller table held a vase with flowers and two or three ornaments. A screen against drafts was folded and stood near the door. Apparently Greville had not felt the need for it. There was a large mirror on the wall. On the opposite side of the room was a marble-topped table with brushes and jars of bath salts and oils.

"One of those?" Pitt suggested. "Perhaps that pink one. It looks about the right size." He stood up and went over to it, leaving Tellman still holding the corpse. He looked at the jar closely without touching it. As far as he could see, there was no mark on it, no smudges of soap to indicate it had been picked up. He put his hand around it experimentally. It was quite easy to grasp. It was also heavy. It would have made an efficient weapon, if wielded with a swing and any weight behind it.

He took it back to the end of the bath and held it carefully against the back of Greville's head. It was the right width, and it was straight.

"Murder?" Tellman said dourly, pursing his lips.

"I think so. Let him down slowly, and I'll see if there is any way the edge of the bath could fit the wound."

Tellman obliged awkwardly, his shoulders hunched to take the weight, his sleeves getting even wetter. "Well?" he repeated sharply.

"No," Pitt replied. "He didn't fall onto the edge of the bath. It was either this jar or one very like it."

"Anything on it?" Tellman asked. "Any blood? Any hair? He's got a good head of hair, poor devil. Not that I liked him!"

Pitt turned the jar over very slowly, pulling a wry face at Tellman's remark.

"No," he said at last. "But this is a bathroom, it wouldn't be very difficult to wipe it clean. And no one would find soap or water odd on a jar of bath salts. Plenty of people must reach for them with wet hands."

Tellman let the body go and it fell back, stiff and clumsy, sliding under the water again, feet sticking out.

"Someone came in an' hit him from behind?" Tellman thought aloud.

"He's facing the door," Pitt pointed out. "So whoever it was, he was not afraid. He didn't cry out, and he allowed the person to pick up the jar of salts and walk behind him."

Tellman gave a sharp little bark of derision.

"Can't imagine it! What kind of man lets someone walk in on him in the bath? Isn't decent, apart from dangerous."

"Gentlemen aren't as prudish as you are," Pitt said with bitter amusement. He saw the look of incredulity in Tellman's face, and the beginning of total confusion. "Who do you think brings the hot water to add to the bath when it gets cold?" he went on.

"I don't know! A valet? A footman? You're saying one of the servants killed him?"

"I think as often as not it's the maids who carry the water or the hot towels," Pitt replied. Then, seeing Tellman's expression, he went on, "Not for me. I am as big a prude as you are. I'd sooner sit in cold water. But Greville may have been used to being waited on by the maids."

"Some maidservant came in with a bucket of hot water and hit him over the head with a jar of salts?" Tellman said in patent disbelief.

"People don't look at the faces of servants, Tellman," Pitt said seriously. "One servant looks pretty much like another, especially in livery, or in a plain black dress, white apron and white lace cap. In some houses the junior servants are even trained to turn their faces to the wall if one of the family passes by."

Tellman was filled with too much anger to speak. His eyes were dark. His lips compressed.

"It could have been anyone, dressed in livery," Pitt concluded.

"You mean an assassin from outside?" Tellman's chin jerked up.

"I don't know. We'll need to ask a lot of questions. At the time Greville had his bath, this house should have been locked up. And the outside staff were watching the grounds."

"I'll speak to all of them," Tellman promised. "You going to tell them who we are?"

"Yes." He had no choice.

"And it's murder?" Tellman went on.

"Yes."

Tellman squared his shoulders.

"We'll have to take the body out of here," Pitt went on. "There'll be an icehouse. Have one of the valets help you carry him there."

When Pitt opened the door Jack was standing outside waiting. His handsome face, with its wide eyes and extraordinary lashes, looked unusually grave, and there were signs of strain around his mouth.

"I'll have to call the Home Office," he said grimly, nodding to Tellman as he passed them and went down the stairs. "And ask them what they want to do. I suppose it's the end of the conference and any chance of success." His voice dropped. "It's damnable! What a wretched mischance. It seems as if the devil is really in the Irish Problem. Just when there was a real hope." He looked at Pitt intently. "Greville was brilliant, you know. He had Doyle and O'Day, at least, talking to each other about issues that matter. There was hope!"

"I'm sorry, Jack, it's worse than that." Unconsciously, Pitt put his hand on Jack's arm. "It was not an accident. He was murdered."

"What?" Jack stared at him as if he refused to comprehend what he had said.

"It was murder," Pitt repeated quietly. "Meant to look like an accident. I think most people would have taken it for such, and I presume whoever did it did not expect to have police on the scene so quickly, if at all."

"What . . . what happened?"

"Someone came in and hit him on the back of the head, possibly with a jar of bath salts, then pushed him under the water. It looked very much as if he had slipped getting out and struck himself on the rim of the bath."

"Are you sure he didn't?" Jack pressed. "Absolutely sure? How can you know it wasn't that?"

"Because in the wound the edge of the bone is straight, and the bath is curved."

"Is that proof?" Jack persisted. "Does the wound have to fit the instrument exactly?"

"No, but it can't be as wrong as this. A curved instrument is going to make a curved indentation when it strikes hard enough to break the bone."

"Who? One of us in this house?" He faced the worst immediately.

"I don't know. Tellman's gone to get help to move the body to the icehouse, then he's going to see if it was possible that anyone came in from outside, but it isn't likely."

"I can't see Greville letting anyone he didn't know into the bathroom without raising an alarm," Jack said grimly. "In fact, what reason would anyone give for interrupting a man in his bath?"

"Well, if I wanted to get in without causing any alarm, I'd dress as a servant," Pitt thought as he spoke. "Carry a pitcher of hot water or one or two towels."

"Of course. So it could be anyone."

"Yes."

"What are you going to do?"

"Get dressed, then call Cornwallis, then, I imagine, begin an investigation. Where is the telephone?"

"In the library. I'd better go and see Emily." His face was pinched with anxiety, and there was bitter laughter in his eyes. "God in heaven, I thought yesterday that this house party was as bad as it could be."

Pitt had no answer, but went back to his bedroom. Charlotte was not there. She must be comforting Kezia still, or perhaps helping Emily. He shaved hurriedly and put on his clothes, then went downstairs to the library and placed a call to London to Assistant Commissioner Cornwallis's office.

"Pitt?" Cornwallis's clear, very individual voice sounded worried already.

"Yes sir." Pitt hesitated only a moment, dreading having to say it. It was such a mark of failure. "I am afraid the worst has happened. . . ."

There was silence at the far end of the line. Then he heard Cornwallis breathing.

"Greville?"

"Yes sir. In the bath, last night. Didn't find out until this morning."

"In the bath!"

"Yes."

"Accident?" He said it as if he were willing it to be true. "His heat?"

"No."

"You're sure?"

"Yes."

"You mean someone caused it? Do you know who?"

"No. At this point it could be almost anyone."

"I see." He hesitated. "What have you done so far?"

"Ascertained the medical facts, as far as his son can tell me—"

"Whose son?"

"Greville's son. He arrived unexpectedly the day before yesterday to tell his parents he is betrothed. She came yesterday."

"How tragic," Cornwallis said with feeling. "Poor young man. I assume he is a doctor?"

"Almost qualified. Down from Cambridge. There was really very little to say."

"Time of death. Cause?"

"Time fixed by the fact he was in the bath. Cause, being struck by a rounded, blunt instrument, probably a jar of bath salts, then held under the water until he drowned."

"You found him under the water?"

"Yes."

"I see."

Again there was silence.

"Sir?"

"Yes," Cornwallis said with resolve. "Take charge of the investigation, Pitt. You have Tellman. If you can, do it without letting the news out for the time being. The Parnell-O'Shea divorce is coming to a climax. If they find against Parnell, it could ruin his career. The Irish Nationalists will be without a leader—until they find a new one. It could very well be one of the men now at Ashworth Hall. What have you told people?"

"Nothing yet, but I shall have to."

"Where's Radley?"

"With Emily."

"Have him telephone me. You can't proceed with the conference for the moment, out of decency, if nothing else. But neither must we abandon it if there is any way whatever of continuing."

"Without Greville?" Pitt was startled.

"I'll speak to the Home Office. Don't let anyone leave."

"Of course not."

"You won't need force to keep them there; to leave would be diplomatic suicide. But if you need assistance from the village police, you have the authority to require it. Have Radley call me in half an hour."

"Yes sir." He hung up the receiver feeling hollow and extraordinarily alone. His sole purpose there had been to keep Greville safe. He could hardly have failed more absolutely. And he had no idea who had killed him. He would have been better to have stayed in London and looked for Denbigh's murderer.

He left the library and went back upstairs. Charlotte was nowhere in sight. Perhaps she was still helping Emily keep some sort of order among the guests, who were all aware of Greville's death but not that it was anything other than a tragic accident . . . except perhaps one of them.

He saw the young Irish valet of Lorcan McGinley closing a bedroom door, a coat over his arm and a pair of boots in his hand. He looked very pale.

"Do you know where Mr. Greville's man is?" Pitt asked him.

"Yes sir, I passed him not two minutes ago, making a cup o' tea, sir. Two doors back that way." He pointed.

Pitt thanked him and followed his directions to the small room where there was a kettle and gas ring for making tea. The man attending to it was in his middle forties, grave and ordinarily very much in command of events. His dark hair was smoothed off his brow and his cravat was perfectly tied, but he looked distinctly ill. He started when he heard Pitt's voice and nearly spilled the jug of hot water he was holding.

"I'm sorry," Pitt apologized. "What is your name?"

"Wheeler, sir. Can I get you something?"

"I'm a superintendent of police, Wheeler. The assistant commissioner has asked me to investigate Mr. Greville's death."

Wheeler set the jug down before he could spill it. His hands were shaking. He licked his lips.

"Yes . . . sir?"

"What time did you draw Mr. Greville's bath yesterday evening?" Pitt asked.

"Ten twenty-five, sir."

"And did Mr. Greville go to it immediately, do you know?"

"Yes sir, within a few moments. He has a great dislike . . . had a great dislike for a cold bath, and water cools off very fast in a big bathroom."

"You saw him?"

Wheeler frowned. "Yes sir. Is there some problem, sir? I understood he slipped as he was getting out." He clenched and unclenched his hands. "I should have been there. I blame myself. He didn't ask for assistance, but if I'd been there, he'd never have slipped."

Pitt hesitated only a moment. There was nothing to be gained by pretending.

"He didn't slip. He was struck by someone."

Wheeler stared at him as if he did not understand.

"How long did Mr. Greville usually spend in a bath before either getting out or sending for more hot water?" Pitt asked him.

"What? You mean . . . deliberate? Why?" Wheeler's voice rose. "Who'd do such a fearful thing? One o' them dammed Irish!" He struggled for breath as the full realization came to him of what Pitt was saying. "They murdered him! What are you going to do about it? You're going to arrest them!"

"Not until I know what happened," Pitt said gently.

"The murdering devils! They tried once before, you know, once that I know of for sure!" Wheeler's voice was losing control, getting louder.

Pitt put his hand on the man's arm, holding him hard.

"I'm going to find out who did it, then I shall arrest him," he promised. "But I need your help. You must keep calm and think very clearly. What you saw and heard may be vital."

"They should be hanged," Wheeler said between his teeth.

"I daresay they will be," Pitt replied with no pleasure. "When we catch them and prove it. How long did Mr. Greville usually spend in a bath before getting out or sending for more water? Did he send for more?"

Wheeler controlled himself with an effort.

"No, sir. It wasn't his habit, especially if he took a bath in the evening. Not more than fifteen minutes. He wasn't a man who liked to lie and soak, except when he'd been riding, which he didn't do often. Soak the ache out of his bones if he'd had a hard day's ride."

"So there would be roughly a fifteen-minute space of time during which one might find him alone in the bath," Pitt deduced. "In this instance between approximately twenty-five past ten and twenty to eleven?"

"Yes sir, that's right."

"You are sure? How do you know the time so exactly?"

"It's my job, sir. You can't look after a gentleman properly if you aren't organized."

"But you didn't notice that he hadn't come out of the bathroom?"

Wheeler looked profoundly unhappy.

"No sir. It was late and I was tired. I knew Mr. Greville wouldn't want more water, because he never did, so I went downstairs to clean the boots he'd taken off and brush his coat ready for the morning. Everything else was already laid out for the day." He stared at Pitt. "When I came back upstairs I was rather later than I expected. I couldn't find the tray. Someone must have moved it. Happens in a big house full of guests. It was long after the time Mr. Greville would have spent in the bath. I knocked on the bathroom door and there was no answer, and when he wasn't in his room, I assumed . . ." He colored faintly. "I assumed he had gone to Mrs. Greville's room, sir."

"Not unnatural," Pitt said with the shadow of a smile. "No one would expect you to pursue it. What time would that have been?"

"About ten minutes to eleven, sir."

"Who else did you see on the landing or corridor?"

Wheeler thought very hard. Pitt could see his desire to be able to blame someone, but racking his memory did not help him, and he could not bring himself to lie.

"I saw that little maid of Mrs. Pitt's going along towards the stairs up to the servants' bedrooms," he said at last. "And I saw that young valet of Mr. McGinley's, Hennessey. He was standing in the doorway of one of the bedrooms along that way."

He pointed. "I think it was Mr. Moynihan's room."

"No one else?"

"Yes, Mr. Doyle said good-night and went to his room. That's all."

"Thank you." Pitt went to look for Jack. He must deliver Cornwallis's message. Jack would have been busy trying to salvage the goodwill of the conference, and Emily would be coping with the domestic catastrophe of death—the house and the bereavement of one of her guests.

He saw Gracie in the hall, looking pale and wide-eyed. There was fear in the stiff, rather proud angle of her head. Just beyond her he saw the slender figure of McGinley's valet. Pitt smiled at Gracie, and she forced herself to smile back, as if everything were all right and she knew he could solve it all in the end.

He passed the open dining room door and glanced in. Charlotte was there, standing still as Iona paced back and forth speaking quietly in great urgency.

Charlotte looked at Pitt and very slightly shook her head, then turned back to Iona, taking a step towards her.

Pitt found Jack in his study with a pile of papers. He had barely closed the door when it opened again and Emily came in. She looked flustered, her color was high and her usually beautiful hair was hastily dressed, as if she could not sit still for the maid. From her expression it was obvious Jack had told her that Greville's death was murder. She was torn between sympathy and fury.

Jack waited for Pitt to speak. "Cornwallis asked me to conduct the investigation," Pitt began, looking at Jack. "Will you telephone him in about fifteen minutes? He will have spoken to the Home Office by then. We have to keep everybody here. . . ."

Emily let out a little groan and went over to stand beside Jack.

"I'm sorry," Pitt apologized. "I know it will be appalling, but I can't let them go. Unless there was a break-in, and Tellman is looking at that now, then someone already here was responsible."

"Even if there was a break-in, it could still involve someone here," Jack said grimly. He put his hand up to Emily's arm and gripped her. "We have no alternative, my dear, except to do everything we can to discover the truth as quickly as possible. At least Mrs. Greville has her brother and son here to care for her. It could have been worse. And Charlotte will help you with the others." He turned to Pitt. "I suppose there is no further danger, is there?"

Emily stiffened till she was almost rigid.

Pitt hesitated. There was nothing they could guard against. Frightening them would serve no purpose.

"Certainly not for the moment. And we'll do all we can to solve it as quickly as possible."

Emily looked at him with disbelief. "Where can you even start?"

"Well, we know he was killed between twenty-five past ten and twenty to eleven, because of his valet's evidence—"

"And you believe it?" Jack cut in.

"The man's been with him nineteen years. But I will have Tellman check. It will be easy enough to know what time the water was taken up for the bath. And he couldn't stay in it longer than a quarter of an hour before sending for more hot."

"Why kill him in the bath?" Jack said, pulling a rueful face. "It seems to add indignity to death, poor devil."

"Best place to be sure of finding him alone." Emily had gathered her wits from her distress and begun to think. "And pretty defenseless. Anywhere else and he could have a valet with him, or someone catching a moment to put some point to him, or be with Eudora. It is the one place a person is alone, and with the door unlocked so more water could be brought. It makes sense, when you consider it. It wasn't a break-in, was it, Thomas?" She said it with certainty. "It was someone here who chose their time very well."

"Do you know where you were?" Pitt asked

"In my own bath," Jack said with a shiver.

"So you don't know where anyone else was?"

"No. I'm sorry."

"Emily?"

"In my bedroom, with the door closed. After that awful day . . ." She smiled tightly, possibly thinking of the day before, then the present. "I was tired. I'm sorry, I can't help either."

Jack looked up at Pitt.

"Don't forget to call Cornwallis." Pitt smiled briefly, then went out again and almost bumped into Tellman. "No break-in," he said, looking at Tellman's expression.

"No break-in," Tellman agreed.

Pitt told him what he had learned from the valet about the time of death.

"Narrows it a bit." Tellman began to look a little more cheerful. At least he was now engaged in his proper employment, not pretending to be some servant. Pitt could see it in his eyes.

"We'll leave Mrs. Greville until last, give her a little time to compose herself," Pitt directed. Questioning the bereaved was one of the worst parts of an investigation. At least this time he did not have to break the news to her. And it was also a political matter, not a personal one, so she should fear no disclosure of ugly relationships and secrets she had not known. There would be no public revelations of dishonor. "See what you can learn from the servants."

Tellman's jaw set hard. "I'll need to tell them who I am!" His look defied Pitt to order him otherwise.

Pitt nodded and Tellman took his leave, moderately satisfied.

Pitt went to find the first of the guests to question.

As he passed the dining room he saw Charlotte was no longer there, nor was Iona.

He went slowly upstairs and knocked on the McGinleys' door. On hearing Lorcan's voice, he opened the door and went in. Iona had returned and was standing by the window, apparently much more composed than when he had seen her in the dining room. Lorcan was sitting over a breakfast tray on the small center table. He had eaten quite well, judging by the empty plate.

"What can we do for you, Mr. Pitt?" Lorcan asked, a little more coolly. His thin face, with its very blue eyes, was full of nervous energy. There were hollows at the bridge of his nose and small lines beside his mouth. Pitt had not thought before of the weight of responsibility which must rest on each of the representatives of the sectarian interests, and the burden of criticism they would bear whatever they achieved, or failed to achieve. And now with Greville's death it was all wasted. It could only be failure and disappointed hopes.

"I am afraid it is very unpleasant news," he said, looking from one to the other of them. "I am with the—"

"I know Greville is dead." Lorcan stood up, almost unfolding himself. He was painfully thin. "That is the end of the conference. We're finished. Another disaster. We should be used to them, but each one still hurts."

"That is not my decision, Mr. McGinley," Pitt replied. "Another chairman might be found. . . ."

"Rubbish! Please don't patronize me, Mr. Pitt! You cannot just substitute someone else at this point, even if you could find anyone with the courage and the skill of Ainsley Greville."

"The courage might be hard," Pitt agreed. "Especially when they know, as they will have to, that Mr. Greville was murdered."

Iona froze, her eyes wide and suddenly truly afraid.

Lorcan looked up at Pitt slowly, as if trying to think of the right thing to say.

"Who told you that?" he asked. "And who the hell are you to come in here saying such a thing?"

"I'm with the police. And nobody told me, I saw it for myself."

Lorcan's eyes did not move from Pitt's. "Are you . . . indeed?"

"What are you going to do?" Iona asked him. "Did someone break in after all? I thought there were men around to make sure we were safe. It's the Protestants. They don't want us to achieve Home Rule. It's the same old thing! When they can't win by reason or the law, they murder us. God knows, the soil of Ireland is steeped in the blood of martyrs—"

"Be quiet," Lorcan said immediately. "If Mr. Pitt's a policeman it's surely a shame he didn't manage to protect Greville, but since he didn't, it is not for us to go flinging blame around. Keep a still tongue. At least you can do that much . . . unless, of course, you know something you should be telling him?" His lip curled. "Your friend Moynihan, for example?" His tone was cruel, sarcastic, but Pitt could hardly blame him for that.

Iona blushed furiously but did not retaliate.

"What time did you retire last night?" Pitt asked.

"I didn't hear anything," Lorcan replied.

"No one broke in, Mr. McGinley. Mr. Greville was killed by someone in this house. What time did you retire?"

"About quarter past ten, or close enough." He looked back at Pitt with a cold, defiant stare. "I didn't come out of my room again." He swiveled to look at his wife, waiting for her to answer as well.

"Were you alone?" Pitt pressed, not hoping for any very helpful answer. A man's wife could not be made to testify against him, and unsubstantiated testimony from her was of no value.

"No," Lorcan said abruptly. "Hennessey, my manservant, was here some of the time."

"Do you know when?"

"About quarter past ten until ten minutes to eleven," Lorcan replied.

"You are very exact?"

"There is a longcase clock on the landing," Lorcan replied. "I can hear it from in here."

"That's a long time for your valet to be here," Pitt observed. "What was he doing for over half an hour?"

Lorcan looked slightly surprised, but he answered readily enough. "We were talking about a shooting jacket I have. I'm fond of it. He thinks I should have it replaced. We also discussed the relative merits of London and Dublin shirtmakers."

"I see. Thank you."

"Does that help?"

"Yes, thank you. Mrs. McGinley?"

"I told you." She regarded him coldly. "I remained in my room.

My maid was with me for a while. She helped me to prepare for the night, and of course put away my gown."

"Do you know what time she left you?"

"No, I don't. But if I had seen anything, I should tell you. I didn't."

Pitt left the subject. There was no reason now to doubt her. But he would check up on Hennessey. He thanked them and went to see Fergal Moynihan.

He found him alone in the billiard room. He looked extremely unhappy and in a considerable temper.

"Police?" he said angrily when Pitt explained who he was. "I think you might have been a little more candid with us, Superintendent. The deception wasn't necessary."

Pitt did not bother to hide a slight smile.

Fergal flushed, but Pitt had the feeling it was more annoyance than embarrassment. He might have been disconcerted at being caught publicly with Iona McGinley, but he was not ashamed of his feelings for her. If anything, he was defensive of them, almost proud. That was part of being wildly in love.

He could account for part of his time between twenty-five past ten and quarter to eleven, but not all of it. He had had opportunity to leave his room unobserved and go as far as Greville's bathroom.

"But I did not," he said firmly.

Pitt next found O'Day.

He was standing in front of the fire, his hands in his pockets. He did not add any comment as to Pitt's lack of success, but it was there in the carefully blank expression in his face. "I don't know how I can assist you. You say it is not an accident? Therefore you are implying that it was murder?"

"Yes, I am afraid so."

"I see. Well, I have no knowledge as to who killed him, Superintendent. Why is not difficult. The conference seemed to have every chance of genuine success. There are many among the more radical and violent of the Nationalist factions who did not want that."

"You mean those Mr. Doyle represents, or those Mr. McGinley does?" Pitt asked. "Or do you believe other factions have infiltrated their staff, perhaps? One of them is unknowingly employing a Fenian disguised as a valet?"

"There is no reason why a valet should not also be a Fenian, Superintendent."

"No, naturally. Why would they wish the conference to fail?"

O'Day smiled. "You are politically naive, Superintendent. Of necessity, any agreement would be a compromise. There are those who would regard even a single concession to the enemy as a betrayal."

"Then why have they come here?" Pitt asked. "Surely their own supporters would consider them traitors?"

"Quite true," O'Day conceded with a flicker of appreciation. "But not everyone is precisely what they seem, or what they affect to be. I don't know who killed Greville, but if I can help you to find out, I shall do everything I can. Although with the conference effectively over, I am not sure how that may be accomplished." His face was smooth, a little grayer than Pitt had thought in the lamplight, and he looked tired and disappointed, as if all his effort were over, and it had left him drained.

"It is not necessarily over," Pitt replied. "We have yet to hear from Whitehall."

O'Day's smile was bitter. There was a lifetime's emotion behind it, passionate, complex, unreadable.

"Yes it is, Mr. Pitt. Tell me, when and how was Greville killed? I thought originally he slipped when preparing to get out of the bath. Now you tell me this is not so."

"He was struck while still in it," Pitt amended. "And then probably pushed under the water. His valet says he drew the bath at twenty minutes past ten, and Mr. Greville would not have been more than five minutes going to it, at the most. Nor would he have remained in it longer than ten or fifteen minutes without calling for additional hot water, which he was not in the habit of doing. When

Wheeler returned upstairs from an errand at quarter to eleven, he knocked on the bathroom door. On receiving no answer, he assumed Mr. Greville had gone to bed. We now know he was dead."

"I see. Then he was killed between quarter past ten and quarter to eleven."

"Probably nearer half past ten. There was a certain amount of soap in the water. He had time to wash."

"I see." O'Day bit his lip on the ghost of a smile, self-mocking. "Unfortunately, I can account at least for McGinley's valet, and for McGinley himself, which is irritating. I came along the corridor and saw the valet standing in the doorway talking to McGinley. He was there for at least twenty minutes. I know, because I left my own door open and I heard him. They were discussing shirtmakers. I confess, I listened with a certain interest. I admire McGinley's linen, but I should dislike him to know it."

Pitt could not help smiling also. He could see O'Day's frustration quite plainly. Also, his information bore out what Lorcan had said. At least it reduced the suspects by three, and three who would not willingly protect each other.

"Thank you," he said sincerely. "You have been most helpful."

O'Day grunted and bit his lip.

Kezia was horrified when Pitt told her as they walked across the gravel drive, the damp wind in their faces. It smelled of newly turned earth, wet raked leaves and clippings from the last mowing of the grass. She swung around to face him, the fresh color fading from her cheeks, her eyes bright.

"I suppose you're sure? You couldn't be wrong?"

"Not about the wound, Miss Moynihan."

"You were to begin with! You thought it was an accident then. Who suggested it wasn't?"

"No one. When I examined it more closely, I saw that the wound could not have been caused by falling and striking the edge of the bath."

"Are you a doctor?"

"You think murder is impossible?"

She turned away. "No, I just wish it were."

She could not help. She had been in her bedroom at the time, alone except for her lady's maid coming and going.

Tellman met him as he was returning to the house.

"Hennessey says he was in McGinley's doorway talking to him about shirts," he said tartly. "Saw O'Day in his room also. That puts them out. Wheeler seems to have been where he said. Footman and housemaid both saw him about downstairs, and he couldn't have got back up again in time to do anything. They confirm the time he took the water up too."

"What about the other servants?" Pitt walked beside him across the gravel and up the steps to the stone terrace.

Tellman looked resolutely ahead of him, refusing to admire the sweep of the stone balustrade or the broad facade of the house.

"Ladies' maids were upstairs, of course. Seems there's not one of the women can get out of their clothes by themselves."

Pitt smiled. "If you were married, Tellman, you'd know better what is involved, and why it would be exceedingly difficult to do it oneself."

"Shouldn't wear clothes you can't get in and out of," Tellman responded.

"Is that all?" Pitt opened the door and went through it first, leaving it to swing.

Tellman caught it. "Your Gracie was up there on the landing. Says she saw Moynihan go to his room about ten past ten. Saw Wheeler go downstairs when he said he did. She was coming back with hot water at about half past ten and passed one of the maids carrying towels."

"Which maid?"

"She didn't know. Only saw her back. But all the maids are accounted for. None of 'em were absent from their duties. It wasn't an outsider who killed Greville, and it wasn't a servant."

Pitt did not reply. It was what he had supposed—and feared.

Now he could no longer put off speaking to Greville's family. He gave Tellman instructions to continue learning all he could and check the accounts of the valets and maids against each other to see if anything further could be learned or deduced, then went upstairs to find Justine.

She was in the small sitting room which served the guest rooms of the north wing. Piers was close beside her and looked anxious. He started up as soon as Pitt entered, his face full of question.

"I am sorry to intrude," Pitt began. "But there are certain things I need to ask you."

"Of course." Piers started as if to leave. "There is no need to distress Miss Baring with details. I'll come with you."

Pitt remained in front of the door, blocking it. "They are not medical details, Mr. Greville, they are just factual observations. And I need to ask Miss Baring as well."

"Why?" Piers looked at him more closely, sensing something further wrong. "Surely . . ." He stopped again.

"I'm sorry, Mr. Greville, but your father did not die by accident," Pitt said quietly. "I am with the police."

"The police!" Involuntarily Justine started, then put her hand to her mouth. "I'm sorry. I thought—" She stopped, turning to Piers. "I'm so sorry!"

Piers moved closer to her. "I was here to try to protect him," Pitt went on. "I am afraid I failed. Now I need to know what happened and who was responsible."

Piers was stunned. "You mean . . . you mean he was . . . deliberately killed? But how? He fell against the bath! I saw the wound."

"You saw what was intended to look like an accident," Pitt pointed out. He glanced at Justine. She looked very white and still, but she was watching Piers, not Pitt. After that momentary outburst, she showed not the slightest sign of hysterics or faintness.

"You expected . . . murder?" Piers had difficulty even saying the word. "Then why did he come? Why didn't you . . ."

Justine stood up and put her hand on his arm. "One can only do so much, Piers. Mr. Pitt could hardly go into the bathroom with him." She looked at Pitt. "Did someone break in?"

"No. I'm sorry, it was someone resident in the house. My sergeant has established that. All the windows and doors were locked and there are men regularly watching the outside of the house, night as well as day. The gamekeeper has dogs out."

"Someone here?" Piers was startled. "You mean one of the guests? You expected this? They are all Irish, I realize that now, but really . . ." Again he stopped. "Was this a political weekend? Is that what you are saying? And I intruded, without knowing?"

"I would not have phrased it so abruptly, but yes. Where were you at that time, Mr. Greville?"

"In my bedroom. I'm afraid I didn't hear anything." It did not occur to him that Pitt could suspect him of involvement. He took his own innocence for granted, and Pitt was inclined to do the same. He thanked them both and went to conduct the last and worst interview.

He knocked on Eudora's door and Doyle answered it. He looked weary, although it was barely midday. His dark hair was ruffled and his tie was a trifle crooked. "I haven't called anyone to make arrangements yet," he said on seeing Pitt. "I shall ask Radley to send for the local doctor. There is no point in calling his own man. The situation is tragically apparent. We'll send a message to his own vicar, though. He should be buried in the family vault. I'm afraid it seems the end of an endeavor for peace in Ireland, at least for the time being. We must make suitable arrangements for everyone to go home. I'll accompany my sister."

"Not yet, Mr. Doyle. I am afraid, although it seemed apparent what had happened, it was not so. It was murder, and Assistant Commissioner Cornwallis has asked me to take charge of the enquiry."

"What competence have you to decide such a thing?" Doyle said very carefully. "Just who are you, Mr. Pitt?"

"Superintendent of the Bow Street Station," Pitt replied.

Doyle's face tightened. "I see. Probably here from the beginning in your official capacity?" He did not make any reference to Pitt's lack of success, but the knowledge of it was in his eyes and the very slight lift of the corners of his lips.

"Yes. I'm sorry." Pitt was apologizing for the failure, not his calling.

"I suppose there is no doubt of your facts?"

"No."

"You said an accident in the beginning. What changed your mind?"

They were still in the doorway. The room beyond was dimmed by half-drawn curtains. Eudora was sitting in one of the large chairs. Now she stood up and came towards them. She looked profoundly shocked. She had the kind of papery paleness and the hollow eyes of someone who has sustained a blow beyond her comprehension.

"What is it?" she asked. Apparently she had overheard none of their conversation. "What has happened now, Padraig?"

He turned to her, ignoring Pitt. "You must be very strong, sweetheart. The news is bad. Mr. Pitt is from the police, sent here to protect us during the conference. He says that Ainsley was murdered after all. It wasn't an accident as we thought." He put both hands on her shoulders to steady her. "We have no alternative but to face it. It was always a danger, and he knew it. We did not expect it here in Ashworth Hall." He half turned back to Pitt. "Was there a break-in?"

"No."

"You sound very sure of that."

"I am."

"Then it was one of us?"

"Yes."

Eudora stared at him with hurt, frightened eyes.

Doyle tightened his grip on her.

"Thank you for doing your duty in informing us," he said firmly. "If there is anything we can do to help, of course we will, but for the time being Mrs. Greville would like to be alone. I'm sure you understand that?"

"I do," Pitt agreed without moving. "I wouldn't disturb her at all if it were not necessary. I am sorry, but no one may leave until we have learned as much as we can and, I hope, proved who is responsible. The sooner that is done, the sooner Mrs. Greville can return to her home and mourn in peace." He felt acutely sorry for her, but he had no alternative. "This was more than the death of your husband, Mrs. Greville, it is a far-reaching political murder. I cannot extend you the sensitivity I would like to."

She lifted her head very slightly. Her eyes were full of tears.

"I understand," she said huskily. "I have always known there was a danger. I suppose I didn't think it would really happen. I love Ireland, but sometimes I hate it too."

"And don't we all," Doyle said, almost in a whisper. "It's a hard mistress, but we've paid too much to leave her now, and when we were so close!"

"What do you want of me, Mr. Pitt?" Eudora asked.

"When did you last see Mr. Greville?"

She thought for a moment. "I don't remember. He often reads late. I go to bed quite early. About ten o'clock, I think. But you can ask my maid, Doll, if you like. She might know. She was here when Ainsley came in to say good-night."

"I will. Thank you. And you, Mr. Doyle?"

"I went to my room, also to read," Doyle replied. "If you remember, it was not an evening when any of us wished to stay up late. The Moynihan business was most uncomfortable."

Pitt flashed him a look of agreement. "I would be most grateful if you would not tell anyone outside Ashworth Hall what happened for the time being."

"If you wish."

"Was your manservant with you, Mr. Doyle?"

Dry, sad amusement flashed in Doyle's face. "You suspect me? Yes, he was, part of the time. He left about half past ten. Have you any idea when Ainsley was killed?"

"Between twenty past ten and twenty to eleven."

"I see. Then no, Mr. Pitt, I cannot account for all that time."

"Padraig . . . don't!" Eudora said desperately. "Don't say that, even lightly!"

"It's not lightly, my dear." He tightened his arm around her again. "I imagine Mr. Pitt is going to be thorough, and that means ruthless, doesn't it?"

"It means very literal, Mr. Doyle," Pitt replied. "Very exact."

"Sure it does. And I didn't kill Ainsley. We differed over a lot of things, but he was my sister's husband. Go and look at some of those fierce, judgmental Protestants, Mr. Pitt, full of the anger and vengeance of their God. You'll find his killer there, never doubting he does God's work . . . poor devil! That's what's wrong with Ireland—too many people doing the devil's work in God's name!"

Emily had an appalling day. She had known from the beginning that there was a possibility of danger to Ainsley Greville, but she had assumed it was remote and would come from outside. And, of course, Pitt and the menservants would deal with it. When Jack had told her Greville was dead, she, like everyone else, had assumed it was accidental.

Her first thought had been for the failure of the conference and what it would mean to Jack's career. Then immediately she was ashamed of that and thought of the grief of the family, especially his wife. She knew the shock of violent bereavement herself only too well. She thought of what she could do to offer any comfort. But fortunately it seemed Padraig Doyle was Mrs. Greville's brother, and he was happy to take control. Why had he not been open about that before? The answer was presumably political. Perhaps they thought others might assume Greville would be biased in his brother-in-law's favor. Or possibly they did not wish everyone to know Eudora was Irish, from the south, and therefore likely to be Catholic, even if not devoutly so. Emily had little patience with such passion over other people's personal beliefs.

But at least Doyle's presence relieved her of the immediate need to spare time offering comfort to someone in such shock or distress. Instead she must try to keep some calm and order among the household staff. Whatever she did, in no time everyone would know there had been murder committed in the house, and there would be hysterics, weeping, fainting and quarreling, and inevitably, at least one person would want to give notice and not be allowed to because no one could leave the hall until the investigation was over.

It would be better to tell them herself and at least be given credit for courtesy and honesty. Jack was occupied with the wreckage of the conference, and anyway, the servants were really her responsibility. She had inherited Ashworth Hall and its staff, and the income to run it, from her first husband, and it was held in trust for her son. The staff all treated Jack with respect, but they still looked to her ultimately, from habit.

She went downstairs and told the butler that she would like to speak to the senior staff in the housekeeper's room immediately. They assembled with due haste and solemnity.

"You all know that Mr. Ainsley Greville died in the bath late yesterday evening." She did not use any of the common euphemisms for death, as she did when speaking to most people. It would be absurd to say that someone who had been murdered had "passed over" or "gone beyond the veil."

"Yes, m'lady," Mrs. Hunnaker said gravely. She still used Emily's title, even though she no longer possessed it because she had remarried. "Very sad indeed, I'm sure. Will that mean the guests will be leaving?"

"Not yet," Emily replied. "I am sorry, but I cannot say how much longer they will be with us. It depends on circumstances—and upon Mr. Pitt, to some extent." She took a deep breath and looked at their polite, attentive faces with a sinking heart. "As most of you know, I daresay, Mr. Pitt is with the police. I am afraid Mr. Greville did not meet his death by accident, as we had first supposed. He was murdered—"

Mrs. Hunnaker blanched and reached for the back of one of the chairs to support herself.

Dilkes gasped, struggled for something to say, and failed to find it.

Jack's valet shook his head. "That'll be why Mr. Pitt was asking about where everyone was. And that Tellman, going around looking at all the windows."

"Nobody never broke in?" the cook said, her voice rising in near panic already. "Gawd 'elp us all!"

"No!" Emily said sharply. "No one broke in." Then she realized that the alternative was worse, and wished she had not been quite so vehement. "No," she repeated. "It is a political assassination. It is all to do with the Irish Question. It has nothing to do with us. Mr. Pitt will deal with it. We must just behave as usual—"

"Behave as usual?" the cook said indignantly. "We could all be murdered in our beds! Beggin' your—"

"Baths," the housekeeper corrected punctiliously. "And we don't take baths, Mrs. Williams. We wash in a basin, like most folks. You can't fall out of a basin."

"Well, I'm not having Irishmen in my kitchen or our hall!" the cook said. "And that's flat!"

Emily was not often caught in two minds where servants were concerned. Once let them see you could be manipulated and you could never govern the house again. She had learned that long ago. But if Mrs. Williams refused to cook now, she would be in a desperate situation. Jack's political career could suffer if his household was considered unreliable. She felt that the fact they had excellent reason would be of no importance whatever.

"They have no occasion to be in your kitchen, Mrs. Williams," she said after a second's hesitation. "And you will be in no danger cooking for everyone, as usual. I am sure you would not wish to judge the innocent along with the guilty, if there are any guilty—"

"They're all guilty of hating each other," Mrs. Williams said with a gleam in her eye. Her hands were shaking and her body began to quiver. "And the Good Book says that's as bad as murder."

"Rubbish," Emily retorted briskly. "We are English, and we don't panic because a collection of Irishmen dislike each other. We have a great deal more fortitude than that!"

Mrs. Williams straightened up noticeably.

"We don't run away from our duty for any reason," Emily went on, realizing she had said the right thing. "But if you prefer to seat the visiting staff separately, then by all means do so. For the sake of the younger maids who may be very naturally upset," she added. "Not for you, of course. You will be perfectly all right. But you will have to look after the junior staff and ensure they don't take fright or behave badly. We have a very important position to maintain."

"Yes, m'lady," Mrs. Hunnaker said, raising her chin. "We mustn't let them Irish think we haven't the stomach for it."

"Certainly not," the butler agreed. "Don't worry, ma'am, we'll make sure everything runs as usual."

But such a task was beyond mortal ability to accomplish. Two of the younger housemaids had hysterics and had to be put to bed, one of them after she had tipped a bucket of water down the front stairs and soaked the hall carpet. One of the junior footmen almost set fire to the library, in absentmindedness piling more and more coals into the grate. The bootboy got into a fight with Fergal Moynihan's valet and they both ended up with black eyes, and three dishes were broken in the scullery, and then the scullery maid had hysterics. One of the laundry maids filled the copper too full and boiled it over, and the senior laundry maid flew at her, whereupon the first one gave notice. No one peeled any potatoes or carrots, and the pies for dessert were forgotten and got burnt.

One of the footmen got drunk, tripped over the kitchen cat, and fell over. The cat was furious but unhurt. Mrs. Williams was in a monumental temper, but she did not give notice. And no one at all was interested in luncheon, so the wreckage of the meal was unnoticed upstairs. Emily was the only person who was ever aware of it.

Gracie, Charlotte's maid, was one sane head amid the domestic chaos, although Emily did observe that every time Lorcan McGinley's very handsome young valet passed by her, which seemed more often than was necessary, she lost her concentration and became uncharacteristically clumsy. Emily was far too astute not to understand the signs.

And Pitt's most disobliging assistant, Tellman, was very busy asking everyone a lot of questions and looking as if someone had broken a bad egg.

In the late afternoon Cornwallis telephoned back and asked to speak to Jack.

"What is it?" Emily demanded as soon as he had replaced the receiver on the cradle. "What did you just agree to?"

They were in the library. He had gone there to answer the call, and she had followed him when she knew from Dilkes who was on the other end.

Jack looked very stiff, his eyes wide. He lifted his chin a trifle, as if his collar were suddenly tight on his throat.

"What is it?" Emily repeated, her voice rising.

Jack swallowed. "Cornwallis has said the Home Office would like me to continue the conference," he replied very quietly, his voice not much more than a whisper. He cleared his throat. "In Greville's place."

"You can't!" Emily said instantly, almost choked with fear for him.

"Thank you." He looked as if she had hit him. She opened her mouth to tell him not to be absurd. This was no time for childish pride. Greville had just been murdered, less than twenty-four hours ago, here in this house. Jack could be next! Then like a drenching of cold water she realized that he thought she had meant that he was not capable of it, he was not fit to take Greville's place.

Was that what he feared himself? Had she pushed him too far, out of her own ambition, her expectations of him? Without meaning to, by her admiration for other people, her dreams, had she tacitly asked of him more than he could give? Was he reaching for this to prove himself to her, to please her, to be, in his own way, all he imagined George Ashworth had been? George had had money, title, charm, but no skills. He had not needed them.

Was Jack trying to excel in political life to match the Ashworth family?

And did he feel he had been driven to take on more than he was capable of fulfilling?

And did he really think she also doubted him?

She looked at him, his handsome face which had earned him his place in society, was now grave, his wide eyes fixed on hers.

He did think she doubted him!

"I mean it's too dangerous!" she said hoarsely. "You must call Cornwallis back and tell him you can't do it . . . until Thomas has found out who murdered Greville. They can't expect you just to pick up where he left it the night he was killed." She moved towards him. "Jack, don't they understand what happened here? These people are murderers—or at least one of them is." She put her hands up to his shoulders.

He took her by the wrists and put her arms down again, still keeping hold of her.

"I know that very well, Emily. I knew it when I accepted. One does not refuse a job because it may be dangerous. What do you think would happen to our country if a general was killed in battle and the next officer in turn refused to take command?"

"You are not in the army!"

"Yes, I am—"

"You're not! Jack . . ." She stopped.

"Emily, don't argue with me," he said with a firmness she had never heard in his voice before. She knew she could not persuade him, and it frightened her, because she admired him more than she wished to. A certain element of control had slipped away from her. Her emotions were racing. There was a shivering of real fear inside her, and it was a terrible feeling. There was nothing exciting about it at all, just a sickness.

"Thank you," he said gently. "You will have a great deal to do.

This is about the worst house party I expect you will ever attend, let alone have to host. I shall not be able to help you. You will have to rely on Charlotte. I'm sorry."

She forced herself to smile. She felt guilty. She had not known his courage, and she had thought him unequal to the task. Worse than that, she had allowed him to see it.

"Of course," she said with far more confidence than she felt. "If you can take over the leadership of the conference, the least I can do is see that the party is . . . bearable. It can hardly be fun, but we can at least avoid any further social disasters."

He smiled back at her with a flash of real humor. "With Iona McGinley in Moynihan's bed, and Greville dead in his bath, unless the cook gives notice, I think we've achieved a full house! Unless of course someone decides to cheat at cards."

"Don't," she said hoarsely. "Jack, don't even whisper it!"

But her brave face did not last far beyond dinner, which she managed with supreme skill. Eudora took it in her room, but everyone else was present, and all behaved with dignity and passably civil conversation. It was afterwards, when she spoke to Pitt in the library, that she lost her composure and all her fear spilled through.

"What have you found out?" she asked sharply.

Pitt looked exhausted and deeply unhappy. His tie was coming undone, his jacket pockets were stuffed with bits of paper and his hair looked as if he had run his fingers through it a dozen times.

"It seems to have been Padraig Doyle, Fergal Moynihan, or one of the women," he said wearily. "Or his son."

"Doyle is his brother-in-law!" she exclaimed with disgust. "And it wouldn't be his son, for heaven's sake. It's a political murder, Thomas. It must be Moynihan. Why not McGinley or O'Day?"

"Because they were seen elsewhere at the time."

"Then it is Moynihan. He's already been caught in bed with McGinley's wife. What makes you think he wouldn't stoop to murder? Arrest him! Then at least Jack will be safe."

"I can't arrest him, Emily. There's no proof he's guilty. . . ."

"You've just said he is!" she shouted. "It has to be him. Or else one of the servants. What is Tellman doing? Can't he find out whether it was a servant? They all have duties. They ought to be able to account for where they were. What have you been doing all day?"

Pitt opened his mouth to speak.

Behind Emily the library door creaked, but she did not bother to turn to see who it was. Her mind was filled with fear for Jack.

"You were no use at looking after Greville, you could at least do something to protect Jack! You shouldn't have let him accept the task. Why didn't you tell Cornwallis how dangerous it was? Arrest Moynihan before you get Jack killed as well!"

Charlotte walked over to the vase of chrysanthemums on the small table and yanked the flowers out, holding the jug of water in her other hand. She stood opposite Emily, her face flushed, her eyes dark with rage.

"Hold your tongue," she said with a low, barely controlled voice. "Unless you want this water all over you."

"Don't you dare!" Emily snapped back. "Jack's in terrible danger, and Thomas won't lift a—"

Charlotte threw the water and Emily was drenched. She gasped in sheer amazement.

Pitt put out his hand as if to restrain someone, then dropped it again, his eyes wide.

"Stop thinking of yourself!" Charlotte said. "Thomas can't arrest anyone until he has proof who's guilty. It might be someone else, and then where will we all be? Use your common sense, and try to think and watch!"

Emily was so furious she was speechless, most immediately because there was nothing at hand to throw back. She spun on her heel and stormed out of the room and strode upstairs, along the landing, and into her bedroom, slamming the door with a resounding crash. Then she threw herself onto her bed and lay there, wretched. She had been unfair to Jack, and now she had been unfair to Pitt as well. He must be feeling dreadful. He could not have foreseen a murder from inside the house, any more than anyone else could have. And she had quarreled with Charlotte, whom she needed more than ever before.

It had been one of the worst days of her life. And tomorrow would probably be no better.

CHAPTER FIVE

Pitt woke with his head throbbing. He lay still in the dark. There was no sound except the tiptoe of a housemaid outside in the corridor. That meant it was past five in the morning.

Then he remembered what had happened the previous day, the screaming, and Ainsley Greville's body with its face under the water. It was someone in the house who had killed him, one of the guests. McGinley had been in his room talking to the valet Hennessey; O'Day had seen them. That meant all three of them were excluded. Physically, it could have been any of the others, although a man was far more likely, which left Fergal Moynihan, brother-in-law Doyle, or Piers. It was beginning to look more and more like Moynihan, except that Moynihan seemed to have abandoned his passionate Protestantism and all its precepts in his affair with Iona McGinley.

Could a man possibly be so double in his thinking? Fergal was committing adultery, a violation of one of the strictest commandments of his faith, and with a Catholic woman. Was it conceivable he would commit murder, against the greatest commandment of all, to preserve his faith from the continuation of popery?

Or was the preservation of Protestantism nothing to do with religion in his mind? Was it simply land, money and power?

There were factors, perhaps major ones, Pitt did not yet know.

Charlotte was still asleep, warm and huddled up. He had been half aware of her moving restlessly during the night, turning over, pushing the pillows around. She was frightened for him. She had not said so. She had pretended she was perfectly confident, but he knew her better than to be deceived. There were mannerisms she had, a way of twisting her rings and tightening her shoulders, when she was worried.

Emily was frightened too, for Jack. He could hardly blame her. Jack was possibly in danger.

He slid out of bed. The fire had long gone out and it was cold. What was worse was that this morning, with the revelation of identity, he could hardly expect Tellman to fetch him any hot water.

He walked barefoot into the dressing room, which was also bitter, and started to put on his clothes. He could shave later. Now he needed to think. A hot cup of tea would help wake him up and clear his head. He knew where the upstairs pantry was, and the kettle.

He was halfway through boiling it, and the sky was graying outside, when Wheeler came in.

"Good morning, sir," he said quietly. He never spoke in a normal voice until the guests were up. "May I prepare that for you?"

"Thank you." Pitt stepped back. He was perfectly competent to do it himself, but he sensed that Wheeler wanted to. He felt more at ease doing his job than permitting someone else to.

Wheeler began with deft hands to lay a tray, which Pitt had not been going to bother with. The valet moved with a kind of grace. Pitt wondered what kind of a man he was when the mask of service was removed. What emotions had he, what interests?

"Would Mrs. Pitt like a tray also, sir?" Wheeler asked.

"No, thank you, I think she's still asleep." Pitt leaned against the door lintel.

"I'm glad I have the chance to talk to you, sir," Wheeler said, watching very carefully as the kettle came to the boil. "You know there was another attempt on Mr. Greville's life, some four or five weeks ago?"

"Yes, he told me. He was run off the road, but he never found out who was responsible."

"That's right, sir. And the outside staff tried everything they could think of. But there were also threatening letters." He poured the water over the tea, then looked at Pitt very directly. "The letters are still at Oakfield House, sir. They are in Mr. Greville's study, in the desk drawer. That's somewhere Mrs. Greville would never go, nor the maids touch."

"Thank you. Perhaps I'll ride over today and have a look. There may be something in them to indicate who is behind this. It is obviously more than one person, because Mr. Greville would have recognized the driver who ran him off the road. He said he had remarkable eyes, wide set, and very pale blue. That man is not here now."

"No sir. I'd put it on the Fenians, myself, but that'd make it Mr. McGinley, and from what Hennessey says, it couldn't have been him. I'd be disinclined to believe Hennessey, except that Mr. O'Day says so too, and knowing how the Protestants like Mr. O'Day feel about Catholics like Mr. McGinley, he'd not say that if he didn't have to."

Pitt nodded rueful agreement and accepted the tea with appreciation.

After having returned to the bedroom and finding Charlotte still asleep, he had an early breakfast. To begin with there was no one else at the table except Jack, and they were able to talk frankly.

"Do you expect to find anything useful?" Jack said with some skepticism. "Surely if the threatening letters implicated anyone, he would have brought them to you already?"

"Possibly nothing," Pitt conceded. "But there is plenty of evidence which is meaningless by itself but makes sense joined with something else. I have to look. I might get a better description of the coachman. There may be something else in the house, letters, papers. One of the servants might know or remember something."

He looked across the wide table at Jack. At a glance he appeared very composed. He was as well-groomed as usual. He was a very handsome man in a casual, dashing way. His gray eyes were long lashed, his smile full of laughter and light. One would have to observe carefully to see the stiffness in his body, the occasion when he hesitated, took a deep breath, and then hurried on with what he was saying, the angle of his head as if he were half listening to hear something beyond the room. Pitt did not blame him for being afraid, both of the physical danger which had already struck Greville, but from which perhaps Pitt and Tellman could save him, and of the danger of failure in a responsibility which was far beyond anything he had approached so far in his very new career.

Doyle came in and greeted them with a smile. He seemed to be a man whom no tragedy or embarrassment could rob of composure. There were times when that was admirable, and others when it was irritating. Pitt wondered if it was a natural lack of ability to feel anything deeply, a shallowness in his emotional nature, or if it were a superb courage and self-control springing from consideration for others, an innate capacity for leadership and a kind of dignity which was all too rare.

As Carson O'Day joined them Pitt excused himself and went to look for Tellman. He found him coming up from the servants' hall, his face dour and pinched in concentration.

"Learned anything?" Pitt asked him quietly, not to be overheard by a housemaid carrying a broom and a pail of damp tea leaves for the carpets.

"How to clean silver knives," Tellman said with disgust. "It's like a madhouse down there. At least six of them have threatened to give notice. The cook's drinking the Madeira as fast as the butler can fetch it up, and the scullery maid's so frightened she screams every time anyone speaks to her. I wouldn't run a household if you paid me a king's ransom!"

"I'm going to Oakfield House," Pitt said with a ghost of a smile. "Greville's home. It's about ten or eleven miles away. I need to look at his papers, especially the threatening letters he received over the past month or two."

"You think there'll be anything in there that matters?" Tellman asked doubtfully.

"Possibly. Even if it is Moynihan, and I'm not sure of that, he certainly didn't act alone. I want to know who's behind him."

"He doesn't need anyone behind him." Tellman also kept his voice down. "He's got enough hatred to kill without prompting. Although he'll be lucky if McGinley doesn't do anything to him before the weekend is through. They're all at their separate prayers down there." He jerked his head towards the way he had come. "The Catholics looking daggers at the Protestants, and Protestants looking daggers back."

His face reflected bewilderment and disgust, his eyes pulled down at the corners. "I've half a mind to stoke the kitchen fires so they can burn each other at the stake, and be done with it all. I can understand greed, jealousy, revenge, even some kinds of madness. But these people are sane—after a fashion."

"Try and keep them from violence while I'm gone," Pitt said, looking at Tellman steadily. He was uncertain whether to be light or to let Tellman know how anxious he felt. "Stay near Mr. Radley. He's the one in most danger now." He could not keep the catch out of his voice. "You can't sit in the conference with him, but you can wait outside. I'll be back not long after dark."

Tellman straightened his shoulders a little, and the criticism dropped out of his voice.

"Yes sir. Ride careful. I suppose you know how to ride a horse?" He looked worried.

"Yes, thank you," Pitt answered. "I grew up in the country, if you recall?"

Tellman grunted and continued on his way.

Pitt went to look for Charlotte to tell her what he proposed to do. He had hardly seen her since they arrived at Ashworth Hall. She always seemed to be with one of the other women, trying to persuade them to keep some kind of peace, or else making idle conversation to mask the social difficulties which were admittedly appalling.

This time it took him a quarter of an hour to find her, and he eventually discovered her in the warming room, a place designed to keep food hot before serving, since the dining room was a considerable distance from the kitchen. It contained a good fire, a steam-heated cabinet, and also a butler's table and a marvelous array of implements for opening and decanting wine. She was listening earnestly to Gracie. They both stopped the instant he came in. Gracie blinked and excused herself.

"What is it?" Pitt asked, looking at her small, retreating form.

Charlotte smiled, her eyes filled with sadness and laughter at once. "Just a few feminine secrets," she answered.

Pitt could see she was not going to tell him any more. He had not thought of Gracie as having feminine secrets. He should have. She was twenty now, even though she was still no taller and very little plumper than she had been when she had come to them at thirteen.

"I'm going to ride over to Oakfield House," he said. "I don't suppose there is anything in the letters Greville received, but there might be. I can't afford to overlook the chance. I'll be back as soon after dark as I can."

She nodded, her eyes anxious. "Ride carefully," she said, then smiled with her head a little on one side. "You'll be stiff tomorrow." She reached up and kissed him very gently. She seemed about to say something else, and then changed her mind. "How will you find your way there?" she said instead.

"I'll ask Piers. I need to get Eudora's permission anyway, and help."

She nodded, and then walked with him as far as the hall.

Pitt found Eudora in the upstairs boudoir with both Piers and Justine. She was not wearing black. Quite naturally, she had not brought black with her. The nearest she could do was an autumnal brown, and in spite of the ravages of shock and grief, she still looked beautiful. Nothing could rob her of the richness of her hair or the symmetry of her bones.

Justine was an extraordinary contrast. She also had not brought black. As a young, unmarried woman she would not wear the shade to such an occasion unless she was at the end of a period of mourning. She had chosen a deep hunting green, and with her dense black hair it was almost a jewel color. She seemed to vibrate with life. Even in repose, as she was now, sitting beside Eudora, Pitt's eyes were drawn to the intelligence in her face.

Piers stood behind the two women, his expression defensive, as if he would protect them from further hurt, were it possible.

"Good morning, ma'am," Pitt said gravely to Eudora. "I am sorry to intrude on you again, but I need your permission to go to Oakfield House and look through Mr. Greville's papers to see if I can find the malevolent letters that he received."

Eudora looked almost relieved, as if she had expected him to say something worse.

"Of course. Yes, naturally, Mr. Pitt. Do you wish me to write something?"

"If you please. And I shall need any necessary keys." He wondered what she had feared from him . . . some further disaster? Or that he suspected someone in particular? Surely, as far as she was concerned, the worst had already happened? "I would also appreciate directions as to the best way to get there," he added. "I shall ride across country, or I shall take far too long. I want to be back before nightfall."

Piers glanced at Justine, then at Pitt. "Would you like me to come with you?" he offered. "That would make it much easier. It would be very difficult indeed to describe to you the best way there, or even to draw a map."

"Thank you," Pitt accepted without hesitation. Apart from the convenience of it, he would welcome the opportunity to speak less formally to Piers, and perhaps learn more of Ainsley Greville. Without realizing it, Piers might know something of meaning.

"What can you learn from his papers?" Justine asked with obvious doubt. "Will they not be state papers anyway, and confidential?" She looked from Piers to Eudora, and back at Pitt. Her voice dropped. "He was killed in this house, and you said it was someone here. No one broke in. Shouldn't we . . . shouldn't we leave him his privacy?"

"It is only Mr. Pitt looking at them, my dear," Eudora said, blinking a little, as if the concern puzzled her. "There won't be any government papers that matter at Oakfield, they would all be at Whitehall. There may be the unpleasant letters which I know he received, and perhaps that will help us"—she took a deep breath—"to learn who is behind this." She looked at Pitt, her eyes wide and dark. "There must be more than one person, mustn't there? There was the incident with the carriage." She was clenching her hands together.

"Of course," Piers agreed. "We should look at those letters. And there may be other things that he didn't mention. . . ."

Justine rose to her feet, taking Piers's arm. "Your father is no longer here to protect himself, his privacy," she said to him, turning a little away from Pitt. "He may have private or personal financial papers, or other letters which it would be preferable were not seen outside the family. He was a great man. He must have dealt with many matters which were confidential. There will have been friends who trusted him, wrote to him of issues which might be embarrassing if they were to become public. We all have . . . indiscretions. . . ." She left it in the air, but she turned to Pitt and met his eyes with a wide stare.

"I shall be discreet, Miss Baring," he assured her. "I imagine he was privy to much information that was sensitive, but I doubt it will be committed to paper in his home. But as has been pointed out, the tragedy was not an isolated incident. There was an attempt to kill Mr. Greville a few weeks ago—"

She turned to Eudora. "You must have been so afraid for him. And then to have this happen. I imagine it was just . . . the sort of threats people make when they want something, empty, bullying." She looked back at Pitt. "Of course, you must find out who sent them. They may very well be behind this, since they have actually attempted before." She looked at Piers. "What happened?"

"Someone tried to drive him off the road. I wasn't there, I was up at Cambridge. Mama was in London." He put his arm around her gently, his eyes on her face. "Will you be all right here if I go with Mr. Pitt?"

She smiled back at him. "Yes, of course I will. And I will look after your mother. I think with the other tensions there are, poor Mrs. Radley could do with all the assistance any of us can offer." A ghost of amusement, and perhaps pity, crossed her eyes and vanished. "I did hear rumors of what the trouble is between the Moynihans and the McGinleys, but I shall pretend I didn't. I think it will be the only way to get through the day, which threatens to feel like a week."

"Surely they will forget all that now?" Piers looked startled. "The future of Ireland may be altered here if Mr. Radley can keep the conference going. After all that has happened, how can anyone care about something so—"

She smiled at him, touching his cheek with her finger. "My dear, we are quite capable of worrying about our own personal grievances and private habits while the whole world is collapsing around us. Perhaps it is easier to think on that scale. I don't doubt the Last Trump will find some of us bickering about the price of a piece of ribbon, or who forgot to pinch out the candle. The end of the world would seem too much to grasp in the mind." She glanced at Pitt. "Don't worry about us, Mr. Pitt, we shall manage the day."

He found himself liking Justine far more than he had expected to. She was anything but ordinary. He wondered what she saw in Piers that so attracted her. He seemed so young compared with her mature humor and balance. But then he was judging on the slightest acquaintance, and it was unfair. He knew very little about any of them, beyond the superficial.

He thanked Eudora and took his leave, arranging to meet Piers in the stables in fifteen minutes.

It was cold but not unpleasant as they set out on two excellent horses, traveling first across the parkland at a brisk canter, then turning along the edge of plowed fields and towards a lane which wound through a patch of woodland. It had been years since Pitt had ridden. One does not forget the feel of the animal. The creak of leather, the smell, the rhythmic movement were all familiar, but he knew he would be painfully stiff the next day. He was using muscles unstretched in a decade. He could imagine Tellman's comments, and see the discreet smile on Jack's face.

They could not converse while they were moving swiftly, but when they were obliged to slow to a walk between the trees it came quite naturally. Piers rode well, with the grace of a man who is both used to the saddle and fond of his animals.

"Will you look for a city practice?" Pitt asked, as much for something uncontentious to say as because he was interested.

"Oh no," Piers replied quickly, lifting his head to look at the bare branches above. "I really don't like London. And I know Justine would prefer a country life."

"I imagine your father's death will change your plans?" They were moving more slowly now along a winding path, Piers a little ahead as they crossed a stream and the horses scrambled up the farther bank, sending a scatter of stones back into the water. The wind caught a flurry of fallen leaves with a rustling sound, and far away to the left a dog barked.

"I hadn't thought of it," Piers said frankly. "Mama will stay on in Oakfield House, of course. It hasn't anything like the lands of Ashworth. There are no farms to manage. She won't need me. Justine and I will find somewhere, perhaps near Cambridge. Of course, financially I will be more fortunately placed, I suppose."

"You probably will not need to practice medicine," Pitt pointed out.

Piers swiveled quickly to stare at him. "But I want to! I know my father would have liked me to stand for Parliament, but I have no interest in it whatever. I am interested in public health." There was a sudden enthusiasm in his face, a light in his eyes which made him quite different from the rather bland young man he had been even moments before. "I care about diseases of nutrition especially. Have you any idea how many English children suffer from rickets? The medical textbook even calls it the English disease! And scurvy. It isn't only seamen who get scurvy. And night blindness. There are too many things we are on the brink of being able to treat, but we don't quite manage it."

"Are you sure you don't want to be in Parliament?" Pitt said wryly, catching up to ride beside him as they emerged into an open field.

Piers was perfectly serious. "You can't make laws until you have proved your case. First you must make them believe, then understand, then care. After that it is time for legislation. I want to work with people who need help, not argue with politicians and make compromises."

Pitt dismounted and opened the gate at the side of the field and held it while Piers took both horses through, then closed it behind them. He remounted a trifle more elegantly than he had mounted the first time.

"That makes me sound very arrogant, doesn't it?" Piers said more moderately. "I know compromise is necessary in a lot of things. I just have no skills at it. My father was brilliant. He could charm and persuade people into all sorts of things. If anyone could have succeeded with the Irish Problem, it would have been he. He had a sort of power, almost an invulnerability. He wasn't afraid of people the way most of us are. He always knew what he wanted out of any situation and how much he was prepared to yield or to pay for it. He never changed his mind."

Pitt thought about it as they moved forward into a canter again over a long stretch of pasture land. He had seen that assurance in Greville, the quiet ruthlessness of a man who can keep his purpose in mind and never waver from it. It was a very necessary quality in his chosen profession, but it was not entirely attractive. Piers had not said that directly, but he had allowed it to be inferred. There was no warmth when he spoke of his father, and very little regret.

Oakfield House was, as he had said, considerably smaller than Ashworth, but it was still a very handsome residence. Approaching it from the west, it looked to be of a size to have ten or twelve bedrooms, and numerous stables and other outbuildings. It was the country home of a man of both taste and position, discreet but of considerable wealth.

They left the horses with the groom and went in through the side door. Pitt was already feeling his leg muscles pull a little. By the next day he would be regretting this.

The butler came across the hall looking disconcerted, his white hair ruffled.

"Master Piers! We weren't expecting you. I'm afraid Mr. and Mrs. Greville are away at the moment. But of course . . ." He saw Pitt and his expression became colder and more formal. "Good morning, sir. May I be of any assistance?"

"Thurgood," Piers said quietly. He walked towards him and took him by one elbow. "I'm sorry, but there has been a tragedy. My father has been killed. Uncle Padraig is with Mama, but it was necessary that I come here with Mr. Pitt." He indicated Pitt while still steadying the swaying butler with the other hand. "We need to look at Papa's papers and letters, and find the threats that were sent recently. If there is anything you know which might be of help, please make sure you tell us."

"Killed?" Thurgood looked startled. Suddenly his slight officiousness vanished and he looked elderly and rather rumpled.

"Yes, I'm afraid so," Piers continued. "But please tell the staff there will be no changes, and they are to continue as usual. They must not discuss it yet, because it has not been in the newspapers, and we have not informed the other members of the family."

It rose to Pitt's tongue to ask Thurgood not to mention it at all, but he realized before he spoke that that would be an impossibility. The man's shock was all too apparent. Others would draw the news from him even if he were unwilling. The air of tragedy and fear was already in the house.

"Perhaps you would arrange a hot toddy for us," Piers went on. "It's been a long ride. And then luncheon at about one. We'll take it in the library. A little cold meat or pie, whatever you have."

"Yes sir. I'm very sorry, sir. I'm sure the other staff will wish me to convey their sympathies also," Thurgood said awkwardly. "When shall we expect the mistress home, sir? And of course there will be . . . arrangements. . . ."

"I don't know yet. I'm sorry." Piers frowned. "Do you understand, Thurgood, this is a government secret at the moment? I think perhaps you had better tell the housekeeper and no one else. Treat it as a family embarrassment, if you like." He glanced at Pitt and smiled with a little twist of the mouth. "Use the same discretion you would if you had overheard a confession to something shameful."

Thurgood obviously did not understand, but his face reflected bland obedience.

When he had withdrawn, Piers led the way to the library, with his father's large desk in one corner. The room was cold, but the fire was laid, and Piers bent and lit it without bothering to call a servant. As soon as he was sure it had caught, he straightened up and produced keys to open the desk drawers.

The first one yielded personal accounts, and Pitt read through them without expecting to find anything of interest. There were tailors' bills, and shirtmakers'; receipts for two pairs of very expensive boots, onyx-faced shirt studs and a fan of carved ivory and lace, an enameled pillbox with a painting of a lady on a swing, and three bottles of lavender water. They were all dated within the last month. It seemed

Greville had been a very generous husband. It surprised Pitt. He had not observed such affection or imagination in him. Eudora was going to find the loss bitter. The private man had obviously been more sensitive and far more emotional than the public politician.

He stood still, holding the papers in his hand, looking around the well-furnished library with its book-lined walls, a few excellent paintings, mostly of scenes from Africa, watercolors of Table Mountain and the sweeping skies of the Veldt. The books in the cases were largely sets of volumes, uniformly bound in leather, but one case seemed to hold odd ones, and from the armchair it was the most easily accessible. He would look at them if he had time. Greville had suddenly become more interesting as a man, a sharper loss now that Pitt had seen his humanity, a sense of his inner emotion.

Piers was looking through the drawers on the further side of the desk. He straightened up, several letters in his hand.

"I think I have them," he said grimly, holding them forward. "Some of them are threatening." He looked puzzled, hurt. "Only two are anonymous or sound political." He stared at Pitt, uncertain what he wanted to say. Twice he started, stopped again, and then simply put out his hand with the papers.

Pitt took them and looked at the first. It was printed in block letters and extremely simple.

Do not betray Ireland or you will be sorry. We will win our freedom, and no Englishman is going to defeat us this time. It will be a simple matter to kill you. Remember that.

Not surprisingly, it was unsigned and undated.

The next was utterly different. It was written in a strong, clear hand, and it was both dated and carried a sender's address.

Oct 20th. 1890.

Dear Greville,

I find it most repugnant to have to address any gentleman

on a matter such as this, but your behaviour leaves me no alternative. Your attentions to my wife must cease immediately. I do not propose to enlarge upon the subject. You are aware of your transgression and it needs no detail from me.

If you see her again, other than as the ordinary demands of civilized society dictate, and in public, I shall take the necessary steps to sue her for divorce, and cite you as an adulterer. I am sure I do not need to spell out what this will do to your career.

I do not write this in idleness. Through her behaviour with you I have lost all regard for her, and while I would not willingly ruin her, I shall do so rather than continue to be betrayed in this fashion.

Yours most candidly

Gerald Easterwood

Pitt looked up at Piers. The image of Greville of only a few moments ago had been shattered.

"Do you know a Mrs. Easterwood?" he said quietly.

"Yes. At least by reputation. I'm afraid it is not much . . . not as good as perhaps Mr. Easterwood would like to imagine."

"Was he a friend of your father's?"

"Easterwood? No. Hardly the same social circle. My father—" he hesitated "—was a good friend to those he liked, or considered his equals. I can't imagine him using another man's wife, not if the man were someone he knew . . . I mean, as a friend. He was very loyal to his friends." He started as if to repeat it again, and realized he had already stressed it.

Pitt looked at the next letter. It was another political threat, and very plainly concerning the future of Ireland, but seemed to be more in favor of the Protestant Ascendancy and the preservation of the estates which had been worked for and paid for by Anglo-Irish landlords. It also promised reprisals if Greville should betray their interests.

The one after was personal and signed.

My dear Greville,

I can never thank you sufficiently for the generosity you have extended to me in this matter. Without you it would have been a disaster for me—deserved perhaps, but nevertheless because of your intervention I shall survive, to behave with more circumspection in the future.

I am forever in your debt,

Your humble and grateful friend

Langley Osbourne

"Do you know him?" Pitt asked.

Piers looked blank. "No."

There were three more. Another was an Irish threat, but so illiterately written it was hard to understand what was desired, except an ill-defined idea of justice. The threat of a most colorful death was contrastingly plain, and mention was made of an old story of lovers who had both been betrayed by the English.

The following one was quite long, and from a friend of some considerable intimacy and length of time. The tone was one of social arrogance, class loyalty, common memory and interest, and deep unquestioned personal affection and trust. Pitt instinctively disliked the writer, one Malcom Anders, and found himself judging Greville less kindly because of it.

The last letter was unopened, even though the postmark was dated almost two weeks before. Apparently it had been of little interest to him. Presumably he had recognized the writing and not bothered to read it. Perhaps he had received it when there was no fire burning and he had not wished to leave it in the wastepaper basket, where a curious housemaid or footman might see it and maybe have sufficient literacy to be able to understand it.

Pitt opened it carefully and read. It was a love letter from a woman who signed herself Mary-Jane. It spoke of an intimate relationship which Greville had ended, according to the writer, abruptly and without explanation, other than the assumption that he had become bored with her. There seemed a callousness about the whole matter which Pitt found repellent. Certainly there was an element of using, and nothing of love. Whether she had loved him, or simply used him also, in a different manner, he could only guess.

He handed the letters back to Piers.

"I can see why he felt the threats were probably irrelevant," he said matter-of-factly. "They could be from anyone at all, and seem to come from Nationalist Catholic and Protestant Unionist alike. It doesn't help us at all. Still, we'll take them."

"Just . . . the threats?" Piers said quickly.

"Yes, of course. Lock the others back in the drawer. You can destroy them later if we find they have nothing to do with the case."

"They can't have." Piers still held them in his hand. "There's nothing political about them. It's simply a sordid affair . . . well, two. But both of them are over . . . were over . . . before this. Can't you just burn them, and keep quiet? My mother has enough to bear without having to know about this."

"Lock them up again," Pitt instructed. "And keep the keys yourself. When the case is over you can come in here and sort anything you want to, and destroy what is better kept discreet. Now, let me look through the rest of the drawers."

The butler returned, looking haggard, bringing the promised hot toddy. He seemed on the brink of enquiring as to their success, then changed his mind and left.

They searched the rest of the library but found nothing more of interest to the case. The books and papers shed more light on Greville's character. He was obviously a man of high intelligence and wide interests. There was the first draft of a monograph on ancient Roman medicine, and Pitt could happily have taken the time to read it, had he had any excuse. It was vividly written. On the shelves there were books on subjects as diverse as early Renaissance painting in Tuscany and the native birds of North America.

Pitt wondered if Eudora had any place in the room, if he had shared some of his interests with her, or if their worlds of the mind had been entirely separate, as was the case in some marriages. All that many held in common were a home, children, a social life and status, and economic circumstance. The imagination, the humor, the great voyages of the heart and intellect, were all made alone. Even the searching of the spirit was unshared.

How much would Eudora really miss him? Had she any idea of the reality of her home, or did she see what she wished to see? Many people did that as a way to place armor around their vulnerability and preserve what they had for survival. He could not blame her if she were one of those.

Luncheon was brought to them in the library and they ate by the fire, saying little. Piers had already learned more about his father in the last two hours than in the preceding ten years, and it complicated the picture he held of him. There was too much to admire and to despise, too much that tore open the emotions and made grief a far more complex thing than simply a sudden loneliness.

Pitt did not intrude with speech.

After they had finished Pitt went out to find the coach driver and question him about the incident on the road. That had been a serious and genuine attempt at murder.

He found the man in the stables polishing a harness. The smell of leather and saddle soap jerked him back in memory to his youth and the estate where his father had been gamekeeper and he had grown up. He could have been a boy again, scrounging winter apples, sitting silently in the corner listening to the grooms and coachmen talking of the horses and dogs, swapping gossip. He could imagine going back to supper in the gamekeeper's cottage, and to bed in his tiny room under the eaves. Or later, after his father's disgrace, after the anger and the rage of injustice had passed, to his room at the top of the big house, when Sir Authur had taken in his mother and himself.

Now he would ride back to Ashworth Hall and sleep beside Charlotte in one of the great guest bedrooms with its four-poster bed and embroidered linen and a fire in the grate. He would not douse himself quickly in the icy water from the pump, but ring a bell, and a manservant would bring him ewers of steaming hot water, enough for a bath if he wanted it. He would have a separate room in which to dress, and then breakfast would be as much as he could eat, with a choice of half a dozen different dishes. He would have silver knives and forks to use, and a linen napkin. And he would sit with people for whom this was the usual and familiar way of life. They had never experienced anything else.

But after he had finished he would not leave for the schoolroom he had been permitted to share with Matthew Desmond, nor for the numerous small tasks around the estate, safely taught or supervised by someone older. He would bear the responsibility for solving the murder of a minister of government, a man whose life he had been sent to safeguard in the first place . . . and failed.

He leaned against the stable wall, his feet in the comfortable, familiar-smelling straw, and heard the horses moving contentedly in other stalls on the farther side.

He had already introduced himself to the coachman and explained to him that Greville was dead. He had wondered whether to try to keep it from him, and decided that if he were a loyal servant, he would tell a stranger little of meaning if he thought his master still alive.

"Describe for me the incident when you were driven off the road," he asked.

The man spoke haltingly, searching for words, all the time his browned hands were working with the leather and soap, rubbing, polishing. His account was in all essentials, exactly the same as Greville's. He also remembered the eyes of the other driver.

"Mad, they looked ter me," he said with a shake of his head. "Starin', like."

"Pale or dark?" Pitt asked.

"Pale, like light coming off water," he answered. "Never seen a face like it afore. Nor again, I 'ope!"

"But you had no success in finding where the horses came from?"

"No." He looked down at the harness in his hands. "Din' try 'ard enough, I reckon. If we 'ad, p'raps Mr. Greville'd be alive now. Lunatics, them Irish. Course, not all of 'em. Young Kathleen were a good girl. Couldn't 'elp likin' er. I were real sorry when she went."

"Who was Kathleen?" It probably did not matter, but he would ask anyway.

"Kathleen O'Brien. She were a maid 'ere. Not unlike our Doll, she were, only dark; dark as night, wi' them blue Irish eyes."

"Was she from Ireland?"

"Oh yes! Voice as soft as melted butter, an' sing real lovely."

"How long ago was that?"

"Six month." His face closed over and his shoulders tightened.

"Why did she leave?" Pitt could not dismiss the thought crossing his mind that she could have had relatives—brothers, even a lover—who were passionate Nationalists.

"There weren't nothing wrong wi' Kathleen," the coachman said, keeping his eyes on his work. "If yer thinkin' she 'ad summat ter do wi' that, yer wrong."

"Why would she have?" Pitt asked quietly. "Did she leave here with a bad feeling? Did she have cause?"

"I've got nothing to say, Mr. Pitt."

"Did you drive Mr. Greville in London as well, or only here?"

"I bin up ter Lunnon lots o' times. There in't much proper carriage drivin' 'ere when both the master and mistress is up in town. John can do all o' that. Learn 'im a bit."

"So you would drive Mr. Greville in London?"

"I said so."

"Do you know Mrs. Easterwood?"

No answer was necessary. The hesitation gave him away, then the angle of his body, the way his fingers stopped on the leather, then started again, digging into it, knuckles white.

"Were there many like Mrs. Easterwood?" Pitt asked quietly.

Again there was silence.

"I understand your loyalty," Pitt went on. "And I admire it . . . whether it is to Mr. Greville or his widow. . . ." He saw the man wince at the word. "But he was murdered, struck over the head and drowned in his own bath, left there all night for Doll to find him in the morning, naked, his face under the water—"

The coachman jerked his head up, his eyes narrow and angry.

"You got no call ter go tellin' me that! It in't decent for folks ter know—"

"Folks don't know." Pitt reached across and passed him a clean cloth. "But I mean to find out who did it. It wasn't just one man, because the coach driver with the staring eyes isn't at Ashworth Hall. There was also a good man murdered in London, a decent man with a family, to keep this secret. I want them all, and I mean to have them. If I have to learn some squalid details about a few women like Mrs. Easterwood, and a good deal about Mr. Greville that the public don't need to know, then I will."

"Yes sir." It was grudging. He hated it, but he saw no alternative. His hands clenched over the harness and his shoulders were tight.

"Were there others like Mrs. Easterwood?" Pitt asked again.

"A few." He kept his eyes on Pitt's. He took a deep breath and let it out in a sigh. "Mostly up Lunnon way. Never wi' wives of a friend. He'd not take anything what's theirs. Only take them as is willin'—" He stopped suddenly.

"And don't count," Pitt finished for him, remembering the tone of Malcolm Anders's letter.

"There's nobody what doesn't count, Mr. Pitt."

"Even whores?"

The coachman's face reddened. "You got no place to go calling any woman a whore, Mr. Pitt, an' I don' care who you are, I won't stand 'ere an' listen to it."

"Even girls like Kathleen O'Brien? Lie with anyone to better their chances and—" Pitt too stopped suddenly, seeing the rage and the hurt in the man's eyes. He had gone too far. "I'm sorry," he apologized. He meant it. He could picture the story. It would be one of a dozen variations on the old theme, a handsome maid, a master who was used to taking anything he wanted and did not think of servants as people like himself, with tenderness and dignity or honor to be hurt. The distinction would not even be intentional.

"She weren't like that." The coachman glared at him. "You've no place saying it!"

"I wanted to provoke you into honesty," Pitt confessed. "What happened to Kathleen?"

The man was still angry. He reminded Pitt of the coachman where he grew up, taciturn, loyal, honest to the point of bluntness, but endlessly patient with animals or the young.

"She got dismissed for thievin'," he said grudgingly. "But it were because she wouldn't have no one touch 'er."

Pitt found himself relaxing. He had not realized until that moment that he had been clenching his hands so hard the nails had scraped his palms, and his muscles ached.

"Did she go back to Ireland?"

"I dunno. We gave 'er what we could, me and Cook and Mr. Wheeler."

"Good. But you are still loyal to Mr. Greville?"

"No sir," he corrected. "I'm loyal to the mistress. I wouldn't 'ave 'er know about them things. Some ladies know an' can live with it, others can't. I reckon as she's one as couldn't. In't nothing sour in her, or some would say realistic. You won't go telling her, will you?"

"I won't tell her anything I don't have to," Pitt answered, and he said it with regret, because he knew it did not mean a great deal. He wished he could have given the assurances the coachman sought.

They rode back through the gathering dusk, the light dying rapidly in the autumn evening, and Pitt was profoundly glad he was not trying to make his way along the hedgerows and through the woods alone. There was little wind, but even so the air was growing colder all the time, and the sharp prickle of frost stung his nose. Twigs snapped under his horse's hooves and its breath was white against the gloom.

It was over an hour and a half before they saw the lights of Ashworth Hall and rode into the stable yard to dismount. In the past Pitt had always had to unsaddle his own horse, walk it cool, rub it down and feed and water it, sometimes Matthew's horse as well. He felt remiss, uncaring, to hand it over to someone else and simply walk away. It was another reminder of how far he was from his origins. Piers, young and slender and full of pain, did it as casually as a man takes off his jacket in his own house.

Pitt followed him in through the side door, scraping his boots on the ornamental cast-iron grid set there for the purpose.

Inside the house was warm, even the hall seemed to embrace him after the sharpness of the night air. A footman was waiting attentively.

"May I fetch you anything, sir?" he asked Pitt first, to Pitt's surprise. He had momentarily forgotten he was a personal guest, Piers only an addition, and a younger one. "A hot drink? A glass of whiskey? Mulled wine?"

"Thank you, a hot drink would be excellent. Is Mr. Radley out of his meeting yet?"

"No sir. I venture to say that they have been going rather better than expected." He looked at Piers. "May I get a hot drink for you also, sir?"

"Yes, thank you." Piers looked at Pitt. He had not asked him what he was going to say. He had already asked for his discretion once, and he had no idea what the coachman had told him. "I'll go up and see Miss Baring." He looked back at the footman. "Is she with my mother, do you know?"

"Yes, sir, in the blue boudoir."

"Thank you." With only another glance at Pitt, he went upstairs and disappeared around the turn of the staircase onto the landing.

"I'll have my drink upstairs too," Pitt instructed. "I think I'll have a bath before dinner."

"Yes sir. I will have some water brought up for you, sir."

Pitt smiled. "Thank you. Yes, please, do that."

It was Tellman who came with it. He did it with a very ill grace indeed. The only reason he did not splash water all over the floor was that he might have found himself mopping it up afterwards. He would be delighted, however, if Pitt were too stiff the next day to move without pain.

"I learned a great deal," Pitt said conversationally, undoing his cravat and laying it on the side table. He began to unfasten his shirt, moving behind the screen which was set up to keep the draft from the door off the bath.

"About what?" Tellman asked grudgingly.

Pitt went on undressing and told him about Mrs. Easterwood and those others like her, about Kathleen O'Brien and what the coachman had said, and not said, about her dismissal.

Tellman stood leaning against the marble-topped table with jug, bath salts and soap dishes on it, his hands deep in his pockets, his face grim.

"Seems like he earned himself a few enemies," he said thoughtfully. "But girls who are wrongly treated don't come back and murder their masters." He moved to keep himself on the other side of the screen from Pitt or the bath. "If they did it would probably do away with half the aristocracy of England."

"It would put a fairly swift stop to the abuse," Pitt said with a shiver as he stepped into the hot water. It was delicious, and he had not realized until that moment quite how cold and stiff he was, or how very tired. It had been far too long since he had done anything so physically strenuous. He eased himself into the steaming, fragrant foam. "I doubt it had any relevance," he went on more seriously. "But we have to consider the possibility that Kathleen O'Brien may have had Nationalist, even Fenian, relatives, and been more than willing to offer information. Heaven knows, it seems she had cause."

"Does it matter?" Tellman opened one of the jars of salts and sniffed it curiously, then wrinkled his nose at its effeminacy. "It was someone in this house now who killed him. It certainly wasn't a disgruntled husband or Kathleen O'Brien. He would have known them. Anyway, we've been told the background of everyone here."

Pitt had no choice but to speak to Eudora. When he was dressed again, not having seen Charlotte, who was busy assisting Emily entertain Kezia and Iona, he went to Eudora's sitting room and knocked.

The door was opened by Justine. There was a flicker of hope in her eyes, and she searched Pitt's face and was uncertain what she saw, except that it would hurt. Piers was not there. Presumably he was still in his bath, or dressing for dinner.

"Come in, Mr. Pitt." She opened the door wide and stood back. She was dressed in deep purplish-blue and was so slender she should have looked fragile, yet her grace instead gave the impression of strength, like a dancer's. It was so easy to understand why Piers was fascinated with her—she had such beauty, arrested suddenly and startlingly by the uniqueness of her nose. He could not even decide whether it was ugly or merely different.

Beyond her, Eudora was sitting in one of the large chairs beside the fire, close to it, as if she were cold, although the room was warm. There was no color in her skin, for all the vividness of her hair. She looked at Pitt guardedly, without interest, as if all he could say would be necessary but tedious, and already familiar.

Justine closed the door behind him and he walked in, without invitation sitting in the chair opposite Eudora. He had thought about this during most of the long, cold ride back to Ashworth Hall, but it still was difficult to know the least painful way to say what he had to, or judge how much could not be held from her. Some of it would become known anyway, and better she learn it privately, and before others did.

The more he looked at her face in the firelight with its gentle lines, its lovely eyes and lips, the more he despised Greville for his betrayals. He knew the judgment was harsh even as he was making it. He had no idea what she was like within such a close relationship, how cold or critical, how silently cruel, how disdainful or remote. And yet he made the judgment just the same, because his mind and his instinct told him different things.

"Mrs. Greville, I read all the letters and papers in Mr. Greville's study and spoke to the coachman about the incident on the road. I understand why he did not show us the letters before. They are of little use, just very general threats, and unsigned. They could be from almost anyone."

"So you found nothing?" She sounded as though she were unsure if she were disappointed or relieved.

"Nothing from those letters," he amended. "There were others, and events which emerged from speaking with the servants."

"Oh? He did not mention other threats to me. Perhaps he was protecting me from the worry."

Justine came back towards the fire.

"I am sure he would. He would not wish you to be afraid if he could avoid it."

Eudora smiled at her. It was obvious the two women had already formed a bond in grief. Justine had barely known Greville, but she seemed deeply sensitive to the loss.

"Do you remember a maid you had called Kathleen O'Brien?" Pitt asked.

Eudora thought for a moment. "Yes, yes, she was a very handsome girl. Irish, of course." She frowned. "You don't think she had anything to do with Fenians, do you? She was from the south, but she seemed a very gentle girl, not in the least . . . I suppose it is absurd to speak of a servant as politically minded. Are you saying she might have been passing information about us to others?" Her face made her disbelief plain.

"She may have had brothers, or a lover," Justine pointed out.

Eudora looked unconvinced. "But the attack happened quite some time after she had left us. She could have told them nothing they could not have gathered for themselves merely by watching the stable yard. I won't have Kathleen blamed, Mr. Pitt, without very good evidence. And she certainly was not here this weekend. I have seen Miss Moynihan's maid, and Mrs. McGinley's. No, this has nothing to do with Kathleen."

"Why did she leave you, Mrs. Greville?"

She hesitated. He saw the lie in her eyes before she spoke.

"Some family matter. She went back to Ireland."

"Why do you say that?"

She looked at him with wide, unhappy eyes.

"She was charged with thieving." He said what she would not.

Justine stiffened, but her expression was unreadable.

"I don't believe she was guilty," Eudora said, but her eyes avoided Pitt's. "I think it was a misunderstanding. I wanted to—" She stopped.

Did she know? Did it matter anyway? Was it necessary to injure her still further by despoiling her husband's memory in her mind? He would much rather not. She looked so crushed already, so easily hurt. Perhaps it did not matter.

Justine had moved closer to Eudora, facing Pitt.

"Surely you don't think this girl had anything to do with it, do you?" she said very calmly. "Even if she went back to Ireland and was a sympathizer with nationalism, even if she told people she had been in service in Oakfield House, she couldn't have told them anything of value. Mr. Greville was killed here, and the attack on the road could have been anyone, but it wasn't a woman." Her eyes were very straight and level.

"No, that is perfectly true," Pitt conceded. Expressed as she had, it dwindled into insignificance. "Mrs. Greville, do you know a Mrs. Easterwood?"

"Yes, slightly." Her expression belied the cautious tone of her voice. She did not care for her. Either she knew about or suspected Greville's connection with her, or she knew her reputation.

Perhaps sensing some nervousness in Eudora, Justine moved an inch or two closer and put an arm protectively across the back of the chair.

"Are these people who might have given information about Mr. Greville's movements, Mr. Pitt?" Justine asked, her tone still polite but with a thread of warning in it. "Do you believe that knowing who they are will lead you to the person in this house who actually committed the murder? Or to whoever killed the poor man in London? Whatever they said was probably unwilling, and they won't even remember to whom they spoke." She smiled very faintly. "It was no intruder, that you already established through Mr. Tellman's questioning of the other servants. It is a political crime, because of Mr. Greville's stand for peace and the skill he brought to the conference table. Someone wants peace only on their terms, or continued violence."

"I know, Miss Baring," Pitt conceded. He could understand, even applaud, her desire to protect Eudora from any further distress. Possibly she guessed that Greville's personal life was not one which would be easy for Eudora to learn of. Pitt felt all the same emotions himself.

But a new and very ugly thought had entered his mind, and he could not dismiss it. If Eudora knew of Greville's liaisons with Mrs. Easterwood and her kind, and suspected what had really happened to Kathleen O'Brien, then she had good cause to hate her husband. Perhaps her brother, Padraig Doyle, also knew these things. Might he see it as yet another betrayal of the Irish by the English? Might this be one wrong he had decided to avenge himself, under cover of a political threat? Or even as part of a political act? No one had broken into Ashworth Hall. Had Doyle been a very willing assassin in Fenian hands? Pitt had thought him less likely before simply because of the family relationship. But that was not now true.

"Mrs. Greville," he said very quietly, "the letters we found, and the information given by the servants, much against their will, show that Mr. Greville had close, intimate ties with several other women. Unless you wish to know, I shall not tell you the details, but they are not capable of any other interpretation. I am sorry."

Justine's elegant body tightened as if he had struck Eudora a physical blow. She stared at him with disgust in her beautiful, wide eyes.

Eudora was very pale, and she had difficulty in finding her voice and keeping it steady. But the look in her eyes as she met Pitt's gaze was not pain so much as fear.

"Many men have frailties, Mr. Pitt," she said slowly. "Especially powerful men in high office. The temptation falls their way more easily, perhaps, and they need the pleasure of having been able for a little while to forget their responsibilities. Those affairs are brief and have no meaning. A wise woman learns very quickly to ignore them. Ainsley never allowed me to be embarrassed in any way. He was discreet. He did not flirt with my friends. Not every woman is so fortunate."

"And Kathleen O'Brien?" He hated having to mention her again.

"She was a maid, you said!" Justine cut in with contempt. "Surely you are not suggesting a man of Mr. Greville's dignity and station would be flirting with a maid, Mr. Pitt? That is insulting."

Eudora turned and looked up at her.

"Thank you, my dear, for your loyalty. You have been extraordinarily helpful to me in this time. But perhaps you should go and be with Piers. He too must be feeling very shaken and disturbed by this. I would go to him myself, but I know he would prefer you." A flicker of regret crossed her mouth and vanished. "You might make sure he has something to eat, after his long ride."

Justine accepted her dismissal gracefully, leaving Pitt alone with Eudora.

Eudora leaned even closer to the fire, as if in spite of the now almost oppressive heat in the room, she were still cold. The yellow light from the flames lit her cheeks and the gentle angle of her chin, and cast the shadows of her lashes on her skin.

Pitt felt brutal, but he had no choice. He forced himself to remember Greville's dead face under the water, the indignity of his body, Doll's screaming; and Denbigh lying dead in a London alley.

"Was Kathleen O'Brien a thief, Mrs. Greville?" he asked.

"No, I don't believe so," she whispered.

"Was she dismissed for refusing to accommodate your husband's wishes regarding her?"

"That . . . may have been part of the reason. She was . . . difficult." She would not be drawn further. He could see it in the set of her shoulders. For all its softness under the draping of her dark dress, her body was rigid. There was much in her form, her auburn coloring, which was like Charlotte, except that she was so much more vulnerable.

"Was your brother, Mr. Doyle, aware of your husband's tastes and his indulgences?"

"I never told him," she said instantly. It was an answer of pride. It was also evasive. "One does not discuss such things. It would be embarrassing . . . and disloyal." There was criticism in her voice, and a huskiness, as if she were close to tears.

He thought of all she had endured in the last few days, the tensions of the pressure upon Greville to succeed in an almost impossible task, the fear for his life which she knew was real. Then Piers had arrived and announced his betrothal, obviously without having even told his family he was deeply in love, let alone consulting them about his plans. The day after that, her husband had been murdered. Now Pitt was forcing her to realize that much of the entire life she had known was false, marred by ugliness and betrayal of her heart, her home, her innermost values. Her pain must be all but intolerable.

And yet she sat by the fire, blank-faced, and remained polite. A lesser woman would have wept, screamed, abused him for his cruelty. He hated being the instrument of her suffering. But it was far from impossible that Padraig Doyle had killed Greville. Greville's treatment of Eudora would free Doyle from the constraints of family loyalties which might otherwise have held his hand. He was Irish, he was Catholic, he was a Nationalist. Greville would trust him above any other man in the house. They might easily have quarreled, but Greville would never have expected violence from him. He would have sat in the bath quite unafraid until the very last moment, when it was too late to cry out.

"Has your brother stayed with you at Oakfield House?"

"No, not for years." She did not look at him.

"In London?"

"Sometimes. A great many people stayed with us in London. My husband has . . . had a very important position."

"Do you go to Ireland from time to time?"

She hesitated.

He waited. The coals settled in the fire.

"Yes. Ireland was my home. I go back occasionally."

There was no point in pressing her. All the questions in his mind were there between them. She understood, and would not answer.

"I'm sorry to have had to speak to you of it," he said after a few moments. "I wish I could simply have burned the letters."

"I understand," she replied. "At least I think I do." She looked up at him. "Mr. Pitt? Did Piers read these letters?"

"Yes . . . but he was not there when I spoke to the servants. He knew nothing about Kathleen O'Brien, or that there were other women in London."

"Will you please tell him only what he has to know? Ainsley was his father. . . ."

"Of course. I have no desire to damage Mr. Greville's reputation in anyone's eyes, least of all his family's. . . ."

She smiled at him. "I know. I do not envy you your task, Mr. Pitt. It must be very distressing at times."

"Because it causes others pain," he said gently. "People who are too much hurt already."

She looked at him a moment longer, then turned back to the fire.

He excused himself and went out and back downstairs to see if Jack was yet free. He was not yet ready to find Charlotte. She was so at home here, so very competent, moving easily in this great house with its high ceilings, exquisite furniture and discreet servants going about their business. He could remember too clearly being one of the servants himself ever to take them for granted. At heart he would always be an outsider.

CHAPTER SIX

Emily was exhausted, and yet she found it hard to sleep except fitfully. The day after Pitt had gone to Oakfield House, she was awake even before the most junior housemaid, although instead of getting up, she lay in the dark going over all the disasters of the weekend in her mind and dreading the day to come.

When she did get up she had a steady dull headache, and her first cup of tea did not help, nor did the hot water her maid brought her to wash in, but the aroma of the oil of lavender she offered was very pleasant. Emily dressed carefully in a teal-blue gown and admired her reflection in the glass, although it gave her no pleasure. She looked perfect. Her figure was completely returned after the birth of her daughter Evangeline, at present safely with her nurse and her elder half brother, Edward, in their London house. The morning dress was the latest fashion, and the color became her, as did any green or blue. Her fair hair, with its soft, natural curl which Charlotte used to envy so much, was elaborately dressed and set exactly as intended. No maid ever had difficulty with it.

But all these things were trivial. Even the wretched thought of having to cajole and persuade the staff to do their duties, calming upset nerves, soothing fears, assuring them there was no lunatic in the house, no one else was going to be killed, was merely the duty of a good hostess. What underlay everything else was her fear for Jack. Cornwallis had asked him, and he had stepped into Greville's position as chairman as if he had no conception of the danger in which he was placing himself. If there were people who cared so intensely about preventing the conference's success that they would murder Greville to achieve that, then they would almost certainly be prepared to murder Jack also.

And Pitt was doing nothing to protect him, except leave that wretched Tellman at Jack's elbow . . . as if that were any use! He did not even know who or what he was protecting him from. They should have canceled the conference. It was the only sane thing to do. Bring in more police and question everybody until the answer was clear. Cornwallis himself should have come.

She could feel the panic rising inside her. She saw pictures in her imagination of Jack lying dead, his face white, his eyes closed, and the tears prickled her eyes, her stomach knotted and suddenly she felt sick. There was no point in any false comfort of saying it could not happen. Of course it could. It had already happened once. Eudora Greville was a widow. She was alone, she had lost the man she had loved. Presumably, she had loved him? Not that that had anything to do with it. Emily loved Jack. This morning, sitting at her dressing table with a brooch in her hand, fingers shaking, she realized how very much.

And she was furious with him for accepting the chairmanship, even though she would have done the same herself, could she ever be in such a position. She had never run away from anything she wanted in her life. She would have despised him if he had. But he would at least have been safe.

And the other fear, which she refused to look at, was that he would fail, not just because the task was probably impossible, but because he was not the diplomat Ainsley Greville had been. He had not the experience, the polish, the knowledge of Irish affairs, simply not the skill.

All that hovered on the edge of her mind, and she would not allow it to the center. She would not permit herself to put it into words. It was disloyal, and it was untrue . . . possibly. She loved Jack for his charm, for his gentleness with her, his ability to laugh, to be funny and brave, to see the beautiful in things and enjoy it, and because he loved her. She did not need him to be clever, to become famous or earn a great deal of money. She already had money, inherited from George.

Perhaps Jack needed to do these things for himself, or at least to try, to find his own measure, succeed or fail. She would rather have protected him . . . from both dangers. Her son, Edward, was George's son, not Jack's, and there were times when she thought of him with the same fierce desire to shield him from harm, even from the necessary pains of growing. She had never considered herself maternal. The idea was ridiculous. Nobody was less so. She was practical, ambitious, witty, quick to learn, she could adapt to almost any situation, and she never told herself comfortable lies. She was a good-natured realist.

And yet that morning she quarreled with Jack. It was the last thing she had intended to do. He came into her dressing room almost the moment Gwen left. He stood behind her, meeting her eyes in the glass and smiling. He bent and kissed the top of her head without disarranging her hair.

She swiveled around on the seat, regarding him very seriously.

"You will be careful, won't you?" she urged. "Keep Tellman with you. I know he's a misery, but just endure it for the present." She rose to her feet, unconsciously putting up her hands to straighten his lapels, although they were perfect, and dust off an imaginary fleck of cotton.

"Stop fussing, Emily," he said quietly. "Nobody is going to attack me in public. I doubt anybody is going to attack me at all."

"Why not? Don't you think you can do whatever Ainsley Greville began? You were there all the time. I'm sure you can do as much as he could have." Then she changed her mind, realizing what she had implied. "Although perhaps all you should really try to accomplish is keeping everyone from giving up. It could always be continued later, in London. . . ."

"When they can appoint a new chairman," he said with a smile, but she saw the hurt in his eyes, self-mocking but very real.

"When they can take better care of your safety," she corrected him, but she knew he did not believe her. What could she say to undo it? How could she make him believe that she had confidence in him, whatever anyone else thought? If she tried too hard she would only make it worse. Why did he have to want something so difficult? Perhaps it was more than he had the skill to achieve?

How could she persuade him she believed something she was not sure of herself? And all the time the sick fear for him crawled around inside her, gnawing away at everything else, stopping her from thinking clearly. She tried to tell herself it was foolish. But it was not foolish. The body of Ainsley Greville, lying in the icehouse, was horrible testimony of that!

"Thomas will take as good care of our safety as can be done," he said after a moment's silence. "The house is full of people. Don't worry. Just see if you can keep Kezia and Iona from quarreling, and look after poor Eudora."

"Of course," she said as if it were a simple task. He did not even appreciate that the real struggle would be to keep the servants from quarreling, having hysterics, or walking out altogether.

"Charlotte will help you," he added.

"Of course," she agreed with an inward shudder. Charlotte would mean well, but her idea of tact could be a disaster. She would have to make sure she did not allow Charlotte anywhere near the kitchen. Charlotte's confronting the cook would be the ultimate domestic catastrophe.

As it happened, breakfast was tense but passed off really quite well. All the men were concentrating on returning to the discussions and were finished and leaving when the women arrived, so Kezia and Fergal were able to avoid each other. Fergal and Iona cast burning looks as they passed in the doorway, but neither spoke. Eudora was still in her room. Piers and Justine were subdued, but Justine at least conducted herself with composure and sustained an agreeable conversation about trivia which drew everyone in, to Emily's relief.

The household management was a different matter. The butler was offended because the visiting valets were not in his control, which he felt they should have been. They dined separately, and it was greatly inconvenient. The laundry maids were overworked because one of them was in bed with the vapors and there was far too much to do. Miss Moynihan's maid gave herself airs and had managed to quarrel with Mrs. McGinley's maid, with the result that an entire bucketful of soap was spilled all over the laundry room floor.

The scullery maid had a fit of the giggles and was perfectly useless, not that she was much good at the best of times. Eudora's maid was so distressed she forgot what she was doing half the time, and poor Gracie was forever picking up after her—when she wasn't watching Hennessey, or listening to him, or wondering when he was coming back again.

Tellman was getting more and more ill-tempered, and Dilkes was fed up with him. He seemed to be neither use nor ornament, although presumably his being a policeman explained that and why Pitt endured him.

But it was Mrs. Williams, the cook, who finally broke Emily's patience.

"It isn't my job to be doin' plain cookin'," she said indignantly. "I'm a professed cook, not a general cook. I do specialities. You'll still be wantin' that Delilah's trifle tonight, and baked goose, no doubt? Them kitchen maids is supposed to fetch after me, not me be runnin' behind them as they get a fit o' cryin', or is hidin' from goblins in the cupboard under the stairs. And I'm not havin' any butler tellin' me how to discipline girls in my own kitchen, an' that's a fact, Mrs. Radley!"

"Who's in the cupboard under the stairs?" Emily demanded.

"Georgina. An' that's no name for a kitchen maid! I told her if she don't come out this minute, I'll send in worse after her than goblins! I'll come in after 'er meself. An' she'll rue the day! I'm not doin' vegetables and rice puddings an' custards. I got venison to do, an' apple pies, an' turbot, an' Lord knows what else. You put a sore trial on a decent person, Mrs. Radley, an' that's a fact."

Emily was obliged to bite her tongue. She would dearly like to have fired Mrs. Williams on the spot, with considerable sarcasm, but she could not afford to. Nor could she afford to lose face. It would never be forgotten, and would open the door to all kinds of future troubles.

"There is a sore trial upon all of us, Mrs. Williams," Emily replied, forcing her expression into one of friendliness she did not feel. "We are all frightened and worried. My greatest concern is that the household should emerge from this awful weekend with honor, so that afterwards people will remember all that was good. The rest will not be associated with us, but with Irish politics."

"Well . . ." Mrs. Williams said, snorting through her nose, "there is that, I suppose. Although I'm sure I don't know what's good about it."

"The food is more than good, it is excellent," Emily replied with something a shade less than the truth. "This is the sort of disaster which sorts the great cook from the merely good. Test under fire, Mrs. Williams. Many people can do well when everything is fine for them and there is no invention called for, no courage or extraordinary discipline."

"Well!" Mrs. Williams straightened up noticeably. "I daresay as you have a point, Mrs. Radley. We'll not let you down. Now, if you'll excuse me, I daren't stay here talking any longer, unless there was something else? I got to be about my work if I'm to do that daft Georgina's as well."

"Yes, of course, Mrs. Williams. Thank you."

On returning upstairs she went into the morning room, where there was a blazing fire, and found Justine talking to Kezia and Iona. The atmosphere was brittle but still within the bounds of civility. But then Kezia had kept her greatest anger for her brother, and Charlotte had explained why. Emily thought that in similar circumstances she might have felt the same.

"I was thinking of going for a walk," Iona said dubiously, staring out of the tall windows at the gray sky. "But it looks very cold."

"An excellent idea," Justine agreed, rising to her feet. "It will be invigorating, and we shall return well in time for luncheon."

"Luncheon!" Iona looked surprised and swiveled to glance at the mantel clock, which said twenty-eight minutes to eleven. "We could walk halfway to London in that time."

Justine smiled. "Not against that wind, and not in skirts."

"Oh, have you worn the bloomers?" Kezia asked with interest. "They look very practical, if a little immodest. I should love to try them."

"Do you ride a bicycle?" Emily said quickly. Bicycling was surely a safe subject. It was appalling having to think so hard before even the slightest remark. "I have seen several different sorts. It must be a marvelous sensation." She was spinning out every comment to make it last. It was pathetic. She hoped fervently that Iona would go for a walk and leave Kezia behind. She must not be seen to try too hard to bring it about. She had never in her life before spent a weekend where almost everyone was so acutely uncomfortable.

They went on discussing bicycles for several more minutes, then Justine led the way, and she and Iona left to collect canes and shawls for their walk. Emily remained with Kezia, struggling to continue some kind of conversation.

After half an hour she excused herself and went to look for Charlotte. Why was she not there helping? She must know how appallingly difficult it was. Emily relied upon her, and she was off somewhere else, presumably comforting Eudora—as if anyone could.

But when she went upstairs to the sitting room which Eudora was using, she found not Charlotte with her, but Pitt. Eudora was sitting in one of the big chairs, and Pitt was bending in front of the fire, stoking it. He should not be doing that. That was what footmen were for.

"Good morning, Mrs. Greville," Emily said solicitously. "How are you? Good morning, Thomas."

Pitt straightened up with a wince as his aching muscles caught him, and replied.

"Good morning, Mrs. Radley," Eudora said with a faint smile. She looked ten years older than she had when she arrived at Ashworth Hall. Her skin had no bloom to it. Her eyes were still wonderful, but the lids were puffed. She had had too little sleep, and her hair no longer shone with the same richness. It was remarkable how quickly shock and misery dulled the looks, as rapidly as any illness.

"Did you manage to sleep?" Emily asked with concern. "If you like, I can have Gwen make you something that will help a little. We have plenty of lavender, and the oil is most pleasant. Or perhaps you would like chamomile tea and a little honey with biscuits before retiring tonight?"

"Thank you," Eudora said absently, barely looking at Emily, her attention upon Pitt.

He stood back from the fire and turned to Emily. He also looked strained, as if he were only too aware of Eudora's distress.

"How about a little vervain tea?" Emily suggested. "Or if we don't have it, basil or sage? I should have thought of it before."

"I am sure Doll will take care of it, thank you," Eudora replied. "You are very thoughtful, but you have so much to do."

It was not dismissal, simply absentmindedness. Her thoughts, even her eyes, were on Pitt.

"Is there anything I can offer which would help?" Emily must try. Eudora looked so deeply troubled, even though Pitt was obviously doing all he could, and seemed profoundly concerned. There was an air of gentleness in him which was even greater than his characteristic compassion.

Eudora turned to Emily, at last looking clearly at her. "I am sorry. I did not realize how shocked I have been. There is so much that—" She stopped. "I cannot seem to think properly. So much has . . . changed."

Emily remembered other violent deaths, and investigations which had discovered whole aspects of lives which were unknown before. A few were creditable, brave; most were ugly, robbing even the safety of what we thought was held inviolable. There was no future, sometimes there was not even any past as one had treasured it. Was this what Pitt had been telling Eudora now? Was that the foundation for his tenderness towards her?

"Of course," Emily said quietly. "I'll have a tisane sent up. And a little food. Even if it is only bread and butter, you should eat."

She withdrew and left them together.

The men were conferring again. Jack would be in charge, trying to get them to some kind of agreement. As she was coming down the stairs she saw the butler carrying a tray into the withdrawing room, and as he opened the door she heard the sound of raised voices. Then the door closed and cut them off. One of them in there had murdered Ainsley Greville, whether he had accomplices outside or not. Why was Pitt sitting and comforting Eudora? Compassion was all very well, but it was not his task. Charlotte should be doing that. Why wasn't she?

Emily went the rest of the way down to the hall and was crossing it towards the conservatory when she almost bumped into Charlotte coming in from the garden.

"What are you doing?" Emily said sharply.

Charlotte closed the door behind her. Her hair was ruffled, as if she had been in the wind, and there was a flush in her cheeks.

"I went for a walk," she answered. "Why?"

"Alone?"

"Yes. Why?"

Emily's temper snapped. "Greville has been murdered by God knows who, but someone in the house, Jack's life is in danger and Thomas is sitting upstairs comforting the widow instead of looking after him, or even trying to find who murdered Greville. The Irish are all at each others' throats while I am trying to keep some kind of peace, the servants are fainting, weeping, quarreling or hiding under the stairs—and you are out in the garden walking! And you ask me why! Where are your wits?"

Charlotte paled, then two spots of color burned up in her cheeks.

"I was thinking," she said coldly. "Sometimes a little thought is a great deal more beneficial than simply rushing around to give the appearance of doing something—"

"I have not been rushing around!" Emily snapped back. "I thought that the past would have taught you, if the present does not, that running a house this size, with guests, takes a great deal of skill and organization. I relied on you at least to keep Kezia and Iona in a civil conversation."

"Justine was doing that—"

"And Thomas to try to guard Jack, as much as it can be done, and he's up there"—she jabbed her finger towards the stairs—"comforting Eudora!"

"He's probably questioning her," Charlotte said icily.

"For heaven's sake, it wasn't a domestic murder!" Emily made an effort to control her voice. "If she knew anything she'd have told him in the beginning. It's one of these men in there."

"We all know that," Charlotte agreed. "But which one? Maybe Padraig Doyle, have you thought of that?"

Emily had not thought of it, she did not think it now.

"Well, at least go and talk to Kezia. She's by herself in the morning room. Perhaps you can persuade her to stop this ridiculous rage against Fergal. It doesn't help anyone." And with that Emily straightened her shoulders and marched back to the baize door and the servants' quarters, although she had forgotten what she was going for.

Gracie was also extremely busy that morning, not essentially on Charlotte's affairs. The dresses she had brought were in little need of attention, and those which had been lent her needed only a slight press here or there with a flatiron. There was personal linen to launder, but that was all. She collected it and took it downstairs and through the corridors of the servants' wing out to the laundry house.

She found Doll already there, looking unhappily at the dull surface of a flatiron and muttering under her breath.

"How is poor Mrs. Greville?" Gracie asked sympathetically.

Doll glanced at her. "Poor soul," she said with a sigh. "Doesn't know whether she's coming or going at the moment. But I daresay it'll get worse before it gets better. Have you seen the beeswax and bath brick?"

"What?"

"Beeswax and bath brick," Doll repeated. "There's plenty o' salt right there. Need to clean this iron before I put it anywhere near a white camisole." She held up the iron critically. The other one on the stove was getting hot.

"Mr. Pitt's very clever," Gracie assured her, seeking to comfort her. " 'E'll find out everythin' there is ter know, an' then 'e'll work out 'oo done it, an' take 'im in."

Doll looked at her quickly, her eyes shadowed. Her hand was tight on the iron.

"Can't need to know everything," she said, beginning to move again, taking the other iron off the stove and putting it on the white petticoat and beginning to work, leaning her weight on it and swinging it gently backwards, smoothing the fabric.

"Yer'd be surprised wot 'as meanin'," Gracie told her. "Ter someone clever enough ter see it an' understand. 'E'll catch 'ooever it is, don' worry."

Doll gave a little shiver and her eyes were far away. Her hand on the iron clenched hard and stopped moving.

"Yer don' need ter look so scared." Gracie moved a step towards her. " 'E's very fair. 'E'd never 'urt them wot don' deserve it, nor tell tales wot don' need ter be told."

Doll swallowed. "Course not. I never thought . . ." She looked down suddenly and moved the iron. The scorch mark was brown on the linen. She took a deep breath and tears filled her eyes.

Gracie snatched the iron up and put it aside on the hearth.

"There must be a way fer takin' that out," she said with more assurance than she felt. "There's a way fer everythin', if yer jus' know it."

"Mr. Wheeler said as Mr. Pitt rode over to Oakfield House yesterday!" Doll stared at Gracie. "Why? What's he want there? It was someone here who killed him."

"I know that," Gracie agreed. " 'Ow do yer get scorch marks out? What's the best way? We better do that afore it's too late."

"Onion juice, fuller's earth, white soap and vinegar," Doll replied absently. "They're bound to have some made up. Look in that jar." She pointed to one on the shelf next to the blue, behind Gracie's head. It was between the bran, rice for congee, borax, soap, beeswax and ordinary tallow candle, used for removing inkspots.

Gracie took it down with two hands and passed it over. It was heavy. Scorches must be quite a common occurrence. But there was something in Doll's unhappiness which was more than ordinary. Gracie felt a need to understand it, not only for the sake of Doll, whom she liked, but because it might be important. Murder was not always as simple as people thought, especially if they were people who had not as much experience as Gracie had.

However, she was foiled in her intent by one of the laundry maids' coming in to iron table linen for dinner that evening, and the conversation suddenly became about the senior groom, and what he had said to Maisie, and what Tillie had said about that, and why the bootboy had repeated it anyway.

At mid-morning Pitt changed clothes. Gracie polished his boots for him. Tellman was otherwise occupied, and anyway he did not really make a good enough job of it, the great useless article! Gracie would not have Pitt leave the hall less well-dressed than any other gentleman there. He took an overcoat and a very smart hat, borrowed from Mr. Radley, and was driven to the railway station to catch the ten forty-eight up to London. She knew it was not a journey he could possibly enjoy. He was going to see the assistant commissioner, who would likely be very upset that Mr. Greville had been murdered after all. She wished there were something comforting she could say to him, but anything she thought of only sounded empty or not her place to say.

And Miss Charlotte was not around to see him off, which she ought to have been. She was busy with that Miss Moynihan who had taken such a temper. If country house parties were usually like this, it was a wonder anybody would go to one.

She decided to throw out the old flowers in the dressing room vase. They were droopy, probably from the fire. She would fill in a little time by going to find the gardener and see if she might pick some fresh ones. Anything would do, even leaves, as long as they were green and crisp-looking.

She obtained permission to choose something, not more than a dozen, mind, from the cold greenhouse. It was just the occasion to put on the new overcoat Charlotte had bought for her. It was even the right size. She went upstairs and found it, and was making her way through the kitchen garden in the general direction indicated when she saw Finn Hennessey. She recognized him immediately, even though he had his back to her. He was watching a ginger-and-white cat walking along the top of the high garden wall towards the branches of the apple tree. From its low, silent tread, she thought it had seen a bird.

She straightened herself a little more, held her chin high, and almost unconsciously swayed her hips a trifle. She must attract his attention without seeming to wish to. She was not very good at playing games; she did not have sufficient practice. She had noticed how skilled the other ladies' maids were. They could flirt so well it came to them like nature. But then they had nothing of real seriousness to do. They couldn't solve a crime if the answer were under their noses. Lot of silly little creatures, sometimes, giggling at nothing.

She was level with Finn Hennessey. She would have to walk past him and say nothing. She ached inside with the frustration of it, but she would not let herself down by playing games any child could see through.

The cat leaped from the tree, an arc of some ten feet. Its claws scraped the bark, sliding another two feet, but it eventually held fast, and it scrambled onto the branch just as the bird flew away.

"Oh!" she gasped involuntarily, afraid it would fall.

Finn swung around. His face lit up with a smile.

"Hello, Gracie Phipps. Looking for herbs, are you?"

"No, Mr. Hennessey, I came for some flowers. The ones we got are lookin' faded so I put 'em out. I don' mind what I get, so long as it's fresh. Sooner 'ave leaves than flowers what's droopin'."

"I'll carry them for you," he offered, moving over to walk beside her.

She laughed. "I'm only gettin' a few. Gardener said I could 'ave a dozen out o' the cold 'ouse. But you can carry 'em for me if you like."

"I'd like," he accepted, smiling back.

They walked side by side along the path, through the gate and the high box hedge, and on towards the cold greenhouses, the gray light reflecting on the glass panes irregularly as it caught them at different angles. The earth was dark and wet, well-manured and ready for planting in the spring. There were cobwebs gleaming in the clipped branches of the hedge, and a gardener's boy was cutting the dead stalks of perennials and putting them into a barrow about twenty yards away. It was chilly, and she was glad not only of the smartness of the coat but of its warmth.

"Smells like winter coming," Finn said with pleasure. "Wood fires, that's something I love, bonfires with old leaves on, and blue smoke in the frosty air, crackle of twigs, breathe out and it hangs white in front of you." He looked sideways at her, keeping step exactly. "How 'bout an early morning, when the sky's all pale blue and the light's as clear as the beginning o' the world, red berries in the hedge, air so crisp it prickles in your nose, tangle of bare branches against the light, and time to walk as long as you like?"

"You 'ave some wonderful dreams," she said hesitantly. She loved the way he spoke, not only the wild things he said but the soft lilt of his voice, foreign and full of music. But she did not begin to understand him.

"That's the things we can have for nothing, Gracie, and if you fight hard enough, no one can take from you. But you have to fight, and you have to hand them on, to your children and your children's children. That's the way we survive. Never forget that. Knowing your dreams is knowing who you are."

She said nothing, just walked beside him, happy that he was there.

They reached the greenhouse and he opened the door for her. It was surprisingly easy to behave like a lady when she was with him, to accept such courtesies.

"Thank you." She went through and stopped in wonder at the rows of flowers all in pots on benches. The colors were vivid, like hundreds of silks. She did not know the names of them, except the chrysanthemums and the Michaelmas daisies and late asters. She let out a long sigh of pure pleasure.

"Do you want a dozen the same, or a dozen all different?" he asked, standing just behind her.

"I never seen anything like this," she said softly. "Even flower sellers in the market in't got this much."

"They'll all be over soon."

"Yeah, but they in't over now!"

He smiled. "Sometimes, Gracie, you're very wise." He put his hand lightly on her shoulder. She could feel its weight, and she imagined she could feel the warmth of it too. He had said she was wise, and yet there was a shadow in his voice.

"You thinkin' about winter?" she asked. "Don' forget there'll be spring too. There 'as to be all sorts, or it don' work."

"For the flowers, yes, but there are winters of the heart there don't have to be, and winters for the hungry. Not everyone lives to see the spring."

She still kept facing the rows of flowers.

"Yer talkin' about Ireland again?" she asked. She did not want to know, but she could not stay there with him and go around the subject as if there were nothing there. She had never avoided the real.

"If you knew the sadness of it," he said softly. "The crying sadness of it, Gracie. Seeing all these flowers makes me think of laughter and dancing, then of graves. They follow each other so quick sometimes."

"That 'appens in London too," she reminded him. She did not know if it was a comfort or a contradiction. But she was going to remember who she was also, and Clerkenwell had seen its share of hunger and cold, landlords who cheated and were greedy, moneylenders, bullies, rats, overspilling drains and bouts of cholera and the typhus. Everyone knew somebody with rickets or tuberculosis. "London in't all paved wi' gold, yer know. I see dead babies in doorways too, all froze up, an' men so 'ungry they'd slit your throat for a loaf o' bread."

"Have you?" He sounded surprised.

"Not in Bloomsbury," she assured him. "In Clerkenwell, where I were before I came ter Mrs. Pitt."

"I suppose there's poverty in most places," he conceded. "It's the injustice that makes you weep."

It rose to her tongue to argue. All kinds of things made her furious, sad, twisted up inside with helplessness. But she did not want to disagree with Finn Hennessey. She would like to be able to share with him everything that mattered, to look at the flowers, smell the damp earth, and talk of good things, of today and tomorrow, not yesterday.

"What sort of flowers are you getting?" he asked.

"I dunno. I in't made up me mind yet. What der you think?" She turned around for the first time and looked at him. He was beautiful, with his black hair as soft as a night and his dark eyes that laughed one minute and drowned you the next. She found herself a little breathless, and confused with feelings.

"How about some of these big shaggy chrysanthemums?" he suggested, but without moving.

She had to concentrate on the room they were to go into. Her mind was a whirl. She could only remember florals. She had better not get lots of colors.

"I'll take them big white ones," she said, with no idea if they would be right, but she had to say something. "They look just about openin' nicely. Them red ones is too far on."

"What about the golden brown?" he asked.

"Color don't go wi' much. I'll take the white ones."

"I'll pick them for you." He stepped around her and started to examine the individual blooms for the best ones. "Funny we should have Padraig Doyle here, and Carson O'Day," he said, smiling at her as he plucked the first flower.

"Is it? In't they the right people for doin' whatever it is?"

"Oh, probably, if there can be 'right people.' It's all happened lots of times before, you know?"

" 'As it? You mean it din't work out?"

He picked another bloom, smelling its earthy fragrance with a sigh, then offering it to her.

She took it and held the damp petals to her face. It was like breathing heaven.

"No, it didn't work," he said in little more than a whisper. "It was a love story. Neassa Doyle was a young Catholic girl, about nineteen she was, same as you."

She did not interrupt to tell him she was twenty now.

"Full of laughter and hope," he went on, holding the flower still as if he had forgotten it. "She met Drystan O'Day by chance. It should never have happened. He was Protestant, as fierce as the north wind in January, all keen, cutting edge, his family was." He laughed but there was no humor in it. "Saw the Pope as the devil on earth and all the church's ways as scarlet as sin itself. They met and fell in love for all the age-old human reasons: they saw the same beauty and magic on the earth, the same tenderness in the sky, loved to sing the old songs, dance till they were too tired even to laugh at themselves."

He was leaning against the door jamb, watching her, searching her eyes as he spoke. She knew he was sharing what mattered to him most, some part of the inner core of himself, the beliefs which drove him. "They hoped for peace, an honorable work," he went on. "A small home and children to raise, same as you might, or me. Long evenings together when the day was done, time to talk, or just to sit and each to know the other was there." He passed her the flower and started to look for another.

"What happened?"

"When it was too late they discovered they were on opposite sides. By then it didn't matter to them, but of course it mattered to everyone else."

"Their families?" she asked in awe. "But 'ow could they stop it? Nobody can stop 'oo you love. Was it her father stopped 'er?"

"No." He looked at her very directly. "It never came to that. The English got to know of it. We were almost at agreement then, but they wanted to keep us divided. Divide and rule." His face was pinched with pain. His voice dropped to a harsh whisper. "They used them both."

" 'Ow?" she whispered.

"It was mainly one English soldier. His name was Alexander Chinnery. He was an officer, a lieutenant in one of the Anglo-Irish regiments. He pretended to be a friend of Drystan O'Day's." His young face was filled with grief and hatred till he looked so different it almost frightened her. "That's the duplicity of it," he said hoarsely. "He was free to carry messages to Neassa as well. No one thought anything of it. He promised to help them both to run away. He was going to get a boat for them. It was summer. Drystan was a good mariner. He could have sailed across to the Isle of Man, that's where they were supposed to go."

She did not take her eyes from his face. She did not hear the gust of wind drive the falling leaves against the glass, or see them flurry over.

"What 'appened?"

"Neassa was beautiful," he said softly. "Like Mrs. Greville, warm as sunlight on the autumn trees." His eyes filled with tears. "Chinnery met her, as he said he would. She trusted him, you see. She went with him to the place where they were to meet Drystan. She couldn't go alone because it was too dangerous." He spat out the last word as if it scorched his tongue. "A woman alone at night."

She waited while he struggled to regain control of himself and continue.

"He took her to the place on the headland where the boat was supposed to be, there with the wind above the sea." His voice cracked. "And he raped her. . . ."

Gracie felt as if she had been struck.

"And cut off her beautiful hair," he went on, his eyes fixed on hers as if the greenhouse with all its reflecting glass, the rows of flowers, the bright color, the wind outside, did not exist. "And left her there for her people to find," he finished.

"Oh, Finn! That's terrible!" She breathed out in horror too great for long and passionate words. She felt numb inside. The betrayal was like a blackness that swallowed everything. "What did 'e do, poor Drystan?" She dreaded the answer, but she had to know.

"He found her," he answered in little above a whisper, his fist clenched white. "He went mad with grief. The poor, trusting soul, he never dreamed even then that it was Chinnery."

A starling hopped across the roof, its feet rattling on the glass, but neither of them heard it.

"What'd 'e do?" she asked again.

"He lost his head completely, and went and attacked the Catholic community, anyone he could find. He'd killed two of her brothers and injured the third before the English army caught up with him and shot him too." He took a deep breath. "That was on the seventh of June, thirty years ago. Of course, in a little while both sides realized what had happened. The English took Chinnery back to England and covered it all up. Nobody ever heard of him again. It was probably for his own protection," he added bitterly. "If any Irishman had found him, he'd have killed him and been hailed as a hero by both sides."

"That's terrible!" Gracie said through a tight, aching throat. Her eyes prickled with tears and she had to swallow hard. "It's awful!"

"It's Ireland, Gracie." He picked another flower and handed it to her. "Even love can't win." He smiled as he said it, but his eyes were full of just as much pain as she felt for the people gone thirty years ago. Time did not matter. The loss was real. It could have been anybody. It could be themselves.

He leaned forward, so close to her she could feel the warmth of his skin, and he kissed her lips, slowly, gently, as if he wanted to count every second and remember it. Then he reached forward and took the flowers from her and laid them on the bench and put his arms around her, holding her softly, and kissed her again.

When at last he moved away Gracie's heart was hammering, and she opened her eyes to look at him, certain that what she saw would be beautiful. It was. He was smiling.

"Take your white flowers back," he said under his breath. "And watch carefully for yourself, Gracie Phipps. There's disaster in this house, and who's to say there won't be others yet. I'd hate more than you can know for you to get hurt." He put up his hand and touched her hair for a moment, then turned and walked past her and out of the door, leaving her to pick another few chrysanthemums and go back to the house with her feet barely touching the ground, and the taste of his lips still on hers.

Charlotte bit her tongue rather than reply to Emily as she felt inclined. What she wanted to say to Kezia Moynihan made excellent sense, but she could hardly say it after quarreling with her own sister, when the better part of her knew exactly what the reason was. Emily was terrified for Jack physically, but also she was afraid he would not measure up to whatever standard she had set for him, or he had set for himself, with this wretched conference.

She found Kezia in the morning room as Emily had said. She was sitting on the padding of the club fender, her skirts puffed out around her. Charlotte went in quite casually and sat down near the fire as if she were cold, when in fact she was merely angry.

"Do you think it is going to clear?" she asked, glancing towards the window and the really quite pleasant sky.

"The weather?" Kezia said with a slight smile.

"That also," Charlotte agreed, sinking back. "It is all rather wretched, isn't it?"

"Absolutely." Kezia shrugged slightly. "And I cannot honestly imagine it getting any better. Have you seen the newspapers?"

"No. Is there something of interest?"

"Only the latest comments on the Parnell-O'Shea divorce. I cannot see Parnell lasting long after this, whatever the verdict is." Her face tightened. Charlotte knew what her thoughts must be, what they had to be, regarding Fergal. The risk he had taken was insane.

As if Charlotte had spoken her thoughts aloud, Kezia clenched her fists and stared into the fire.

"When I think what he's thrown away, I could hate him," she said bitterly. "I understand why men punch each other. It must be very relieving to be able to strike out as hard as you can when someone exasperates you beyond endurance."

"I'm sure," Charlotte agreed. "But I think the relief would last a very short time, then it would have to be paid for."

"How very sensible you are," Kezia said without an iota of admiration.

"I've cut off my nose to spite my face too often to think it's clever," Charlotte replied, keeping her temper.

"I find that difficult to imagine." Kezia picked up the poker and leaning sideways, prodded viciously at the fire.

"That is because you leap to judgments about other people and find it very difficult to imagine their feelings at all," Charlotte replied, letting go her temper with considerable satisfaction. "It seems to me the fault you criticize in your brother is exactly the one you suffer from yourself."

Kezia froze, then turned around very slowly, her face red, although it was impossible to tell whether it was with anger or the heat from the fire.

"That is the stupidest thing you have said so far! We are exact opposites. I followed my faith and was loyal to my people at the cost of the only person I have ever loved, as Fergal commanded me to. But he's thrown everything away, betrayed all of us, and committed adultery with a married woman, as well as a Roman Catholic actually representing the enemy!"

"I meant the inability to place yourself in anyone else's situation and imagine how they feel," Charlotte explained. "Fergal did not understand that you truly loved Cathal. He saw it only as a matter of obedience to your faith and loyalty to your people's way of life. Without any compassion at all, he ordered you to give him up."

"And I did! God forgive me."

"Perhaps he has never been really in love, wildly, utterly and madly in love, as you were—until now?"

"Is that an excuse?" Kezia demanded, her pale eyes blazing.

"No. It is a lack of understanding, or even the effort to imagine," Charlotte answered.

Kezia was surprised. "What are you saying?"

"That you have been so in love, why can't you imagine how he feels now about Iona, even if you can't condone it?"

Kezia said nothing, turning away again, the flames' reflection warm on her cheek.

"If you are honest, absolutely honest," Charlotte went on, "would you be so bitterly angry if you had not loved Cathal and been forced to give him up? Isn't a lot of your rage really your own pain?"

"What if it is?" Kezia still had the poker in her hand, gripped like a sword. "Is that not fair?"

"Yes, it is fair. But what will be the result?"

"What do you mean?"

"What will be the result of your not forgiving Fergal?" Charlotte elaborated. "I don't mean you should say it is all right—of course it isn't. Iona is married. But that will carry its own cost. You don't need to exact it. I mean your cutting yourself off from Fergal."

"I . . . I don't know. . . ."

"Will it make you happy?"

"No . . . of course not. Really, you ask the strangest questions."

"Will it make anyone happy, or wiser, or braver, or kinder, or anything you want?"

Kezia hesitated.

"Well . . . no . . ."

"Then why are you doing it?"

"Because . . . he's so . . . unjust!" she said angrily, as if the answer should have been apparent to everyone. "So self-indulgent! He's a total hypocrite, and I hate hypocrisy!"

"Nobody likes it. Although it is funny, sometimes," Charlotte rejoined.

"Funny!" Kezia's brows rose very high.

"Yes. Don't you have any sense of the ridiculous?"

Kezia stared at her. At last her turquoise eyes began to sparkle a little and her hands unclenched.

"You are the oddest person I ever met."

Charlotte shrugged lightly.

"I suppose I shall have to be content with that."

Kezia smiled. "Not a wholehearted compliment, I admit, but at least there is no hypocrisy in it!"

Charlotte glanced at the newspaper lying on the table where it had been left.

"If Mr. Parnell loses his leadership, who do you think will succeed him?"

"Carson O'Day, I imagine," Kezia answered. "He has all the qualities. And he has the family as well. His father was brilliant, but he's an old man now. He was a great leader in his day. Absolutely fearless." She relaxed, retreating into memory, her inner vision far away. "I remember my father taking Fergal and me to hear him at a political meeting. Papa was one of the finest preachers in the north. He could stand there in the pulpit and his voice rolled all around you like a breaking sea with all the foam white and the tide so strong it took you off your feet." Her voice grew stronger, rich with feeling. "He could make you see heaven and hell, the shining pavements and the angels of God, the endless joy and the singing; or the darkness and the fire which consumes everything, and the stench of sin like sulfur which chokes the breath out of you."

Charlotte did not interrupt, but she found herself wanting to move closer to the fire. That kind of passion frightened her. There was no room for thought in it, and certainly no room for considering the possibility you might have something wrong. When you take a stand like that in public, you can never go back on it, no matter what you learn afterwards. You have left yourself no room to change, retreat or grow.

"He was a marvelous man," Kezia repeated, perhaps as much to herself as to Charlotte. "He took us to see Liam O'Day. It was his brother, Drystan, who was shot by the British, so they said, for his love of Neassa Doyle."

"Why? Who was she?"

"A papist. It's an old story. She and Drystan O'Day fell in love. This is thirty years ago. A British soldier called Alexander Chinnery was a friend of Drystan's, and he betrayed him, raped and murdered Neassa, then fled back to England. Drystan went to her brothers and there was a terrible fight. Two of her brothers were killed, and so was Drystan, by the English, of course, to cover up what Chinnery had done. But neither side ever forgave the other for their part in it. The Doyle family felt Drystan had seduced her, and will talk of nothing else. The O'Days thought she had seduced him. And the O'Days all hate the Nationalists. Carson is the second son, but Daniel, the eldest, is an invalid with tuberculosis. He was supposed to be the one who rose to lead the cause, but now it's all fallen to Carson. He hasn't the fire of Daniel." She smiled. "I saw Daniel when he was young, before he became ill. He was so handsome, like his father. But maybe

Carson is better anyway. He has a steadier head. He's a good diplomat."

"But you don't agree with him entirely, do you?"

Kezia smiled widely. "No, of course not. We're Irish! But close enough to face the papists beside him. We'll fight among ourselves afterwards."

"Very wise," Charlotte agreed.

Kezia gave her a quick glance, then laughed abruptly. "Yes, I see what you mean."

Later that morning Charlotte was not far from Jack, standing on the terrace outside the withdrawing room doors, when one of the urns on the balcony above crashed down. It missed him by about three feet and broke to smithereens on the flags, sending earth and ivy over several yards.

Jack was very pale, but he made light of it and forbade her to say anything whatever to Emily.

She promised, but found herself shaking and suddenly desperately cold when she went inside, in spite of the sharp sunlight.

Pitt traveled on the train up to London. It was a journey which in the usual circumstances he would have enjoyed. He liked watching the countryside flying past, he liked the steam and the clatter and the sense of incredible speed. But today he was thinking of what he would say to Cornwallis, and he wanted to get it over with as quickly as possible.

There were no excuses. He had failed to protect Ainsley Greville, and three days later he could not offer any proof as to who was responsible. By process of elimination it looked to be either Doyle or Moynihan, and he had no idea which.

"Good morning, Pitt," Cornwallis said gravely when Pitt arrived and was shown to his office.

"Good morning, sir," Pitt answered, taking the seat that was offered beside the fire. It was a courteous act. Rather than having Pitt sit in front of the desk with Cornwallis behind it, in a gesture he had placed them in the same situation. This did not, however, ease Pitt's conscience or diminish his sense of having failed a trust.

"What happened?" Cornwallis asked, leaning forward a little and unconsciously placing the tips of his fingers together. The firelight glistened on his cheeks and head. He was a man in whom baldness seemed completely natural. It became him, throwing into strong relief his powerful features.

Pitt told him everything he knew that was pertinent. It seemed a lot, and yet it amounted to nothing that was conclusive.

When he had finished Cornwallis stared at him thoughtfully.

"So it might be Moynihan, for political reasons. His father was certainly a rabid enough Protestant. Conceivably, he has the idea that any settlement will reduce the Protestant Ascendancy, which I suppose it will. But it will also create a far greater justice, and therefore peace, and a greater safety and prosperity for everyone." He shook his head. "But the hatred runs deep, deeper than reason or morality, or even hope for the future." He bit his lip, regarding Pitt steadily. "The other possibility is Padraig Doyle, either for political reasons again, or because of Greville's treatment of his sister." He looked doubtful. "Do you really think it was gross enough to prompt murder? A great many men treat their wives badly. She wasn't beaten or kept short of money, or publicly humiliated. He was always extremely discreet. She had no idea, you say?"

"No . . ."

Cornwallis leaned back and crossed his legs, shaking his head very slightly. "If she had found him in bed with a serious rival for his affections, she might have killed him on impulse, a crime of passion. Although women don't often do that, especially women of the breeding of Eudora Greville. She had far too much to lose, Pitt, and nothing whatever to gain. Unless you have some idea she wanted her freedom to marry elsewhere, and you've shown nothing of that . . . ?" He left it as a question.

"No," Pitt said quickly. He had never suspected Eudora. He could not imagine her in such violence. "She is . . . Have you met her?"

Cornwallis smiled. "Yes. Very beautiful. But even beautiful women can have powerful feelings at having been betrayed. In fact, especially so, because they do not think it will happen to them. The outrage is greater."

"But he didn't do anything at Ashworth Hall," Pitt said sharply. "All we discussed was the past, and nothing which threatened her position as his wife. As you say, it was all simply indulgence of appetite, not love."

"Then why should Doyle murder Greville on her account?"

Pitt had no reply.

Cornwallis narrowed his eyes. "What is it, Pitt? There's something else, or you wouldn't have raised it. You are as capable as I am of seeing the fallacy of your argument; more so."

"I think she is afraid it was Doyle," Pitt said slowly, putting words to it for the first time himself. "But maybe I have the motive wrong. Perhaps it is political . . . Irish nationalism, like everything else."

"Not everything." Cornwallis shrugged. He looked faintly embarrassed. There was a very slight flush in his lean cheeks. "The O'Shea divorce verdict is due in today."

"What will it be, do you know?"

"Legally, I think they'll grant Willie O'Shea's petition. His wife was unquestionably guilty of a long-standing adultery with Parnell. The only question was did Captain O'Shea collude in the affair, or was he actually a deceived party."

"And was he?" Pitt had read little of it. He had not had time, and until now, not the interest either. He was still uncertain what bearing it had upon events at Ashworth Hall.

"Thank God it's not mine to judge," Cornwallis replied unhappily. "But if it were . . ." He hesitated. This sort of thing made him acutely uncomfortable. He thought there were aspects of life a man should keep private. He was embarrassed by the exposure of that part of a man's life which should be personal to himself.

"But I would find it hard to believe anyone as gullible as he claims to be," he finished. "Even though some of the evidence seems to border upon the farcical." His lips twitched in a curious mixture of irony and distaste. "Climbing out of fire escapes while the husband came in at the front door, then a few minutes later presenting yourself at the same front door as if you have just arrived, is beneath the dignity of anyone who would presume to lead a national movement for unity and represent his people in the Houses of Parliament."

Pitt was astonished. It must have shown in his face.

Cornwallis smiled very slightly. "It isn't even as if the man had a sense of humor and could be presented as a charming rogue who got away with it. He has done it with a sanctimoniously straight face and been caught!"

"Will it ruin him?" Pitt asked, watching Cornwallis closely.

"Yes," Cornwallis replied unequivocally, then thought for a moment. "Yes, I am almost sure it will."

"Then the Nationalist movement will be seeking a new leader?"

"Yes, if not immediately, then within a relatively short time. He may stagger on as long as he can, but his power is finished . . . I believe. Others must believe so too, if that is what you mean. But either way, the case will have set back the cause of Irish unity, unless the Ashworth Hall Conference can come to an agreement. That rests primarily upon Doyle and O'Day, helped or hurt by Moynihan and McGinley."

Pitt took a deep breath. "The first morning I was there Moynihan's sister went to talk to him about their strategy—apparently she is just as politically minded as he—and she found him in bed with McGinley's wife."

"What?" Cornwallis looked as if he had not understood.

Pitt repeated what he had said.

Cornwallis stared into the fire and rubbed his slim, strong hand over his head, then he turned and looked at Pitt.

"I'm sorry, but I cannot send you more men," he said quietly. "We're keeping Greville's death secret for the moment. I hope by the time we have to make it public we will be able to say that we have also caught the man who killed him."

Pitt had known he must say that, but it still tightened the knot inside him, the sense of being pressed into a steadily decreasing space.

"Any further information about Denbigh?" he asked.

"A little." Now it was Cornwallis's turn to look apologetic. "We've traced his movements for several days before he was killed, and we know that that evening he was at the Dog and Duck on King William Street. He was seen talking with a young man with fair hair, and then they were joined by an older man, broad-shouldered with an unusual walk, from the sound of it a bit bowlegged." He looked at Pitt steadily. "The barkeeper said he had unusual eyes, very pale and bright."

"Greville's murderous coach driver . . ." Pitt let out his breath with a sigh. "That gives me two reasons for finding the devil."

"Us, Pitt," Cornwallis corrected. "We'll find him in London. You put all your mind to proving which of those four Irishmen killed Ainsley Greville. We need to know that before they leave Ashworth Hall, and we can't keep them there more than another few days."

"Yes, sir."

CHAPTER SEVEN

Gracie arranged the white chrysanthemums and placed the vase on the table in the dressing room, then drifted downstairs in a vague, delicious daydream. In the hallway she did not see the ancestral portraits or the wood paneling; she saw light on glass and smelled the earth and the damp leaves and rows and rows of flowers. One moment she wanted to remember every word of the conversation, the next it did not matter in the slightest; the way she felt, the warmth of it was everything. Examine it too closely and it might disappear, like taking a tune apart. She had seen the black notes written on the page, and they meant nothing. The magic was gone; it was not music anymore.

She had Charlotte's dress for the evening over her arm, and it was difficult to hold it high enough to keep the long skirts at the back from trailing on the floor.

"Gracie!"

She only dimly heard the voice.

"Gracie!"

She stopped and turned.

Doll was running down the stairs after her, her face pinched with anxiety.

"What is it?" Gracie asked.

"What are you doing here?" Doll said, taking her by the arm. "We aren't supposed to carry clothes along these stairs! What if someone came to the door! It'd look terrible. That's what back stairs is for. You only come down these if you're sent for to one of the front rooms."

"Oh. Oh, yeh. O' course." She had known that. She was not thinking.

"Where's yer wits?" Doll asked more gently. "Yer out woolgathering?"

"What? What's woolgathering?" Without realizing it, her arms were lowering and the blue dress was trailing on the floor.

Doll took it from her. She was six inches taller and it was an easy task for her.

"Picking bits o' sheep wool that's got caught in the hedges. I mean your wits are wandering." She shook her head. "Yer going to iron this? If you weren't before, you'd better now . . . and clean the hem of that skirt train." She looked at the silk appreciatively. "It's a lovely color. I always imagine the sea looks like that 'round desert islands and such."

Gracie had no time for desert islands. The best things happened in gardens in England, in the dying blaze of the year. Green and white were the most beautiful colors. She followed Doll obediently through the baize door, along the passageway, turned left, and then past the stillroom, the footmen's pantry, the room where they hung the pheasants and other game, the coal room, and on to the various laundry rooms and ironing rooms.

Doll put the blue dress on a hanger and inspected it carefully, flicking off specks of dust, wringing out a cloth till it was barely damp, and then wiping the places where Gracie had inadvertently let the hem of the dress brush on the floor.

"It doesn't look bad," she said with a slight lift in her voice. "Let it dry a minute or two, then iron it. Mrs. Pitt won't find fault. You've got a good place. You're lucky."

Suddenly Gracie put Finn Hennessey from her mind and remembered the moments of unhappiness she had seen in Doll's face, the deep, searing loneliness and sense of pain, not fleeting, but there all the time, breaking through in an unguarded instant.

"In't you lucky?" she said very quietly. She nearly asked if Mrs. Greville found fault, but she did not think that was the answer. It seemed too surface, too insubstantial. And although one could not judge someone's private treatment of their servants by the public face they presented, she had not felt that Eudora was of that nature. Mr. Wheeler was not in the least nervous in his duties. He was deeply shocked at his master's death, and aware of at least some of what murder meant, but that was not the same thing.

Doll's back was stiff, her shoulders set as if all her muscles were locked.

"In't you lucky, then?" Gracie repeated. It was important; it had suddenly come to matter very much.

Doll started to move again, reaching up to the cupboards as if she were looking for starch, or blue, or some other laundry aid, although they were all there in labeled jars, and she took none of them.

"You been very pleasant to me," Doll said, choosing each word, then delivering it as if it were of no importance. "I wouldn't like to see you hurt." She moved a couple of jars around to no purpose, still keeping her back to the room. "Don't go falling in love, Gracie. Kiss and a cuddle's all right, but don't ever let no one take it further than that. There's grief in it you wouldn't think to imagine . . . for the like of us. Don't take offense. It isn't my business. I know that."

"I don' take no offense," Gracie said softly. Although she felt the hot blood surge up her face, it was embarrassment. If Doll could read her so well, maybe everyone could. Maybe even Finn could! She must concentrate her mind. She should know how to be a detective. She had had enough example. "Did you fall in love, then?"

Doll laughed, a bitter, tearing sound close to a sob.

"No . . . I never fell in love. I never met anyone . . . anyone I felt like that about, not as'd be likely to look at me."

"Why wouldn't anybody look at you?" Gracie said frankly. "You're one of the prettiest girls I seen."

Some of the rigidity eased out of Doll's back. "Thank you," she said quietly. "But that's not all a man wants. You've got to be respectable too, have your character."

"You mean your reputation?" Gracie asked. "Well, I s'pose so, mostly. But it don't always count."

"Yes, it does." Doll's voice was flat, allowing no argument, as if she had already hoped and been beaten.

Gracie was almost sure she must have someone in particular in her mind.

"Is that why you stay, even though it in't a good place?"

Doll froze. "I didn't say it wasn't a good place!"

"I in't goin' ter go an' tell anyone you said that," Gracie protested. "Anyway, maybe she'll change now. Things is goin' ter be different now Mr. Greville's dead, poor creature."

"He wasn't a poor creature." She almost choked on the words.

"I meant 'er. She looks terrible pale and scared, like she knew 'oo done it."

Doll turned around very slowly. Her face was white; her hands gripped the marble ledge of the sink top as though if she let go she might fall.

" 'Ere!" Gracie started forward. "Yer goin' ter faint?" She looked around but there was no chair. "Sit on the floor. Afore yer fall over. Yer could hurt yourself rotten on this stone." Against Doll's will, Gracie clasped her and threw her inconsiderable weight to catch her and made her ease downwards instead of falling.

Doll crumpled, carrying Gracie down with her. They sat together in a heap on the cold stone floor.

Gracie kept her arm around her, comforting, as she would have one of the children. "You know 'oo done it too, don't yer?" she pressed. She could not afford to let it go.

Doll started to shake her head, gasping to catch her breath.

"No! No, I don't know!" She gripped Gracie's hand, holding it hard. "You have to believe me, I don't know! I just know it wasn't me!"

"Course it wasn't you!" Gracie kept her arms around Doll. She could feel her shaking as the fear ran through her and seemed to fill the air.

"It could have been," Doll said, clinging to her, her head bent low, her fair hair beginning to straggle out of its pins and its cap. "God knows, I wished him dead often enough!"

Gracie felt the chill take hold of her, as if something dreaded had become real. "Did yer?" She had to ask. She needed to know for Pitt, who was in bad trouble, and anyway, Doll could not keep it all tied up inside her anymore. "Why were that?"

Doll did not answer but just wept quietly as if her heart would break.

Gracie thought of the maid she had seen in the passage near the Grevilles' bathroom. She hurt almost physically with her desire that it should not have been Doll and her fear that it might have been. She did not want to remember, but the question of denying it did not arise. Apart from the fact that she had seen her, she had told Pitt. He would not forget. Not even if she could let him.

She did not even want the picture cleared in her mind, but she had to see it if she could.

Still Doll said nothing, just huddled there, consumed with pain and fear.

Gracie tried hard to remember, to recapture the picture in her mind. Perhaps there would be something to prove it was not Doll? Nothing came at all. The harder she tried the more elusive it was. She took a deep breath.

"Why did you wish 'im dead, Doll?" she said with far less fear than she felt inside. "What'd 'e do to yer?"

"My child . . ." Doll said in an agonized whisper. "My baby."

Gracie thought about all the babies she had known, the living ones and the dead, the unwanted, the loved and cherished who still got sick or had accidents, the ones she cared for at home in Bloomsbury, although they were hardly babies now, only in moments when they were tired and frightened or hurt. Perhaps everyone was then.

She held Doll as if she too was a child. There was nothing absurd in the fact that Doll was taller, older, handsomer. In this instant it was Gracie who had the strength and the wisdom.

"What'd 'e do to yer baby?" she whispered.

For another long moment there was silence. Doll could not bring herself to say the words. Gracie knew what it would be before Doll did at last manage to say it.

"He made me . . . have it killed . . . before it was born. . . ."

There was no possible answer. The only thing she could do was hold her closer, rock her a little, nurse the grief.

"Were it 'is baby?" she said after a few moments.

Doll nodded her head.

"Did yer love 'im, afore that?"

"No! No, I just wanted to keep my job. He'd have thrown me out if I'd said no to him. Then if I kept the baby he'd have put me out without a character. I'd have ended up walking the streets, in a whorehouse, and the baby would probably still have died. Least this way it never knew anything. But I loved that baby. It was mine—just as much as if it'd been born. It was part of my body."

"Course it was," Gracie agreed. The coldness inside her was now a hard, icy anger, like a stone in her stomach. " 'Ow long ago were it?"

"Three years. But it doesn't hurt any less."

That was some small relief. At least it was not so very recent. If she had been going to kill him in revenge, she had already had three years and not done it.

" 'Oo else knows about it?"

"No one."

"Not Mrs. Greville or the cook? Cooks can be awful observant." She nearly added "so I hear," then realized that would give away that Charlotte had no cook.

"No," Doll answered.

"They must 'a thought summink. Yer must 'a looked like yer'd broke yer 'eart. Yer still do."

Doll gave a sigh that ended in a sob, and Gracie held her tighter.

"They just thought I'd fallen in love," Doll said with a fierce sniff. "I wish I had. It couldn't hurt this much."

"I dunno," Gracie said softly. "But if you din't kill 'im, 'oo did?"

"I don't know, I swear. One of the Irishmen."

"Well, if I were Mrs. Greville, an' I knew wot yer just told me, I would 'ave killed 'im, no trouble," Gracie said candidly.

Doll moved back and sat up. Her eyes were red, her face tear-stained.

"She didn't know!" she said vehemently. "She didn't, Gracie! She'd never 'ave been able to hide it. I know. I was with her every day."

Gracie said nothing. Doll was right.

"Come on," Doll urged, her face full of urgency now, her own fear temporarily forgotten. "You're a lady's maid. You know everything in your house, don't you? Everything about your mistress. You know her better than anyone, better than her husband or her mother!"

Gracie did not want to argue that point. Her house was not like Doll's, and Charlotte was certainly nothing like Eudora Greville.

"I suppose," she said with a sigh.

"You won't tell no one." Doll gripped her arm. "You won't!"

" 'Oo'd I tell?" Gracie shook her head a little. "Could 'appen ter anyone, if they was pretty enough."

But it ate at Gracie all day and she could not get her pity or her anger at it out of her mind. And more than that, Doll's trust in her tore at her loyalty to Pitt. She had made up her mind that she could say nothing. She really did believe that Doll had not killed him, and Doll would surely know if Eudora knew of Greville's treatment of her. How could any woman hide the knowledge that her husband had behaved that way and hide it from the victim, of all people? If Charlotte had had such a terrible secret, Gracie would have known.

Pitt came back after dark, his clothes grimy after the long train journey. He was still horribly stiff from his horseback ride across country, and now he was so tired he looked as if he would rather go to bed than change and go downstairs again to the dining room with the effort of civility that would entail. He had to watch what was said all the time, the emotional tension. He looked defeated, and Gracie could only guess at what they had said to him up in London.

Charlotte had already dressed in the blue silk and gone down for dinner, looking wonderful. She felt it was best if she watched and listened as much as possible, just in case she observed something, but it left her no time to do more than welcome him home and ask anxiously what Cornwallis had said.

Only Gracie knew what an effort it had cost her. She was so tensed up it was a hard job to lace up her straps tight enough, her back hurt, and she had the kind of headache no amount of lavender oil or feverfew would lift for long. Half an hour after you thought you got rid of it, it was back again. But Charlotte did not mention it.

Gracie stood in the dressing room doorway and watched Pitt fiddle to put the studs in his shirt. That Tellman was useless. He should have been doing it.

"I'll do that for yer, sir," she offered, coming forward.

"Thank you." Pitt handed the shirt to her, and she picked up the studs and threaded them through, her fingers quick and supple.

"Sir?"

"Yes, Gracie?" He swiveled to face her, his attention complete.

She had not been going to tell him, but she found herself doing so. The words spilled out and it was impossible to equivocate or pretend she had not asked Doll the next question, and the next.

She felt guilty. It was too late to draw any of it back. She had betrayed Doll, who had already suffered so much. But what if Mrs. Greville had killed her husband? She had good reason, if she knew what he had done. And Gracie could not lie to Pitt, and saying nothing would be the same as a lie. She owed him far more than that, and Charlotte too. She could never forgive herself if she knew the truth and Pitt were blamed for failure, when all the time Gracie could have told him what he needed to find the answer.

And Pitt also had no choice. He sat all through dinner turning over in his mind what Gracie had told him. He was only vaguely aware of the conversation around him, of Emily bright-eyed and nervous, trying to watch everyone and the servants at the same time, of Jack being immeasurably more genial than he must have felt, and of Charlotte looking a little pale, not eating much, and trying to fill in the gaps in the conversation.

He took no pleasure in the food on his own plate, exquisite as it was, food he could normally only imagine. Gracie's words filled his thoughts and drove out everything else. It was one of the most wretched stories he had ever heard, and only over the gooseberry tart and iced meringues did he realize with surprise that he had never doubted it. It was a reflection on his personal estimate of Ainsley Greville that he had not even considered that Gracie had been lied to. It was too much like the man revealed in the letters in the study in Oakfield House. The arrogance was there, the callousness towards women. He would regard Doll as his own, paid for with every week's wages. That he had used her was bad enough, if not as uncommon as one would wish. Forcing her to have the child aborted or face a life alone on the streets was beyond forgiveness.

He could not ignore it, neither could he forget it, and it was too powerful a motive for murder for him to leave it unexamined.

He excused himself from the table before the port was passed. He went to the servants' hall to find Wheeler. If he had no knowledge of it, it would be brutal to tell him. But murder was brutal, so were the fear, misery and suspicion that fell on innocent people, their lives taken apart, then other, irrelevant, secrets torn open.

"Yes sir?" Wheeler said with a frown when Pitt took him aside to the butler's pantry, Dilkes being occupied in the withdrawing room.

Pitt closed the door. "I wouldn't ask you this if it were not necessary," he began. "I regret it, and if I can keep it from going any further, then I will."

Wheeler looked anxious. He was really a very agreeable man, perhaps younger than Pitt had supposed earlier, when he had first seen him on the morning of Greville's death. He was serious, but there was something gentle in his face, and perhaps in other circumstances he could laugh or dance like anyone else.

"Wheeler, you must know Mrs. Greville's maid, Doll?"

Wheeler's expression changed almost imperceptibly, perhaps no more than a tightening of muscles.

"Doll Evans? Yes, sir, of course I do. She's a very good girl, hard-working, good at her job, never gives any trouble."

Pitt sensed the defensiveness in Wheeler. The answer had been too quick. Was he fond of her, or simply protecting his own household?

"Did she have an illness about three years ago?" Pitt asked.

Wheeler was guarded. A sharpness in his eyes betrayed a need to be careful. Pitt was sure in that moment that he did know.

"She was ill for a while, yes sir." He did not enquire why Pitt asked.

"Do you know what she suffered from?"

There was a slight flush of pink in Wheeler's cheeks.

"No sir. It was not my place to ask, and she did not say. That kind of thing is personal."

"Was she changed in any way when she recovered?" Pitt pressed.

Wheeler's face smoothed out until it was bland, almost defiant, but the long-trained courtesy did not vanish, only became remote, a thing of habit.

"Was she?" Pitt asked again.

Wheeler looked straight at him. His eyes were gray—and completely guarded.

"She took a long time to recover herself, sir, yes. I think she must have been ill indeed. Sometimes it can take a person that way." He took a breath and made a decision to go on. "When you have to work to support yourself, it can be very frightening to be seriously ill, sir. There's no one'll look after a girl like Doll if she can't work, and we all know that. You try not to think of it, but sometimes circumstances makes you."

"I know," Pitt said quietly, meaning it. "I think you forget, Mr.

Wheeler, I am a policeman, not one of the gentry here. I have no private income. I have to earn my way just as you do."

Wheeler flushed very slightly. "Yes sir. I did forget that," he apologized without retreating an inch. "I don't know why you're asking about Doll, but she's an honest and decent girl, sir. She'd tell you the truth about anything, or keep silent, but she wouldn't lie."

"Yes, she would," Pitt said gently. "To protect Mrs. Greville's feelings, and when the harm can't be undone."

Wheeler stared at him. Pitt saw in his face he was never going to admit he knew. It might be for Eudora's sake, but Pitt thought it was for Doll's. There was a color in Wheeler's cheeks which was emotion, not mere loyalty. Pitt did not need to press it any further. He had seen all he wanted to, and Wheeler knew he had.

"Thank you," he said with a little nod, and opened the pantry door.

He went up the servants' staircase, then through the baize door upstairs. He did not want to chance meeting anyone on the main staircase who would ask him where he was going. This was something he had to do, though he dreaded it. But like Gracie, the knowledge left him no alternative.

He knocked on Eudora's door. She had left the dining room even before he had, so he knew she would be there. He hoped she would be alone. Doyle would be with the other men, probably still drinking port, and if Piers were not there also, he would probably be with Justine.

He heard her answer, and went in.

She was sitting in the large chair near the fire again. Her dark gown spilled around her in a dense shadow against the delicate pastels of the room with its flowers and curtains and linens.

Her face tightened when she saw him, and he felt a knot of guilt inside himself. He closed the door.

"What is it, Mr. Pitt?" she asked, the tremor still in her voice. "Have you learned something?"

He walked over and sat down opposite her. He would like to have been able to talk about anything else. She was frightened, perhaps for Doyle. Surely it could not be for Piers? Why did she imagine Doyle might have killed her husband? How violent was his Irish nationalism? On the surface he seemed the most rational of the four of them, certainly more amenable to reason and compromise than Fergal Moynihan or Lorcan McGinley.

"Mrs. Greville," he began a little awkwardly, "when someone dies, one can discover many things about him one did not know before, sometimes things which are very painful and at odds with what one saw of him, and loved."

"I know," she said quickly, putting out her hand as if to stop him. "You do not need to tell me. I appreciate your gentleness, but I already realize that my husband had affairs with women which I knew nothing about. I would prefer not to know now. I daresay in time I will hear all sorts of things, but just at the moment I feel too . . . confused. . . ." She looked at him earnestly. She seemed to care very much what he thought. "I expect you find that weak of me, but I simply don't know exactly who it is I have lost. Some of what I have learned has horrified me." She bit her lip, staring up at him. "And what horrifies me almost as much is that I didn't know. Why didn't I? Did I deliberately close my eyes, or was it really hidden from me? Who was the man I thought I loved? Who am I, that he chose me, and that I did not see it all those years?" She blinked, as if to close out something, only to find it was within her. "Did he ever love me, or was that false too? And if he did, when did it die? Why did it?" She searched Pitt's eyes. "Was it my fault? Was it something I did . . . or didn't do? Did I fail him?"

He drew in breath to deny it, but she waved her hands. "No, don't answer that. Above all, don't tell me kind lies, Mr. Pitt. I have to come to the truth one day, but let me do it slowly . . . please. I can answer my own question. Of course, I failed him. I did not know him. I should have done. I loved him . . . not passionately, perhaps, but I loved him. I can't suddenly stop that feeling, no matter what I learn about him. It is the habit, the pattern of thought and feeling, of more than half my lifetime. I shared so much with him . . . at least I did with him whether he did with me or not. In a few days everything I thought I knew has been thrown into chaos." She smiled bleakly. "Please, Mr. Pitt, don't tell me anything more yet. I don't know how to change so quickly."

She looked very vulnerable. She was a woman over forty, yet the softness of youth was still in her face, the curve of her cheek, the unbroken line of her chin and throat, the full lips. She was probably Pitt's own age. She could have given birth to Piers before she was twenty.

He must remember why he was there: to uncover the truth. He could not afford to protect everyone who needed or deserved it. No matter what his own feelings, he had no right to choose whom to guard and whom not to, nor could he foresee what the results might be of such an act.

"Mrs. Greville, you already know that your husband had liaisons with certain women which were of a physical nature and had nothing to do with any kind of affection." How could he phrase this to cause as little distress as possible? She was the kind of woman in front of whom even the more violent realities of the daily news should not be discussed, far less the coarseness of private appetite, even if it were of a stranger and not her husband. He felt guilty for forcing her to know something so repugnant. He was about to shatter her memories, her world, to even smaller pieces, so what was left was beyond salvaging.

"Yes, I know, Mr. Pitt. Please don't tell me. I prefer not to imagine it." She was quite open about it, not hiding behind any pride, as if she trusted him as the friend he had appeared to be before she knew who he was.

He hesitated. Did she have to know about Doll? He had to investigate it. The motive for murder was intense. The other philanderings were not enough to draw most men to murder, even on a sister's account, but this was. Even more was it motive for Doll, or anyone who loved her. Could that be Wheeler? He thought not, but it was not impossible.

"Your husband was murdered, Mrs. Greville. I cannot refuse to look at anybody who had a powerful motive for that, no matter how much I would prefer to."

Unconsciously, her body tensed. "Surely you know the motive? It was political." She said it as if there could be no doubt. "Ainsley was the one man who might have drawn the two sides together to agree on some compromise. Some of the Irish extremists don't want a compromise." She shook her head, her voice gathering strength and conviction. "They would rather go on killing and dying than give up an inch of what they think is theirs. It goes back centuries. It has become part of who we are. We have told ourselves we are a wronged race so often and so long we can't let go of it."

She was speaking more and more rapidly.

"There are too many men, and women, whose whole identity is bound up in being people who fight for a great cause. To win would make them nobodies again. What does a war hero do in peacetime? How do you become great when there is nothing to die for? Who are you then, how do you believe in yourself anymore?"

Without intending to, perhaps without even thinking of herself, she had discussed her own confusion and grief as well, the loss of what she had believed her life and her values to be. In the space of hours it had dissolved and taken new and horrible shape. What had she built with her life? She would not be embarrassingly frank enough to say that to him, it would be indelicate, and she would never be that, but it was there in her eyes, and she knew it was understood between them.

He ached, almost physically, to be able to offer her the strength and the comfort, the protection she needed, and he could not. He was going to do the very opposite, make it almost immeasurably worse. Perhaps he was even going to take from her the one person she had left to believe in who cared for her, her brother. Even Piers offered her largely duty and no real understanding. He was too much in love with Justine to see anyone else, and too young to comprehend her distress. He had not yet truly discovered himself, not had time to invest so much of himself in anything that disillusion could tear apart his identity.

He began with the easiest question, the first thing to eliminate.

"When your husband was in the bath, you were here in your room, weren't you?"

"Yes." She looked puzzled. "I already told you that when you asked before."

"And your maid, Doll Evans, was with you?"

"Yes, most of the time. Why?" There was a shadow in her eyes. "Even if I had known how Ainsley was behaving, I would not have harmed him." She smiled. "I had imagined you understood me better than that, Mr. Pitt."

"I did not imagine you hurt him, Mrs. Greville," he said honestly. "I wanted to know where Doll was."

"Doll?" Her delicate eyebrows rose in disbelief. It was almost laughter. "Why on earth would Doll wish him any harm? She is as English as you are, and completely loyal to me. She has no cause to hurt us, Mr. Pitt. We looked after her when she was ill, and kept the position for her return. She would be the last person to harm either of us."

"Was she with you all that quarter hour when your husband was in the bath?" he repeated.

"No. She went to fetch something, I don't recall what. It may have been a cup of tea, I think it was."

"How long was she away?"

"I don't know. Not long. But the idea that she would attack my husband in the bath is absurd." It was plain in her face that she had no fear it could be true. She sincerely thought it was preposterous.

"Did Mr. Doyle visit you often, either in London or at Oakfield House?"

"Why? What is it you are seeking after, Mr. Pitt?" She was frowning now. "Your questions do not make any sense. First you ask about Doll, now Padraig. Why?"

"What illness did Doll suffer? Did Mr. Doyle know of it?"

"I don't remember." She tightened her hands in her lap. "Why? I don't know what illness it was. What can it matter?"

"She was with child, Mrs. Greville—"

"Not by Padraig!" She was horrified, denial was fierce and instant.

"No, not by Mr. Doyle," he agreed. "By Mr. Greville, and not willingly . . . by coercion."

"She . . . she had a child!" She was really finding it difficult to catch her breath. Unconsciously, she put her hand up to her throat as though her silk fichu choked her.

He wanted to lean forward and take her hand, steady her, but it would have appeared like an overfamiliarity, even an intrusion. He had to remember where he was, formal, removed, going on hurting her, watching her face to judge whether she had known this before or not.

"No," he answered. "He insisted that she abort it, and she could not afford to defy him. She would be out on the street with no money and no character. She could not have cared for a child. He had it done away with." He chose the words deliberately and saw her face lose every shred of its color and her eyes darken with horror. She stared at him, trying to probe into his mind and find something that would tell her it was not true.

"She was . . . different . . . when she came back," she said slowly, more to herself than to him. "She was . . . sadder, very quiet, almost slow, as if she had no will anymore, no laughter. I thought it was just because she was not yet fully recovered."

Once she saw he was sincere, she did not fight against it. She was looking backward, trying to remember anything which would disprove it, and there was nothing. It was almost like examining a wound. Part of her was clinical, logical, exact. And yet she was looking at the death of part of herself.

"Poor Doll," she said in a whisper. "Poor, poor Doll. It is so awful I can hardly bear to think of it. What worse thing could happen to a woman?"

"I wish I had not had to tell you." It sounded lame, an excuse where there was none. He was certain she had not known. But then neither did she disbelieve it now. Had Doyle known, and would he have cared? Not on Doll's behalf. She was a servant. Servants frequently get with child.

"Who else might have known?" he asked. Wheeler had. He was the only one of the Greville servants at Ashworth Hall, apart from Doll herself. Unless they had brought a coachman. They were close enough not to have taken the train. He had not asked. "Did you drive over?"

She understood immediately. "Yes . . . but . . . but no one else knew. We thought she was ill . . . a fever . . . I feared it might have been tuberculosis. People with tuberculosis can have those flushed cheeks, the bright eyes. She looked so . . ."

"Wheeler knew."

"Wheeler?" Again she was not afraid. She did not even consider it possible. "He would . . . never . . ."

"What?"

"He would never have hurt Ainsley."

"What were you going to say, Mrs. Greville?"

"That once or twice I thought perhaps he did not like him, but he was far too well trained to show it, of course." She shook her head to dismiss it. "It was just an impression I had. And he did not have to stay with us. He could easily have found a position elsewhere. He was excellent at his job."

Pitt thought it was his feeling for Doll which had kept him in the house of a man he despised, perhaps even hated, but he did not say so. He would have Tellman make sure Wheeler's time was as closely accounted for as they had supposed.

There was a knock on the door.

"Come in," Eudora said reluctantly.

Justine appeared, followed immediately by Charlotte. They both looked flushed and tired, as if they had been too close to the withdrawing room fire and had found the evening's forced conversation trying. But even weary and with a few tendrils of her hair escaping Gracie's coiffure, Charlotte looked marvelous in the blue silk gown. It was one of Vespasia's. Pitt wished he could afford to buy his wife clothes like that. Again he was reminded how naturally she fitted in here. It was the life she could so easily have had if she had married a man of her own social station, or rather better, as Emily had.

Justine was quick to notice Eudora's pallor and the tension in her hands as they twisted together on her lap. She came over immediately, filled with concern.

Charlotte remained in the doorway. She had the feeling that she and Justine had intruded. It was not specific, just a look on Pitt's face and something of regret in Eudora, a way in which she turned back to him before speaking to Justine.

She asked Pitt about it later, when they were preparing to go to bed. She tried to sound casual. As usual he was ready before she was. Gracie had gone, and Charlotte was combing her hair. There were considerable knots to get out after the way it had been dressed, and they would be worse by morning. Also there was rose milk to smooth into her skin, and she loved the luxurious feel of that, whether it did any good or not.

"Eudora seemed distressed," she said, avoiding meeting Pitt's eyes in the glass. He had already told her what little had transpired in his meeting in London, but she knew there was something else since then, something which had moved him far more deeply. "What have you discovered since you returned home?" she asked.

He looked so weary there were shadows around his eyes, and he sat up against the pillows awkwardly. He was still very stiff.

"Greville forced himself on Doll and got her with child," he said quietly. "Then he insisted she do away with it or he would have her put out on the street with nothing."

Charlotte froze. She heard the rage in his voice, but it barely matched the horror she felt, as if something icy had torn a wound inside her. She thought of her own children. She remembered the first time she had held Jemima, fragile, immeasurably precious, herself and yet not herself. She would have given her life to protect her daughter, given it without thought or hesitation. If Doll had killed Ainsley Greville, then Charlotte would do all she could to save her, let the law go to perdition.

She turned around slowly on the stool and stared at Pitt.

"Did she kill him?"

"Doll or Eudora?" he asked, staring at her.

"Doll, of course!" Then she realized that it could also be Eudora, from the same act, for different reasons. Was that why Pitt had looked so very gentle with her? He understood and pitied her? She was beautiful, vulnerable, so desperately in need of strength and support. Her world had been shattered, the present, the future, and some of the past too. In a space of days she had been robbed of all that she was. No wonder he was sorry for her. She called out to all that was best in him, the gentleness, the ability to see without judgment, to pursue truth—and yet still suffer for the pain it brought.

There was much of the knight errant in him, the hunger to be needed, to struggle and to rescue, to measure his strength against the dragons of wrong. Eudora was the perfect maiden in distress. Charlotte was not, not anymore. She was vulnerable in quite different ways, only inside herself. She stood in no danger, just a faint sense of not being entirely included, not factually but in some depth of the emotions.

"No, I don't believe so," he said, answering her question about Doll.

"Does it have anything to do with Greville's death?"

"I don't know . . . directly or indirectly. I hope not."

She turned back to the dressing table, reaching for the rose milk. She was not ready to go to bed yet. She smoothed the milk into her face over and over again, then into her neck, then her face once more, pressing her hands up to her temples, regardless of getting it into her hair. It was ten more minutes before she turned out the gas lamp and crawled into bed beside Pitt. She touched him gently, but he was already asleep.

Breakfast was extremely trying. Charlotte made the effort to rise early, though she did not feel in the least like it, but she could not leave Emily to cope alone. As it was, she was the first to arrive, followed almost immediately by Padraig Doyle. She welcomed him, watching with interest as he helped himself to food from the sideboard and took his place. As he had been every day since he arrived, he was immaculately dressed, and his sleek, dark hair was brushed almost to a polish. His long face, with its humorous eyes and mouth, was set in lines of perfect composure.

"Good morning, Mrs. Pitt," he said with a slight lift to his voice. She was not sure if it was genuine indifference to the distress in the house, a determination to overcome it, a natural will to fight despair and the courage to sustain the battle, or simply the music of the Irish brogue. She could not help responding to it. Regardless of its reason, one felt better for it. She liked him so much better than Fergal Moynihan, with his somber, rather dour air. If she had been Iona, looking for someone to fall in love with, she would have chosen Padraig Doyle far sooner, regardless of the twenty years or so between them. He would have been so much more interesting, more fun to be with.

"Good morning, Mr. Doyle," she replied with a smile. "Have you seen what a clear sky it is? It will make walking in the woods very pleasant."

He smiled back; it was a gesture of understanding as well as friendship.

"A relief," he agreed. "It is rather difficult to find sufficient to do on a wet day, when conversation is as full of pitfalls as ours."

She allowed herself to laugh very slightly, and reached for the toast and apricot preserves.

Iona came in, greeting them both and taking her place. As usual, she declined the food on the sideboard and took instead toast and honey. She was dressed in a deep, romantic blue which heightened the shadowed blue of her eyes. She ate without speaking again. She was remarkably self-contained. Her beauty was dramatic, almost haunting, but it had a remoteness to it which to Charlotte was cold. Was it because she was absorbed in her own problems and they consumed everything else she might have felt? How deeply did she love Fergal Moynihan? Why? Had she ever loved her own husband, or had it been a marriage made for other reasons? Charlotte did not know how old Iona had been at the time of her marriage. Perhaps only seventeen or eighteen, too young to have realized much of the woman she would become in the next fifteen years, or what hungers would waken in her during that time.

Did Lorcan love her? He had seemed angry and embarrassed at the awful scene in the bedroom, rather than emotionally shattered. If she had been deceived by Pitt like that, her world would have ended. Lorcan looked far from so destroyed. But then, people do not always wear their emotions where everyone else can see them. Why should they? Perhaps his way of dealing with such pain was to hide it. It would be natural enough. Pride was important to most people, especially men.

Was Iona lurching from one disaster to another, looking for companionship, some passion or shared charm, where she would never find it? Was it to fire Lorcan with jealousy, to waken in him a hunger or a need which had grown stale? Or was it the simple outrageousness of it, something no one else would do, something to make her talked of, a name to run like fire on every tongue, a bid for her own immortality, another Neassa Doyle, only alive?

As Charlotte was thinking, Fergal came in. "Good morning," he said politely, looking at each of them in turn. Everyone murmured a reply, Iona glancing up quickly and then down again.

Fergal took a portion of eggs, bacon, mushrooms, tomatoes and kidneys, and sat down almost the length of the table away from Iona, but where he could look at her—in fact, where he could hardly avoid it. His face in the hard morning light was smooth, only the faintest of lines around his eyes, and a deeper score from nose to mouth. There seemed an inner complacency about him. If any emotion tore him apart, he hid it with a consummate skill. There were slight shadows under his eyes, but no tension, not the ravages of sleeplessness Charlotte thought she would have suffered in a like situation.

Was that what Iona saw in him, what she needed, some cold challenge to thaw with the heat of her dreams, some icebound heart upon which to exercise her magic?

Or was Charlotte being unfair because she did not like Fergal herself? And was that because she saw him through Kezia's eyes, through her hurt and anger?

"Looks like another agreeable day," Padraig observed, regarding the sky beyond the long windows. "Perhaps we shall have an opportunity for a little walk after luncheon."

"The rain might hold off," Fergal agreed.

"I don't object to a touch of autumn rain." Padraig smiled. "Patter of it among the fallen leaves, smell of the damp earth. Better than the conference room!"

"You'll not get away from the conversation," Fergal warned. He did not look at Iona, but Charlotte had the sense that he was acutely conscious of her, as if he had to exercise an effort of will to keep his eyes from her.

Iona was concentrating on her tea and toast as single-mindedly as if it were a complicated fish full of bones.

No one had brought in the morning newspapers. Was that because the verdict of the Parnell-O'Shea divorce would be in them?

The atmosphere was crackling stiff, like overstarched linen. Charlotte could not decide whether she should try to say something, artificial as it would sound, or if that would only make it worse.

Justine came in, greeting everyone.

"Good morning. How are you?" She hesitated a moment for the tacit reply of nods and half smiles.

"Well, thank you," Padraig answered. "And you, Miss Baring? This can hardly be what you expected when you arrived here."

"No, of course not," she said gently. "No one ever expects

tragedy. But we must support each other." She took a small serving from the sideboard and then sat opposite Charlotte, smiling at her, not blindly in mere politeness, but with a sharp light of understanding, and not without a dry humor.

"I noticed a wonderful bank of hawthorn beyond the beech trees to the west," she observed, mostly to Charlotte. "That must be wonderful in the spring. I love the perfume of them, it is almost intoxicating in the sun."

"Yes, it's marvelous," Charlotte agreed. She had no idea because she had never been there in the spring, but that was irrelevant now. "And the flowering chestnuts," she added for good measure. "Do you have them in Ireland?" She looked directly at Iona.

Iona seemed surprised. "Yes, yes, of course we do. I always think it's a pity we can't bring them inside," she added.

"Why can't you?" Fergal took the excuse to speak to her.

"It's bad luck to bring the May blossom into the house." She fixed him with her brilliant blue gaze, and he seemed unable to turn himself away.

"Why?" he whispered.

"It's unlucky for the housemaid who has to clean up after them," Charlotte said quickly. "They drop hundreds of little petals . . . and little black dots of something too. . . ."

"Insects," Justine offered with a smile.

Padraig winced, but not with distaste.

Suddenly the conversation was easier. Charlotte found herself relaxing a little. By the time Lorcan and Carson O'Day joined them there was even a glimmer of laughter, which did not stop even when Piers came in.

Jack, Emily and Pitt came not long after, and everyone was drawn into at least a semblance of involvement.

O'Day was either in very optimistic spirits or was determined to appear so.

"Have you ever been to Egypt?" he asked Jack with interest. "I have recently been reading some most fascinating letters. They are quite old. I cannot think how I came to miss them." He smiled at Emily, then at Charlotte. "Written by women. One was Miss Nightingale, whose name we all know, of course. But there were several other extraordinary women who traveled as far and were profoundly moved by their experiences." And he proceeded to repeat what he had read of Harriet Martineau and Amelia Edwards, to everyone's interest. Justine in particular was obviously fascinated. At another time, Charlotte would have been also.

Kezia was the last to come, dressed in pale green with a trimming of flowered silk. They were Emily's colors, if not her style, and with her similarly fair hair and skin she was extremely handsome. Charlotte wondered what would happen to her. She was far nearer thirty than twenty. She was highly intelligent, at least politically if not academically. She had fallen in love once, passionately and utterly, and her family and her faith had denied her a consummation. She then made a sacrifice of her heart in order to further her conviction. Would she now feel that something bought at such a price must be made to yield her a return?

Or would she feel that Fergal's betrayal had freed her from her own obligation?

Sitting across the table from her, Charlotte was still sharply aware of the anger in her movements, the tightness with which she gripped her fork, the rigidity of her shoulders, and the fact that she spoke pleasantly to everyone else but did not speak to her brother at all, or to Iona.

The discussion had moved from Egypt, the Nile and its temples and ruins, its hieroglyphics and tombs, to Verdi's recent opera on the story of Othello.

"Very dark," O'Day said appreciatively, passing the orange marmalade to Charlotte. "A truly heroic voice is required, and immense stamina."

"And a fine actor too, I should have thought," Justine added.

"Oh, indeed." O'Day nodded, helping himself to more tea. "And for Iago also."

Kezia glanced across at Charlotte, as if about to speak, then hesitated. Her thoughts on adultery, betrayal, jealousy and villains in general were plain in her eyes.

"An equally great baritone role," Justine said with a smile, looking to left and right. "I assume Othello is the tenor?"

"Naturally." Padraig laughed. "The heroes are always tenor!"

"In *Rigoletto* the tenor is appalling!" Emily rejoined, then blushed with anger at herself.

"Quite," Kezia agreed. "A hypocritical womanizer with no morals, no honor and no compassion."

"But sings like an angel," Padraig interrupted almost before she had finished speaking.

"If angels sing," Fergal said dryly, "perhaps they dance, or paint pictures."

"Is there paint and canvas in heaven?" Lorcan asked. "I thought it was all insubstantial . . . no body, parts or passions?" He looked sideways at Fergal, and then at Iona. "Sounds like hell to me . . . at least for some."

"They take messages," Charlotte stated decisively. "Which would be very difficult to make clear if you had to dance them!"

Justine burst out laughing, and almost everyone else did also, at the release in tension if nothing else. Absurd pictures of mime filled the imagination, and one or two offered suggestions in good humor. When they sobered a little, O'Day asked Jack about the local countryside.

Charlotte wondered as she watched them all if O'Day would be the next leader of the Nationalist cause if Parnell were forced to resign.

He seemed far more open to reason and to compassion. And yet he had a heritage, just as they all had, and a powerful man's shoes to step into. His elder brother was crippled by tuberculosis, or it would have been his duty; now Carson had to achieve it for both of them. It was a heavy burden.

She looked sideways at his face, with its straight angles, smooth, rather heavy cheeks and level brows. It was in every way different from the face of Padraig Doyle; there was imagination in it, but not the wit or sudden laughter. Instead there was a directness, a concentration and a clarity. He would be a very difficult man to get to know, but she felt that once you had it, his loyalty would be complete. She would have understood it had Iona ever pursued him for the challenge. Except that challenges were no fun unless you believed there were some chance of success, however remote. Charlotte did not think anyone manipulated Carson O'Day, except for his own inner compulsions to succeed.

Pitt also found breakfast difficult, but not for the same reasons as Charlotte. He felt no duty to try to ease the social difficulties, although he was sorry for Emily's predicament. He would not willingly have distressed her. His mind was absorbed in the problems of who had killed Ainsley Greville, and his fear that in spite of her protestations, Eudora did know something that she resolutely refused to say, perhaps even to herself.

He could not blame her. She had been hurt so very much; if she chose to be loyal to her brother, even in thought, it was easy to understand.

Pitt looked around the table also, weighing and judging. Doyle was talking eloquently, his face full of concentration, his hands held a little up from the white linen cloth with the Ashworth crest embroidered in self-color on the edges. He used his hands to emphasize what he was saying.

Fergal Moynihan was listening as if he were interested, but every few moments his eyes would go to Iona. He was not very good at covering his feelings.

If Lorcan McGinley noticed, he was far cleverer. His thin face with its intense expression and almost-cobalt-blue eyes stared into the far distance, then when Padraig made some especially telling point he would smile suddenly, illuminating his face, making himself dazzlingly alive. When the moment was past, he would relapse into his private world again, but it did not seem one of pain so much as dream, and not one which hurt or displeased him.

Pitt caught Charlotte's eye several times. She looked lovely in the sharp, autumn light, her skin the warm color of honey, her cheeks very slightly flushed, her eyes dark with anxiety. She seemed to be worried for everyone. Many times she looked at Kezia, nervous of what she might say in her still-smoldering temper. She was busy supporting Emily, guiding the conversation, attempting to be cheerful and avoid the pitfalls of controversy.

He was delighted when he could acceptably excuse himself and go to look for Tellman, who would be curt and still ruffled by his situation, by the house and its wealth, by the fact that four-fifths of the people in it were servants, but Pitt would not have to defer to his feelings. He could be blunt.

He was followed from the room almost immediately by Jack, and he stopped until Jack drew level with him at the foot of the stairs.

Jack pulled a slight face and smiled at him ruefully. He looked tired. Standing close to him now as Pitt was, he could see the fine lines about Jack's eyes and mouth. He was not the same elegantly fashionable young man with whom Emily had fallen in love, and whose easy charm had rather frightened her, fearing him too shallow. His eyes were just as beautiful, his lashes as long and dark, but there was a substance to him that had been lacking before. Earlier in his life he had had no money, only a silken tongue, a quick wit and the ability to flatter with sincerity and to entertain without ever appearing to have to try. He had moved from one home to another, always a welcome guest. He had made it his business to be liked, and taken no responsibility.

Now he had Ashworth Hall to worry about, a seat in Parliament, and far deeper than that, a standard he had set himself to live up to. He was discovering the exact nature of its weight this weekend, and Pitt had not heard him complain once. He had accepted the burden of it with unobtrusive grace. If it frightened him he gave no sign, except now, as Pitt met his eyes, there was a shadow in their depths, something he was hiding even from himself.

"My collar's too high," Jack said with self-mockery. He ran his finger around inside it, pulling it away from his throat. "Feels as if it's strangling me."

"Is it as bad in conference as it is around the meal table?" Pitt asked.

Jack hesitated and then shrugged. "Yes. You need the patience of Job even to bring them to the point where they will discuss anything that actually matters. I don't know what Greville thought could be accomplished by this. Every time I think I have them to the brink of some kind of agreement, one of them will change direction and it all falls apart again." He put his hand on the newel post and leaned a little against it. "I never realized the power of old hatreds until now, how deep they run. They are in the blood and the bone of these people. It is part of who they are, as if they have to cling to the old feuds or they would lose part of their identity. What do I do about that, Thomas?"

"If I knew, I would have told you already," Pitt answered quietly. He put his hand on Jack's arm. "I don't think Greville could have done any better. Gladstone didn't!" He wanted to say something better, something that would let Jack know the warmth of respect he felt for him, but none of the words that came to his mind seemed appropriate. They were too light, too flippant for the reality of the hatred and the loss that filled the conference room, and which Jack had to fight alone every morning and every afternoon.

He took his hand away and pushed it into his pocket.

"I don't know where I am either," he confessed.

Jack laughed abruptly. "Trying to keep our heads above a sea of insanity," he replied. "And probably swimming in the wrong direction. I must get a better collar. By the way, yours is crooked, but don't bother to straighten it. It's a touch of familiarity in a world that is frighteningly unfamiliar. Don't do up your cuff either, or take the string out of your pocket." He smiled quickly, as lightly and easily as used to be characteristic, then before Pitt could say anything further, went up the stairs two at a time.

Pitt moved away, but as he was crossing the hall and about to turn towards the green baize door to the servants' quarters, he heard quick footsteps on the wood behind him and his name called.

He turned to see Justine coming towards him, her face filled with concern. Instantly he was afraid it was for Eudora. She had not been at breakfast, but of course no one had expected her.

Justine caught up with him.

"Mr. Pitt, may I speak with you for a few moments, please?"

"Of course," he agreed. "What is it?"

She indicated the morning room, which was opposite where they stood and next to Jack's study.

"May we go in there? No one else will wish to use it so early, I think."

He obeyed, walking ahead of her and holding the door while she went in. She moved with a unique kind of grace, head high, back very straight, and yet with more suppleness than most women, as if dancing for sheer, wild pleasure would come easily to her.

"What is it?" he asked when the door was closed.

She stood in front of him, very earnest. For the first time he noticed signs of strain in her, a momentary hesitation, a small muscle working in the side of her jaw. This must be appalling for her. She had arrived at the house of strangers, at the invitation of the man she intended to marry, in order to meet his parents. They had stumbled into a political conference of the most delicate and volatile nature. And the very next morning they had awoken to the murder of Greville, and then the long, draining task of trying to comfort and sustain Eudora when Justine should have been the center of attention and happiness herself.

He admired her courage and her unselfishness, that she had borne it not only with dignity but considerable charm. Piers had found a remarkable woman. Pitt was not surprised he was determined to marry her—and had informed his parents rather than sought their permission. He respected Piers for that more than he had previously realized.

"Mr. Pitt," Justine began quietly, "Mrs. Greville told me what you have been obliged to tell her about her maid, Doll Evans." She breathed in deeply. He could see the fabric of her gown tighten as her body stiffened. She seemed to be weighing her words with intense care, uncertain even now whether to say this or not.

"I wish it had not been necessary," he said. "There is much I wish she did not have to hear."

"I know." The ghost of a smile crossed Justine's face. "There are many truths it would be better to hide. Life can be difficult enough with what we have to know. Things can be rebuilt more easily if we do not shatter them before we have the strength to cope with the magnitude of it. When you see the whole task, it can be too much. One loses the courage even to try, and then you are defeated from the beginning."

"What is it you want to say, Miss Baring? I cannot take back what I told her. I would not have spoken at all without having done all I could to make sure it was true."

"I understand that. But are you sure it was, Mr. Pitt, really sure?"

"Doll told Mrs. Pitt's maid. Gracie hated breaking the confidence, but she realized that it might be at the core of this crime. It is a very real motive for murder. Surely you can see that?" he asked gently.

"Yes." Her face was tight with emotion. "If he really did that to her, then I can . . . I can see how she might have felt he deserved to die. And it seems he did . . . have affairs with other women, acquaintances . . . but, Mr. Pitt, they are none of them here in this house now! Isn't all that matters who is here now, and could have killed Mr. Greville? Can't you let all the past indiscretions be buried with him, for Mrs. Greville's sake, and Piers . . . and even for poor Doll? After all, Doll was with Mrs. Greville almost all the time you are speaking about. And . . ."

"And what?"

Again she stiffened, her face tight with anxiety.

"And you do not know that the story is true. Yes, of course Doll was with child, and unspeakable as it is"—her eyes were hard with suppressed fury—"she had little chance but to have the child aborted. That would be a better death than any other it faced. But you don't know that Mr. Greville was responsible."

He stared at her, for a moment taken aback.

"But she said it was Greville. Who . . . what are you saying? That she blamed him when it was someone else? Why? Greville's dead . . . murdered. To blame him makes her a suspect when no one would have thought of her otherwise. It makes no sense."

She looked back at him with wide eyes, almost black, her body tense like an animal ready to fight. Was she so in love with Piers she must defend his father with this fierceness and determination? He admired her for it. The uniqueness of her face was no accident, the sudden strength where one had expected only beauty.

"Yes it does," she argued. "If she had already said it was Greville, before, she couldn't go back on it now. And better she tell someone first, before anyone else did, and she appear to have hidden it and lied. So she told Gracie, knowing it would come back to you."

"She didn't know it would. Gracie very nearly didn't tell me."

She smiled with a flash of humor. "Really, Mr. Pitt! Gracie's loyalty to you would always win in the end, for a dozen reasons. I know that. Doll must know it too."

"But Doll didn't know that anyone else was aware of her tragedy," he argued back.

"She said so?" Her eyebrows arched delicately.

"Perhaps that is not true," he conceded. "At least one other servant knew, although I doubt she told him."

"Him?" she said quickly. "No, more likely she confided in another woman, or they guessed. It is one of the first things that would come to a woman's mind, Mr. Pitt. They would know something was wrong at the time she was raped . . . if it was rape. Or seduced, which is more likely. Women are very observant, you know. We notice the slightest change in other people, and we can read our own sex very clearly. I would be surprised if the cook and the housekeeper didn't know, at least."

"So she told them it was the master, rather than say who it really was?" He still found the idea difficult, but it was making more sense all the time. "Why? Wouldn't that be a very dangerous thing to say? What if it were reported back to him?"

"Who would do that?" she asked. "And if it were one of the menservants, surely they would be willing to protect their own? After all, she didn't say it outside the house. Mr. Greville himself never knew of it, and certainly neither Mrs. Greville nor Piers did."

He thought about it a little more seriously. It was not impossible.

She saw his indecision in his face.

"Do you really think a politician and diplomat of Mr. Greville's standing is going to seduce a maid in his own household?" she urged. "Mr. Pitt, this is a political murder, an assassination. Mr. Greville was brilliant at his task. For the first time in a generation it seems there may really be some improvement in the Irish Problem, and he was responsible for that. It was his skill at diplomacy, his genius at the conference table that was bringing it about. This is what was unique about him. Surely that was why he was killed . . . here . . . and now?"

Her face became suddenly more grave. There was a new and greater tension in her body. "Perhaps he did not tell you—he may have wished not to frighten anyone further—but there was a very unpleasant happening yesterday when an urn was crashed onto the terrace only a yard away from Mr. Radley. If it had struck him he would unquestionably have been killed. That can only be because he has been out to step into Mr. Greville's place in the conference. It is political, Mr. Pitt. Please give his family the opportunity to recover from their grief, and mourn for him, without destroying the memories they have."

He looked at her earnest face. She meant passionately what she said, and it was easy to understand. He would like to protect Eudora himself.

"You have a high opinion of Mr. Greville," he said gravely.

"Of course. I know a lot about him, Mr. Pitt. I am going to marry his son. Look for the person who envied his brilliance, who was afraid of what he could achieve . . . and above all, in whose interest it is to keep the Irish Problem unsolved."

"Miss Baring—"

He got no further. There was an explosive crash. The walls shook, the ground trembled. The looking glass above the mantel shattered outwards, and suddenly the air was full of dust.

The gas mantles fell in shards onto the floor, and out in the hall someone started screaming over and over again.

CHAPTER EIGHT

The noise died away. For seconds Pitt did not move, too dazed to realize what had happened. Then he knew. A bomb! Someone had exploded dynamite in the house. He spun around and lunged out the door.

The hall was full of smoke and dust. He could not even see who was screaming, but the door of Jack's study was hanging on one hinge and the small table that had stood outside was lying in splinters on the floor. The dust was clearing already. The cold draft which came from the shattered windows was blowing it in billows through the doorway. Finn Hennessey was lying on the floor, crumpled and dazed.

The woman was still screaming.

Jack!

Sick at heart, Pitt staggered in without even bothering to steady the remains of the door. He could see shards of wood everywhere, and smell gas and burning wool. The curtains were flapping into the room, filled like sails and then snapped empty, their bottoms torn. Books lay in piles and heaps on the carpet. The burning was getting worse. The coals must have been thrown out of the fire by the blast.

There was someone on the carpet behind the ruins of the desk, spread-eagled, one leg bent under him. There was blood all over his chest and stomach, bright scarlet blood.

Pitt could barely force himself to pick his way through the debris, treading on papers and the wreckage of furniture and ornaments.

The jaw was broken, the throat torn, but the rest of the face was remarkably undisfigured. It was Lorcan McGinley. He looked faintly surprised, but there was no fear in him, no horror at all. He had not seen death coming.

Pitt climbed to his feet slowly and turned back to the door. The wind filled the curtains and sent them flying up. One caught a picture swinging on its broken hook and sent it crashing to the floor, glass exploding.

Emily was standing in the doorway, her body shaking, her face gray.

"It's McGinley," he said clearly, walking over towards her, slipping on books, loose papers, glass, splintered wood.

Emily shook more violently. She was gasping for breath as if she were choking, unaware that she was beginning to sob.

"It's McGinley!" Pitt said again, taking hold of her shoulders. "It's not Jack!"

She raised her fists, tightly clenched, and started to beat against him, lashing out blindly, terrified, wanting to hurt him, to share some of the intolerable pain inside her.

"Emily! It's not Jack!" He did not wish to shout. His throat was sore with the dust and smoke. Somewhere behind him the study carpet was beginning to burn. He took her shoulders and shook her hard. "It's Lorcan McGinley! Stop it! Emily, stop it! I've got to put the fire out before the whole damn house is alight!" He raised his voice to a shout, coughing violently. "Somebody get a bucket of water! Quickly! You!" He pointed to a dim figure through the settling dust. The maid had stopped screaming at last. Other people were coming, frightened, not knowing what to do. One of the footmen stood as if paralyzed, his livery filthy. "Get a bucket of water!" Pitt shouted at him. "The carpet's on fire in there."

The footman moved suddenly, swinging around as if to escape.

Emily was still shaking and crying, but she had stopped hitting him. Her hair was coming undone and she looked ashen pale.

"Where's Jack?" she said hoarsely. "What have you done with Jack? You were supposed to look after him! Where is he?" She jerked back as if to strike at him again.

There was a clatter of feet, and loud voices.

"What is it?" O'Day demanded. "Oh, my God! What happened? Is anyone hurt?" He swung around. "Radley?"

"I'm here." Jack pushed his way past Doyle and Justine. Other people were coming down the stairs, and more from the baize door at the far end of the hall.

Emily did not even hear Jack. She was still furious with Pitt, and he had to hold her hard to prevent her from hurling herself at him again.

One of the footmen was cradling Hennessey in his arms, and he appeared to be slowly regaining his senses.

Jack strode forward, glancing at the wreckage of the study, and his face paled.

"McGinley," Pitt said, meeting his eyes. "There was an explosion—dynamite, I should think."

"Is he . . . dead?"

"Yes."

Jack put his arm around Emily and held her, and she began to cry, but softly, as of relief, the terror slipping out of her.

O'Day came forward to stand almost between them, his face grim. They must all be able to smell the smoke now.

"Where the devil is the footman with the water?" Pitt shouted. "Do you want the whole house on fire?"

"Here, sir!" The man materialized almost at his elbow, staggering a little under the weight and awkwardness of two buckets of water. He moved past Pitt to where the curtain was now rising slightly and gusting out towards them on the draft from the broken windows, and they heard the furious hiss of steam as he threw the water, then the smoke belched and lessened. He came out covered in smut and with his face scalded bright pink.

"More water!" he gasped, and two other footmen ran to obey.

Pitt stood in the doorway, shielding the sight behind him. Everyone seemed to be present, white-faced, shocked and frightened. Tellman came forward.

"McGinley," Pitt said again.

"Dynamite?" Tellman asked.

"I think so." Pitt looked to see Iona. She was standing between Fergal and Padraig Doyle. Perhaps she had already guessed the truth from Pitt's face, and the fact that Lorcan was not in the hall while everyone else was.

Eudora moved towards her.

Iona stood still, shaking her head from side to side. Padraig put his arm around her.

"What happened?" Fergal asked, frowning, trying to see beyond Pitt. "Is it a fire? Is anyone hurt?"

"For God's sake, man, didn't you hear the noise?" O'Day demanded angrily. "It was an explosion! Dynamite, by the sound of it."

Fergal looked startled. For the first time he noticed Iona's fear. He swung around to glare at Pitt, the question in his face.

"I am afraid Mr. McGinley is dead," Pitt said grimly. "I don't know what happened beyond the fact that the explosion seemed to center behind Mr. Radley's desk. The fire is incidental. The blast blew the coals out of the grate and they fell onto the carpet."

As he spoke a footman came struggling back with more water, and he stood aside for him to pass.

"Are you sure there is nothing I can do for McGinley?" Piers asked anxiously.

"Quite sure," Pitt assured him. "Perhaps you could help Mrs. McGinley."

"Yes. Yes, of course." He moved back and approached Iona gently, talking to her as if there were no one else there, his voice quivering only very slightly.

Padraig Doyle walked over to Pitt, his face creased with concern.

"A bomb in Radley's study," he said with his back to the others so they could not hear. "And it exploded and caught poor Lorcan. It is a very bad business, Pitt. In the name of the devil, who put it there?"

"In the same name, Doyle, what was McGinley doing in there?" O'Day said grimly, looking around each in turn as if he thought someone might answer him.

Iona was silently clenching and unclenching her hands. Fergal had moved closer to her and surreptitiously slid his arm around her shoulders.

"Looking for Radley?" Padraig suggested, his eyes sharp and dark. "Borrowing paper, ink, wax, who knows?" He turned to Finn Hennessey, who was struggling to his feet with the assistance of the same footman who had held him before. "Do you know why Mr. McGinley was in Mr. Radley's study?" Padraig asked.

Finn was still dizzy, blinking; his face was dark, smudged with dust, and his clothes were covered in it. He seemed barely able to focus.

"Yes sir," he said huskily. "The dynamite . . ." He swiveled to stare at the shattered study door and the clouds of dust and smoke.

"He knew the dynamite was there?" Padraig said incredulously.

"Is he . . . dead?" Finn stammered.

"Yes," Pitt answered him. "I'm sorry. Are you saying McGinley knew the dynamite was there?"

Finn turned towards him, blinking. It was obvious he was still dazed and probably suffering physical as well as emotional shock. He nodded slowly, licking dry lips.

"Then why in God's name didn't he send for help?" O'Day said reasonably. "Anyway, how did he know?"

Finn stared at him. "I don't know how he knew, sir. He just told me . . . to stand guard, not to let anyone go into the study. He said he knew more about dynamite than anyone else here. He'd be the best person to deal with it." He looked at O'Day, then at Pitt.

"Then who put it there?" Kezia asked, her voice rising towards panic. She swung around, staring at each of them.

"The same person who murdered Mr. Greville," Justine answered her, her face pale and tight. "It was obviously intended for Mr. Radley because he has had the courage to take his place. Someone is determined that this conference shall not succeed and is prepared to commit murder after murder to see that it doesn't."

The fire in the study was out now. There was no more smoke, but the wind blowing through carried the rank smell of wet, charred wool and the still-settling dust.

"Of course it was intended for Mr. Radley," Eudora said with a gulp. "Poor Lorcan saw someone put it there, or realized someone had, we shall never know now, and he went in there to try and disarm it before it could explode . . . only he failed."

Iona looked up sharply, her eyes wide and suddenly filled with tears.

"He was betrayed, like all of us! He was one of the immortal Irishmen who died fighting for peace and trying to bring it to reality." She faced Emily and Jack, standing close to each other. "You have a terrible responsibility, Mr. Radley, a debt of honor, incurred in blood and sacrifice. You cannot let us down."

"I will do anything in my power not to, Mrs. McGinley," Jack replied, meeting her gaze steadily. "But no sacrifice buys my conscience. I wish Lorcan McGinley were the only man who had died for Irish peace, but tragically he is only one of thousands. Now, there is much to do. Superintendent Pitt has another crime to investigate—"

"He hasn't achieved much with the last one," O'Day said with sudden bitterness, uncharacteristic of him until now. "Perhaps we should call in more help? This is lurching from bad to worse. McGinley's is the second death in three days—"

"The third in a week," Pitt cut across him. "There was a good man murdered in London because he had penetrated the Fenians and learned something of their plans—"

O'Day swung around, his face coloring, his eyes sharp. "You never mentioned that before! You never said you had information that the Fenians were planning all this. You knew that . . . and still you didn't prevent it?"

"That's unfair!" Charlotte intervened for the first time, coming forward from the shadows, where she had been standing near Emily and Jack. "This house wasn't broken into by Fenians. Whoever did this"—she gestured towards the open study door and the wreckage within—"is one of us here. You brought murder with you!"

Someone gave a little cry. It was impossible to tell who. The room was as thick with fear and grief as it was with dust and the smell of burning.

"Yes, of course," O'Day apologized, composing himself with difficulty. "I am sorry, Mrs. Pitt, Superintendent. I had hoped so much of this conference, it is hard to see one's dreams dashed and not want to blame someone you can see and name. But it is nonetheless unworthy." He looked around them, especially at Padraig. "Come. I think we should all leave Mr. Pitt to his gruesome duty, and ourselves return and see what we can do to foil this madman's violence by preparing to continue the best we may."

"Bravo." Padraig applauded, raising his hands as if to clap, then turning to walk away.

"Certainly," Jack agreed, after glancing at Pitt. "We shall all go to the morning room, when the fire is lit, and have Dilkes bring us a hot punch with a little brandy in it. I'm sure we could all do with it. Emily . . ."

She was still ghostly white, but she made an effort to respond.

"Yes . . . yes . . ." she said hesitantly, walking as if she were not sure of the ground under her feet. She went straight past Iona. It was Justine who took Iona by the arm and offered to go with her up to her room, fetch her maid and have a tisane sent up, with brandy if she wished, and to sit with her. Charlotte was standing beside Finn Hennessey, talking to him quietly, gently, trying to help his shock and confusion. He was still staring around him as if he barely knew where he was and could not comprehend what had happened or what he was doing there. Gracie was there also, white-faced.

Pitt watched Charlotte with a sudden admiration which was oddly painful. She was so competent, so strong. She did not seem to need support from anyone else. If she was frightened, she hid it. Her back was straight, her head high; her concern was all for Hennessey and Gracie.

He turned back to the business in hand. Tellman was at his elbow. He had been unaware of him until now.

Everyone else followed Jack to the morning room—except Eudora and Tellman, standing close to the study door. Eudora was staring at Pitt, her face white, smudged across the cheek with dust.

"Mr. Pitt, I'm so sorry," she said gently. "What Mr. O'Day said was unforgivable. No one can defend us from each other. This is terrible, but it does look as if we have great goodness among us, as well as evil. Lorcan gave his life trying to defuse the bomb. Perhaps we have still the will to succeed, if you can find who . . . who it was who laid it there." She stared at him fixedly. "Can . . . can you? I mean, is there anything? Can anyone tell from what is left?"

"Not from the study," he replied. "Anyone in the house could have done that, but we shall question the servants and everyone else, and see who came this way, where everybody was. We may learn something."

"But . . . but we could all have come across the hall," she protested. "That doesn't prove . . . I mean—" She stopped, her throat tight, her voice thin and high. "I mean . . ." She shook her head quickly and walked after the others, her dark skirts pale with dust.

Tellman sighed and stared into the study, hesitated a moment, then started to pick his way through the debris towards the desk and the body of Lorcan McGinley. He squatted down and peered at it thoughtfully, then at what was left of the desk.

"I think the dynamite was in the top drawer on the left, or the second," Pitt said, following after him.

"That's what it looks like," Tellman agreed, chewing his lip. "Judging from the way all the splinters and debris are lying. It would all fall outward from the blast, I suppose. What a mess. Whoever put it here wanted to be sure an' kill Mr. Radley, no mistake. I wouldn't be a politician trying to sort this lot out." He moved his attention from the desk to Lorcan's body. "He must've been right in front of it, poor devil."

Pitt stood with his hands in his pockets, brow furrowed. "It would have been on a wire of some sort, rather than a clock," he said thoughtfully. "No one could be sure when Jack would come in here. It might simply have blown up with no one, or if it were on top of the desk, under papers and books, it might have been moved by a servant tidying up."

"D'you think that lot would care?" Tellman said bitterly. "What's one English servant more or less?"

"Possibly nothing," Pitt agreed. "But it would achieve no purpose. It would be a risk and an outrage that would serve no end. No, it would have been designed specifically for Jack, put in one of the drawers no one else would open."

He reached over and searched among the debris for the remains of the drawers. He found one and examined it without success, then a second. He turned it over very carefully, feeling it with his fingertips. There was one side, and a shard of the bottom left more or less attached. He examined the underneath. Across the bottom was a straight line of flat-topped furniture tacks. There was a broken piece of wire under one of them.

"I think we have found where the mechanism was," Pitt said quietly. "Pinned under the drawer to detonate when the drawer was opened. It must have taken a few minutes to do this. Empty the drawer out, tack this across the bottom, and then replace it all."

Tellman's eyes widened and he stood up, his knees cracking as he straightened them. "It's a great pity McGinley's dead," he said slowly. "He could answer some important questions."

"He was a very brave man." Pit shook his head. "I would dearly like to know what he deduced, and we didn't."

"Damn fool should've told us," Tellman said angrily. "That's our job!" Then he colored very faintly. "Not that we've exactly done it well this time. I don't know anything about dynamite. Do you?"

"No," Pitt confessed. "I've never dealt with a murder by dynamite before. But somebody put it here and set it up to explode when the drawer was opened. We ought to be able to find out who that was. McGinley did."

"Same person as killed Greville," Tellman replied. "An' we know that wasn't McGinley, O'Day or the valet Hennessey, but it could be just about anyone else."

"Then we had better find out when the bomb was placed here. Obviously it was after the last time Jack used the drawer. Speak to the servants, housemaids, butler, footmen, anyone who came in here or was around the hall. See where everyone was all morning, who can substantiate it, who they saw and when, especially Finn Hennessey. I'll go and speak to Mr. Radley, and then to the other guests. But before you do that, you had better have someone help you put poor McGinley in the icehouse." He turned around. "You can carry him on the door. It's only hanging by one hinge. Then we'd better see if anyone can at least tack a curtain over the doorway, something to keep the sight from distressing anyone still further. And board up the window too, in case of rain."

"Mess, isn't it . . ." Tellman said, puckering his brow. He disapproved of wealth, but he hated to see beauty spoiled.

Gracie had heard the blast, as had almost everyone else in the house. At first she thought of some domestic accident, but only for a moment. Then her better sense told her something was very seriously wrong. She put the jug of water in her hand on the marble-topped table bench in the stillroom, where she was helping Gwen prepare a remedy for freckles, there being no mending to do.

"What's that?" Gwen said nervously. "That wasn't trays or pans dropped."

"I dunno, but I'm goin' ter see," Gracie replied without hesitation. She almost ran out of the stillroom door past the coal room and the room where the footmen cleaned the knives and along the passageway towards the baize door.

Tellman came out of the boot room, his face pale, his eyes wide and bright. He ran after her and caught her just short of the baize door, taking her by the arm.

"Stop, Gracie! You don't know what it is."

She was swung around by the strength of his hold.

"I know it didn't oughter be," she said breathlessly. "It's summink bad. Is it a gun?"

"Guns don't make that noise," he argued, still gripping her arm. "That's more like dynamite. You wait here. I'll go through and see what's happened."

"I in't waitin' 'ere! Mr. Pitt could be 'urt!"

"There's nothing you can do if he is," he said briskly. "Just wait here. I'll tell you—"

She wrenched herself away and flung the baize door open. Immediately she saw the dust and the shattered door of the study. Her heart lurched so violently she thought she would suffocate. Then she saw Pitt standing up and the relief was almost too much. Dizziness overwhelmed her. She was going to faint like some silly little housemaid if she wasn't careful. She had to hold on to the side table for a moment.

There was another crash and she nearly jumped out of her skin. It was only a looking glass falling and breaking. There was a horrible smell, and dust everywhere, clouds of it. It would take weeks to get rid of all this.

People were coming from every direction. Thank heaven there was Mr. Radley. Mrs. Radley was flying at Mr. Pitt, shouting at him. Understandable, perhaps, but she still didn't ought to do it.

Tellman was standing close behind her. "You all right?" he demanded.

"Yes, course I'm all right!" she assured him with an effort. Pitt was safe, and Charlotte was coming across the hall, white-faced but unhurt. "Thank you," she added.

"There's nothing you can do here," he went on. "There'll be a lot of tidying up to do later, but for now we need to know what happened, and we don't want anything moved."

"I know that!" she said hotly. Of course she knew it. Did he think she was stupid?

Someone spoke McGinley's name.

Doyle's valet was standing next to the stairs.

There was a smell of burning. Someone was calling for water.

Suddenly Gracie saw Finn half sitting on the floor, a footman supporting him and Charlotte close by. Her stomach lurched. She slipped past Miss Moynihan and Miss Baring and went over to Charlotte.

"Wot 'appened?" she asked as loudly as she dared. "Is 'e . . . all right?" She was looking at Finn.

"Yes, he's all right," Charlotte whispered back. "Mr. McGinley went into the study and somehow triggered off a bomb made of dynamite."

"Is 'e dead?"

"Yes, I'm afraid so. He must have been right by the blast."

Gracie caught her breath and nearly choked from the dust in the air.

"That's terrible! Them Irish is mad! 'Oo's this goin' ter 'elp?"

"No one," Charlotte said softly. "Hennessey says Mr. McGinley knew it was there and was trying to make it safe, but it must have been so finely balanced it went off anyway."

"Poor soul." Gracie was wrenched by sadness for him. "Per'aps 'e were so brave 'cos o' Mrs. McGinley bein' off wi' Mr. Moynihan, like? Maybe 'e were 'urt so bad—" She stopped. She should not have said that. It was not her place. " 'E were very brave," she added. She looked at Charlotte, then at Finn.

Charlotte gave her a little nudge.

Gracie went over and knelt down beside Finn. He seemed stunned, still only partially sensible of where he was. His face and clothes were filthy from the dust and smoke, and beneath the soot he was ashen skinned.

"I'm ever so sorry," she said softly. She put her hand out and slid it over his, and he gripped it gratefully. "Yer gotta be brave, like 'e were," she went on. " 'E were a real 'ero."

He stared at her, his eyes wide, almost hollow with shock and hurt.

"I don't understand it!" he said desperately. "It shouldn't have happened! He knew dynamite! He should . . ." He shook his head as if to clear it. "He should have been able to . . . to make it all right."

"D'yer know 'oo put it there?" she asked.

"What?"

"D'yer know 'oo put the dynamite there?" she repeated.

"No. No, of course I don't," he replied. "Or I'd have said, wouldn't I?"

" 'Ow'd poor Mr. McGinley know it were there?"

He turned away. "I don't know."

Instantly she was ashamed. She should not be asking him all these questions when he was shocked and bruised and grieved. She should be trying to comfort him.

"I'm sorry," she whispered. " 'Cos you don't understand it. I don't s'pose nobody does, 'ceptin' 'im wot put it there, an' maybe not even 'im neither. Yer'd better come away and sit down for a while, quiet like. Mr. Dilkes won't mind if yer 'ave a drop o' 'is brady. Gawd knows, yer need it. Everybody needs time an' a spot o' 'elp ter get an 'old o' themselves."

He looked back at her. "You're very sweet, Gracie." He swallowed, took a very deep, shaky breath, and swallowed again. "I just don't know how it could have happened!"

"Mr. Pitt'll find out," she answered him, trying to convince herself as well. "Come back ter Mrs. Hunnaker's room an' sit down. There'll be lots o' things ter do soon enough."

"Yes . . ." he agreed. "Yes, of course." And he allowed her to help him to his feet and, after thanking the footman, to lead him out of the dusty hall back through the green baize door and to Mrs. Hunnaker's sitting room, where there was nobody to give or deny them entrance. She made him sit down, and then in the absence of the butler to grant her brandy, went to the cooking cupboard and helped herself to a stiff glass of sherry and took it back. Let Mrs. Williams quarrel about that later. She sat opposite him, watching him carefully, trying to comfort him, aching for his confusion and his loss.

By the time Tellman came to ask both of them where they had been all morning, and what they had seen, Finn was almost himself again.

Tellman stood just inside the doorway, his body angular, his shoulders stiff. He looked thoroughly disapproving as he stared at Gracie, sitting perched on the housekeeper's second-best chair, and Finn, slumped in the best.

"I'm sorry, Mr. Hennessey," he said grimly. "I don't like having to ask you when you just lost someone you're close to, but we got to know what happened. Someone put that dynamite there. Probably the same person as killed Mr. Greville."

"Of course . . ." Finn agreed, looking up at him. "I don't know who it was."

"Maybe not outright, or you'd have said." Tellman was holding a pencil and paper in his hands, ready to write down what was said. "But you may 'ave seen more than you realize. What did you do from seven o'clock this morning?"

"Why seven?"

"Just answer, Mr. Hennessey." Tellman's temper was shorter than he was willing to have known. There was a muscle flicking on his temple and his lips were white. Gracie realized with sudden surprise what a weight of responsibility Tellman had and how worried he must be. He knew exactly how far he and Pitt were from finding a solution, what a failure this whole task had been so far, and how it was getting no better even as the minutes passed. She should be helping him. After all, he was Pitt's assistant. That was her real duty. She certainly should not be allowing his manner to put her off.

"You want to know who done that to Mr. McGinley, don't yer?" she said urgently to Finn. "Any of us may 'ave seen summink." She turned back to Tellman.

"I din't come down till long after seven. First off, o' course, I got up and dressed meself, then I made sure the mistress's dressin' room fire were lit an' burnin' proper. Then I fetched 'ot water for 'er ter wash in. I asked 'er if she wanted a cup o' tea, but she didn't. Then I got a cup o' tea for Mr. Pitt, seein' 'is valet were neglectful." She gave him a meaningful look. He glared back at her but refrained from saying anything, although she could see his response in his eyes.

"And . . ." he prompted.

"An' I 'elped 'er ter dress an' do 'er 'air. . . ."

"How long did that take?" he asked with what she was sure was an edge of sarcasm.

"I don' sit an' watch the clock, Mr. Tellman. But since I were doin' the work fer two, longer than most."

"You never helped the superintendent to dress?" he said with final incredulity.

"Course I didn't! But I fetched water and brushed 'is shoes an' 'is jacket, seein' as 'is valet's a useless article and were nowhere ter be seen. Then I came downstairs ter bring down the laundry an' I passed Doll, that's Mrs. Greville's maid, on the stairs an' 'ad a word wif 'er—"

"That doesn't help," Tellman interrupted.

"An' about quarter ter nine I go to find Mrs. Pitt ter ask 'er about what she'd like ter wear for dinner, an' I sees Miss Moynihan come down the front stairs and go ter the mornin' room, an' Mrs. McGinley in the conservatory wi' Mr. Moynihan, standin' much too close ter the door for the likes o' wot they were doin'. . . ."

Tellman pulled a face, from which his contempt was obvious.

Finn smiled as if he saw some bitter humor in that love affair.

"Go on," Tellman said sharply. "Did you see anyone else?"

"Yeh. Mr. Doyle were leavin' the 'all an' goin' ter the side door."

"To where?"

"Ter the garden, o' course."

"What time?"

"I dunno. Ten minutes afore nine, mebbe?"

"You sure it was Mr. Doyle?"

"Don' look funny at me like that! I know better than to say it were if I wasn't sure. You jus' remember I work in Mr. Pitt's 'ouse, an' I know as much about some of 'is cases as whatever you do."

"Rubbish," he said derisively.

"Oh, yes I do! 'Cos I knows wot Mrs. Pitt does, an' Mrs. Radley . . . an' that's more'n wot you do."

He glared at her. "You got no business meddlin' in police cases. Like as not you'll do more harm than good and get yourself hurt, you stupid little girl!"

Gracie was cut to the core. She could think of no retaliation which was even remotely adequate to the insult, but she would remember it, so when the opportunity arose, she would crush him.

Tellman turned to Finn. "Mr. Hennessey, would you please tell me what you did, and anybody you saw, from seven o'clock onwards, and when you saw them. And don't forget Mr. McGinley himself. That may help us to know how he learned about the dynamite but no one else did."

"Yes . . ." Finn still looked very shaky. He had to make a considerable effort to keep his voice steady. "Like Gracie, the first thing I did was get up and shaved and dressed, then I went to Mr. McGinley's dressing room to make sure the housemaid had lit the fire, which she had, and it was all cleaned and dusted properly. The servants here are very good."

He did not see Tellman's lip curl or see him take a long breath and let it out in a sigh.

"I prepared the washstand, laid out the hairbrush, nail brush, toothbrush, and fetched the ewer of hot water, laid out the dressing gown and slippers in front of the fire to warm. Then I sharpened the razor on the strop as usual, but Mr. McGinley likes to shave himself, so I just left it all ready for him."

"What time was this?" Tellman said sourly.

"Quarter before eight," Finn replied. "I told you."

Tellman wrote it down. "Do you know when Mr. McGinley left his room?"

"For breakfast?"

"For anything."

"He went down for breakfast about quarter past eight, I imagine. I don't know because I left him just before that to clean his best boots. I needed to make more blacking."

"Make it? Don't you buy it, like anyone else?"

Finn's face showed his disdain. "Bought polish has sulfuric acid in it. It rots leather. Any decent gentleman's gentleman knows how to make it."

"Not being a gentleman's gentleman, I wouldn't know," Tellman responded.

"Twelve ounces each of ivory black and treacle, four ounces each of spermaceti oil and white wine vinegar," Finn informed him helpfully. "Mix them thoroughly, of course."

"Where did you do this?" Tellman was unimpressed.

"Boot room, of course."

"You went down the men's stairs at the back?"

"Naturally."

"See anyone?"

"Wheeler, Mr. Doyle's man, the butler Dilkes, and two footmen whose names I don't know."

"Did you go into the front of the house at all?" Tellman persisted.

"I went across the hall to fetch the newspapers to iron."

"What?"

"I went across the hall to fetch the newspapers to iron them," Finn repeated. "I wanted to see if there was anything in them about Mr. Parnell. I saw Mr. Doyle coming downstairs."

"Alone?"

"Yes."

"Where did he go? Into the dining room?"

"No. He went in the other direction, but I don't know where to. I went back through the baize door with the newspapers."

"Then what?" Tellman had his pencil poised, his eyes on Finn.

Finn hesitated.

"Yer gotta tell 'im," Gracie urged. "It's important."

Finn looked wretched.

Gracie longed to lean forward and touch his hands again, but she could not do it in front of Tellman.

Tellman licked the end of his pencil.

"Mr. McGinley sent for me," Finn said shakily.

"From where? Where was he?" Tellman asked.

"What? Oh, in his room, I expect. Yes, in his room. But I met him as he was coming across the landing. He told me to go with him and to stand in the hall while he went into Mr. Radley's study. He said someone had put dynamite there and he was going to . . . to make it safe."

"I see. Thank you." Tellman took a deep breath. "I'm sorry about Mr. McGinley. Looks like he died a hero."

"Somebody murdered him," Finn said between his teeth. "I hope you get the son of the devil who did it and hang him as high as Nelson's column."

"I expect we will." Tellman looked at Gracie as if he wanted to say something further, but he changed his mind and went out. Gracie turned back to Finn, longing to be able to help. She could guess at the grief and shock which must be tearing at him, and soon it would be fear for himself also. With McGinley dead he would have no position. He would have to start looking for a new place, with all the difficulty, hardship and anxiety that was. She smiled at him tentatively, not to mean anything, except that she understood and she cared.

He smiled back and reached up with his hand to touch hers.

Pitt found Tellman about an hour later, standing in the havoc of the study.

"What did you learn?" he asked quietly. The door had not yet been replaced.

Tellman recounted to Pitt what Finn had told him.

"That's more or less what we know." Pitt nodded. "Anything else?"

"Maid came in and lit the fire just after seven this morning," Tellman replied, consulting his notebook. "She dusted the desk and refilled the inkstand and checked there was enough paper, wax, sand, tapers, and so on. She opened the drawer down this side because that's where they're kept. There was nothing wrong with it then. And she's been with the house since Lord Ashworth's time."

"So it was after seven this morning, and the bomb went off at about twenty-five to ten. That's two and a half hours."

"All the servants were either upstairs or in the servants' hall having their own breakfast," Tellman replied. "Or else about their duties in the laundry, the stillroom or wherever it is they do these things. I never imagined there was so much to do to keep half a dozen ladies and gentlemen turned out as they like to be, and fed, housed and entertained." His face expressed very clearly his opinion of the morality of that.

"Could any of them have come through and put the dynamite in here?" Pitt made no comment on the number of the servants.

"No. It'd take a fair while to set up a bomb with dynamite, and something to trigger it off when Mr. Radley opened the drawer. You couldn't just put it in and run away."

"It seems all the women were either with their maids or else at breakfast, and then with each other," Pitt said slowly. He had spoken to them all, although he had never seriously thought that it would turn out to be a woman who had put the dynamite in Jack's study. "Except Mrs. Greville. Not unnaturally, she still likes to spend some time alone."

Tellman said nothing.

"That leaves the men," Pitt said somberly. "Which means either Moynihan or Doyle. Piers Greville was with Miss Baring."

"Moynihan was in the conservatory with Mrs. McGinley," Tellman said with a shake of his head. "Your Gracie saw them there. Of course, there's nothing to say they didn't do it together, to get rid of McGinley so they could marry each other . . . if that sort like to marry."

"They'd marry," Pitt said dryly, "if they could ever settle on which church . . . if either would have them. I gather both sides feel very strongly about not marrying the other."

Tellman rolled his eyes very slightly. "He's daft enough about her he would have killed her husband, and I wouldn't swear she'd not have helped him. Then there is Doyle," Tellman pointed out. "He was seen in the hall twice, once by Hennessey and once by Gracie."

"I think I had better go and speak to Mr. Doyle," Pitt said with reluctance. He knew Eudora was afraid for her brother. She had been since Greville's death. With McGinley's death she would be more so . . . perhaps with cause. Pitt did not want to think so, for he had liked the man. But the fact that McGinley had been the only one aware of the dynamite, apart from whoever placed it there, made it look more and more as if it could have been Doyle. Had they quarreled about the ways of bringing about the ends they both sought? And had Doyle been prepared to use more violence, and McGinley guessed it?

They met in the boudoir, Eudora standing by the window. She watch them both, her eyes going from Padraig's face to Pitt's and back again.

"Yes, I crossed the hall," Padraig admitted, a flash of anger in his eyes. "I did not go into the study. I went from the front door to the side door to see what the weather was like, then I went back upstairs."

"No, you didn't, Mr. Doyle," Pitt said quietly. "You were seen in the hall after Hennessey collected the papers to iron them."

"What?" Doyle demanded.

Eudora looked terrified. She stood like a cornered animal, as if she would flee if there were only a way past them. She looked at Padraig, then at Pitt, and he felt the force of her plea for help even though she did not speak it.

"McGinley's valet took the papers to be ironed before you were seen in the hall by my wife's maid," Pitt explained. He glanced at Eudora and back again. "You have made a mistake in your account. . . . You had better think again, Mr. Doyle. Did you go into Mr. Radley's study?"

Padraig stared at him.

Pitt thought for a moment he was going to refuse to answer. The blood rose hot in his face.

"Yes, I did . . . and I swear before God there was nothing in the drawer when I was there. Whoever put the dynamite in there did it after I left. I was only there a minute or so. I took a piece of paper from the drawer. I'd used all mine. I was making notes for the conference."

Eudora moved over to stand beside him, slipping her arm through his, but she was shaking, and whether Padraig knew it or not, Pitt knew she did not believe him. She would be on the brink of tears if she had had the emotional energy left, but she was exhausted. He longed to be able to help her, but he could not except by pursuing the proof against Padraig and finding a flaw in it.

"Did you pass the conservatory?" Pitt asked.

A bitter smile flashed across Padraic's face. "Yes. Why?"

"You saw Fergal Moynihan and Iona McGinley?"

"Yes. But I doubt they saw me. They were extremely occupied with each other."

"Doing what?"

"For god's sake, man!" Padraig exploded, his arm tightening around his sister's shoulders.

"What were they doing?" Pitt repeated. "Exactly! If it's not fit for Mrs. Greville's ears, then I'm sure she will excuse us."

"I am not leaving you," Eudora stated, staring at Pitt and at the same time tightening her grasp on Padraig's arm.

"When I passed to go to the study they were having a rather heated argument," Padraig said, watching Pitt closely, his eyes narrowed.

"Describe it," Pitt commanded. "What did you see?"

At last Padraig understood. "Moynihan was standing in front of the camellia bush and leaning forward a little with both his hands spread wide. I could not hear what he was saying, but he appeared to be exasperated. He was speaking with very exaggerated care, as one does when one is about to lose patience. He waved his arms around and hit an orchid. He knocked off a stem of flowers and was very annoyed. He picked it up and threw it behind one of the potted palms. She was standing in front of him. That is all I saw."

"And on the way back, with the paper?"

"They had obviously made up the disagreement. They were in each other's arms and kissing very . . . intimately. Her clothes were in considerable disarray, especially her bodice." He winced with distaste and glanced at Eudora and away again, perhaps sensitive to the fact that she might find passionate adultery a painful subject. "I have no intention of describing it further."

"Thank you," Pitt acknowledged it. Then he saw Eudora's smile and hoped profoundly that Fergal Moynihan would bear out what Padraig had said.

He found Moynihan in the morning room with Carson O'Day. He was profoundly embarrassed but faced Pitt rather belligerently.

"Yes, I did break the orchid, quite accidentally. We had a . . . a slight disagreement. It lasted only a moment. It was nothing at all, really."

"You made it up again very quickly?" Pitt asked.

"Yes. Why? How do you know about it? What in heaven's name does one broken orchid matter?"

"Quite a bit, Mr. Moynihan. You made it up very quickly? How long after you broke the orchid? Five minutes? Ten minutes?"

"No, not at all! More like two or three minutes—why?" He was growing angrier because he did not understand, and he plainly hated having the discussion in front of O'Day. His color was heightening with every moment, and he moved jerkily, as though eager to escape, even physically. It made Pitt more inclined to believe Padraig's account. It was acutely embarrassing behavior in which to be observed—and to later have described to a man who was, after all, from the police.

"Would you please tell me how you made it up, Mr. Moynihan?" Pitt requested with some satisfaction. There was something supercilious in Moynihan he did not like.

Fergal glared at him. "Really, Mr. Pitt! I have no intention of satisfying your prurience. I will not."

Pitt met his eyes squarely. "Then you leave me no alternative but to ask Mrs. McGinley, which will be considerably more indelicate. I would have thought in view of your professed affection for her you might have spared her that necessity." He ignored the look of loathing in Moynihan's face. "Particularly now that her husband has just been murdered, whether she cared for him or not."

"You're despicable!" Fergal said.

Pitt raised his eyebrows. "Because I require you to describe your actions in order to vindicate others from suspicion of murder, or not? Are you not as eager as the rest of us to discover the truth?"

Moynihan swore at him under his breath, briefly and viciously.

"If you please?" Pitt smiled back.

"We kissed," Fergal ground between his teeth. "I . . . I think I opened the bodice of her . . . of her gown. . . ." His eyes were daggers.

"You think?" Pitt said curiously. "You don't find it something you remember?"

"I did!" He turned to give O'Day, who was clearly amused, a look of loathing.

"Thank you," Pitt acknowledged it. "It seems, from the other description I have already heard, that McGinley could not have been in the study long enough to have wired up the dynamite."

"I hope you appreciate that it also means I didn't?" Fergal said sarcastically.

"Of course I appreciate it." Pitt still smiled. "That is of the utmost importance. You were naturally the first in my mind to suspect. You have a classic motive."

Fergal blushed scarlet.

"And Mrs. McGinley too." Pitt opened his eyes very wide. "A

trifle ungallant for me to have to remind you it also removes her from suspicion."

Fergal was incredulous. "You couldn't have thought . . . that she . . ."

"She would not be the first woman to murder an unwanted husband in order to elope with someone else," Pitt pointed out reasonably. "Or to conspire with a lover to that end."

Fergal was too angry to reply, nor could he think of an argument, which was plain in his face.

"Then who did?" O'Day asked, wrinkling his brow. "You seem to have reasoned yourself into an impasse, Mr. Pitt."

It was true, although it was not pleasant having O'Day point it out.

Fergal smiled for the first time.

"Then we shall just have to go over everyone's movements again," Pitt replied. "And verify them again. Obviously there is a mistake somewhere." And with that he left and went to search for Tellman.

Charlotte left the scene of the explosion and found herself physically shaking and a little dizzy. Her eyes stung from the dust in the air and she was gulping, which made the dust catch in her throat as well, and she started to cough. For a moment the hallway swayed around her and she thought she was going to fall. She grasped the arm of a big wooden settle and sat down hard. She was obliged to lean forward and lower her head until the swimming sensation cleared.

She straightened up slowly, her eyes prickling with tears. This was ridiculous. She wished Pitt were beside her, warm and strong and concerned, to comfort her fear and assure himself she was all right, not frightened, not distraught. But of course he was trying to do his job, not look after a wife who ought to be strong enough to look after herself. There was nothing in coping with death or fear of death which a woman should not be able to do just as well as a man . . . even violent death and the blasting apart of a room. It did not require any physical strength or specialized knowledge, just self-control and a greater concern for others than a concentration upon oneself. She should be supporting Pitt, helping, not looking for him to help her.

And Emily. She should be thinking how to comfort Emily, who was obviously terrified, and with good reason. That dynamite had been intended to kill Jack. It was only the most extraordinary chance that Lorcan McGinley had gone to the study and, without asking, opened the drawer.

Or had he known the dynamite was there and, as some people were already suggesting, tried to defuse it—and given his life in the attempt?

Poor Iona. She must be feeling riddled with guilt. And even worse than that, did she even wonder if Fergal had had something to do with it?

The most helpful thing Charlotte could do would be to discover who had killed Greville and tried to kill Jack, but she had no idea where to begin. Pitt had confided unusually little in her this time. Perhaps that was because he had not discovered much of meaning, but more probably it was because she had been so preoccupied with trying to help Emily with this ghastly party that she had seen him so seldom, and then for only moments.

She had not asked him about Greville's death. She only knew that he had been hit over the head and then pulled under the water in the bath, and everyone knew that by now. She also knew that the valet Finn Hennessey, whom Gracie had mentioned several times, Carson O'Day and Lorcan McGinley all accounted for each other, so they could not be guilty. Eudora was obviously afraid it was Padraig Doyle, and after Charlotte had found how Greville had behaved towards Eudora, it would not be surprising if her brother had a powerful hatred of him. Although killing him would not necessarily make Eudora's life easier or happier. But how often did people with violent and uncontrolled tempers ever think like that?

And Eudora did seem to be a woman who awoke in men a strong desire to protect her. She looked so feminine and so vulnerable. Of course, some women could affect that when actually they were as capable of defending themselves as anyone. But she did not doubt the reality of Eudora's pain and fear, or the sincerity of her behavior. It might have been easier if she had.

Eudora's need for comfort was real, and Pitt was responding to it as he always did. It was part of the reason Charlotte loved him so much. Were he to lose that quality it would be as if a coldness had entered her life, a darkness that would shadow everything and take the heart from the happiness she possessed.

Pitt needed to give, to support and help and protect. Charlotte sat on the settle and looked across the dust-clouded hall and saw Pitt's concern as he looked at Eudora. It was so much of what was best in him. And yet she wished it was she he was comforting, not Eudora. But he did not see Charlotte as in need of him. And in truth she was not. Wanting was different.

Should she pretend to need? Would he be happier, love her more, if she pretended to be more fragile, more dependent than she was? Was she pushing him away by her independence? Was Eudora weaker or only cleverer—and more lovable?

But it was dishonest to pretend. Would Pitt not hate her if she affected to need him when she really could have managed and been useful, instead of an additional burden to him?

Perhaps she could do both if she were only a little subtler? Emily always seemed to manage it . . . which was a humbling thought.

But she had to be herself, at least for the time being. She was too uncertain to try anything else yet. If she could only help solve this wretched crime, then things could return to something like normal. Eudora Greville would go away. Pitt would have helped her, and that would be the end of her need of him.

Charlotte wished there was someone she could talk to, but Emily had walked past her without even seeming to see her. She had no time to give attention to Charlotte or be bothered with her emotions.

All her thoughts were centered on Jack. In her place Charlotte would have been the same.

No one was threatening Pitt's life, but this miserable failure would not help his career. He would be held responsible for not preventing Greville's death. Never mind that nobody could have. No policeman in the world, no matter how brilliant, would have followed Greville into the bath to stop someone from coming in and drowning him. It was hopelessly unfair!

She wished Great-Aunt Vespasia were there. But of course she was in London.

Pitt had been to London yesterday on the train. There was no reason why she should not go on the train today. She stood up and walked towards the library and the telephone.

CHAPTER NINE

Having made the decision to go to London, Charlotte wasted no time whatever in completing the necessary arrangements. She told Pitt she was going to visit Vespasia.

"Now?" he said incredulously.

"Yes. There are things with which I think she may be able to help." She could not tell him what. If he pressed her, she would have to invent something.

"What about Emily?" he argued. "She needs you here. She's terrified for Jack. And with reason." He stopped suddenly. "I think you should be here."

"I'll come straight back." She would not be persuaded out of it. The scene with Eudora was sharp in her mind. If she were going to fight, she needed to talk with someone first, and Vespasia was the only person who might understand. She felt just as vulnerable as Eudora or Emily, although for entirely different reasons. "I won't be long," she promised, then kissed him quickly on the cheek and turned and left.

Emily was occupied, which was excellent. Charlotte left a message with Gwen. Then, after having spoken briefly to Gracie, she requested Emily's second-best carriage to take her to the railway station for the next train. At the station she made enquiries as to the hour of the return trains in the evening and arranged to have the carriage meet her from the one which arrived in Ashworth at three minutes before ten.

"Well, my dear," Vespasia said with interest, regarding her carefully. Charlotte was very smart in her deep hunting green traveling suit and cape with fur trim, borrowed from Emily. Although the chill wind had stung some color into her cheeks, Vespasia was quite capable of seeing the anxiety beneath the surface well-being.

"How are you, Aunt Vespasia?" Charlotte enquired, going forward into the withdrawing room with its warm, delicate colors and old-fashioned, almost Georgian lines. There was far more light in it, more simplicity, than the modern design fashionable ever since the Queen came to the throne fifty-three years before.

"I am as well as I was when you spoke to me on the telephone this morning," Vespasia replied. "Sit down and warm yourself. Daisy can bring us tea, and you can tell me what concerns you so much you are prepared to leave Ashworth Hall and return to London for a day." Her eyes narrowed a little and she regarded Charlotte with some gravity. "You do not look at all yourself. I can see that something exceedingly unpleasant has happened. You had better tell me about it."

Charlotte realized she was still trembling very slightly at the memory of it, even though she had exercised her mind on other things for the entire duration of the journey on the train, but the effort had been immense. Now it was all as vivid as the moment after it happened. She even found her voice a little high.

"Someone exploded a bomb at Ashworth Hall this morning, in Jack's study. . . ."

Vespasia went very pale.

"Oh, my dear, how dreadful!"

Charlotte should have been more thoughtful. She should never have told Vespasia like this. She clasped her quickly.

"It's all right! Jack isn't hurt! He wasn't there at the time."

"Thank you," Vespasia said with some dignity. "You may let go of me, my dear. I am not going to faint. I presume if Jack were hurt, you would have told me so immediately and not in this roundabout fashion. Was anyone else injured? Who was it who did such a fearful thing, and why?"

"Someone was killed, an Irishman named Lorcan McGinley." She took a deep breath, steadying herself with an effort of will. "And we don't know who did it. It is all part of a long story."

Vespasia indicated the large chair to one side of the fire, burning high up in the grate and sending warmth throughout the room.

Charlotte sat down gratefully. Now that she was there it was less easy to put her fears into words. As always, Vespasia sat upright, straight-backed, her silver hair curled and braided in a coronet, her silver-gray eyes under their hooded lids bright with intelligence and concern. Lady Vespasia Cumming-Gould was an aristocrat from an ancient family with many lands, obligations and knowledge of honor and privilege. She could freeze an impertinence at twenty feet and make the unfortunate trespasser wish he or she had never spoken. She could trade wit with philosophers, courtiers and playwrights. She had smiled at dukes and princes and made them feel honored by it. In her eighties the bones of her face were still exquisite, her coloring delicate, her movements a good deal stiffer but not without the pride and assurance of the past. One could easily believe that half a century ago she had been the greatest beauty of the age. Now she was old enough and rich enough not to care in the slightest what society thought of her, and she was enjoying the exquisite freedom it gave her to be utterly herself.

It was Charlotte's immense good fortune that Emily's first husband had been Vespasia's great-nephew. Vespasia had become fond of both Emily and Charlotte, and more remarkably, considering the chasm between their situations, of Pitt as well.

Vespasia was looking more closely at Charlotte. "Since it is apparently so serious," she said gravely, "perhaps you had better begin at the beginning, wherever you believe that to be."

That was easy. "It started with going to Ashworth Hall to protect Ainsley Greville," Charlotte replied.

"I see." Vespasia nodded. "For political reasons, I assume? Yes, of course. One of our more notable Catholic diplomats; discreetly Catholic, naturally. He is not a man to allow his religion to get in the way of his career. He married Eudora Doyle, a very beautiful woman from one of the outstanding Irish Catholic Nationalist families, but they have always lived here in England." A ghost of irony crossed her features. "Is it to do with this absurd Parnell-O'Shea business?"

"I don't know," Charlotte replied. "I don't think so. Although perhaps indirectly it is. I'm not sure. . . ."

Vespasia put her long, thin hand with its moonstone rings very gently on Charlotte's lap.

"What is it, my dear? You seem very deeply troubled. It can only be some person for whom you care very much. From the tone in which you told me of his death, I assume it is not the unfortunate Mr. McGinley, and I cannot imagine that it is Mr. Greville. He is not a very pleasant man. He has great charm, considerable intelligence, and certainly diplomatic skill, but a basically self-serving nature."

"He did have," Charlotte agreed with the shadow of a smile.

"Don't tell me he has had a sudden conversion to the light," Vespasia said incredulously. "That I must see. . . ."

Charlotte laughed in spite of herself, but it ended abruptly.

"No. Thomas was there in order to protect him from threats of assassination, and I am afraid he did not succeed." She took a deep breath. "He was murdered. . . ."

"Oh." Vespasia sat very still. "I see. I am sorry. And I assume you do not yet know who is responsible?"

"No . . . not yet, though it will be one of the Irishmen who are staying there this weekend. . . ."

"But that is not what you have come to see me about." Vespasia put her head a little to one side. "I am tolerably well-acquainted with Irish politics, but not with the identity of individual assassins."

"No . . . of course not." Charlotte wanted to smile at the idea, but the reality was too painful. She remembered that morning vividly, the physical shock of the explosion, and then the realization a moment later of what it was. She had not been close to such powerful violence before. There was something quite new and terrible about an actual room being blown apart.

"I think you had better leave the beginning and come to the middle." Vespasia slid her hand over Charlotte's. "It is obviously very serious. Ainsley Greville has been murdered, and now this Mr. McGinley, and so far you do not know who has killed them, except that it is someone still at Ashworth Hall. You have experienced crimes before, and Thomas has solved some exceedingly difficult murders. Why does this trouble you so much you have left Ashworth and come here?"

Charlotte looked down at her hands, and Vespasia's older, thinner, blue-veined hand over them.

"Because Eudora Greville is so vulnerable," she said quietly. "In the space of a few days she has lost everything, not only her husband—and therefore her safety, her position, and whatever he earned, if that matters—but what really hurts is that she has lost what she believed he was." She looked at Vespasia. "She has been forced to learn that he was a philanderer, and uglier than that, a man who used people without any regard for their feelings, or even for what happened to them as a result."

"That is very unpleasant," Vespasia agreed. "But, my dear, do you suppose she really had no suspicion? Is she completely naive?" She shook her head a little. "I doubt it. What hurts is that the rest of the world will know it too, or at least that part of the world with which she is familiar. It will become impossible for her to deny it to herself any longer, which is something we all tend to do when the truth is too painful."

"No, there is more than that." Charlotte looked up and met Vespasia's eyes. In hard, angry words full of pain she told her about Doll.

Vespasia's face was bleak. She was an old woman and she had seen much that was hideous, but even so, this twisted deep in her, in her memory of holding her own children, in the miracle and the fragility and the infinite value of life.

"Then he was a man with much evil in him," she said when Charlotte had finished. "That will be very difficult indeed for his wife to learn to live with."

"And his son," Charlotte added.

"Very difficult indeed," Vespasia agreed. "I feel more deeply for the son. Why is it Eudora who bothers you more?"

"She doesn't." Charlotte smiled at her own vulnerability. "But she does Thomas. She's the perfect maiden in distress for him to rescue."

The seconds ticked past on the clock on the mantel, its black filigree hands jerking forward with each one. The maid brought the tea and poured it, hot and fragrant, then withdrew and left them alone.

"I see," Vespasia said at last. "And you want to be a maiden in distress too?"

Charlotte was prompted to laugh and cry at the same time. She was closer to tears than she had realized.

"No!" She shook her head. "I don't need rescuing. And I'm no good at pretending."

"Would you like to be?" Vespasia passed Charlotte her tea.

"No, of course I wouldn't!" Charlotte took the cup. "No . . . I'm sorry. I mean . . . I mean, I don't want games, pretending. If it isn't real, it's no good."

Vespasia smiled. "Then what are you asking?"

There was no purpose in putting it off any longer, refusing to put words to her fear did not make it any less real.

"Perhaps Thomas needs me to be more like Eudora? Maybe he needs someone to rescue?" She searched Vespasia's face for denial, hoping to find it.

"I think he does," Vespasia said gently. "You ask a great deal of him in your marriage, Charlotte. You ask him to strive very high. If he is to be all that you need of him, if he is to live up to what you could have had in your own social class, then he cannot ever be less than the very best he is able. There can be no easy choices for him, no allowing himself to relax, or commit to second best. Perhaps sometimes you forget that." Her hand tightened over Charlotte's. "You may at times remember only the sacrifices you have made, the gown you don't have, the servants, the parties you don't attend, the savings and economies you have to make. But you don't have an impossible yardstick to measure yourself against."

"Neither does Thomas," Charlotte said, aghast at the thought. "I don't ever ask for—"

"Of course you don't," Vespasia agreed. "But you are at Ashworth Hall, your sister's house . . . or to be more correct, one of her houses. I imagine poor Jack does not always find that comfortable either."

The coals settled in the fire and burned up more brightly.

"But I can't help it," Charlotte protested. "We are there because Thomas was called to go, not for me. It is his position that took us there."

"Not because Emily is your sister?"

"Well . . . yes, of course that made him the obvious person . . . but even so . . ."

"I know you did not choose it." Vespasia smiled very slightly and shook her head. "All I am saying is that if Thomas finds it agreeable that Eudora Doyle—I mean, Greville—should lean upon him and find comfort in his strength, it is not surprising, or discreditable, in either of them. And if it hurts you, or you are troubled by it, then you have the choice of pretending to be in distress yourself and masking your strength in weakness so that he will turn his attention to you instead." She lowered her voice a little. "Is that what you wish?"

Charlotte was appalled. "No, it would be despicable! I should hate myself. I should never be able to meet his eyes."

"Then that is one question answered," Vespasia agreed.

"But what if . . . what if that is what he . . . wants?" Charlotte said desperately. "What if I lose part of him because I don't . . . don't need . . . that. . . ."

"Charlotte, my dear, nobody is everything to someone else, nor should they seek to be," Vespasia said gently. "Moderate your demands at times, disguise some of your less-fortunate attributes, learn to keep your own counsel in certain matters, sometimes give more generous praise than is merited, but be true to the core of yourself. Silence does not hurt, at times, nor patience, but lies always do. Would you wish him to pretend for you?"

Charlotte closed her eyes. "I should hate it. It would be the end of everything real. How could I ever believe him again?"

"Then you have answered your own question, haven't you?" Vespasia sat back a little. "Allow him to rescue others. That is part of his nature, perhaps the very best part. Don't resent it. And don't underestimate his strength to love you as you are." The fire collapsed still further, and she ignored it. "Believe me, from time to time you will find in yourself enough weaknesses to satisfy him." Her eyes flickered with amusement. "Do your best. Never be less than you are in the hope of earning someone else's love. If he catches you in it he will hate you for what you have judged of him, and far worse than that, you will hate yourself. That is the most destructive of all things."

Charlotte stared at her.

Vespasia reached for the bell to ask the maid to come to stoke the fire.

"Now we shall have luncheon," she said, rising to her feet with the use of her silver-topped ebony cane, declining Charlotte's arm. "I have poached salmon and a few vegetables, and then apple tart. I hope that will satisfy. And you can tell me about this wretched Irish business, and I shall tell you about the absurd divorce of Mrs. O'Shea. We can laugh about it together, and perhaps weep a little."

"Is it sad?" Charlotte asked, walking beside her to the smaller, wood-floored breakfast room, where Vespasia more often ate when she was alone. It had a row of floral-curtained windows looking onto a paved corner of the garden. On two sides glass-fronted cases of porcelain, crystal ornaments, vases and plates. A cherrywood gateleg table was set for two.

"Yes it is," Vespasia answered when the butler had helped her to her seat and she had unfolded her linen napkin.

Charlotte was surprised. She had not thought Vespasia would grieve over such a thing. But then perhaps she did not know Vespasia as well as she had presumed. More than seventy years of her life had passed before Charlotte had even met her. It was an impertinence to imagine she could guess at most of it.

The butler served them a light consommé and withdrew.

Vespasia saw Charlotte's face and laughed.

"Sad for Ireland, my dear," she corrected. "The whole thing is so patently ridiculous!" She began her soup. "Parnell is a humorless devil at the best of times. He takes himself so terribly seriously. It is a Protestant failing. It is certainly not an Irish one. Love or hate them, you cannot accuse the Irish at large of a lack of wit. And yet Parnell has behaved like someone in a badly written farce. Even now he still does not believe that his audience will laugh at him and, of course, cease to take him seriously."

Charlotte began her soup also. It was delicious.

"Will they?" she asked, thinking of Carson O'Day, his ambitions, and what his family would expect of him, his father, and the elder brother whose place he had to fill.

"My dear, would you?" Vespasia's fine brows arched even higher. "Apparently when Captain and Mrs. O'Shea took a house in Brighton, within two or three days a Mr. Charles Stewart appeared, wearing a cloth cap over his eyes." She kept her face straight with difficulty. "He called quite often, but almost always when Captain O'Shea was out. He always came up via the beach way and took Mrs. O'Shea out driving, never in daylight, always after dark."

"In a cloth cap," Charlotte said incredulously, forgetting her soup. "You said he had no sense of humor. Mrs. O'Shea cannot have had either!" Her voice rose in disbelief. "How could you possibly make love with a man who crept up to your door at night when your husband was out—disguised in a cloth cap, using a false name that would fool nobody? I should be hysterical with laughter."

"That isn't all," Vespasia went on, her eyes light. "Five years ago—this affair has persisted for some very considerable time—he went to an auctioneer in Deptford who was acting as agent for a landlord in Kent." She held up her hands as she spoke. "Parnell went calling himself Mr. Fox. He was told the house in question belonged to a Mr. Preston. Parnell then said he was Clement Preston. The agent replied that he had thought he said he was a Mr. Fox. Parnell then said he was staying with a Mr. Fox, but his own name was Preston, and he would take the house for twelve months, but refused to give any references"—her eyebrows rose—"on the grounds that a man who owned horses should not be required to do so."

"Horses?" Charlotte nearly choked on her soup. "What have horses to do with it?" she demanded. "You can sell horses, or they can fall ill, or be injured, or even die."

"Nothing whatever. The music halls are going to have a wonderful time with it," Vespasia said with a smile. "Along with the cloth cap and the business of the fire escape. It is all so unbelievably grubby and incompetent." Her face became serious again. "But it is sad for Ireland. Parnell may not have realized it yet, and his immediate supporters may give him a vote of confidence, out of loyalty and not to be seen to desert him, but the people at large will never follow him now." She sighed and permitted the butler, who had returned, to remove the last of her soup and to serve the salmon and vegetables.

When he was gone she looked at Charlotte again, her eyes grave. "Since Ainsley Greville is dead, I presume the political issues for which he worked are now sacrificed, which will have been the reason for his murder."

"No, Jack has taken his place, at least temporarily," Charlotte replied. "It was almost certainly to kill Jack that the dynamite was placed in the study this morning. Poor Emily is terrified, but Jack has no honorable choice but to continue in Greville's place and do the best he can."

"How very dreadful," Vespasia said with considerable alarm. "You must all be most distressed. I wish there were some way in which I could help, but the Irish Problem is centuries old, and bedeviled by ignorance, myth and hatred on all sides. The tragedies it has caused are legion."

"I know." Charlotte looked down at her plate, thinking of the tale Gracie had told her. "We have Padraig Doyle and Carson O'Day with us."

Vespasia shook her head and a flicker of anger crossed her face.

"That miserable business," she said grimly. "That was one of the worst, typifying everything that is wrong with the whole sordid, treacherous affair."

"But we betrayed them," Charlotte pointed out. "Some soldier called Chinnery raped Neassa Doyle and then fled to England." She did not try to keep the rage and disgust out of her voice. "And Drystan O'Day was his friend! No wonder the Irish don't trust us. When I hear something like that, I'm ashamed to be English."

Vespasia leaned back in her chair, her face weary, her salmon forgotten.

"Don't be, Charlotte. We have certainly done some dreadful things in our history, things that sicken the heart and darken the soul, but this was not one of them."

Charlotte waited. If Vespasia did not know the truth of the matter, perhaps she did not need to. She was an old lady. It would serve no purpose to harrow her with it.

"You have no need to be gentle with me," Vespasia said with the ghost of a smile. "I have seen more to haunt one's dreams than you have, my dear. Neassa Doyle was not raped. She was followed by her own brothers, and it was they who cut off her hair because they thought she was a whore, and with a Protestant man at that. . . ."

Charlotte was appalled. It was so horrible, so utterly unlike the story she had heard and accepted, instinctively she drew breath to deny it.

"It was they who killed her and left her for Drystan O'Day to find," Vespasia went on. "In their eyes she had betrayed them, their family in front of its peers, and their faith before God. She deserved not only death but shame as well."

"For falling in love?" Charlotte was confused, full of anger, darkness and quarreling emotions in this calmly elegant room with the sunlight slanting across the polished floor, the flowered curtains at the windows with their Georgian panes and the honeysuckle tangled beyond, and the white linen on the table, the silver and the trail of dark leaves in the cut glass vase.

"For being prepared to elope with a Protestant," Vespasia answered. "She had let down her tribe, if you like. Love is no excuse when honor is at stake."

"Whose honor?" Charlotte demanded. "Hasn't she the right to choose for herself whom she will marry, and if she is prepared to pay the price of leaving her own people to do it? I know there is a cost, we all know that, but if you love someone enough, you pay it. Perhaps she didn't believe their faith? Did they ever think of that?"

Vespasia smiled, but her eyes were tired, pale silver.

"Of course not, Charlotte. You know better than to ask. If you belong to a clan, you pay the price of that too. The freedom not to be answerable to your family, your tribe, is a very great loneliness.

"You were more fortunate than most women. I think sometimes you don't fully appreciate that. You chose to marry outside your class, and your family's choice for you, but they did not blame you for it or cut you off. Your social ostracism was a natural result of your marriage, not the act of your family. They remained close to you, never criticizing your choice or seeking to change your mind." Her expression was sad and tired, her eyes far away. "Neassa had the courage to make her choice too, but her family did not understand. To them, to her brothers, it was a shame they would not live with."

"But what about Alexander Chinnery?" Charlotte had forgotten him for a moment. "What did he do? How did you know it was not he who killed her, as they said?"

"Because by June eighth, Alexander Chinnery was already dead," Vespasia said softly. "He was drowned in Liverpool Harbour trying to save a boy who had caught his leg in a rope and been pulled into the water."

"Then why did both the Catholics and the Protestants believe it was he who killed Neassa Doyle?" Charlotte pressed. "And why did they think she was raped if she wasn't?"

"Why do stories grow around anything?" Vespasia picked up her fork and began to eat again, slowly. "Because someone leaps to a conclusion . . . a conclusion that suits the emotions they feel and wish to arouse in the others. After a while everyone believes it, and then even if the truth is known, it is too late to tell it. Everyone has too much invested in the myth, and the truth would destroy what they have built and make liars of them."

"They aren't lying, they really believe it." Charlotte picked up her wineglass, full of clean, cold water. "I suppose it was thirty years ago, and there's no one about now who was involved, at least not in present-day politics. And they aren't going to tell people they lied then."

"Nobody would believe them if they did," Vespasia argued. "The powers of the legends which tell us who we are, and justify what we want to do, is far too great to take notice of a few inconvenient facts and dates."

"You are sure?" Charlotte urged, her fork held up in one hand. "Couldn't Chinnery have died later? Maybe the same date, but the following year? To think her own brothers murdered her like that, cutting off her hair first, and then his people let Drystan think it was the Doyles, so he attacked them and was shot! Or did they know it was the Doyles?" She found her hand clenching on her fork, and her stomach knotted.

"Yes, they told Drystan it was," Vespasia answered. "With the obvious result that he went mad with rage and grief and attacked them." Her voice was hard. "That way the Catholics could blame the Protestants for seducing one of their women and for allying with an English traitor, which resulted in her rape and murder; and the Protestants could blame the Catholics for roughly the same thing; and they could all blame us. And there was no one left alive to say otherwise."

"Did they know Chinnery was dead?"

"No, I doubt that." Vespasia shook her head. "But they knew his denial would convince no one, and after that he would be withdrawn from Ireland, which was all that mattered."

"But what about Chinnery's family?" Charlotte asked. "Don't they want his name cleared? That's a monstrous crime he is accused of."

"It is cleared, as far as they are concerned. He died a hero's death in Liverpool Harbour."

"But no one knows that!" Charlotte protested angrily.

"Yes, they do. It was in the Liverpool newspapers at the time, and his family lived in Liverpool."

"In the newspapers?" Charlotte let her fork drop. "Then it can be proved."

"To whom?" Vespasia asked dryly. "The people who tell stories about Drystan and Neassa? The poets and harpists who sing songs by hearths and by moonlight to keep the myths alive? My dear, Macbeth was actually the last High King of Scotland, when Scotland extended as far south as Yorkshire, and he ruled for seventeen peaceful and prosperous years." Her silver eyes were full of irony. "And when he died his people buried him in the sacred isle of the kings. He was succeeded by Lady Macbeth's son Lulach, as the rightful heir through his mother's line. She was a remarkable woman who instituted many reforms for the care of the widowed and orphaned." She shrugged, then speared her fork into the salmon on her plate. "But to accept that would spoil one of Shakespeare's best plays, so no one wishes to know."

"Well, I am going to find that newspaper and show people that

that particular story is a monstrous fabrication," Charlotte said with total conviction. "Macbeth is academic now, but this is still real!"

Vespasia looked at her steadily. "Are you sure that is wise? Or even that it will make any difference? People get very angry when their dreams are shown to be false. The emotion is what matters, the force which sustained the dream. We believe what we need to believe."

"The illusion fed the hatred—" Charlotte started.

"No, my dear, the hatred fed the dream. Take that dream away and another will be created to take its place." Vespasia sipped her water. "You cannot solve the Irish Problem, Charlotte. But I suppose perhaps you may make a difference to one or two people. Although I doubt very much that they will accept your word for what is in a newspaper, and how you may convince them I don't know."

Actually, neither did Charlotte. Her intention was rather more practical, but she did not wish to involve Vespasia in it, even by committing her to the knowledge. She merely smiled and continued with her meal.

When Charlotte left in the early afternoon, after having thanked Vespasia for her help and her counsel, and above all for her friendship, she took a hansom to the British Museum. She went to the reading room and asked the grim and very formal attendant if she might see the Liverpool newspapers of June of the year of 1860, and then the Irish newspapers for the same period. Fortunately, she had a very small pair of nail scissors in her reticule, something she frequently carried with her because they served in a number of emergencies, along with a file, a needle and thread, a thimble and several gold safety pins.

"Yes, miss," he said gravely. "If you will follow me, miss." He led the way along narrow aisles between enormous banks of books and papers until he found her a reading desk, then promised to return with the requested newspapers.

At the table next to her was a young man with a fierce mustache and a deadly earnest expression. He seemed utterly absorbed in a political pamphlet; he barely seemed to breathe, so intent was he upon it.

On the other side of her was an elderly gentleman of military aspect who glared at her as if she had intruded in some gentleman's club, and considering what she had it in mind to do, his suspicion was more than justified.

Her newspapers were brought, and she thanked the attendant with a charming smile—but she hoped not so charming that he would remember her.

It took her a quarter of an hour of diligent reading of print to discover both the articles she needed. It was a much more difficult thing to devise a way of cutting them out without being seen. For all she knew, to steal the pieces of newspaper might very well be a criminal offense. It would be most unfortunate to find herself under arrest and hauled off to Pitt's police station charged with vandalism and common theft!

She turned and smiled at the military gentleman.

He looked uncomfortable and swiveled to face the other way.

The student of revolution did not appear to notice either of them.

Charlotte rattled the newspaper and sniffed loudly.

The military man was startled and looked at her with disapproval.

She smiled at him radiantly.

He was profoundly unhappy. He blushed red and fished for a handkerchief to blow his nose.

She pulled out a lace handkerchief and held it out towards him, smiling even more brightly.

He regarded her with utter horror, rose from his seat and fled.

Charlotte bent very low over the newspaper, shielding it from the side of the revolutionary, and clipped out first one piece she wanted, and then the other. She was shaking and her face was hot. She was stealing and she knew it, but there was no other way to prove the truth of what she was saying.

She closed the huge ledgers and left them on the table. She glanced around to see if she could find the attendant. He appeared to be chastising an elderly lady in a mauve-colored hat. Charlotte put her head down, the pieces of paper in her reticule along with the scissors, and walked rapidly and as nearly silently as possible out of the reading room, her hand over her mouth as if she were about to be ill.

A young man made a halfhearted attempt to apprehend her, then abandoned the idea. He might have been going to ask her to replace her reading material, or account for it, but he may simply have been going to offer her assistance. She would never know.

Outside the cold air of the street was marvelous, but she was still burningly aware of the papers in her reticule and the dour face of the senior attendant. She wanted to laugh aloud at the military man, and then to run as fast as she could and be lost among the crowd. She did have a quiet chuckle, and then walked as rapidly as she could, and not attract undue attention to herself, until she saw a hansom, which she hailed, and directed it to take her to the railway station.

It was dark and bitterly cold when Charlotte arrived back at Ashworth Hall and was met by a tired footman. All the rest of the household had retired early, shaken and frightened after the day's events. The hall had been swept and dusted and mopped again, but the dust was still settling, and no amount of housework by maids with brooms or cloths could disguise the splintered wood of the study door, now rehung but still badly scarred, and definitely a trifle crooked.

"Thank you," she said politely, annoyed with herself that she was too tired to remember his name. She had been told it.

"Can I bring you anything, ma'am?" he asked dutifully.

"No, thank you. Lock up and go to bed. I shall go upstairs."

"Your maid is waiting for you, ma'am."

"Oh . . . oh, yes. Of course." She had forgotten that Gracie would be taking her lady's maid duties so seriously. She had not the heart or the strength to tell her tonight that the story Finn Hennessey had told her was substantially untrue. She had to know, but the next day would be time enough. She stopped on the stairs and turned back.

"Is everything all right?" she asked, wishing again she could recall the footman's name.

"Yes ma'am, nothing new has happened, not since this morning."

"Thank you. Good night."

"Good night, ma'am."

Upstairs, Gracie was curled up in the big chair in the dressing room, sound asleep. Her scrubbed face was free of any lines, but her skin was pale, even in the light of the single lamp, and she looked like a worn-out child. She still had her cap on, but it had slid sideways and her hair was coming undone, straight and fine, shiny and impossible to curl. She had been with Charlotte and Pitt for seven years. She was as close as a member of the family, closer than most.

It was a shame to wake her up, but she would not thank anyone for assuming she was not up to her duty. And anyway, she would waken some time in the night, stiff from lying curled up, and then she would wonder what had happened. She might be terrified Charlotte had not come home.

"Gracie," Charlotte said, touching her sleeping hand where it lay curled under her chin. It was as small as a child's, scrubbed clean like her face. "Gracie!"

Gracie stirred and slipped back into sleep again.

"Gracie," Charlotte said more firmly. "You can't stay there, you'll wake up stiffer than Mr. Pitt."

"Oh!" Gracie opened her eyes and relief flooded her face as she saw Charlotte. She straightened up and scrambled to her feet. "Oh, I'm real glad yer safe, ma'am! Yer didn't ought ter go on them trains all by yerself. The master's in bed, ma'am, but I'll lay anything 'e in't asleep yet neither."

"Thank you for waiting up for me," Charlotte replied, hiding her smile and taking off her cape as Gracie reached for it to hang it up.

"That's me job," Gracie said with satisfaction. "Yer like some 'ot water ter wash in?"

"No, cold will do very well." Charlotte shook her head. She was not sending Gracie downstairs to heat water and carry jugs up at this time of night. "And trains are perfectly safe, you know," she added. "You shouldn't worry. How was everything here?"

"Terrible." Gracie helped her unlace her boots, then undo her dress and slip it off. The boots could be cleaned in the morning, and the mud taken off the hem of her skirt, and of course her underclothes would be laundered. "Everyone's scared o' their own shadows," she said, taking the heavy skirt. "Footman popped a cork and the parlor maid near screamed the place down. Wonder she didn't shatter the gas mantles, them what's left!"

"Oh dear." Charlotte took the pins out of her hair and felt the wonderful relief as the weight of it fell and she ran her fingers through it.

Gracie unlaced her stays for her.

"I want to sleep until ten!" Charlotte said, knowing it was impossible.

"Yer like breakfast up 'ere?" Gracie asked helpfully.

"No . . . no, thank you. I shall have to get up in the morning and go down, even if only to watch and listen, or try to help Mrs. Radley."

"We in't doin' a very good job o' detectin', are we?" Gracie said unhappily. "We in't bin no 'elp ter the master at all."

"Not so far," Charlotte agreed with a sharp stab of unhappiness. "I've been more concerned about Emily and this wretched weekend." She kept her voice low, not to disturb Pitt, in the next room, if by chance he were asleep. "I don't know where to begin." She frowned. "Usually we are more use if there are women involved, families, something ordinarily human. I don't understand the issues of religion and nationalism." She poured water from the jug into the bowl and splashed it over her face. It was cold and clean, but it took her breath away.

"I can understand 'ating wot's done to yer family 'cos o' religion and nationalism," Gracie responded, handing the towel to her. "Some of them things is just tragedy like any other."

"I know," Charlotte said quickly, not wanting to get drawn into the Neassa and Drystan story tonight. "We'll have to think about it tomorrow. You must be tired now, and I know I am. Good night, Gracie, and thank you for waiting up."

"It in't nuffink, ma'am," Gracie replied, stifling a yawn, but she was pleased nonetheless.

Pitt was half asleep, too exhausted to stay awake but not able to rest properly until Charlotte was home.

"How was Vespasia?" he mumbled, hunching the blankets over himself and, without realizing it, pulling them away from her half of the bed.

"Very well," she answered, climbing in and tugging back her portion.

He grunted and allowed them out of his grasp, shivering as she let in the cold air, then moved closer to him with her cold hands and feet.

"I learned a lot," she went on, knowing he wanted only to sink back into sleep. But there might be no time the next morning, before she told Gracie. "About the old tragic romance of Neassa Doyle and Drystan O'Day."

He took a deep breath. "Does it matter?"

"It might. Alexander Chinnery didn't rape or kill her. He was already dead in Liverpool two days before."

He said nothing.

"Are you asleep?" she demanded.

"I would like to be," he replied. "It's just one more piece of tragic farce in this whole situation."

"And the Parnell-O'Shea divorce is finished, and Parnell seems to have behaved like a complete fool," she went on. "And Vespasia says he'll lose the leadership, if not straightaway, then soon. I suppose that affects the people here?"

He grunted.

"Did you learn anything?" she went on, unconsciously warming herself close to him, and making him chill. "It was very brave of Lorcan McGinley to try to defuse the bomb. Did you discover how he knew it was there?"

"No." He opened his eyes at last and turned over onto his back. "We did everything we could to trace his movements all morning, who he spoke to, where he went. None of it is any use so far."

"I'm sorry. I haven't been much help, have I?"

"It would help a lot if you would be quiet and go to sleep," he said with a smile, putting his arm around her. "Please!"

Obediently she snuggled even closer and put her head on the pillow, not speaking again.

In the morning it could no longer wait. As soon as Charlotte was dressed and the more physical and distracting part of preparing for the day was accomplished, she sat down in front of the glass and Gracie began to dress her hair. It could not be put off any further.

"I saw Lady Vespasia when I was in London yesterday . . ." she began.

" 'Ow was she?" Gracie asked without stopping what she was doing. It was part of a lady's maid's job to be able to conduct a pleasant conversation while at the same time doing something useful. Anyway, she had an immense admiration for Lady Vespasia, and was more in awe of her than of anyone else she could think of, even the commissioner of police . . . perhaps not the Queen. But then she had never met the Queen, and she might not even like her. She had heard she was rather critical and hardly ever laughed.

"She was very well, thank you," Charlotte replied. "I told her what was happening here, of course."

"I expect she was upset," Gracie said, pursing her lips. "It bein' so nasty for the master, an' all, an' for Mr. Radley."

"Yes, of course she was. She knows quite a lot about Irish politics, and all the things that have happened."

"I wish she 'ad an answer for it," Gracie said with feeling. "Some of them things is enough to make the angels weep." Her face tightened as she spoke, and an overwhelming sadness engulfed her. "When I think o' that poor girl wot got raped an' killed 'cos she were beautiful and loved someone on the other side, an' wot we English done to 'er, I'm fair ashamed."

"You don't need to be," Charlotte said clearly. "We—"

"Oh, I know it weren't us," Gracie interrupted, her voice urgent and a little hoarse. "But it were still English, so that's kind of us."

"No, that's what I mean." Charlotte swiveled on the seat till she was facing Gracie. "Listen to me! We've done plenty of things that are wrong in Ireland. There's no arguing that. But the murder of Neassa Doyle was nothing to do with us. Look!" And she stood up and went to her reticule, from which she pulled the two pieces of newspaper she had stolen in London. "You can read this, most especially you can read the dates. Alexander Chinnery died in Liverpool two days before Neassa Doyle was killed by her own brothers. And thank God, she wasn't raped at all."

Gracie looked at the pieces of paper, sounding out the words. She stared at them so long Charlotte was on the verge of offering to read them for her, if perhaps she found the print difficult or some of the words too long.

Then Gracie looked up, her eyes wide and troubled.

"That's wicked, that is," she said slowly. "Think of all them people wot believed that lie. All them songs an' stories, an' all them people 'atin' Chinnery, an' 'e never done it at all. Wot about all them other stories? 'Ow many o' them is lies?"

"I've no idea," Charlotte answered. "Probably some, not all. The thing is that hatred can become a habit until you do it for its own sake, long after you've forgotten the reason. You begin to look for reasons to justify the way you feel, and then you create them. Don't let them make you feel guilty for something that has nothing to do with you, Gracie. And don't accept that all the songs and stories are true."

"Do you think that if they knew the truth, Mr. Doyle and Mr.

O'Day would feel better about each other?" Gracie asked with a very faint lift of hope in her voice.

"No," Charlotte answered without hesitation. "Their families were in the wrong. Nobody ever feels better for knowing that."

"Even if it's the truth?"

"Especially if it's the truth."

Nevertheless, when she had time, after breakfast, Gracie went up to Charlotte's room and took the two pieces of newspaper, then went to look for Finn Hennessey. Surely he would want to know the truth? Charlotte might be right about some people hating from habit, but Finn was not like that. He hurt for the real suffering of his people, not the imaginary.

She found him in the boot room, but she waited until Mr. O'Day's valet had gone and he was alone before she went in. He still looked pale after his concussion, and he was very grave. He had no job anymore, no reason to polish boots or brush coats or see to any of the other tasks of a gentleman's gentleman, but he did it automatically. It was better than standing around idle. He had a pair of boots now. Perhaps they were somebody else's and he was merely helping.

" 'Ow yer feelin'?" she asked, standing in the doorway and looking at him anxiously. "I bet yer got a crackin' 'eadache."

He smiled thinly. "Sure I have, Gracie. Like a dozen little men with hammers were shut in there an' trying to get out. But it'll pass. That's a lot more than can be said for some."

"Yer got anythin' for it?" she asked sympathetically. "I'll get yer summink if yer like."

"No, thank you," he declined, relaxing rather more. "I took something already."

"I'm terribly sorry about Mr. McGinley," she said, looking at him as he leaned against the bench, the light shining on his dark head. There was a grace in him unlike that in anyone else, almost a kind of music. And he cared so much. There was nothing in him that was lukewarm, nothing indifferent or callous to the pain of others. It must be terrible to be part of a people who had suffered so much, being the victim of such deep wrongs. She admired him for his compassion, his anger and his courage. He was a bit like Pitt, really, fighting for justice in his own way. Perhaps she should care for her own people more, be concerned to fight for better things for them? Who were her own people? The poor in London? Those who had grown up cold and hungry and ignorant like herself, fighting for every scrap of food, for a place of shelter and a little warmth, fighting to stay alive without stealing or going into prostitution?

Here she was in Ashworth Hall, living like a lady and trying her best to forget about them. Would Finn despise her if he knew that? She did not want to go back to Clerkenwell or anything like the people she had left behind. How do you fight for change for them, except by changing yourself?

"Mrs. Pitt went up ter town yesterday, ter see 'er great-aunt," she said aloud. Thinking of Vespasia always gave her a little lift of excitement, like a beam of sunshine.

Finn looked surprised. "Did she? All the way up to London, after what happened yesterday morning?" Perhaps he did not mean there to be, but there was criticism in his voice, as if he thought she had somehow abandoned her duty and she should have remained here with them at Ashworth.

Gracie was immediately defensive.

"Lady Vespasia's very special indeed! She's one o' the greatest ladies in the 'ole country. Wot she don't know in't worth bothering wif."

"Well, if she knows how to get us out of this mess, I wish Mrs. Pitt had brought her back here," he said grimly.

"In't nobody can get us out o' this mess 'ceptin' Mr. Pitt," she answered with more conviction than she felt—and was ashamed of herself; of course Pitt would succeed . . . sooner or later. " 'E'll find out 'oo killed Mr. Greville and 'oo put the bomb there wot killed poor Mr. McGinley," she added forcefully.

He smiled. "You're loyal, Gracie. I wouldn't have expected any less from you."

She took a deep breath. "But 'e can't sort out the way you all 'ate each other. But Lady Vespasia did some o' it. She told Mrs. Pitt the truth about that story o' Neassa Doyle and Drystan O'Day, an' it in't wot yer bin told all them years."

He stood very still.

Outside someone walked along the passage and went on to the knife room. A footman swore under his breath as he lifted a heavy coal bucket.

"And what would an English lady in London know about a murder on an Irish hillside thirty years ago?" he asked carefully, his voice soft, his eyes steady.

She saw the defensiveness in him. But he was not weak enough to prefer a lie to the truth.

"Just wot anybody knows wot can read," she replied, her eyes not wavering from his.

"And you believe it, Gracie? Written where? By whom?"

"In the newspaper," she replied without wavering. "It's writ in the newspaper. I read it meself."

He almost laughed. "What newspaper? An English newspaper?" There was derision and contempt in his face and his voice. "Would you really expect them to print the truth? That one of their own, a soldier in their army, a lieutenant, raped and murdered an Irish girl and betrayed his own best friend. Of course they wouldn't say that! I'm sorry the truth is hard, Gracie, but you have to face it!" He came towards her, his eyes gentle. He lowered his voice and it was sad rather than angry, but he did not waver. "Gracie, sometimes our own do things that we're so ashamed of we can hardly bear to think of it, and it's like a little bit of us dying to have to admit it's true. But if it is . . . then running away or saying it isn't doesn't change anything, it just makes us part of whatever it was, because we haven't the courage to face the truth, however terrible it is. You don't want to be part of a lie, Gracie. That's not you.

However it hurts, be part of the truth. It's a cleaner wound, and it heals."

"Yeah," she whispered. "But it in't easy, Finn. It 'urts like yer tearin' yerself apart, sometimes."

"Be strong." He smiled and held out his hand.

She did not take it. She hesitated even more. She had the two pieces of newspaper clenched in her pocket. She closed her eyes. It was easier to say it not looking at him, but she did not turn her face away.

"You said Neassa Doyle were raped and murdered on the night of the eighth o' June."

"Yes. It's a date none of us will ever forget. Why?"

"By Alexander Chinnery, an Englishman wot were the best friend o' Drystan O'Day, or pretended to be?"

"Yes. You know that!"

"Yeh. It says so in the newspaper wot Mrs. Pitt got up in London."

"So what is it you're saying? It's true! We all know it's true!"

"I got another piece." Now she opened her eyes. She did not mean to, it just happened. "A Liverpool newspaper o' sixth o' June, two days before."

He looked a trifle puzzled.

"Saying what?"

"Sayin' as 'ow Lieutenant Alexander Chinnery jumped into the 'arbor o' Liverpool ter try ter save a young lad wot was drownin'—"

"So he was brave when it suited him," Finn said quickly. "I never said he was a coward. Only a betrayer and a murderer and a rapist."

"An' a bleedin' miracle." She nearly choked on the words. " 'E were dead, Finn! 'E din't save the boy, nor 'isself! They was both drowned. They got the bodies out, but it were too late. When Neassa Doyle were killed, Finn, Chinnery were two days dead. An' there were dozens o' people wot saw 'im. Dozens of 'em were tryin' ter get 'em out an' save 'em."

"That's not true!" His face was blank with shock. "It isn't! It's a lie to try to protect him."

"From wot?" she demanded. " 'E 'adn't done nothin'!"

"That's what you say!" He stepped back, his cheeks flushed now, his eyes brilliant and angry. "The English would say that. They're hardly going to admit it was one of their own."

"One o' their own done wot?" Her voice was rising higher, and she had to try hard not to shout. "That were two days before Neassa got killed. There weren't nuffink to protect 'im from. You sayin' they drowned 'im in Liverpool 'arbour ter save 'im from bein' blamed fer summink wot 'adn't 'appened yet?"

"No! Of course I'm not. But it can't be the truth. It's a lie somewhere. It's a very clever one—"

"It in't a lie, Finn! The only ones wot's lyin' is Neassa Doyle's brothers, wot really killed 'er an' shaved 'er 'ead fer bein' an 'ore an' goin' after a Protestant. They blamed Chinnery 'cos they din't 'ave the stomach ter stand up an' be counted for wot they believed in."

"No! No, they didn't—"

"Then 'oo did? 'Cos it weren't Chinnery, lessn'n 'e come back from the grave an' scared 'er ter death."

"Don't speak about it like that!" he shouted, raising his hand as if to strike her. "It isn't funny, God damn you!" His voice was thick with emotion. Anger and confusion were all but choking him. "Haven't you even a decent respect for the dead?"

"What dead? Only Irish dead?" she shouted back, refusing to retreat. "Course I 'ave! Enough ter want the truth fer 'em. But I got respect fer English dead too—if Chinnery didn't do it then I won't stand 'ere an' 'ave anyone say as 'e did! It in't honest." She drew in her breath in a gasp. There were tears running down her cheeks, but she could not stop. "You told me ter face the truth, no matter 'ow much it 'urt. You said it were like a little bit of us dyin' if we 'ad to admit our own 'as done summink terrible." She waved her arm in the air, pointing at him. "Well, you gotta do it! Them Doyles killed 'er an' let

Chinnery take the blame 'cos they 'adn't the guts ter say as they done it to 'er theirselves 'cos she let 'em down by fallin' in love wi' O'Day. Well, they did, an you denyin' it in't going ter make it different."

"It's a lie," he repeated, but there was no belief left in his voice, only anger and hurt and confusion. "It can't be true." She fished in her pocket and brought out the newspaper clippings. She pushed them at him without letting go of them. "Look fer yerself. Can yer read?"

"Of course I can read." He stared at them without touching them. "We've known all about it for years! Everybody knows!"

"Everybody knowin' don't make it true," she argued. "They only know it 'cos someone said so. They weren't there, were they?"

"No, don't be stupid!" he said with scalding disgust. "That's an idiotic thing to say—"

"Then 'ow could they know?" Her reasoning was impeccable. "They know 'cos them Doyle brothers said so. Drystan O'Day must a' thought it were them, or 'e wouldn't a' gorn an' attacked them, would 'e?"

"He was a Protestant," he said with vicious logic. "Of course he would."

"No, 'e wouldn't! Not if 'e thought it were Chinnery. 'E'd a' gorn after Chinnery. Be honest! Wouldn't you?"

"I'm not a Protestant!" His chin jerked up and his eyes blazed generations of loathing.

"Yer just the same!" she retorted with agonized conviction. "There in't no difference, lyin' and 'atin' and killin' each other—"

His reaction was instant.

"There's all the difference in the world, you stupid girl!" he shouted thickly. "Don't you listen to anything? You're so . . . English! You can't see Ireland at all." He took a step forward, jabbing his finger at her. "You're just typical, arrogant English, thinking all Ireland is the same, there for you to rob and plunder and then turn your back on and ignore when the people starve and die and the hate goes on from generation to generation and century to century! You make me sick! No wonder we hate you!"

Suddenly she saw the tragic stupidity of it, and the rage disappeared out of her, leaving her choked with grief.

"I in't sayin' we're right," she answered him with a quiet level voice, completely in control. "I'm sayin' Alexander Chinnery din't kill Neassa Doyle an' you bin lyin' ter yerselves all them years because the lie served you better than the truth, 'cos yer want ter blame somebody else, an' best be it's the English." She shook her head. "Yer'd sooner live in a dream. An' yer in't never goin' ter get peace wif each other long as yer'd sooner feed yer old 'atreds 'cos yer think yer some kind o' romantic victims o' somebody else."

He made as if to fight back, but she drew in her breath and shouted over him. "I don't know why yer want ter be somebody else's victim! If it in't yer own fault, yer can't even fight it! Can yer? I don't want all me troubles ter be someone else's fault. Wot do that make me but an 'elpless little article pushed all over the place? In't 'elpless. I makes me own mistakes an' I takes the truth an' I puts 'em right or I lives wif 'em." And she turned on her heel and ran out, gasping for breath, throat aching, hardly seeing where she was going for the tears, the cuttings still clutched in her hand.

She was running down the corridor towards the women's stairs when she pitched full tilt into Tellman. He caught hold of her to prevent her from falling.

"What's the matter?" he said immediately.

"Nuffink!" she shouted back, but her voice caught in a sob. Tellman was the last person she wanted to see just then. "In't nuffink wrong! Let go o' me!"

He kept hold of her, searching her face. "You're upset. Something has happened. What is it? Did someone hurt you?" He sounded anxious.

She snatched at her wrists, trying to drag away from his hand, but he refused to let go. Surprisingly for the firmness of his grip, he was quite gentle.

"Gracie?"

"Nobody 'urt me," she said desperately. She knew the tears were running down her cheeks. She could hardly see him through them. She was bursting with rage and grief and loneliness over Finn and the whole idiotic business. She did not want Tellman to know that she could ever be hurt, let alone see it in her. He was a useless creature, full of anger and resentment himself. "And it in't nuffink ter do wif yer if they 'ad. It in't p'lice business, if that's wot yer thinkin'."

"Course it isn't police," he said awkwardly. "Are you frightened, Gracie?"

"No, I in't frightened." She managed to snatch her hand away at last. She sniffed fiercely and gulped.

He produced a handkerchief, quite a nice, clean white one, and gave it to her.

She took it only out of necessity, poking the cuttings into her pocket first. She really did have to blow her nose and wipe away the tears.

"Thank you," she said grudgingly. She would not let Tellman, of all people, catch her out in bad manners.

"Do you know something, Gracie?" he persisted, grasping her again. "If you do, you've got to tell me!"

She glared at him and blew her nose a second time. It was infuriating not to be able to control tears. She hated having him see her weakness.

"You have to!" His voice rose, as if he were frightened himself. "Don't be so stupid!"

"In't stupid!" she burst out, pulling away from him. "You watch 'oo yer callin' names! 'Ow dare yer—"

"How can I protect you if you don't tell me wot the danger is?" he said angrily, and suddenly she knew it really was fear in his voice, even in his face and the locked muscles of his body as he braced himself to hold on to her against her will. "Do you think they won't blow you up too, or push you down stairs, or just wring your neck, if they think you know enough to get them hanged?" He was shaking now too.

She stopped abruptly, staring at him.

He blushed very faintly.

"I don't know nuffink, I swear," she said honestly. "If I did, I'd tell Mr. Pitt. Don't yer know that? Now 'oo's stupid?" She blew her nose for a last time and looked at the handkerchief. "I'll wash it an' give it yer back."

"You don't need to . . ." he said magnanimously, then blushed more deeply.

She took a deep breath and let it out shakily.

"I gotter go an' do me work. If'n yer remember, I got extra jobs ter do, seen' as the master's valet in't much use." And with that she stuffed the handkerchief into her pocket and marched off, leaving him standing in the corridor looking after her.

CHAPTER TEN

Emily knew that she had been unfair to both Charlotte and Pitt after the explosion. Part of her had realized it even as she was striking out, but she was so terrified and angry and overwhelmed with immediate relief that she had lost control of her emotions. Now, a day later, she knew she must apologize.

She went to look for Pitt first. There was a sense in which he would be the easier. It was he whom she had attacked. It was Charlotte, on his behalf, because he was vulnerable in that he had so far failed, who would find it harder to forgive. She was walking along the passage towards the stillroom and laundry rooms, where Dilkes had said Pitt was, when she was waylaid by the kitchen maid, carrying an empty basket.

"I in't goin' in there, m'lady, if we're 'ungry the rest o' the week. I in't goin' in there if we starve, an' that's a fact." She stood with her feet apart and one hand on her hip, fist clenched, almost as if she expected someone to try to carry her forcibly wherever it was.

"Where aren't you going, Mae?" Emily asked reasonably. She was used to the vagueness of maids. It could almost certainly be sorted out with a little reason and a great deal of firmness.

"Ter fetch the meat," Mae answered resolutely. "I absolutely in't." She stared at Emily, and her eyes did not waver, which was a bad sign.

Servants did not defy their employers like that if they wanted to keep their places.

"It's your job," Emily pointed out. "If Cook sent you. Did she?"

"I don't care if God hisself sent me, I in't going!" Mae stood her ground without blinking.

This was not the time to be having to dismiss a kitchen maid, especially a good one. And Mae had been good until now. What on earth had got into the girl? Perhaps there was some point in trying reason.

"Why not? You always have before."

"In't bin corpses o' dead men in the ice'ouse afore," Mae answered in a husky voice. "Men as was murdered an' don't lie easy. Dead wot went afore their time an' wants vengeance."

Emily had forgotten the bodies were there.

"No," she said as calmly as she could. "Of course not. Anyway, you don't have the keys. I expect Superintendent Pitt has them. I'll go and fetch the meat myself."

"You can't do that!" Mae was horrified.

"Well, somebody has to," Emily replied. "I didn't kill anyone, so I'm not afraid of dead bodies. I must offer my guests food. Go back to the kitchen and tell Mrs. Williams I'll bring the meat."

Mae stood motionless.

"Go on," Emily ordered her.

Mae was white-faced.

"Yer can't carry meat, m'lady." She took a huge gulp of air. "It in't fittin'. I'll come an' carry it, if yer swear yer'll come in wi' me? I'll be all right if yer come wi' me."

"Thank you," Emily said gravely. "That is very brave of you, Mae. We'll get the keys from Mr. Pitt and go together."

"Yes, m'lady."

They found Pitt five minutes later, returning from speaking with Padraig's valet and going to look for Kezia.

"Thomas," Emily said quickly. She could not apologize for her earlier behavior in front of the kitchen maid. She smiled at him as meekly as she could and saw the surprise in his eyes. "Thomas, we have run out of meat in the kitchen and need to fetch some from the icehouse. I believe you have the keys, since . . ." She let the sentence hang unfinished. "Would you please come with us? Mae is nervous to go alone, and I promised to stay beside her."

Pitt looked at her steadily for a moment without answering, then slowly he smiled back. "Of course. I'll take you there now."

"Thank you, Thomas," she said softly. She did not need to say more. He knew that was an apology.

Finding Charlotte proved more difficult, and when she did, knowing what to say was even harder. Charlotte was obviously still angry and upset. She had been up to London, without telling anyone why, and returned so late everyone else had already been in bed. Normally, of course, at a country house weekend like this they would remain up enjoying themselves, possibly until two or three in the morning. But there was nothing usual about this weekend. No one wished to be in general company any longer than was obligatory for the most basic good manners.

Now they were standing in the first open space in the conservatory between the potted palms and the orchid which Fergal had broken, although they did not know it. Emily had been passing in the hall when she had glanced across and seen Charlotte, and gone in. Now she did not know how to begin.

"Good morning," Charlotte said a trifle stiffly.

"What do you mean 'Good morning'?" Emily responded. "We saw each other at breakfast."

"What else would you like me to say?" Charlotte asked, raising her eyebrows. "It doesn't seem the time for light conversation, and I'm not going to discuss the case with you. We will only end up quarreling again. If you don't know what I think of your treatment of Thomas, then I'll tell you." It was a threat; it was implicit in every angle of her body and line of her face.

Emily's heart sank. Could Charlotte not understand how terrified she was for Jack, not only for his life—which must be obvious to anyone—but that he would fail the challenge of making some kind of success of this conference and his career would be over before it began? They had asked too much of him far too soon. It was grossly unfair. Pitt was not the only one faced with failure, and no one was threatening his life. She needed Charlotte's help and companionship, her support, not her anger. But if it had to be begged for, it was of no use. Suddenly she felt more in sympathy with Kezia Moynihan than she would have thought possible.

"No, thank you," she said stiffly. This was not the apology she had intended. "You have already made it quite plain in your manner." Nothing was going the way she had planned.

They stood in stiff silence facing each other, neither sure what to say next, temper and pride dictating one thing, deeper emotion another.

Fifteen feet away, on the farther side of a dense, tangled vine with yellow trumpet flowers, one of the outside doors of the conservatory opened. Emily turned instantly, but she could not see anyone through the foliage, although their footsteps were plain.

"You're being unreasonable!" Fergal Moynihan's voice came heatedly.

The door closed with a sharp snap.

"Because I won't agree with you?" Iona's voice retorted, equally hard and angry.

"Because you won't be realistic," he answered, lowering his tone a little. "We both have to make accommodations."

"What 'accommodations,' as you put it, are you making?" she demanded. "You won't listen to me about the core and the soul of it. You just say they are mysteries, folklore. You laugh at the most sacred things of all."

"I don't laugh at them," he protested.

"Yes, you do! You mock them. You pay lip service, because you don't want to make me angry, but in your heart you don't believe—"

Emily and Charlotte glanced at each other, eyes wide.

"Now you're accusing me not for what I say or do but for what you imagine I believe?" Fergal was growing angry again. "It's impossible to please you! You are just looking for a quarrel. Why can't you be honest—"

"I am honest! It's you who's lying, not only to me but to yourself. . . ." Iona's voice retaliated.

"I am not lying!" he shouted. "I'm telling you the truth! That's the problem. You don't want truth because it doesn't fit with your myths and fairy stories and the superstitions you let govern your life—"

"You don't understand faith!" she shouted back. "All you know is rules and how to condemn people. I should have known better. . . ." There was a sound of quick clattering footsteps and the door opening.

"Iona!" Fergal called out.

Silence.

"What?"

His footsteps followed hers to the door.

"I love you."

"Do you?" she asked quietly.

"You know I do. I adore you."

There was a long silence, again broken only by sighs and the rustle of fabric, and then eventually two lots of footsteps, and the outside door closing.

Emily looked at Charlotte.

"Not so smooth a path," Charlotte said very quietly. "Kissing isn't a resolution to an argument, not a real one."

"Kissing isn't an answer at all," Emily agreed. "It's something you do if you want to, not to resolve a problem. In a way it only clouds the issue. It can be very nice to kiss someone, but it can stop you thinking clearly. When you've finished and pull apart, what is left?"

"In their case, I don't think they know yet." Charlotte shook her head. "And it will be very sad if they pay too much for their chance together and then discover it isn't what they really want and it won't work. Then they'll have nothing."

"I don't think they want to hear that," Emily pointed out.

Charlotte smiled for the first time. "I'm sure they don't. I wonder how Kezia will feel? I hope she can find it in herself not to be too satisfied."

Emily was surprised. "Why? Do you like him? I thought you didn't much."

"I don't. I think he's cold and pompous. But I like her. And whatever he is, he's the only brother she has, the only family. She'll hurt herself horribly if she doesn't offer him some gentleness, whatever he does with it."

"Charlotte . . ."

"What?"

Now it was not so hard. There would never be a better time. "I'm sorry I flew at Thomas yesterday. I know it was unfair. I'm terrified for Jack." She might as well say it all now. "Not only in case they try again to kill him, but because they've given him an impossible task and they might blame him if he can't succeed."

Charlotte held out her hand. "I know you are. The whole situation is horrible. But don't worry about Jack not solving the Irish Problem. In three hundred years nobody else ever has. They might hate him if he did!"

Emily almost laughed, but she might too easily cry if she let go her control right at that moment. Instead she took Charlotte's hand and held it tightly, then put her arms around her and hugged her.

After helping get the meat out of the icehouse for Emily, Pitt changed his mind about seeing Kezia and instead went to find Tellman. They needed to start again from the beginning.

"Back to Greville?" Tellman said with raised eyebrows. "I'd like to go back to Denbigh, myself, but I don't suppose they'll let us do that. I hate conspiracies."

"What do you like?" Pitt asked wryly. "A nice domestic murder where the people have known each other for years, perhaps all their lives, lived under the same roof in open love and secret hate? Or someone who has been abused beyond bearing and has finally retaliated the only way they knew how?"

They were walking outside through the stable yard entrance and across the gravel path to the long lawn. The grass was wet, but the feel and smell of it was clean, and the air was still and not unpleasantly cold.

"How about simple greed?" Tellman replied grudgingly. "Someone hit over the head and robbed, then I can work out who did it and be happy to take them in and see them hanged. Well, not happy, but satisfied."

"I shall be extremely satisfied to see this one taken," Pitt rejoined.

"And hanged?" Tellman asked, looking sideways at him. "That's not like you."

Pitt shoved his hands into his pockets. "I might make an exception for people who plot political overthrow and random violence," he replied. "I take no joy in it, but I think I can grant the necessity."

"Got to catch him first." With a faint smile Tellman put his hands in his pockets also.

"Who killed Greville?" Pitt said.

"I think Doyle," Tellman replied. "He had the best reason, personal as well as political . . . at least as much sense in the political reason as any of them. It's all stupid to me." He frowned. His boots were soaking in the heavy dew on the grass, but he was used to wet feet. "Besides, Doyle has a weight about him, a passion which could carry through his beliefs."

"Moynihan's daft enough," Pitt said, mimicking Tellman's tone of a few moments earlier.

Tellman shrugged. "His sister has more real nerve than he has."

"I agree." Pitt nodded as they walked under the shadow of the huge cedar, their feet falling softly on the bare earth. "And I don't suppose he killed McGinley. That looks like an accident, the bomb meant for Mr. Radley."

"O'Day?" Tellman asked.

"Not Greville," Pitt replied. "Both McGinley and his valet saw him in his own room at the relevant time. And he overheard their conversation about shirts."

"Doyle," Tellman said again. "Makes sense. That's how McGinley knew about the dynamite, because they're on the same side. Doyle must have said something and given himself away. Either that, or McGinley was in it from the beginning, then he had second thoughts . . . changed his mind."

Pitt said nothing. Tellman was right, it did make sense—much as he fought against the thought, for Eudora's sake. They were at the far side of the cedar now and the sun shone through the cloud in bars making a glittering surface on the wet grass.

"Can't prove it, mind," Tellman added irritably. "Could be they'd all lie to protect each other. Even Mrs. Greville maybe, though it was her husband. If she knew anything about his goings-on, she can't have had any love for him. And she's Irish, isn't she? Catholic . . . and Nationalist."

"I don't know," Pitt said crossly. "She may have wanted peace just as much as Greville did himself." He sighed. "I'd like to know who the maid was that Gracie saw on the landing."

"No one that I can find," Tellman said bluntly. "I've asked them all, and no one admits to being there."

"Might be frightened." Pitt stared at the grass thoughtfully. They were approaching the rugosa hedge and the fields beyond, rolling gently towards a stand of elms, most of their leaves gone now. Over to the west a shaft of sunlight shone silver on the wet village roofs, and the spire of the church stood out darkly against the sky.

"Because they saw something?" Tellman asked, looking at Pitt skeptically. "Didn't say anything then, and scared now?"

"Possibly. More likely didn't see anything, just frightened of being involved at all. I refuse to say this is unsolvable. There's only a limited number of people it could be. We've got another two days at least. We're going to find the answer, Tellman."

Tellman smiled, but there was no humor in it at all.

Pitt turned around and faced the gracious mass of Ashworth Hall again. It really was very beautiful in the autumn light. On the west facade the creeper was a scarlet stain against the warm color of the stone. It was a pleasure just to look at it. He glanced sideways to see Tellman's face and was satisfied to catch a moment's softness in it, as the loveliness moved him, in spite of himself.

They started back to the house together, roughly in step over the grass, feet soaked and now thoroughly cold.

"Gracie, I want you to remember exactly what you saw on the landing the evening Mr. Greville was killed," Pitt said half an hour later when he found her alone in the ironing room. She looked terribly unhappy, as if she had been crying and would like nothing more than to creep away and be alone, had her duties allowed. He guessed it was something to do with the fondness he had seen her show for the young Irish valet, Finn Hennessey. Charlotte had warned him to be careful about that, and he had resented the fact that she thought such a warning necessary. Then he realized afterwards that he had not honestly been aware of it. He liked Gracie profoundly. He would hate to have hurt her, and he was unnecessarily angry that Hennessey should have, however unintentionally. He was not sure whether to let her know he was aware of her misery, or if it would be more tactful to pretend he had not noticed.

She sniffed and attempted to concentrate.

"I already told Mr. Tellman wot I saw. Din't 'e tell yer? 'E's a useless valet, 'e is. In't 'e no good as a policeman neither?"

"Yes, he is good," Pitt replied. "Although I daresay you are a better detective than he is a valet."

"I in't no use this time." She stared down at the iron, although it was cold and she was not even pretending to use it. "We in't none of us no use to yer this time. I'm really sorry, sir."

"Don't worry, Gracie, we'll solve it," he said with a certainty he did not feel. "Tell me about the maid you saw with the towels."

She looked up at him with surprise. Her eyes were red-rimmed, and he had no doubt she had been crying.

"In't yer found 'er yet? Stupid article! She in't got nuffink ter be afraid of. She weren't doin' no wrong . . . just carryin' towels, like I said."

"But perhaps she saw something, or someone," he pointed out. "She is the only person we can't account for. Try and remember, Gracie. We haven't got much to go after at the moment. Almost anyone could have put the dynamite in Mr. Radley's study . . . except Mr. McGinley, I suppose . . . or Hennessey."

She sniffed. "Yeah, I s'pose." She brightened considerably. "I dunno 'oo she were, sir, or I'd 'a said."

"Describe her, as exactly as you can."

"Well, she were taller'n me. But then I s'pose everyone is. She stood tall, proud like, 'ead very straight—"

"What color hair?"

She screwed up her face. "I don' remember seein' 'er 'air. She 'ad a lace cap on. Real big sort o' cap, not like mine wot sits on top o' me 'ead. 'Ers were allover lace. Too big, if yer ask me, but some folks like 'em like that. She could 'e bin any color underneath it."

"Have you seen any of the maids wearing caps like that?"

"Yeah. Mrs. McGinley's maid wears one like it." Then the eagerness died from her face. "But it weren't 'er. Least, I don't think it were. She's sort o' got narrow shoulders, like a bottle, an 'er wot I saw 'ad good shoulders, more square."

"Was she large or small, Gracie? Slender or plump?"

"I'm thinkin'!" She screwed up her face, eyes closed, trying to bring back the picture.

"Start at the top," he encouraged. "What after the lace cap and the shoulders? Neat waist or plump? Did you see her hands? How was her apron tied? Anything you can think of."

"Din't see 'er 'ands." She kept her eyes closed. "She were 'oldin' a pile o' towels. Goin' ter someone's bath, I s'pose. Not a bad waist, but not as good as some. She weren't slender, not real slender. Solid enough, I'd 'a' said. Come ter think on it, 'er apron weren't tied real well. Not like Gwen's, say. She showed me 'ow ter tie 'em real pretty. I'm goin' ter keep on doin' that w'en I get 'ome again." She looked at him hopefully.

"Good." He smiled. "We'll impress Bloomsbury. So she didn't tie her apron well?"

"No. Mrs. 'Unnaker'd 'ave torn strips orff anyone 'oo'd done a sloppy job like that, so it weren't one o' the Ashworth 'All maids."

"Good!" he said enthusiastically. "Very good. What else?"

Gracie said nothing but stood with a look of fierce inner thought on her face, her eyes wide open, staring beyond him into the distance.

"What?" he demanded.

"Boots," she whispered.

"Boots? What about them?"

"She weren't wearin' boots!"

"She was barefoot?" he said with disbelief.

"No, o' course she weren't barefoot. She were wearin' slippers, like wot ladies wear. She'd took someone's slippers!"

"How do you know? What did you see . . . exactly?"

"She were facin' away from me, like she was going inter the doorway. I just seen the side o' one foot, an' the 'eel o' the other."

"But it was a slipper? What color? How do you know it wasn't a boot?"

" 'Cos the foot were stitched. It were embroidered, like a slipper, an' the 'eel were blue." Her eyes widened. "Yeah, the 'eel were blue."

Pitt smiled. "Thank you."

"It 'elps?" she said hopefully.

"Oh, yes, I think so."

"Good."

Pitt left the ironing room with the feeling that for the first time since he had found Ainsley Greville's body he had a real and tangible piece of evidence to follow. One of the women was part of the conspiracy. It was not hard to believe. In fact, it made excellent sense, only too excellent. His mind was weighed down with it. Eudora

Greville, born Eudora Doyle, Irish to the blood and bone, helping her brother Padraig to fight for the freedom of their country in the way he thought would work. Her hatred for Greville would make it easy. And how could she not hate him, if she had had the slightest idea how he had treated Doll. Pitt could imagine the way Charlotte would feel towards anyone who treated Gracie that way! He would be lucky if a crack over the head and a slide under the water was the worst that happened to him.

Eudora could easily have slipped out of her room in Doll's dress and a cap, perhaps borrowed earlier from the laundry room.

The large lace cap was an obvious choice, to hide the vivid color of her hair should anyone see her. She would be too easily recognizable by that alone. She would walk along the landing with a pile of towels, perhaps her own towels, and be virtually invisible. It was only the slightest chance that Gracie, the most observant of maids, had seen her, and noticed her feet, and then remembered them afterwards.

She could have gone into the bathroom, keeping her face averted. Greville would have taken no notice until it was too late. If he had seen her, realized who it was, he would have wondered what on earth she was doing in a maid's dress and cap, but he would still not have been afraid, not have cried out, attracted attention, or called her name.

But Padraig could not have placed the bomb in Jack's study. Pitt's heart sank. Could that have been Eudora also? Why not? It required nerve and dexterity, not any physical strength. Why should Eudora not care as passionately or as bravely about the fate of her country as any politician—or Fenian sympathizer?

He must speak with Charlotte. She would be able to look at the slippers of the various women in the house without arousing the sort of suspicion which would make someone seek to hide or destroy them. She might even know already whose they were. She would remember what people had worn, who might have blue heels.

But he did not find the opportunity to speak with her alone until an hour before luncheon, when she was about to go for a short walk with Kezia, who looked surprisingly gentle, as if the anger had slipped from her. He wondered what Charlotte had managed to say to her that she forgave Fergal at last. He would ask her later.

"Charlotte!"

She turned, and was about to reply when she must have seen the anxiety in his face, and perhaps the sadness.

"What is it?"

"I have discovered something which I need to discuss with you," he said quietly enough he hoped Kezia did not hear him. It could be her. Perhaps conspiring with Fergal. The other brother and sister. It was a hope!

Charlotte turned back to Kezia, just outside the door on the terrace.

"Please excuse me," she called. "I must take this chance to speak with Thomas. I'm so sorry!"

Kezia smiled and lifted her hand in acknowledgment, then walked onto the grass and away.

"What is it?" Charlotte said quickly. "I can see it is unpleasant."

"Discovering who committed a crime is usually unpleasant," he answered a little bleakly. Then, seeing her eyes widen, he added, "No, not completely, just an excellent piece of observation by Gracie. She remembered more about the 'maid' she saw on the landing about the time Greville was killed."

"What? Who was it?" She gulped, her face suddenly wretched. "Not—Doll?"

"No," he said quickly. "No, it wasn't Doll. It was someone wearing slippers with stitched fabric sides and blue heels."

"What?" For a moment she looked confused; the instant after, understanding flew to her. He knew she also thought of Eudora. He watched the conflicting emotions in her face, a light of relief, almost satisfaction, as swiftly overtaken by pity, and then wiped clean again. He found he understood, or thought he did. He was surprised. Was she more vulnerable, underneath the independence, than he had assumed?

"Oh," she said soberly. "You mean it was one of the guests, wearing a maid's dress over her own? Then she had to be involved."

"Over her own?" He was momentarily puzzled.

"Of course," she said quickly. "Thomas, it takes ages to get in and out of a dinner gown. They all do up at the back, for a start! She could get a maid's dress large enough to put on top of her own and long enough to cover it completely. An inch or two of satin underneath it would give her away in a second. It was only coincidence that Gracie saw a piece of the shoe and that she remembered it, but satin anyone would have seen."

He should have thought of that.

"Which means she was probably slimmer than she appeared to be to Gracie," Charlotte went on. "Two dresses would make a lot of difference. Blue slippers?"

"Yes. Can you remember who wore blue that evening?"

She smiled weakly. "No. But Emily might. I'll ask her. If not, we'll have to start looking. We'll find a way."

"Without them knowing," he warned. "If they know before we get to them, they'll hide them or destroy them. There's a furnace for the conservatory heaters, at least. Then we'd never have proof."

"I'll start by asking Emily. And don't worry, I'll be discreet. I can, you know!"

"Yes, I know." But nevertheless he watched her with anxiety, although he was not quite sure why. Perhaps it had more to do with the emotion he sensed in her, and his sudden awareness of it, than any danger she could be in or misjudgment she might make regarding the slippers.

"Blue-heeled slippers," Emily said quickly. "Then it was one of us! I mean, it wasn't a maid. Oh . . . I see. You mean that was who killed

Greville." She looked startled and very sober. Charlotte had found her coming back from the kitchens, where she had been consulting with Mrs. Williams about the next day's dinner and how much longer the guests were likely to be there, which of course she did not know. Now they were walking across the hall towards the long gallery overlooking the formal garden, a place where there was unlikely to be anyone else at this time of the afternoon. The men were back to their discussions, for any good it might serve, and the women were all about their separate pastimes. Since two of them were very newly widowed, any attempt at social entertainment was impossible.

Emily opened the door to the gallery, a long room with ranks of windows to the south, and at the moment filled with a wavering light as the wind chased the clouds across the sun and away again.

"Who wore blue?" Charlotte pressed, closing the door behind them.

"I can't remember," Emily answered. "Anyway, you might wear blue slippers under another color, if it was the closest you had, or the most comfortable. None of them, except perhaps Eudora, have enough money to buy slippers for every dress."

"How do you know?"

Emily gave her a sideways look. "Don't be naive. Because I'm observant. You may not, but I know what is this season's fashion and what is last . . . and what things cost. And I know good silk from cheap, or wool from bombazine or mixture."

"So who wore blue?"

"I'm trying to think!"

"I don't think it was Kezia."

"Why not? Because you like her? I think she could have just the nerve to do it," Emily argued. "I don't think Iona McGinley would. She's all dreams and romantic notions. She'd rather talk about things and prompt other people than do them herself."

"Maybe," Charlotte conceded. "Although that could be a pose. But I had a rather more practical reason for thinking it was not Kezia. She's rather well built. With a maid's dress over her own she'd look . . . well, pretty enormous. Gracie would have noticed her size.

Anyway, whose dress would go over hers? Are any of the ladies' maids really stout?"

"No. Maybe you're right. That leaves Eudora herself, which is very likely, or Iona."

"Or Justine," Charlotte added.

"Justine? Why on earth would Justine kill Ainsley Greville?" Emily said derisively, her eyes wide. "She isn't Irish. She'd never even met him before the previous day, and she was going to marry his son, for heaven's sake!"

"I can't think of any reason at all. I don't think there is even very much money."

"Don't be squalid." Emily's mouth turned down at the corners.

"People have been known to kill for money," Charlotte pointed out.

Emily ignored her, which expressed her opinion very clearly.

"Blue gown," Charlotte repeated.

"I'm thinking! I haven't seen Eudora in blue. She prefers warm colors and greens. I don't think blue would suit her." She shrugged. "Not that that means she wouldn't wear it, of course. People wear the most awful things sometimes. Do you remember Hetty Appleby, with the mouse-colored hair, wearing yellow? She looked like a cheese!"

"No."

"Really, you are so unobservant sometimes," Emily said in disgust. "I don't know how you are ever the least use to Thomas."

"Justine wore cream with blue," Charlotte replied.

"I think we agreed Justine had no earthly reason. And I remember now, Iona wore blue, dark blue like the sea at night. All very romantic. Fergal Moynihan could hardly take his eyes off her."

"He'd have been like that whatever she wore. We'd better go and look at their shoes."

"Now?"

"Why not?"

"Because Iona will be in her room, for a start," Emily pointed out. "We can hardly interrupt her and say 'Please may we look through your wardrobe to see if we can find a pair of blue-heeled slippers, because we think you were wearing them when you killed Ainsley Greville in his bath?' "

"I didn't mean—"

"You go when we are all at luncheon," Emily commanded. "I shall keep everyone occupied at the table. You excuse yourself, blame a headache or something."

"What do you mean 'keep everybody occupied'?" Charlotte said with a touch of sarcasm. "If they are at luncheon, they will be occupied anyway."

"I'll see they don't leave. I can't very well plead a headache, even if I have a real one. What's the matter? Are you afraid?"

"No, of course not," Charlotte replied indignantly. "I don't want it to be Eudora, for Thomas's sake, and I don't want it to be Justine, because I like her."

"I don't want it to be anybody," Emily agreed. "Because I think Ainsley Greville was a complete bounder. But wanting has nothing to do with it."

"I know that! I'll find the slippers during luncheon."

When Pitt had left her, Gracie's brief moment of feeling better vanished. There was only one good thing about it. She was quite sure the "maid" she had seen was not Doll Evans. She had not been tall enough for Doll, she was sure of that now. And she did not think Doll would take anyone's shoes, but if she had worn slippers with heels like that, she would have been even taller. Only now did she realize how afraid she had been that Doll had gone into the bathroom and hit Greville over the head and then pulled him under the water. She had certainly had provocation. Gracie had no sympathy with Ainsley Greville at all. Anyone who could do that to a girl, and to his own child, deserved a lot of pain in return. It was just a pity so many other people had to suffer as well. But maybe nobody ever suffered without taking other people with them.

She could not keep Finn from her mind. His pain engulfed her.

Disillusion was one of the hardest things to bear. If he had been so wrong about the murder of Neassa Doyle and what he believed of his own people, then what else had he been wrong about? What else was lies? If they could murder their own sister, who and what were they? What was the cause they were really fighting for? If Finn had given so much of his emotional loyalty to them, how could he cope with it if they were unworthy of him, or of anyone? How much of it all was lies?

He must be asking himself that now. He would be terribly alone and confused. In one brief quarter hour or so, she had robbed him of his lifetime's beliefs, belonging to his people, loyalties, angers, all that he thought he was. She should not have done that. Some truths should be told gently, maybe even little by little.

She had no urgent jobs. Charlotte's clothes were all in excellent repair. And Charlotte certainly did not want Gracie to sit and talk to her, read to her, which was sometimes a real lady's maid's job. Charlotte always had more to do than she had time for anyway. But then her life was not like that of a lady. Gracie would find it terrible to look after real gentry after the excitement of being with the Pitts. How did people like Gwen and Doll bear the sameness of it?

She should go and find Finn and make up her quarrel with him. He would need all the friendship she could offer now. And she wanted to apologize. She had acted without thinking hard enough.

The decision was made. She left the ironing room and went to look for him.

He was not in any of the places where he would normally be carrying out his duties. She did not like to ask for him. It was bad enough to imagine people knew how she felt. She was painfully self-conscious. She knew how observant she was of other people's behavior. There was rather a lot to be said for working with only a casual woman who came in to do the "heavy," as she did at home. One had a great deal more privacy, even if there was less company, and most of the time less day-to-day interest in others. All told, it was better.

After three quarters of an hour searching, inside and out, there was only one place left, his bedroom. She had never been there, of course. But perhaps on this extraordinary occasion it would be the best place. Even if she were caught, Charlotte would not dismiss her for such a thing when Gracie explained to her why she had gone there. And McGinley couldn't dismiss Finn because he was dead anyway, poor creature. The worst thing that could happen would be the others whispering and laughing. And even that would be better than leaving Finn to suffer his loss and disillusion without telling him she was sorry.

She looked very carefully to see there was no one around before she ran up the first staircase. The regular Ashworth Hall servants had the rooms nearest the stairhead; the senior ones had the best, naturally. The footmen, bootboy and the like had the smaller ones, further away. Visiting valets and other servants were another floor up again, right under the roof.

But which was Finn's room? Think! Everything in the servants' hall went by order of precedence. The servants went in to dinner, sat down, were served, even served the sweet, in order of the importance of their masters. That would make Mr. Wheeler the most senior up here. He belonged to Mr. Greville, the chairman of this miserable conference. Who was next? Be quick! Mustn't get caught up here. No one was going to believe she was stupid enough to be lost.

Mr. Doyle and Mr. O'Day. That meant Finn and Mr. Moynihan's valet would be further away, then probably Tellman. The thought of running into Tellman by mistake was enough to knot up her stomach so tight she could hardly breathe!

Maybe it was not worth it after all?

Come on! Don't be a coward! Take a chance. Try one. Don't just stand here like one of the pieces of statuary in the garden! Knock!

There was no answer.

She tried the next one, her hands shaking.

There was a moment's silence, then footsteps.

Her heart was beating so loudly it seemed to pound in her ears.

The door opened. It was Finn.

Thank heavens! Now, what was she going to say?

"I'm sorry!" she burst out.

"Gracie!" He looked startled, and momentarily confused, uncertain what to say or do.

"I'm sorry I told you about Chinnery," she explained. If she did not say it now she might lose her courage. "I shouldn't oughter said it out like that. Perhaps maybe I shouldn't oughter said it at all. One lie don't make the 'ole cause wrong."

He stared at her, his dark eyes wide and puzzled.

There was nothing more she could say. She could not deny the truth, and he had no business to expect that. Perhaps it was not such a good idea to have come. But he did look so miserable, surely there was something she could do? Love had to be worth something?

He smiled very slowly.

"You'd better come in." He stood aside. "If they catch you up here you'll be in trouble."

She hesitated only a moment. They had not said all there was to say between them yet. And he was right. Anyone else could possibly go up there at this time in the afternoon. If she were caught it would be very embarrassing. She stepped past him into the room. It was simple, like her own, a place made comfortable for a short time, almost warm enough, a bed with sheets and blankets, a wooden chair, cotton curtains at the garret window, a washstand with a jug and basin, a small cupboard for coats and trousers, a three-drawer chest for underclothes and anything else which might fold. There was a knotted rag mat on the floor. There was a small desk against the wall to the right and a second wooden chair in front of it. There was a paper on the desk now, with writing like a short letter, and beside it an envelope, an open book, a leather satchel, some blue paper and a heap of candles.

He stood still, looking at her.

"I don't care what anyone says the Doyle brothers did, or what it looks like," he said a little stiffly. "Perhaps they were wrong when they said it was Chinnery, but the spirit is true. The hunger and the tragedy is real." He faced her as if she were denying that, his eyes bright and hard, his chin raised a little, jaw tight.

She must be patient. She must remember how hurt he was. It was easy for her. No one had broken her dreams about her people, the ones she most admired and cared for, the people who defined who she was and what she had given her time and care to.

She took a deep breath.

"Course," she agreed. "I spoke 'asty if I said diff'rent."

He relaxed a trifle.

She must be careful she did not give so much away he thought she was weak, or disloyal to her own. He would not admire that, and she would not do it anyway. It was very painful to care so much about someone who was on the other side of such a division of beliefs, of honor, of loyalties which could not now be changed. There were too many debts, too many shared experiences, losses to be comforted and borne together, wept over. How were Mr. Moynihan and Mrs. McGinley ever going to manage?

"You don't understand at all," he said thoughtfully. "You can't, and that isn't your fault. You'd have to be Irish to have seen it, the suffering and the injustice."

"Everybody suffers, one way or another," she said reasonably. "It in't just the Irish wot gets cold and 'ungry, or scared, or lonely, or wot gets put out on the street, or locked in gaol for summink they din't do, or couldn't 'elp doin'. It 'appens to all sorts. Sometimes even English gents gets 'ung for summink wot they din't do."

He regarded her with open disbelief.

"Course they do!" she said urgently. "I work for a policeman. I know fings wot you don't. You in't got the 'ole world's lot o' sufferin' all to yerself, yer know."

His face darkened.

"Not that yer in't right ter fight for fings better!" she went on quickly. "Or that it in't important that Ireland be free ter look arter itself any way it wants. But wot about folk like Mr. O'Day and Mr.

Moynihan? They got ter be done fair ter as well. Yer wouldn't want it unfair, would yer?"

"Irish freedom is not unfair," he said with an effort to control the anger in his voice. "Gracie, listen to me!" He sat down on the edge of the bed and pointed to the chair for her to sit, which she did. "You can't understand in a week, or in a year, all the stealing of land, the killing of people that has gone on in Ireland over the centuries, or why the hatred runs so deep." He shook his head, his face pinched and tense. "I can't tell it to you. You would need to see it to believe people could treat other living, breathing beings that way, people who are their own kind, who hunger and shiver like they do, who work and sleep and love their children the same, who have the same dreams and fears for the future. It's inhuman but it happened for hundreds of years, and it's still happening." He leaned further forward, his eyes brilliant, his voice urgent and angry. "We've got to put a stop to it, for all time, whatever it costs. All the past cries out to us not just to think of ourselves, but to think of those who are children now, or who are to be our children in the future."

She said nothing, staring at him.

"Listen, Gracie!" His hand trembled with emotion. "Nothing precious is bought without a price. If we care enough, we must be prepared to pay!"

"O' course," she said quietly. But his words troubled her the instant after she had agreed with them.

He was going on, not seeing the hesitation in her face.

"History can be cruel, Gracie." He was smiling at her now, some of the shadows gone from his eyes. "We have to have the courage of our beliefs, and sometimes that can be very difficult, but great changes are not made by cowards."

Privately she thought that sometimes they were made by men without consciences, but she did not say so.

"Thank you for coming," he said warmly. "I didn't like quarreling with you." He held out his hand.

She put hers out and his fingers closed over it, strong and gentle. He pulled her towards him and she yielded willingly. Very softly he kissed her lips, then let her go. She sat back feeling a peace and happiness settle inside her. The argument was not over. She still thought he was wrong in some of his ideas, but the feeling was right, and other things would be dealt with later. Caring was what mattered. She smiled back at him, letting her fingers slip from his and sitting back on her chair. She put her hand on the table to steady herself and glanced sideways as she accidentally moved the blue paper and the candles.

"Don't touch that!" Finn started forward, his face tight and hard, his body stiff.

She froze, staring at him. She had never seen him like this before, such anger in him, and something else, uglier and more alien. She had touched two of the candles. They had felt different from each other. One was waxy, like any candle she was used to. The other was vaguely sticky, not the same.

"Leave it alone," he said between his teeth.

"Sorry," she said shakily. "I didn't mean no 'arm."

"No . . . no, of course not." He seemed to be struggling for words, driven by a consuming emotion that he fought against—and lost. "It . . . you just . . . you shouldn't . . ."

A prickle of horror ran through her. Maybe it was not a candle, as she had assumed. She had seen no wick in it. Could that be what dynamite was like?

She looked at his face and knew with a sick misery that she was right. Were it just a candle, her seeing it, touching it, would never have made them suddenly strangers.

She folded her arms, unconsciously hiding her hands and the fact that she was trembling.

He was still watching her. He must have seen the change in her face. Did he guess the fearful thought that beat in her mind?

"Gracie?"

"Yes!" She had answered too quickly, she knew it the moment

the word was out of her mouth. She saw it in his eyes. Finn had had the materials for the bomb which had exploded in the study and killed Lorcan McGinley, his own master. How could he be part of such a betrayal? Had he meant to kill him all the time, and not Mr. Radley at all?

She had stood up without realizing it.

"I gotta go," she said, her voice almost choking her. She gulped and swallowed air. She scrambled towards the door and only remembered to stop and turn around to face him just as she touched the handle. She must explain herself, her flight. Anything but the truth. "If anyone come 'ere an' finds me, we'll both be in trouble," she blurted. "I only wanted to say I were sorry. I shouldn't 'a spoke."

"Gracie . . ." He stood up too and moved towards her.

She forced herself to smile. It must have been sickly. She knew it was false, and he must know it too. But she had to get out . . . now . . . this minute. Her mind was in chaos. She could not believe it, it was too horrible. There must be another answer, but she could not stay there to ask him.

She pulled the door open, her hands shaking, and almost tripped over and fell, banging against the jamb as she went out.

"Gracie!" He came after her.

She fled without looking back, clattering down the steps to the main men's landing, then down again to the corridor, and almost bumped into Doll.

"Sorry," she gasped. "Didn't mean ter tread on yer."

"Gracie! You all right?" Doll asked anxiously. "You look awful."

"Got an 'eadache," Gracie said, putting her hand up as if in pain. She heard footsteps behind her. It must be Finn. But he would not come in here, not with Doll. "I'll just go an' get a . . . a bit o' lavender oil, or summink. A cup o' tea, p'raps."

"I'll get you one," Doll offered immediately. "No wonder you've got a headache, with all that's going on. Come with me, I'll look after you." She would not take a denial.

Gracie accepted, though she had no choice short of an argument, and her head was in too much fever of thought to master any reasoning. Obediently she followed Doll along to the pantry where the kettle was, and the small hob. She saw no one in the corridor. She sat down in the chair while Doll fussed over her.

What had Finn done? How had he gotten the dynamite? Had he made the bomb himself? Hadn't Pitt proved he was not there? He would have thought of that, he thought of everything. And Finn could not have killed Mr. Greville. Mr. O'Day had been watching or listening to him all the time.

Doll was making tea. The kettle was singing.

She must think properly, she must have this straight in her mind. Her head was throbbing like a drum. Finn must be helping someone. It made most sense if it was Mr. Doyle. He was on the same side. Finn must be only pretending to be on Mr. McGinley's side.

"Gracie?"

She did not hear Doll's voice. There must be some other explanation. Finn was not the kind of person to want something so violent and so cruel. Someone far more wicked was using him, telling him these false stories about people like Neassa Doyle, Drystan O'Day, and getting him to do terrible things without understanding what the end of it would be.

"Gracie?"

She looked up. Doll was standing in front of her with a cup of tea in her hand, her face creased with worry.

"Thank you." She took it gingerly. It was very hot and it smelled like daisies.

"It's chamomile," Doll said. "It's good for headaches and feeling upset. You really do look poorly. Now, you better go and lie down for a while. I'll look after Mrs. Pitt for you, if she needs anything, if you like?"

Gracie forced herself to smile. "It's all right, thank yer, I'll be good in a minute or two. It's just . . . all this . . . all the 'ating people, gets yer down. Yer don't know 'oo yer can trust or 'oo's secretly plannin' summink 'orrible."

"I know." Doll sat down on the other chair, a cup of tea in her hands. "I think maybe we shouldn't trust anyone, 'cepting maybe your Mr. Pitt."

Gracie nodded, but in her mind she made the decision not to tell Pitt yet what she thought she had seen in Finn's room. Perhaps she was wrong. She did not really know anything about dynamite. Maybe she had only imagined the look on Finn's face.

She sipped the tea slowly. It was too hot, but it was rather nice, and gradually she began to feel a little better.

But for the rest of the afternoon she could not get the fear out of her mind. Should she tell Pitt after all? Maybe he should be the one to decide if it was dynamite, or whether Finn knew what he was doing or was being used by someone else. After all, Finn had seemed as shocked as anyone by Mr. McGinley's death. Gracie knew that. She had seen his face. Surely if he knew that the bomb in the study would go off, he would not have stood so close to the door that he was caught by the blast when it exploded?

It all made no sense.

She was in the laundry rinsing petticoats when she looked up and saw Finn in the doorway. There was no one else around just at the moment. Gwen had been and gone, the laundry maids were at tea. She had chosen the time on purpose, not wanting to have to talk to anyone. Now she ached for there to be someone else there, anyone at all.

"Gracie!" He took a step forward; his face was dark, his eyes troubled. "We have to talk about things. . . ."

"This isn't the place," she said quietly, gulping, realizing with a kind of sick misery that she was actually afraid of him. It was not just that she did not want to face the truth, or hear him try to explain with what might be lies, she was actually physically afraid. "Someone might come in." She heard her voice, high-pitched, almost a squeak. "Them other girls is only 'avin' tea. They'll be back any second now."

"No they won't," he said levelly, coming further towards her. "They only went five minutes ago, and they'll take half an hour easy, longer if they don't have much work waiting for them." He glanced around and saw a few items of personal linen, a little repairing, no sheets, no towels. They had all been done earlier, and it was a windy day. Everything was blown nearly dry and brought in and hung on the rails. The room smelled of clean cotton.

"Yeah, they will," she lied, holding on to the wet petticoat and wringing it as hard as she was able, as if she could somehow use it to protect herself.

He was coming closer. There was a curious expression in his face, as if he hated what he was doing but could find no way of avoiding it.

She backed away from the tub, still holding the petticoat in her hands.

"Gracie . . ." he said reasonably. "Stop . . ."

"It in't the place," she said again, still moving backwards. The petticoat was wrung hard. Maybe it would have been better wet?

"I only want to talk to you," he said earnestly.

She edged around the wooden tubs towards the farther door, past the copper boilers, still warm.

He was still coming towards her.

She picked up the big wooden pole the laundry maids used to stir the sheets.

"Gracie!" He looked hurt, as if she had struck him already.

It was ridiculous! She should have pretended she had seen nothing and conducted herself with some dignity. What did she imagine? That he was going to strangle her there in the laundry room?

Yes, she did! Why not? Mr. Greville had been drowned in his own bath, and Mr. Radley would have been blown up sitting at his desk in his study if Mr. McGinley hadn't been blown up first!

She threw the pole at him, then turned and fled, her feet clattering on the stone floor, her skirts flying, tangling around her legs, slowing her down. He must be behind her, chasing her. She could hear him, hear his feet, hear his voice calling out behind her. What would he do if he caught her? He was angry now, and hurt. She could hear that too.

She had never known she could run so fast. Her feet were sliding over the linoleum of the passageway. She barged around a corner, lurching against the wall, regained her balance with difficulty, arms flailing, and cannoned straight into someone. She let out a shriek of terror.

"Hey now! What's the matter with you? Anyone'd think the devil himself was behind you!" It was a man's voice, an Irish voice. He was holding on to her.

She looked up. Her heart almost stopped. It was Mr. Doyle. He had hold of her wrists and he was smiling.

She swung the wet petticoat hard and caught him across the side of the face, then kicked him as hard as she could on the shins.

He let go of her with a gasp of pain and astonishment.

She snatched her arms away and fled, charging through the green baize door into the hallway, leaving the door swinging on its hinges.

A footman looked at her in amazement.

"You all right, miss?" he said with a frown.

Grace was still holding the wet petticoat. Her cap had gone and she must be scarlet in the face.

"Yeah, perfickly," she said with as much dignity as possible. "Thank yer, Albert." She took a deep breath and decided to go upstairs to Charlotte's room. It was probably the only place where she was safe.

CHAPTER ELEVEN

It was not easy searching for the slippers with the blue heels. Charlotte excused herself from the luncheon table, pleading an unnamed indisposition. Let people assume it was a discomfort of the stomach. That was something about which no one would enquire too closely, nor would anyone feel compelled to follow her. For such things one wished privacy above all.

As soon as she was out of earshot of the dining room, she ran across the hall and up the stairs. A footman looked at her anxiously but said nothing. It was not his place to query the eccentric behavior of guests.

It had not been Kezia that Gracie had seen on the landing, of that Charlotte was almost certain. Kezia was too handsomely built. It could have been any other one of the three remaining female guests. She feared it was Eudora. She, above all, had a reason any woman could understand.

Charlotte already knew which was each person's room. She would start with Eudora, who, thank goodness, had been persuaded to join everyone else for luncheon. It would have been dreadfully awkward if either of the two recently widowed women had decided to remain in their rooms, which they could well have done without needing to offer any further explanation. Emily had had to work hard to achieve that. But Emily was a good diplomat, and she was certainly fully persuaded of the necessity for solving this crime most urgently. She was still finding it very hard to keep her composure and not give way to her fear for Jack. At least there was something she could do, some outlet for her physical and mental energies, a way of helping.

Charlotte knocked on Eudora's bedroom door, just in case Doll should be there.

There was no answer.

She opened the door and went in, and straight through to the dressing room. There was no time to consider anything now except which cupboard housed Eudora's boots and shoes. She looked in the first and saw rows of gowns. It was horrible searching through another woman's clothes without her knowledge. They were beautiful, heavy silks and taffetas, fine quality laces, smooth wools and gabardines. There was a rich fur collar on a traveling cape. They were colors which would have suited Charlotte perfectly. And none of these would be borrowed! She felt a prick of envy.

That was absurd! Who would want a queen's ransom of clothes at the price of being married to a man like Ainsley Greville?

The boots and shoes were on the rack below the dresses and on shelves to one side. They were as she had thought, all earth colors and warm tones, nothing blue or with blue heels.

She did not know if she was relieved or not. That meant it was either Iona or Justine. She would like it to be Iona.

It was a grubby thing searching through other people's bedrooms. They were so personal. It was the one place where you were most yourself, when your secrets and pretenses were taken away, where you let down your guard and allowed yourself to be vulnerable, naked in every sense, and asleep. Eudora's room had a faint odor of lilies and something heavier, spicier. It must be a perfume she liked.

Charlotte went to the door and opened it, looking outside cautiously, which she realized was pointless as soon as she did it. If anyone saw the door move at all, they would see her. She had no possible excuse. There was nothing she could say to justify being in Eudora's room.

There was no one there.

She slipped out just as Doll came around the corner. She looked prettier than Charlotte had seen her before, and for the first time she was smiling. Her head was high and she moved easily and lightly. Charlotte had no idea what had caused the change, but her start at being seen gave way immediately to a surge of happiness. If anyone in this house deserved a little joy, it was Doll.

"Afternoon, Mrs. Pitt," Doll said cheerfully. "Can I help you? Do you need something?"

Charlotte was a long way from her own room, and she could hardly claim to be lost. She scrambled for a lie which would be credible—and failed to find one.

"No, thank you," she said simply, and then hurried past Doll towards the end of the corridor and the landing. It was a nuisance. She wanted to search Justine's room, but Doll would still be around. They might be finishing luncheon, and Emily could not hold them indefinitely. Searching Eudora's room had already taken some time, long enough for a complete course at least.

She could not afford to hesitate. She had better try Iona's room.

She glanced around just to make sure there was no other servant in sight, then opened the door and went in. The floral curtains were drawn wide and the room was full of sunlight. Lorcan's brushes and his personal effects like collar studs and cuff links were gone from the tallboy, but when she went across to the wardrobes his clothes were still hanging there, and his boots beneath. It was an unpleasant sensation, a reminder of the closeness of life and death. An instant and one was changed into the other. Yesterday morning he had been alive. He had been far braver, more selfless than she had imagined him. Now it was too late to get to know him or know anything of the man he had really been behind the rather brittle exterior and the passionate hatreds and ambitions behind which he had hidden his virtues. He had seemed so cold, and yet he could not have been.

How did Iona feel now? Was that part of the beginning of the end of her romance with Fergal Moynihan? And it did seem as if they were feeling a sudden chill, a realization of the differences between them which no amount of fascination could overcome.

She tried the next wardrobe. It held gowns, but not as many as she had expected. There were dark blues, dark greens, a rich, lush purple which she envied. They were dramatic colors, highly flattering to dark hair and blue eyes. Iona knew how to make the best of herself. From the shawls and blouses, she also knew how to make a relatively small wardrobe look much larger.

There were three pairs of boots, brown, black and fawn, and one pair of slippers, mid-green.

She closed the door and took another quick glance around. There was nothing else of interest. Her eye caught the wastepaper basket, a pretty thing of woven wicker with a flower motif on the side. There were pieces of torn paper in it. It was an appalling thing to do, but she went over and picked up two or three of them. She looked at them. It was inexcusable. They were part of a love letter from Fergal. There were only a few words, but it was unmistakable.

She dropped them again quickly, her face hot. Kezia was going to have a lot to be generous over, if she could find it in her. Perhaps Fergal would have learned something about infatuation, and about love and loss, and how easy it is to follow one's desires, and need the compassion of those you have treated lightly, when your own time of loneliness and defeat comes.

Out on the landing there was nothing left but to go back to Justine's room. Unless it was Kezia after all, it must be Justine.

She looked very carefully from left to right to see if Doll were still anywhere in sight, but thank heaven she was not.

Charlotte ran along the corridor and, after the very briefest rap on the door, threw it open and slipped inside, closing it behind her as quickly as she could.

It was smaller, prepared in haste for an unexpected guest. The dressing room was barely big enough for the wardrobes, dressing table, and small central table with a lace cloth and a low easy chair beside it, and a pleasant fireplace. She looked in the first wardrobe. There were several dresses, all of very good quality and apparently bought within the last year or two. The colors varied but were suitable for a young, unmarried woman. Justine might lack family; she certainly was not without funds. Her parents, or some other relative, had left her very well provided for.

She looked at the shoes and boots. They too were of very fine make and style. None were blue or had blue heels.

She could not stay there any longer. Anyone could leave the table for a dozen different reasons, and she would be caught here. She would look like a petty thief at worst, or at best an unpleasantly nosy woman who snooped through other people's clothes and personal belongings.

On second thought, perhaps it was better simply to be thought a thief!

She went out into the corridor and had only just reached the landing when she saw Justine at the head of the stairs.

"Are you feeling better?" Justine asked solicitiously.

Charlotte felt as if she must be blushing scarlet. "Yes . . . yes, thank you," she stammered. "Much better. I . . . I wasn't nearly as ill as I thought. Maybe the room was a little warm. A . . . a drink of water." That was a stupid remark. There was plenty of water available in the dining room. It was the easiest place to find it. And the room had not been hot. Her guilt must be standing out like spilled wine on a clean tablecloth.

Justine smiled.

"I'm so glad. I expect it is just the distress of the last few days. I am sure it will affect all of us, one way or another."

"Yes," Charlotte said gratefully. "Yes, that will be what it is."

Justine walked past her. She moved extraordinarily gracefully, back straight, head high, a very slight swing to her skirts. One side brushed against one of the chairs on the landing. Charlotte, who was staring after her, saw a glimpse of heel, blue heel. Justine's gown was smoky gray-blue, with darker patterning on it. Blue slippers were right. On the first evening she had been there, when Greville had been killed, she had worn another blue dress.

Charlotte stood on the spot as if she truly were faint. She found herself gripping the railing to steady herself. Perhaps Gracie had been mistaken? She had seen the heel only for an instant. Maybe it had been gray or green? Gaslight could be misleading. It could alter colors, everyone knew that, certainly every woman. There were colors which suited perfectly in the daylight, and by gaslight made one look a hundred and jaundiced into the bargain.

She was still in the same spot when Emily came up the stairs towards her.

"What's the matter?" Emily demanded. "You look terrible. You aren't really ill, are you?"

"No. I saw the shoes. . . ."

Emotion crowded Emily's face—elation, fear, anxiety.

"Good! Whose are they?" she demanded.

"Justine's. She's wearing them right now."

Emily stared at her. "Are you sure?"

"No . . . yes. No, I'm not sure. Except I am, because they aren't anyone else's."

Emily said nothing. She looked suddenly sad, hurt, as Charlotte felt.

"I must go and tell Thomas," Charlotte said after a moment or two. "I wish it were not her."

"Why?" Emily shook her head.

"Because I like her. . . ." Charlotte said lamely.

"No . . . I mean why would she kill Greville," Emily clarified. "It doesn't make any sense."

"I know that." Charlotte started to move at last. "But she had the shoes. That's what I'm going to tell Thomas . . . just that she had the shoes."

As soon as Charlotte entered the withdrawing room Pitt stood up, excusing himself to the others, and came towards her, his face intent.

"Are you all right?" he asked her in barely more than a whisper. "You do look rather pale. Did you find the shoes?"

"Yes . . ."

"Well? Where are they?" Now he looked pale as well, his eyes hollow, dark-ringed from lack of sleep. "Are they Eudora's?"

She managed the ghost of a smile. She would have preferred it if they were.

"No . . . they are Justine's. She's wearing them now."

He stared at her. "Justine's?" He said exactly what Emily had. "Are you sure? It makes no sense! Why on earth would Justine want to kill Ainsley Greville? She only met him—" he stopped.

Padraig Doyle moved forward from the fire where he had been standing. "Are you all right, Mrs. Pitt?" he asked with some concern.

"I'm sure she will be," Pitt said quickly, putting his arm around Charlotte. "I think it would be better if she went upstairs and lay down. The long journey to London yesterday must have been too much for her. Please excuse us both?" And with a charming smile he guided Charlotte out of the room and closed the door behind them as Kezia also politely wished Charlotte restored health.

"You make me sound like some drooping lily," she said hotly the moment they went out of earshot. "One trip on the train and I faint all over the place. They'll think I'm too feeble for words."

"We can't afford to care what they think," he replied impatiently. "Come on upstairs. We have to reason this through and make some kind of sense out of it."

She went obediently. She had no desire to sit through an afternoon's polite conversation in the withdrawing room, and if Justine returned she would not be able to hide the confusion or the sadness she felt. She thought she was quite a good actress and could mask her feelings rather well, but Emily said she was awful. On reasonable consideration, with some honesty, it was possible Emily was right.

Up on the landing Pitt turned not towards their room but in the opposite direction, towards the Grevilles' bathroom. He opened the door and went in. She followed with a shiver, although in fact it was not cold, except to the mind.

"Why in here?" she said quickly. "I can think just as well in the bedroom."

"I want to re-create exactly what happened," he replied, closing and locking the door.

"Will that help?" she asked.

"I don't know. Perhaps not." He looked at her with raised eyebrows. "Have you got a better idea?"

She felt a kind of desperation welling up inside her. She tried to steady her mind. Whatever the outcome was, there must be reason in it, emotional reason. Nobody was mad, acting from unconnected, irrational motives, it was simply that there was something important that they did not know.

"She must have had a reason," she said, not directly in answer. "I don't think it's anything to do with Ireland. It must be personal. Perhaps we were wrong in assuming they don't know each other?"

"They neither of them showed the slightest sign of recognition when she came in that first time," he pointed out, sitting on the edge of the bath.

"Which only means that they did not want anyone else to know they knew each other," she said reasonably. "Which in turn means it was not a relationship they could acknowledge."

He frowned. "But the types of women he was used to were servants and the looser-moraled wives of acquaintances. Justine doesn't appear to be either of those."

"Well, if she did know him in that way," she said with a shudder, "it would provide an excellent reason for her wanting him dead before he could perhaps tell Piers and ruin her prospects of marriage. Added to which, I think she really loves Piers, and I am certain he loves her."

Pitt sighed. "I have little doubt that Greville would have told him when he had the opportunity. He wouldn't want his only son marrying a woman who used to be his own mistress, if that word could be used of the way he regarded women."

"Well, not for Doll Evans, poor creature," she said bitterly. "And from what you said, possibly not for some of the others he discarded."

He bent forward and started to unfasten his boots.

"What are you doing?" she asked him.

"Going to reenact what happened," he replied. "I don't want to scratch the bath. I'll take Greville's part, you take Justine's." He took off his boot and began to undo the other.

"I'll start from the door," she said. "I'm not going outside. You can pretend I have towels."

He looked up at her with a bleak smile and took off his other boot. He stood up and climbed into the bath. He lay down gingerly, trying to arrange himself as he remembered Greville.

She watched from the door.

"All right," he said after a moment. "Come in as if you had a pile of towels."

She held up her arms and walked forward. He was looking straight at her.

"This doesn't work," he answered. "You had better get towels and come in here properly, holding them in front of you. The screen wasn't up; the room was just like this. He was lying with his head a little to one side, I think."

"Shouldn't I get Tellman?" she suggested. "To make sure it was just the same? Maybe he could take Greville's part and you could watch?"

"He isn't tall enough," he agreed. "But yes, fetch him, by all means. And get the towels. If we are right about them knowing each other, he would have said something, surely, if she had come into the bathroom? Didn't he suspect what she might do?"

"I doubt it," she said with a slight smile. "He was an arrogant man. He'd used and thrown aside a lot of women. Maybe he thought she was going to plead for his mercy or his discretion."

"Then she was a bigger fool than I take her for," Pitt said grimly.

She went out, leaving him lying in the bath looking glum, and went to find Tellman. It did not take her long, and she returned less than ten minutes later with him and also a pile of half a dozen towels.

"Don't see what it'll accomplish," Tellman observed with a shrug and a wary look at Pitt, who did look somewhat odd. Charlotte had told him about Justine and the blue slippers. He had been surprised, and she thought disconcerted also, but she was guessing from the expression in his face. He had not said anything.

Pitt did not reply, but slid back down to the position he thought Greville had occupied and looked at Charlotte to begin again.

She held the towels on one arm and closed the door behind her, as if she had just entered.

"You're not lying right," Tellman criticized Pitt. "He had his head a bit more to that side."

"It wouldn't make any difference," Charlotte pointed out. "He could still see me unless I held the towels up in front of my face." She did it in demonstration. "And I wouldn't have to look towards him."

"You would as you passed him to go behind." Tellman was thoroughly argumentative. He looked back at Pitt. "And you still aren't in the right position. You are too straight."

Pitt obligingly slid further sideways.

Tellman regarded him. "Now you've changed your shoulders as well. He had his head more to one side—"

"Does it matter?" Charlotte interrupted. "It wouldn't affect what he could see."

"Maybe he was asleep?" Tellman said without conviction. "That would account for why he didn't react or call out."

"She couldn't rely on that," Pitt pointed out. "And Justine wouldn't leave anything to that kind of chance."

"It was a crime of opportunity." Tellman was still disposed to argue.

"No it wasn't," Charlotte contradicted him. "She was dressed as a maid. That meant she thought about it and planned it. She must have brought the lace cap up from the laundry room, even if she took a dress from somewhere closer. She chose the only style of cap which would hide her own hair."

"Well, you still aren't lying right." Tellman was immovable. He went over to Pitt and put his hand on the side of Pitt's head. "You should be another three inches over that way." He pushed gently.

"Oh!" Pitt let out a cry. "Three inches that way and my neck would be broken!" he said sharply.

Tellman froze. Then he straightened very slowly, his body rigid.

Pitt let out a long sigh, then sat up in the bath, staring at Charlotte.

"Are you sure?" Charlotte whispered. "Absolutely sure?"

"Yes!" Tellman replied sharply, but his very stubbornness was a doubt.

"Only one way." Pitt climbed out of the bath, characteristically without bothering to straighten his clothes. "We'll have to go to the icehouse and have a look at the body." He walked towards the bathroom door.

"Boots," Charlotte said quickly.

"What?"

"Boots," she replied, pointing to his boots at the end of the bath.

He came back and put them on absentmindedly, smiling at her for a moment, then following Tellman.

But he got no further than the landing when he met Gracie, her face pinched with anxiety, her cap gone, her apron crumpled.

"Please sir, I gotter see yer!" she said desperately, her eyes on Pitt's, completely ignoring Tellman beside him, and Charlotte standing in the bathroom doorway. "It's private. . . ."

He could see the importance of it to her, whether it proved to be real or not to anyone else. He did not hesitate.

"Yes, of course. We'll go back into the bathroom." He turned and walked past Tellman, leaving him on the landing, and caught Charlotte's eye, hoping she would understand. He closed the door after Gracie. "What is it?"

She looked absolutely wretched, her small hands clenched in her apron, making it like a rag.

"Wot does dynamite look like, sir?"

He controlled his surprise with an effort, and the immediate leap of both hope and fear.

"White and solid, a bit like candle tallow, only a bit different to touch."

"Sort o' . . . sweaty?" she asked, a catch in her voice.

"Yes . . . that's right. They sometimes wrap it in red paper."

"I seen some. I'm sorry, sir, I went there, but I can explain. It weren't nothin' wrong." She looked thoroughly frightened.

"I hadn't thought it would be, Gracie," he said, more or less honestly. This was sounding like Charlotte's area of jurisdiction. He certainly was not going to interfere. "Where was it?"

"In Finn 'Ennessey's room, sir." She colored painfully. "I went ter tell 'im I were sorry for makin' 'im look at the truth about Neassa Doyle an' Drystan O'Day and Mr. Chinnery. You see, I made 'im look at the newspaper pieces."

"What newspaper pieces?"

"Them wot Mrs. Pitt brought back from Lunnon. It proved Mr. Chinnery couldn't a' done it, 'cos 'e were dead."

"But that was thirty years ago. It wouldn't be in today's newspapers," he said reasonably. "Are you sure you have that right, Gracie?"

"Yes sir. They was old newspapers . . . just pieces like."

"Old newspaper cuttings?" he said in disbelief.

"Yeah. She brung 'em back from Lunnon." Her face was completely innocent and full of fear.

"Did she indeed? I'll speak to Mrs. Pitt about that later. So you saw what looked like dynamite in Finn Hennessey's room?"

"Yes sir."

"Does he know you saw it?"

"I . . ." She lowered her eyes. She looked wretched. "I fink so. 'E came after me later on, ter try an' explain, I fink. I . . . I din't listen . . . I jus' ran."

"How long ago did you see this dynamite, Gracie?"

She did not look at him. "About two hours," she whispered.

He did not need to tell her that she should have reported it to him straightaway. She knew it already.

"I see. Then I had better go and speak to him about it. You stay here with Mrs. Pitt. And that's an order, Gracie."

"Yes sir." Still she did not look up.

"Gracie . . ."

"Yeah . . ."

"He might have hidden it, because he knew you'd seen it, but he can't have taken it off the premises."

She looked up slowly.

He smiled at her.

Her eyes filled with tears which spilled over down her cheeks.

He put his hand on her shoulder very gently. "I know it's hard," he said. "But you did the only thing you could."

She nodded and sniffed.

He patted her, wishing he could do more, and went out to find Tellman.

Charlotte looked at him inquiringly.

"I think we have to arrest Finn Hennessey," he said almost under his breath. "I wish I didn't."

Her face crumpled with sorrow, and she turned to the bathroom to go immediately to Gracie.

"Come on." Pitt strode ahead along the corridor, leaving Tellman to follow behind, torn whether to stay or go, hating every step of it.

At the top of the main stairs they found Wheeler looking surprisingly cheerful. For a man whose employer had just been murdered and who therefore was about to be without a position, his general air of well-being was extraordinary. He seemed to glow with some inner secret which buoyed him up and filled him with joy.

"Do you know where Hennessey is?" Pitt asked him.

"Yes sir," Wheeler said instantly. "He is in the stable yard talking to one of the grooms. Seems to have made friends. Poor young man has nothing much to do now that Mr. McGinley is dead."

"Rather like yourself," Pitt observed.

Wheeler looked faintly surprised. "Why yes, I suppose it is." He did not seem greatly perturbed by it, and having ascertained that that was all he could do to be of assistance, he continued on his way.

"What's wrong with him?" Tellman demanded angrily, catching up with Pitt to walk side by side with him along the passageway towards the side door. "He looks like he ate the cream instead of a man without a job."

"I don't know," Pitt replied. "I would guess it has something to do with Doll Evans. I hope so." He shot Tellman a dazzling smile, then went out of the door and strode across the ground towards the stable gates, leaving Tellman to follow after.

Finn Hennessey was standing in the yard talking to a groom who was lounging against the stable door. They were sheltered from the wind and it was quite mild out there in the late afternoon. Pitt dropped his pace to an amble. He did not want Finn to run, and then have to chase him in an unpleasant scene. It would all be painful enough. He saw Tellman walk past and go to the far side of the yard, as if he intended going through the gates and into the drive.

"Mr. Hennessey," Pitt said, stopping in front of him.

Finn looked around and straightened up, throwing away the straw he had been chewing. The groom seemed unaware of anything untoward.

"Yes?" Finn said, then saw something in Pitt's eyes, in his face, or even the tension in his body. For a second of prickling silence he stood poised on the edge of flight, panic in his face. Then he realized there was nowhere to run to, and he relaxed. A curious rigidity took hold of him. His body stiffened as though in anticipation of a blow, and a veil came over the directness of his eyes. "Yes?" he said again.

Pitt had seen that look before. He had not really expected Hennessey to tell him anything, but the faint hope of it died that moment.

"Finn Hennessey, I would like to question you about the dynamite placed in Mr. Radley's study and exploded by Mr. McGinley, we assume, in an attempt to make it safe. Do you know where that dynamite came from?"

"No," Finn said with a faint smile.

"I have reason to believe there may still be some in your room," Pitt said grimly. "I intend to go and look. If, of course, you have removed it and placed it somewhere else, then it would be better for you if you tell me where it is before it explodes and hurts someone else . . . almost certainly someone who has no part in your quarrel."

"I'm saying nothing," Finn replied, then stood still, his head lifted, his eyes straight ahead.

Tellman came up behind him and slipped on the handcuffs. The groom looked aghast. He opened his mouth to speak and then found he had nothing to say.

Pitt turned and left to go and search Hennessey's room. He took the butler, Dilkes, with him, in case he should find something and later require a witness to the fact.

Dilkes stood in the doorway somberly, deeply unhappy at the whole affair. Pitt went into the room and began methodically to go through cupboards and drawers. He found the candles and the one stick of dynamite inside a tall boot at the back of the wardrobe. It was out of sight, but hardly hidden. Hennessey had either been sure enough of Gracie or had thought it not worth trying to hide in some other place less obviously his. Maybe his type of loyalty extended to not attempting to lay the blame on anyone else. He was a passionate believer in his cause, not a murderer for hire or for personal satisfaction.

There was paper ash in the bowl. It could have been anything, possibly the letter Gracie saw on the table. He had taken care at least to destroy everything to link him to someone else. That was worth a kind of oblique respect.

Pitt showed the dynamite to Dilkes, then replaced it and requested the butler to lock the door and give him the key. If there was another key, he was to find that and give it to Pitt also. There was a storeroom with a grille window and a stout door where Hennessey could remain until the local police took him away, perhaps tomorrow or the day after.

Pitt went back to Finn again, with Tellman, and told him about finding the dynamite.

"I'm not saying anything," Finn repeated, looking directly at Pitt. "I know my cause is just. I've lived for Irish freedom. I'll die for it if I have to. I love my country and its people. I'll just be one more martyr in the cause."

"Being hanged for a murder you committed is not martyrdom," Pitt replied tartly. "Most people would regard murdering your employer, a man who trusted you, another Irishman fighting for the same cause, as a pretty shabby and cowardly betrayal. And not only that, but pointless as well. What did killing McGinley achieve? He wanted exactly the same as you did."

"I didn't kill McGinley," Finn said stubbornly. "I didn't put the dynamite there."

"You expect us to believe that?" Pitt said with disdain.

"I don't care a damn what you believe!" Finn spat back. "You're just another English oppressor forcing your will on a defenseless people."

"You're the one with the dynamite," Pitt retaliated. "You're the one who blew up McGinley, not me."

"I didn't put the dynamite there! Anyway, it wasn't meant for McGinley, you fool," Finn said contemptuously. "It was for Radley! I'd have thought you'd realize that—" He stopped.

Pitt smiled. "If you didn't put it there, how do you know who it was meant for?"

"I'm saying nothing," Finn repeated angrily. "I don't betray my friends. I'll die first."

"Probably," Pitt agreed. But he also knew that he would get little more from him, and grudgingly he respected his courage, if little else. "You are being used," he added from the door.

Finn smiled. His face was very pale, and there was a sweat of fear on his lip. "But I know by whom, and what for, and I'm willing. Can you say as much?"

"I believe so," Pitt replied. "Are you as sure that those you've used feel as certain?"

Finn's jaw tightened. "You use who you have to. The cause justifies it."

"No, it doesn't," Pitt replied, this time with absolute certainty. "If it destroys what is good in you, then it is a bad cause, or you have misunderstood it. Everything you do becomes part of it and part of you. You can't take it off, like old clothes, when you get there. It's not clothes, Finn, it's your flesh."

"No, it isn't!" Finn shouted after him, but Pitt shut the door and walked slowly back towards the kitchens and then into the main part of the house. He was miserable, and inside him there was a deep, hard anger. Finn had been gullible, like thousands of others. The worst in him had been wooed and won, then used by more cynical people. Certainly he had been willing to choose violence to right the wrongs he perceived. He had not cared who was hurt by it. But he had had the courage of his beliefs. He had taken at least some of the risks himself. Behind him were other men, hidden, who had prompted him to his acts, who had perpetuated the old legends and lies and used them to motivate the repeating violence.

He would dearly like to have known who wrote the letter Finn had burned. That was the man he wanted. And it was probably someone in this house. He feared it was Padraig Doyle.

He went to the library, where what was left of the conference was still proceeding. He knocked and went in. Moynihan and O'Day were sitting at one side of the table, Jack and Doyle on the other. They all looked up as Pitt came in.

"Excuse me, gentlemen," he apologized. "But I must speak with Mr. Radley. I am sorry, but it cannot wait."

Moynihan glanced at O'Day, who was watching Pitt.

"Of course," Doyle said quickly. "I hope nothing further unpleasant has happened? No one is hurt?"

"Were you expecting something?" O'Day demanded.

Doyle merely smiled and waved his hand in dismissal.

Outside in the hall, Pitt told Jack about finding the dynamite and arresting Finn Hennessey.

Jack looked deeply unhappy. "What does it prove?" he said with a frown. "Who is behind him?"

"I don't know," Pitt admitted.

Jack was puzzled. "But we have O'Day's word that neither McGinley nor Hennessey could have killed Greville!"

"I know. That was Justine—"

Jack's jaw dropped. "What? Oh come, Thomas! You've made a mistake there. You must have. You're not saying she's behind this? She's Irish?"

"No—no, that had nothing to do with politics." Pitt sighed. "I don't know the answer to that yet, only the evidence. She was seen by Gracie. . . ." He saw Jack's face. "Her shoes were," he tried to explain. "She was dressed as a maid. Gracie saw her back, but today remembered seeing her shoes as well. . . ." He stopped again. Jack's expression made continuing unnecessary.

"I must tell Iona and Mrs. Greville that I have arrested Hennessey," he said quietly. "If you can keep the men talking a little longer it would be very helpful."

"Doyle?" Jack asked, his voice hard and sad.

"Probably," Pitt agreed. He did not add that he wished it were not. He could see it in Jack's face as well. But being likable and having a sense of humor and imagination were not mitigating factors in murder, simply coincidences, just added hurt after the difficulty and the ugliness and the waste of it.

Pitt found Iona alone in the long gallery staring out into the wind and the gathering dusk. She did not turn, and for several moments he stood watching her. Her face was completely immobile, her expression impossible to read. He wondered what was occupying her mind so intensely she was apparently unaware of anyone else having come into the room, let alone of being observed.

At first he thought it was a calmness in her. She seemed almost relaxed, the lines and tension somewhat gone from her features. There was no sense of pain in her, no torment, no violence of emotions, certainly not the anger which so often accompanied loss. There was no struggle to deny the reality, to go back and recapture the past before the bereavement.

Did she really not care, feel no pain or grief at the heroic death of her husband? For all her romantic songs, her poetry and music, was she essentially quite cold inside, a lover of the beauty of art, but dead to reality? It was a peculiarly repellent thought. He found himself shivering although the gallery was not cold.

"Mrs. McGinley . . ." He wanted to break the moment.

She turned towards him, not startled, simply mildly surprised.

"Yes, Mr. Pitt?"

He saw sadness and confusion in her eyes. She was lost, uncertain what she felt, only that it hurt. There was no excitement, no relief that she was free to go to Moynihan, or even resolution that she wanted to. Perhaps her emotion in seeking him had not been love so much as loneliness?

"I am sorry, Mrs. McGinley, but I have had to arrest your manservant, Finn Hennessey. He was in possession of dynamite."

Her eyes widened. "Dynamite? Finn was?"

"Yes. It was in his room. He has not denied it, simply refused to give any explanation or say where he got it, though he denies making the bomb or placing it in the study."

"Then who did?"

"I don't know, yet, but it is only a matter of time now." That was a lie, he felt no such certainty, but he wanted her to believe he did. She might even have been the one behind Finn, although he doubted it. He knew she had not placed the bomb herself; her time was accounted for by Moynihan and by Doyle. "I am telling you simply so you know why he is no longer available to you. I'm sorry."

She turned away from him, looking out again towards the dusk beyond the window where rain now spattered the panes.

"He was always passionate about Ireland, about our freedom. I suppose I shouldn't be surprised. But I really never thought he would hurt Lorcan. He loved Ireland as much as anyone."

She was silent for a moment and when she continued there was a different kind of pain in her voice. "As long as I knew Lorcan, it was what he cared about most . . . more, I think, than he ever loved me. Freedom for Ireland was what he talked about, planned for, worked for all his life. No sacrifice of time or money was too much. I know it was meant for Mr. Radley, but if Finn knew it was there, you would think he would have stopped Lorcan going to try to . . ." She shook her head. "No, I suppose not. Perhaps they quarreled. He may have tried to stop him, and Lorcan was determined to defuse it anyway. I don't know. I don't even know why." She blinked. "I seem to find there is so much confuses me now . . . things I thought I was certain of."

He did not know what to say. He wished there was something comforting, an assurance that it would pass, but there was none. It would not necessarily resolve.

She looked at him and suddenly smiled very slightly. "I thought you were going to say something trite. Thank you for not doing so."

He found himself coloring, immensely relieved he had not spoken. He looked at her for a moment longer, then turned and went.

In the evening, after dinner, Pitt was obliged to face the necessity of looking more closely at the body of Ainsley Greville. If Tellman were correct and he had lain in the bath at the angle described, then his neck had been broken. Perhaps it was possible the blow to the back of his skull had accomplished that, but he found it hard to believe, and he would not accept it without detailed examination. The blow, as he had seen it, would have been enough to concuss but not to cause death—unless it were a great deal harder than it had appeared to him. It did not seem at the right angle. If Greville's neck were broken, then he had not drowned. Pitt needed to resolve it. Perhaps it made no difference to the charge, or to Justine's guilt, but it was unexplained, and he would not leave it so.

He needed Piers's help. And if it were necessary to do more than examine from the surface, then it would have to be Piers who did so. He should have Eudora's permission. That was something he dreaded, but there was no alternative.

Charlotte saw him as he was starting up the stairs.

"Where are you going?" she asked, catching up with him, searching his face anxiously.

"To ask Piers to help me look at the body again," he answered. "He's upstairs with his mother. Anyway, I need her permission, or more properly, I would rather not take the time and trouble to apply for a legal writ."

Her face tightened. "An autopsy?" she said huskily. "Thomas, you can't ask Piers to do an autopsy on his own father! And . . . and when are you going to tell him it was Justine? What are you going to do about her?"

"Nothing yet," he answered, meeting her gaze. She looked frightened and worried, and still her composure was complete. If she wanted or needed comfort there was no sign of it.

"Do you want me to come with you?" she offered. "In case Eudora is very distressed? Some people find the invasion of an autopsy very dreadful . . . as if in some way the person they loved could know about the . . . the intimacy of it."

Instinct told him to decline.

"No, thank you. I think this is something better done with as few people involved as possible. I won't even take Tellman." He changed the subject. "How is Gracie? She's taken this matter of Hennessey very bad."

"I know," she said softly, her face bleak with sadness and anger. "It will be hard for her for a while. I think the best thing we can do is say as little as possible. It will just take time."

"By the way, Charlotte." He looked very directly at her. "Where did you get the newspaper cuttings that Gracie showed to Hennessey?"

"Oh . . ." She colored uncomfortably. "I think . . . all things considered . . . you might prefer not to know that. Please don't ask, then I shall not have to tell you."

"Charlotte . . ."

She smiled at him dazzlingly, and before he could argue, she touched his hand, then turned and went downstairs.

Charlotte turned in the hall and watched him disappear around the newel at the top. Her momentary happiness vanished. She felt so alone she could have cried, which was ridiculous. She was tired. She seemed to have spent weeks trying to make things run smoothly, to prevent quarrels from becoming permanent rifts, trying to make light conversation when all any of them wanted to do was scream at each other, or weep with grief and fear, and now confusion and anxiety as well, and the dark pain of disillusion as things they thought they had known fell apart.

Emily was still terrified for Jack, and she had good cause. She was looking paler and more tired with each day. It was all pointless anyway; nobody was going to solve the Irish Problem. They would probably still be hating each other in fifty years. Was it worth one more life lost or broken?

And what about Eudora? How was she going to find the strength to comfort Piers when he heard the truth about Justine . . . whatever that truth was? Could he ever find peace within himself once he knew the woman he loved so much now had been his own father's mistress—and then murdered him? His world was about to end.

And Eudora had not been close enough to him to give the gentleness, the silent understanding he would need. She had not been a large enough part of his experiences in the past to travel through this with him. He would not be able to allow her. Charlotte knew it already from the small things Eudora had said, but more from the way Eudora had watched him with Justine and not known how he would react, what would make him laugh or touch his emotions. Charlotte had felt Eudora's sense of exclusion, as she felt the sudden chill of her own now.

She watched Pitt's back as he reached the top of the stairs and wondered if he would turn and look at her. He must know she was still standing by the newel at the bottom.

But he did not. His mind was on Eudora and Piers, and what he must ask of them. So it should be. Perhaps hers was at least in part on Emily.

Aunt Vespasia's advice seemed hollow. There was probably honor in it, but very little comfort. She turned away and went back to the withdrawing room. Kezia was alone. She ought to talk to her, not simply leave her.

"What do you need to look at him again for?" Piers asked with a shiver. He looked pale and tired, like everyone else, but in no sense afraid. It was perhaps the last evening he was going to have such an innocence.

"I would prefer to see if I am correct before I tell you," Pitt replied, looking apologetically at Eudora, who had risen and was standing in front of the boudoir fire. She had not taken her eyes from Pitt's face since he had come in. Thank heaven Justine was not there. She had apparently chosen to retire early.

"I suppose," she said slowly. "If you must?"

"It matters, Mrs. Greville, or I would not ask," he assured her. "I really am very sorry." He was apologizing not only for the present, but for the future as well.

"I know." She smiled at him, and there was a warmth in her he found it impossible to disbelieve. If it was indeed Doyle behind Finn Hennessey and the bomb, she was never going to heal from this. It would be a mortal wound. Half of him wanted to stay and offer whatever understanding or compassion was possible, the other half wanted to escape before he said or did something, or what he feared for her was betrayed in his face. He hesitated a moment.

She looked at him with increasing anxiety, as if she read his indecision and perceived the reasons.

He turned to Piers.

"There is no point in delaying what must be done," he said grimly. "It is best to begin."

Piers took a deep breath. "Yes, of course." He glanced at his mother, seemed on the edge of saying something, then it eluded him. He moved to the door ahead of Pitt and held it open for him.

They went together, without speaking again, down the stairs, across the hall, through the baize door and along the passage past the kitchens and servants' hall. Pitt collected the lanterns and led the way past the stillroom, gameroom, coal room, knife room, and general other storage and workplaces to the icehouse. He put the lantern down and took out the keys. Beside him Piers was standing rigidly, as though his muscles were locked. Perhaps Pitt should not have asked this of him? He hesitated with his hand on the key.

"What is it?" Piers asked.

Pitt still could not make a certain decision.

"What's wrong?" Piers said again.

"Nothing." It would not make any difference in the end. He put the key in the lock and turned it, then bent and picked up the lantern and went in. The cold hit him immediately, and the damp, slightly sickly smell. Or perhaps it was his imagination, knowing what was there.

"Is there a light?" Piers asked with a tremor in his voice.

"No, only the lanterns. I suppose they usually get the meat out during daylight," Pitt replied. "And I expect leave the door open."

Piers closed it and held the other lantern high. The room was quite large, stacked with blocks of ice. The floor was stone tile, with drains to carry off the surplus water. Carcases of meat hung on hooks from the ceiling: beef, mutton, veal and pork. Offal sat in trays, and several strings of sausages looped over other hooks.

A large trestle table had been moved in, and the outlines of two human bodies were plainly visible under an old velvet dining room curtain, faded now.

Pitt took the curtain off and saw the white, oddly waxy face of Ainsley Greville. The other face, Lorcan McGinley's, was so swathed in the remains of the study curtain to hide the blood and the injuries that it looked far less obviously human.

Piers took a deep breath and let it out slowly.

"What am I looking for?" he asked.

"His neck," Pitt replied. "The angle of his head."

"But he's been moved. What does it matter now? He was hit from behind. We already know that." Piers frowned. "What are you thinking, Mr. Pitt? What do you know now that we didn't then?"

"Please look at his neck."

"That blow wouldn't break it." Piers was puzzled. "But if it had, how does that alter anything?"

Pitt looked down at the body and nodded very slightly.

Piers obeyed. There was a very slight moment of reluctance, the knowledge of who it was he was touching so professionally, then he placed his fingers on the skull and moved it gently, then again, exploring, concentrating.

Pitt waited. The cold seemed to eat into him. No wonder meat kept well here. It was not far above freezing, if at all. The damp from the ice seemed to penetrate the flesh. The taste of dead things filled his mouth and nose.

The lanterns burned absolutely steadily. It was totally windless, almost airless in there.

"You're right!" Piers looked up, his eyes wide and dark in the uncertain light. "His neck is broken. I don't understand it. That blow shouldn't have done that. It's in the wrong place, and at the wrong angle."

"Would that blow at the back have killed him?" Pitt asked.

Piers looked unhappy. "I'm not absolutely certain, but I don't think so. I don't see how it could." He swallowed, and Pitt could see his throat jerk. "There would be no way of knowing if he was dead when he slid under the water. . . ."

Pitt waited.

"I could find out if there is water in the lungs. If there isn't, then the broken neck killed him and he was already dead before he went under."

"And the blow at the back?" Pitt asked again.

"I might be able to tell from that if it happened when he was alive, or dead, by the blood and the bruising. The bathwater washed the outside clean, of course." Piers seemed hunched into himself, his face shadowed starkly in the lanternlight. "But if I . . . if I did a post-mortem examination . . . at least . . . I don't know if I . . . I am really qualified to give an opinion. I couldn't in court, of course. . . . They wouldn't accept my judgment."

"Then you had better be very careful how you treat the evidence," Pitt said with a bleak smile. "It could make a lot of difference, one way or the other."

"Could it?" Piers sounded disbelieving.

Pitt thought of Justine, of Doll, and of Lorcan McGinley.

"Oh, yes."

"I can't do it here," Piers said grimly. "I can't see, for a start. And I'm so cold I can't hold my hands still."

"We'll use one of the laundry rooms," Pitt decided. "There's running water and a good wooden scrubbing table. I don't suppose you have any instruments with you?"

"I'm only a student." Piers's voice was tight and a little high. "But I'm very nearly qualified. I take my final exams this year."

"Can you do this? I don't want to send for the village doctor. He won't be trained for this kind of thing either. To send to London for someone I would have to do it through the assistant commissioner, and it will take too long."

"I understand." Piers looked at him unwaveringly in the lantern-light. "You think it was my Uncle Padraig, and you want the proof before he leaves."

There was no purpose in denying it.

"Can you work with the best kitchen knives, if they are sharpened?" Pitt said instead.

Piers flinched. "Yes."

Carrying the body from the icehouse was a miserable and exceedingly awkward matter. It must not be handled roughly, or damage might be done which would destroy the very evidence they were looking for. Geville had been a large man, tall and well built. To place him on a door would make him impossibly heavy for Pitt, Tellman and Piers to carry unassisted.

"Well, we can't get anyone else," Tellman said tartly. "We'll have to think of another way. I've seen enough of these servants to know what would happen if we used a footman. We'd be branded ghouls or ressurectionists by tomorrow morning."

"I'm afraid he's right," Piers agreed. "We could try boards. There'll be some in one of the outbuildings, like the ones they used for the study window."

"We'd never balance him on boards," Pitt dismissed the idea. The thought of struggling along the passageway in the half dark trying to keep a corpse from falling off a plank was grotesque. "The door is the only thing."

"It's too heavy!" Tellman protested.

"Laundry basket," Piers said suddenly. "If we're really careful how we put him in it, we won't disturb the evidence."

Pitt and Tellman both looked at him with approval.

"Excellent," Pitt agreed. "I'll fetch one. You get him ready."

It was after eleven o'clock by the time Tellman stood by the laundry door, which naturally did not lock, and Pitt watched as Piers Greville very slowly began cutting into the body of his father, holding Mrs. Williams's best kitchen knife in his right hand. The ordinary lights were turned up as high as they could go, and there were three extra lanterns placed so as to cast as little shadow as possible.

It seemed to take hours. He worked slowly and extremely carefully, cutting tissue, hesitating, looking, cutting again. He obviously loathed the necessity of what he was doing. But once he had become engrossed in it, his professionalism asserted itself. He was a man who loved his calling and took a kind of joy in the delicate skill of his hands. Never once did he complain or suggest that it was unfair of Pitt to have asked him. Whatever fears he had as to what the evidence might show, he hid them.

It was warm in the laundry, and damp from the steam of the coppers boiling heavy linen and towels. It smelled of soap, carbolic and wet cloth.

Tellman stood with his back to the door. No one in the house had been told what they were doing. They had brought the body themselves, after making sure all the servants were elsewhere. Most had already gone upstairs. If they heard even a whisper that there had been a body cut up in the laundry, the stories would grow until they were monstrous, and no servant would come to work in Ashworth Hall ever again.

It was now half past eleven.

"Will you hold that, please?" Piers asked, indicating the bones of the chest he had cut with Mrs. Williams's meat cleaver. Pitt obeyed. It seemed callous to be holding a part of a man's body, and yet he knew as well as anyone that it was no longer animate, but it still seemed peculiarly personal.

Another ten minutes went by. No one spoke again.

There was no sound but the hissing of the gas. The entire house seemed silent, almost as if there was no one else in all the dozens of rooms.

"There is no water in the lungs," Piers said at last, looking up at Pitt. "He didn't drown."

"Did the blow to the back of the head kill him?"

Piers did not answer, but closed up the chest as well as he could. He wiped the blood off his hands, then, after Pitt had helped him roll the body over so he could see, he turned his attention to the wound at the back of the neck.

Another twenty minutes passed.

"No," he said with a lift of surprise. "There's no bleeding, no real bruise at all, just a crushing of bone . . . there." He pointed. "And there." He screwed up his face in confusion. "He was killed . . . twice . . . if you see what I mean? First by breaking the neck, which was a very expert blow, exactly right. It must take some skill, and strength, to break a man's neck with one blow. And there was only one. There's no other bruising or damage."

Tellman had come inside earlier, silently, and now he came forward from the door, his eyes wide open, looking first at Piers, then at Pitt.

"Then someone hit him over the back of the head and pushed him under the water," Piers finished. "I haven't the faintest idea why. It seems . . . crazy. . . ." He looked totally bewildered.

"Are you sure?" Pitt felt a soaring of spirit that was out of all proportion to any good there could possibly be. "Are you absolutely sure?"

Piers blinked. "Yes. You can get a proper police surgeon to check after me, but I'm sure. Why? What does it mean? Do you know who killed him?"

"No," Pitt said with a catch in his voice. "No . . . but I think I know who didn't. . . ."

"Well, it looks like two people did." Tellman stared down at the body on the bench. "Or meant to!"

Pitt did not move. He was wondering if he could make a case

against someone for hitting the head of a corpse and holding it under the water. What could the crime be? Defilement of a dead body? Would the courts bother with it? Did he even want them to?

"Sir?" Tellman prompted him.

Pitt jerked his attention back. "Yes . . . Yes, tidy up here, will you, Tellman. I have something to do upstairs . . . I think. Thank you." He looked at Piers. "Thank you, Mr. Greville. I appreciate both your courage and your skill . . . very much. Put the body back in the ice-house, will you, and for God's sake, lock the door and don't leave any traces of what we've done here. Good night." And he went to the door, opened it, and strode back towards the main house and the stairs.

CHAPTER TWELVE

Charlotte was asleep when Pitt reached the bedroom, but just as she had been on her return from London, he was unable to wait until morning to share with her what he had learned. He was less gentle about waking her. He made no pretense at diplomacy. He walked straight in and lit the main gaslamp and turned it up.

"Charlotte," he said in a normal voice.

She grunted at the brightness of the light and turned over slowly, hiding her face under the coverlet.

"Charlotte," he repeated, going over and sitting on the bed. He felt abrupt, but it was not a time for approaching softly. "Wake up. I need to speak to you."

She caught the urgency in his voice even through the remnants of sleep. She sat up, blinking and shielding her eyes, her hair too loosely braided to stay in place, and now falling over her shoulders.

"What is it? What's happened?" She stared at him, not yet alarmed because there was no fear in him. "Do you know who did it?"

"No . . . but it wasn't Justine."

"Yes, it was." She was awake now, still blinking in the light, but feeling curious. "It had to be. Why else would she be on the landing in a maid's dress? It doesn't make any sense."

"She went in and hit him on the head, then pulled him under the water," he agreed. "But she didn't kill him . . . he was already dead!"

She glanced at him as if she were not sure if she had grasped what he had said.

"Already dead? Are you sure? How do you know?"

"Yes, I am sure, because Piers said so—"

"Piers?" She was sitting up now. "If he knew, why didn't he say before?" Her face darkened. "Thomas . . . maybe he knew it was Justine and he is—"

"No." He was quite certain. "No, he does not know what it means. He merely told me the evidence. . . ."

"What evidence?" she demanded. "What evidence does he know now that he didn't know before?" She was shivering as the bedclothes fell from around her.

"We took the body to the laundry and did something of an autopsy. . . . Charlotte, Justine had every intention of killing Ainsley Greville, but someone else got there before her and broke his neck . . . with a single, very expert blow . . . someone who knows how to kill and has probably done it before."

She shuddered, but seemed to have forgotten the bedclothes within a hand's reach of her.

"You mean an assassin," she said in a whisper. "One of the Irishmen here."

"Yes, I can think of no other answer," he agreed.

"Padraig Doyle?"

"I don't know. Possibly."

"Eudora will never get over it." She stared at him. "Thomas . . ."

"What?" He thought he knew what she was going to say, something about pity and that it was not his fault; not to be too hurt for her, grieved, and above all guilty. He was wrong.

"You must prepare yourself for the possibility that she already knows," she answered.

Everything in him was repelled by the idea—it was appalling. It was unimaginable that behind those soft features and wounded eyes was an accomplice, even a silent one, in cold, indiscriminate political murder.

Charlotte was looking at him with hurt and sorrow in her face, but for him, not for Eudora. "She is very close to her brother," she went on quietly. "And she is as Irish as any of them, even if she doesn't seem like it or hasn't lived there for twenty years. She might still carry the old hatreds and the unreason which seems to infect everybody in this issue."

She put out her hand and laid it softly over his. "Thomas . . . you've seen them, you've heard them argue. You can see what happens to people once they start talking about Ireland. One man's freedom is seen as another man's exploitation and loss, or theft of all he has built up over the generations, and far worse than that, and far more justifiable to defend, as loss of his freedom of faith. A Nationalist independent Ireland would be Roman Catholic. Its laws would be Catholic, whatever the beliefs of the individual. There would be censorship of books according to the Papal Index. All sorts of things would be banned."

She grasped the coverlets and pulled them half around her.

"I resented it when my own father told me what to read and what not to. I should rebel if the Pope did. He's not anything to do with me. But in a Catholic Ireland some books would be illegal. I wouldn't even know they existed. . . . I'd learn only what the Church decided I should hear. Maybe I don't want to read them. . . . I might even agree . . . . I just want the choice to be mine."

He did not interrupt.

"On all things, I want laws my own people can vote on. . . ." She smiled lopsidedly. "Actually, I'd even like to vote on them myself. But either way, I won't be told by a lot of cardinals in Rome what to do."

"You're exaggerating . . ." he protested.

"No, I'm not. In a Catholic state the Church has the last word."

"How do you know all this?"

"I've been talking to Kezia Moynihan. And before you say she is exaggerating too, she told me proof of it. There's a lot they say which I think is nonsense. They blame the Catholics for all kinds of things, but that much is true. Where the Church of Rome has power, it is absolute. You can't force religion on other people, Thomas. Mostly I think the Americans have it right. You should keep church and state separate. . . ."

"What do you know about the Americans?" He was startled. He had never thought of her as having the slightest interest in, let alone knowledge of, such things.

"Emily was telling me. Do you know how many millions of Irish people have emigrated to America since the potato famine?"

"No. Do you?"

"Yes . . . about three million," she replied unhesitatingly. "That's about one in three of the whole population, and it's largely the young and able-bodied. Nearly all of them went to America, where they could find work—and food."

"What is that to do with Eudora?" He was shaken by the information, and by the fact that Charlotte apparently knew it, but nothing could take the image of Eudora entirely from his mind.

"Only that the situation is desperate," she answered, still looking at him with the same gentleness. "There are many people who think when issues are so large that the end justifies any means, even murder of those who stand in the way of what they see as a larger justice."

He said nothing.

She hesitated, seeming on the brink of leaning forward and putting her arms around him, then changed her mind. Instead she climbed out of bed and went for her dressing robe.

"Where are you going?" he said in surprise. "You're not going to Eudora?"

"No . . . I'm going to Justine."

"Why?"

She put her robe on and tied the long sash. She was completely awake now, but she did not bother to wash her face from the ewer of cold water or run the brush over her tangled hair.

"Because I want to tell her she didn't kill Ainsley Greville. She thinks she did."

He stood up. "Charlotte, I don't know that I want Justine to know. . . ."

"Yes you do," she said firmly. "If you have to arrest Padraig Doyle tomorrow, you need this dealt with tonight. Don't come with me. I can speak to her better on my own. We need to know the truth."

He sat frozen on the bed. She was right in that they needed the truth, but he also dreaded it.

She went quietly along the corridor, across the landing and into the other wing. The whole house was silent. Everyone had long since gone to bed, apart from Pitt and Tellman, and presumably Piers. But he would not go to Justine's room at this hour, and certainly not after what he had just been involved in. He would not take the smell and the emotional chaos of such a thing to her.

It was dim in the corridor, the gaslamps on very low, only sufficient to guide anyone who might wish to get up for any personal reason. She knocked on Justine's door once, sharply, then without waiting for a reply, went in.

It was in darkness and complete silence.

"Justine," she said in a soft voice, but well above a whisper.

There was a faint sound of movement, then a crinkle of bedclothes.

"Who is it?" Justine's voice was tight, afraid.

"It's Charlotte. Please turn up the light. I can't see where it is."

"Charlotte?" There was a moment's silence, then more movement and the light came on.

Charlotte could see Justine sitting up in bed, but wide awake, her ink-black hair over her shoulders and a look of anxiety and puzzlement in her face.

"Has something happened?" she said quietly. "Something more?"

Charlotte came over and sat on the end of the bed. She must learn the truth from Justine, but she could think of no subterfuge with which to trick her in any way, nor did she want to trick her.

"Not really," she said, making herself comfortable. "But we know more than we did at dinnertime, although we knew quite a lot then."

Justine's face reflected no emotion except relief that no further disaster had happened.

"Do you? Do you know who killed Mr. McGinley yet?"

"No." Charlotte smiled in sad irony. "But we know who did not kill Mr. Greville. . . ."

"We already know who did not," Justine said, still keeping a suitably good temper in the circumstances. "Mr. O'Day and Mr. McGinley, and the valet Hennessey, if you had considered him. I hope you would know it was not Mrs. Greville, or Piers, but I suppose you cannot take that for granted. Is that what you have come to say . . . that it was not Mrs. Greville?" She put her hand on the covers as if to get out.

Charlotte leaned forward and stopped her.

"I don't know whether it was Mrs. Greville or not." She met Justine's dark eyes levelly. "But I should think it unlikely, although she might very well know who did. It was someone very skilled, very professional at killing." She watched Justine closely, her eyes, her movement. "It was done with one very accurate blow."

Justine sat absolutely motionless, but she could not keep the start of shock from her eyes. The instant after came a shadow of fear as she wondered how much Charlotte knew, what she had seen in her face. Then it was gone again.

"Was it?" she asked, her voice very nearly steady. Any huskiness in it could easily be attributed to the unpleasantness of the subject and the fact that she had been awoken from the first deep sleep of the night.

"Yes. His neck was broken."

This time the surprise was accompanied by bewilderment, and for all her iron will and practiced composure she could not hide it. She masked it the instant she saw the recognition in Charlotte's eyes. She shuddered in revulsion.

"How horrible!"

"It is cold-blooded," Charlotte agreed. She clenched her hands in her lap where Justine could not see them. "Less understandable than the person who came in after that, with a maid's cap on and a maid's dress over her own, and walked behind him with a jar of bath salts in her hand and hit him over the back of the head, then, believing him senseless from the blow, pushed him under the water and held him there."

Justine was white. She grasped the sheets as if they kept her afloat from drowning.

"Did . . . somebody . . . do that?"

"Yes." Charlotte kept all doubt out of her voice.

"How . . ." Justine swallowed in spite of her effort at control. "How do you . . . know that?"

"She was seen. At least her shoes were seen." Charlotte smiled very slightly, not a smile of triumph or blame. "Blue fabric slippers, stitched on the sides, with blue heels. Not a maid's shoes. You wore them today at luncheon, with your muslin dress."

This time Justine made no pretense. She would not lose her dignity so far as to continue to fight when the battle was over.

"Why?" Charlotte asked. "You must have had a very powerful reason."

Justine looked drained, as if the life had ceased inside her. In a few words Charlotte had ended everything she had longed for and worked for, and almost had within her grasp. There seemed nothing she could say which would alter or redeem even a portion of the loss. There was no anger in her, only resignation in the face of absolute disaster.

Charlotte waited.

Justine began in a low, quiet voice, not looking at Charlotte, but down at the embroidered edge of the linen sheet under her fingers. "My mother was a maidservant who married a Spanish sailor. He died when I was very young. He was lost at sea. She was left with no money and a small child to bring up. Because she had married a foreigner, against her family's wishes, they would have nothing to do with her. She took in laundry and mending, but it barely kept us alive. She didn't marry again."

She smiled a curious, half-amused smile. "I was never beautiful. I was too dark. They used to call me names when I was a child: gypsy, dago, and worse. And make fun of my nose. But as I got older I had a kind of grace, I was different, and it interested some people . . . especially men. I learned how to be charming, how to awaken interest and to sustain it. I . . ." She kept her eyes studiously away from Charlotte's. "I learned how to flatter a man and make him happy." She did not specify in what way she meant.

Charlotte believed she understood.

"And Ainsley Greville was among them?"

Justine jerked her head up, her eyes bright and angry.

"He was the only one! But when you are desperate, and it is your way of surviving, you can't pick and choose. You take who has the money, and doesn't knock you around or carry disease, at least that you can see. Do you think I liked it?" She was defiant, as if Charlotte were judging her.

"You poor soul," Charlotte said, slightly sarcastically.

Rage blazed in Justine's eyes for an instant as they sat staring at each other. It never crossed Charlotte's mind that she was in any danger. She had in all practical senses forgotten that Justine had only a few days ago attempted to murder a man. She had failed only because he was already dead. She had thought until ten minutes before that she had succeeded.

Charlotte looked at the gorgeous embroidered lace on Justine's nightgown. It was immeasurably prettier than her own, and more expensive.

"I like your nightgown," she remarked dryly.

Justine blushed.

Again they sat in silence for several moments.

Justine looked up. "All right . . . I did it to survive, to begin with. Then I learned to like the luxuries I could afford. Once you've been poor, really hungry and cold, you never feel safe enough. You always know it can happen again tomorrow. I was always thinking I'd give it up, do something respectable. It just . . . never seemed the right time."

"So why murder Ainsley Greville? Did you hate him so much? Why?"

"No, I didn't hate that much!" Justine said angrily, contempt hot in her black eyes. "Yes, I hated him, because he despised me just as he despised all women," she said viciously. "Except when he couldn't be bothered with us at all. Yes, there was a way in which he was typical of all the men who use women and loathe them at the same time. But I killed him because he would have told Piers what I am—what I was. . . ."

"Does that matter?" Charlotte did not ask as a challenge this time, simply a question.

Justine closed her eyes. "Yes . . . it mattered more than anything else in the world. I love him . . . not just to get out of being a—a whore!" She made herself say the word, and her face showed that it was like stabbing herself. "I love him because he is kind and funny and generous. He has hopes and fears I can understand, dreams I can share and the courage to seek them. And he loves me . . . most of all, he loves me." Her voice was strained so tight it cracked with her effort to keep control. "Can you imagine what it will do to him if he hears? Can you see the scene . . . Ainsley laughing at him, telling him his precious betrothed was his father's whore? And he would have enjoyed that. He could be very cruel."

Her hands were knotted on the edge of the sheet. "He resented anyone's happiness, especially if he knew them well, because they had something he didn't. He couldn't find happiness in any woman because he didn't know how to love. He didn't permit the gentleness in himself, so he couldn't see it in others. He only saw his own reflection, unsatisfied, seeking the weakness to exploit, using his power to hurt, before anyone hurt him."

"You did hate him, didn't you?" Charlotte said, feeling not only the emotion behind Justine's words but the knowledge and the reason.

Justine met her eyes. "Yes, I did, not only for what he did to me, but to everyone. And I suppose for a moment to me he was all men like him. What are you going to do now?"

Charlotte made her decision as she was speaking the words.

"You didn't kill him, but that was only chance, your good fortune, if you like. You meant to."

"I know that. What are you going to do?" Justine repeated.

"I don't know what kind of a crime it is to attack a man who's already dead. It's bound to be some sort."

"If . . . if Mr. Pitt is going to arrest me . . ." Justine took a shuddering breath. She did not weep. Perhaps that would come later, when she was alone and it was all over, and there was nothing left ahead but the regret. She regained her control and started again. "If Mr. Pitt is going to arrest me, may I please go and tell Piers myself why? I think I would rather . . . at least . . ."

Again there was silence. The gas hissed gently in the bracket. There was no other sound in the house.

"I'm not sure if I can!" It was a cry of despair. Her body was rigid. She really was very slight, almost thin. She looked tight and tense, every muscle in her was knotted. One would have thought physical pain racked through her.

"Yes, you can," Charlotte assured her. "It may be dreadful, but whatever it is, if you don't, you will ever afterwards wish you had. Even if you have nothing else left, have courage."

Justine laughed abruptly, a bitter sound close to hysteria.

"You say that so easily. But it isn't you facing the only man you've ever loved, perhaps the only person, apart from my mother, and she's dead now, and telling him you are a whore, and a murderess at heart—but not in fact only because some mad Irishman got there first."

"Do you prefer the alternative?" Charlotte said gently. "That is that someone else tells him. I will, if you want, but only if you make me believe you can't."

Justine sat still, staring back at her.

"What do you want?" Charlotte repeated. "Time? It isn't going to alter what must be done, but I'll wait here if you like."

"It isn't going to change, is it?" Justine said after a moment or two. "I am not going to wake up and find you were only a nightmare?"

Charlotte smiled. "Perhaps I'll wake up, and it will be Kezia or one of the maids who hit him." She shrugged. "Or perhaps the Red King will wake up and we'll all disappear."

"What?"

"*Alice Through the Looking Glass*," Charlotte explained. "Everybody in it was supposed to be part of the Red King's dream."

"Then can't you waken him?"

"No."

"Then I had better go and tell Piers," Justine replied.

Charlotte smiled very slightly without saying anything.

Justine climbed out of the bed, hesitated, as if debating whether to dress or not, then put on her robe. She went to the dressing table and picked up the brush. She stood with it in her hand, looking at her reflection in the glass. She was tired, pale with shock and strain; her hair was twisted and had come out of the braid she had placed it in on going to bed.

"I wouldn't," Charlotte said, before she realized it was not her place, now of all times, to try to influence such a decision.

Justine put the brush down and looked back at her. "You're right. It is hardly the time for vanity, or anything that looks like forethought." She bit her lip. Her hands were not quite steady. "Will you come with me?"

Charlotte was surprised. "Are you sure that's what you want? This is about the most private thing you will ever do."

"No, I'm not sure. If I could think of any other way, I'd take it. But someone else there will help to keep it rational and . . . and honest. It is not a time for trying to use the emotions. It will stop either of us from saying things we might later wish we had said differently, or not at all."

"Are you certain?"

"Yes. Please, let us go before I lose my courage."

Charlotte did not argue any further but stood up and followed Justine out into the passage and the short distance to Piers's room. Justine stopped, drew in her breath and knocked.

The door opened and Piers looked out. He had obviously only just got into bed and had not yet fallen asleep, which, considering what the evening had already held for him, was not surprising. He saw Justine first.

"Is something wrong?" he said in immediate alarm. "Are you ill?" His face in the dim light from the landing was full of concern.

"Yes," Justine answered with irony. "I must speak with you. I'm sorry it is so late. But tomorrow there will be other things . . . perhaps."

"I'll get dressed." He was about to retreat when he saw Charlotte. "Mrs. Pitt!"

"I think it would be as well if we came in," Charlotte said decisively. "We can sit in the dressing room—"

"It's quite small . . . there are not three chairs. . . ."

"In the circumstances it hardly matters," she murmured, leading the way through the door and inside. "We do not wish to awaken anyone else by speaking outside in the corridor," she went on. "Or by walking around more than we have to."

"Why?" He was trying not to look alarmed now. He was very pale and tired. There were heavy shadows like bruises around his eyes, his hair falling forward over his brow at the front and standing up in spikes at the crown. "What has happened, Mrs. Pitt? No one else is . . . dead . . . are they?"

"No," she assured him quickly. Although, considering what Justine was about to tell him, he might prefer someone were. "Please sit down. I can stand."

Now thoroughly fearful, he obeyed, turning from Charlotte to Justine.

Justine sat on the other chair and Charlotte stood in the shadows by the wall. There was a single lamp burning. Piers must have lit it before he answered the door.

Justine glanced at Charlotte once, then she began.

"Piers, we don't know who killed your father by breaking his neck. I imagine it was one of the Irishmen, but I don't know which." Her voice was very nearly steady. Her effort of will must have been immense. "But it was I who hit him over the head with the jar of bath salts and pushed him under the water—" She stopped abruptly, waiting.

There was utter silence but for the faint hiss of the gas.

Twice Piers opened his mouth as if to speak, then realized he did not know what to say. It was left to Justine to continue. Her voice was harsh with pain. Charlotte knew from the tightness of her back, the rigidity of her shoulders, that she had kept some kind of hope until this moment, and now she had at last let it go. She was speaking from despair.

"I meant to kill him," she went on flatly. "I didn't actually, only because he was already dead. I had been his mistress . . . for money . . . and he was going to tell you." She smiled with a bitter mockery at herself. "I thought I couldn't bear that. I still love you, and I wanted you to love me more than I wanted anything else in the world. It would have been much easier to bear than this . . . having to tell you myself, and not only tell you what I was but what I have done as well. I'm sorry . . . I'm sorry I did this to you. You will never be able to understand how sorry. . . ."

He stared at her as if he had not seen her before.

She looked back in silence, without evasion, almost without blinking.

Charlotte was locked immobile. She would have felt intrusive if she had thought either of them had the slightest awareness of her.

"Why?" he said at last, his face almost bruised with shock and incomprehension at what he had heard. "Why did you live that . . . that kind of . . . life?"

This time Justine did not use the word *whore*. If she were tempted to make excuses, she resisted it. Charlotte would never know if it was her presence there which accomplished that.

"At first it was to survive," Justine answered, her voice low, expressionless, as though the feeling in it were too great to be allowed through. "My father was killed at sea, and my mother and I had nothing. She was ostracized because she had married a foreigner. Her family would do nothing for us. Later I got used to the things it could buy me, the safety, the warmth, and in time the beauty, the freedom from worrying every day where the next week's food and rent would come from."

She took a deep breath and went on. "I knew it wouldn't last. Women get old, then no one wants them. You can't earn much past thirty, even less past thirty-five. I wanted to save so I could buy a business of some sort. I kept meaning to get out, but it was too easy to stay in. Until I met you at the theater. I came to love you, and I realized what I had paid for my safety. I stopped from that day on." She did not make any protestations that it was the truth.

Again he sat silent, only shivering a little, as from physical shock.

Minutes passed by—five, ten, a quarter of an hour. Neither of them moved or made a sound.

Charlotte was getting stiff and, in spite of her gown, thoroughly chilled. But she must not interrupt. Justine had not looked at her. She would, if she wanted her to take any part.

At last Piers drew in a breath and let it out in a long sigh. "I . . ." He shook his head a little. "I can't . . ." He looked wretched, shattered, confused, hurting too much to know how to express it. "I can't think what to say . . ." he confessed. "I . . . I'm sorry. I need a little time . . . to think. . . ."

"Of course," Justine said quickly in a curiously flat tone. It was an acknowledgment of defeat, of a kind of little death inside. She rose to her feet and at last looked at Charlotte. "Good night," she said to

Piers with a formality which was at once absurd and yet understandable. What else was there to say? She turned and went to the door, leaving him also standing helpless, watching her go.

Charlotte followed her and closed the door behind them both. They went back along the passage to Justine's room. Charlotte was not sure if Justine might want to be alone, but she was afraid to leave her, knowing the despair she must now feel. Without asking, she went into the room after her.

Justine was walking in a nightmare, as if unaware even where she was anymore. She walked into the corner of the bed, bruising herself against the wood and barely registering the pain. She sat down suddenly, but she was too numb to weep.

Charlotte closed the door and went over to her. There was nothing to say which would mean anything. It would be ridiculous and painful to talk about hope or even to imagine plans. There was nothing which could have been done differently or better as far as Piers was concerned, and anyway it was all past. She did not know whether Justine would find touch comforting or intrusive, but it was her instinct to reach out. She sat beside her on the bed and very gently put her arms around her.

For minutes they sat unmoving, Justine rigid, locked inside her own pain. Then at last she relaxed and leaned against Charlotte's shoulder. The wound was no less, but she consented to share it for a space.

Charlotte had no idea how long they sat. She grew stiff and even colder except where Justine's body kept her warm. Her arm started prickling with pins and needles. When she could bear it no longer and her muscles were beginning to jump, she spoke.

"You might try to sleep a little. I'll stay with you if you like—or go, if you'd prefer?"

Justine turned around slowly. "How selfish of me," she answered. "I've sat here as if there were no one else in the world. You must be exhausted. I'm sorry."

"No, I'm not," Charlotte lied. "Do you want me to stay? I can sleep here anyway."

"Please . . ." Justine hesitated. "No, that's stupid. I can't expect you to stay with me forever. I brought this on myself."

"We bring a lot of our griefs upon ourselves," Charlotte said honestly. "It doesn't make it hurt any less. Lie down and get warm. Perhaps then you'll sleep a while."

"Will you lie down too? Under the covers, or you'll be frozen."

"Yes, certainly I will." Charlotte suited the act to the words, and Justine turned out the gas. They lay in silence. Charlotte had no idea how long it was before sleep overtook her at last.

She woke with a start to hear knocking on the door. It took her a moment to remember that the person beside her was not Pitt, but Justine, and then to remember why.

She slid out of bed. She was still wearing her robe. She had climbed into bed without bothering to remove it. She made her way over to the door gingerly, feeling where she went in the dark. She opened it and saw Piers standing in the passage, the gaslight yellow behind him. There was no hint of daylight yet from the windows of the landing beyond. He looked haggard, as though he had been pacing all night, but his gaze met hers directly, without flinching.

"Come in," she whispered, standing aside for him.

Justine sat up slowly, reaching for the candle. She lit it, and Charlotte closed the door.

Piers walked over to the bed and sat on it facing Justine, Charlotte temporarily forgotten.

"You know at first I thought it might have been Mama," he said with a crooked, painful smile. "She would have had as good a reason. Or Doll Evans; I think she had an even better one. Poor Doll."

Justine stared at him, searching his eyes, last night's despair suddenly, agonizingly quickened with hope again.

"Haven't you noticed?" she asked softly. "Wheeler is in love with her, perhaps he has been for ages, but she thought after what happened with Greville that he wouldn't have anything to do with her. . . ."

"Why not?" he said with a jerky laugh. "It wasn't her fault. You can be fascinated by someone, and then revolted if they don't live up to your ideal." His eyes were very steady on her face. "But if you love them, you expect them to be real, as you are yourself, to have the power and the possibility to be stupid and angry and greedy, and make terrible mistakes . . . and to have the courage to keep on trying, and the understanding to forgive. Not that Wheeler has anything to forgive Doll for."

She looked at him with a blaze of hope like a scald of light across the darkness.

"Those are brave words," she whispered. "Do you think we can live up to them?"

"I don't know," he admitted frankly. "Have you the courage to try? Do you think it's worth it? Or would you rather not take the risk, and leave now?"

For the first time she looked down.

"I don't think I shall have the chance . . . although I would like it if I had. I'm all kinds of things, but I'm not a coward. There isn't anything else I want, except to be with you. There's nothing else to take as second best."

"Then . . ." he started, leaning forward and holding her hands.

She pulled them away.

"Mr. Pitt won't allow that, Piers. I'm guilty of a crime . . . not the crime I intended, but a crime all the same. He'll arrest me in the morning, I expect. If not then, later, after he solves the real murder and the death of Mr. McGinley."

"Maybe he won't," Charlotte intervened. "It's legally a crime, of course, but it isn't one which matters a lot." She looked at Piers. "Unless, as the nearest relative of the deceased, you want to press a charge of defiling the dead? I don't know what he'll do. And I don't know about Tellman either. I don't know what they have to do."

Piers turned to Charlotte, his eyes wide. "What will they do to her? A few months in prison at the worst, surely?" He looked back at Justine. "We can wait. . . ."

She lowered her head. "Don't be ridiculous. What medical practice would you have married to a wife who had spent time in prison, let alone for defiling the bodies of the dead?"

He said nothing, trying to muster an argument.

"You wouldn't get a single patient," Charlotte agreed, hating to have to be realistic. "You would have to go abroad, perhaps to America. . . ." The thought began to look better. "That way you would also run no risk of meeting anyone you had known previously."

Justine turned her head and looked at Charlotte with a wry smile. "How very tactfully put." She looked at Piers again. "You can't marry a defiler of bodies, my dear, and you can't marry a whore either." She winced at the word, using it to wound herself before he could. "No matter how exclusive or expensive." She laughed. "I know a lot of respected ladies of rank and wealth have extremely loose morals, but they do it for gifts, not for money, and there is all the difference in the world in that. I don't really understand why. They don't do it to earn their living. They have plenty of money; they do it because they are bored. I suppose it is the old difference between amateurs and players." Her voice was rich with mockery. "Trade is so vulgar, after all."

They all laughed, jerkily, a little too close to hysteria.

"America," Piers said, looking at Justine, then at Charlotte.

"America," Justine agreed.

"What about your mother?" Charlotte asked. "What if she needs you?"

"Me?" Piers looked surprised. "She's never needed me."

"And if your uncle Padraig is the one who really killed your father and Lorcan McGinley?"

His face darkened and he looked down again. "It's pretty possible, isn't it?"

"Yes. It looks as if it could be either him or Fergal Moynihan, and frankly, I don't think Fergal has the stomach."

Piers seemed very slightly amused by her bluntness, but it was the humor of despair.

"No, neither do I. But I think Padraig has. And he had plenty of cause, at least where my father is concerned. But I'm not staying here, so if Mama doesn't want to go back to Ireland, to the Doyle family, who'll probably make her welcome, then she'd better come to America with us. I can't see the far west suiting her, but we'd all have to make the best of it. At least there they will have plenty of need for doctors, and they won't care very much if we are Irish, English, or half-and-half, and they certainly won't care what our religion is. And as you said, there won't be much chance of one running into old acquaintances, not if we go to the frontier."

His voice dropped a little. "But we'll be poor. All I have won't last us very long. People may not pay doctors much out there, and they may take a long time to get used to me and accept me. It will be hard work. There'll be none of the luxuries we take for granted here. Certainly no servants, no pretty gowns, no hansom cabs to call, no sophisticated theater, music or books. The climate will be harder. There may even be hostile Indians. . . . I don't know. Are you still willing?"

Justine was torn between hope and terror of the unknown, the grim and dangerous, perhaps beautiful, but hideously unfamiliar. But it was all she had. She nodded slowly, but with absolute certainty.

"We still have to tell your mother something."

He nodded also. "Of course. But not yet. Let us see what Mr. Pitt does about Uncle Padraig first, and what he has . . . decided."

Charlotte moved away from the shadows at last. "It will be dawn soon. The maids will be up already." She looked at Piers. "I think we should go back to our rooms and try to get ready for the day. We will need all our strength and whatever courage and intelligence we can bring to it."

"Of course." Piers went to the door and opened it for her. He turned and looked at Justine. Their eyes met in something almost like a smile.

"Thank you," Justine said to both of them, then she spoke to Piers. "I know there is a very great way to go yet, even if I am not prosecuted. I shall have to prove to you that I am what I am trying to be. There is no point in saying I am sorry over and over again. I will show it by being there, every hour, every day, every week, until you know it."

Charlotte and Piers went out, glanced at each other, then turned their separate ways.

When Charlotte reached her own room the small light was still on in the dressing room, but the bedroom door was ajar and it was dark inside. She was about to take off her robe and creep in when she was startled by a noise and whisked around to find Pitt standing just inside the room, his face drawn with exhaustion. "Where the hell have you been?" he demanded, his voice rough-edged with anxiety.

Guilt washed over her in a wave. She had not even thought of telling him where she was.

"I'm sorry," she said, aghast at herself. "I stayed with Justine. She was so . . . so devastated. She told Piers. It took him all night, which in the circumstances is no time at all, but I think it will be all right." She took a step towards him. "I'm sorry, Thomas. I didn't think."

"No," he agreed. "She tried to kill Greville. You can't protect her from that."

"So what are you going to do?" she asked. "Arrest her for killing a corpse? I'm sure it is a crime, but does it matter? I mean . . ." She shook her head. "I know it matters, but will it really help anyone to prosecute her?"

He said nothing.

"Thomas . . . she won't go unpunished. She can't stay here, and she knows that. She wants to leave her old life, and she and Piers can go to America, to the west, where nobody will know her."

"Charlotte . . ." He looked crumpled and worn out with sadness.

"You can't stop him marrying her . . . if he wants to," she said quickly. "And she did tell him. . . ."

"Are you sure?"

"Yes. I went with her. I don't know whether it will be all right or not, maybe no one will for years. But he'll try. Can't you just . . . turn a blind eye? Please?" It crossed her mind to say something about Eudora, and what it would mean to her, but she dismissed it as unworthy. This was between herself and Pitt, and Eudora Greville had nothing to do with it. "It will be hard enough for them," she added. "They will leave everything they know behind them and take only their love, their courage and their guilt."

He leaned forward and kissed her long and very close, and then again, and then a third time. "Sometimes I haven't the slightest idea what you are thinking," he said at last, looking puzzled.

She smiled. "Well, that's something, I suppose."

Gracie woke up, and it was a moment before she remembered what had happened the day before, the strange, sweaty candle in Finn's room, the look in his eyes when she had touched it . . . the guilt which had betrayed to her what it was, and then his anger when she had run away, then his arrest. It was hard to feel different about him quickly. There was too much memory of sweetness. One could not turn off emotion in a few hours, not when it had run so deep through you.

She got up and washed and dressed. She did not care how she looked. Clean and tidy was all that mattered, good enough for the job. Pretty wasn't important anymore. Only the day before it had mattered so much.

She went downstairs and passed Doll looking busy but with a faraway smile on her face, and Gracie found it in herself for a moment to be glad for her.

In the servants' hall she met Gwen, taking a quick cup of tea before going up with hot water for Emily to wash.

"I'm sorry," Gwen said with a little shake of her head. "He seemed like a nice fellow. But far best you're out of it now, and not later. One day you'll maybe find someone decent, and you'll forget all about this. At least you've still got your character, and no one thinks the worse of you."

Gracie knew she meant well by it, but it was no comfort. The broken ache of loneliness inside her was just as deep—in fact, in ways deeper, because other people knew about it. Better they were sympathetic than not, probably. But it was surprising how kindness could hurt, make you want to sit down and cry.

"Yeah, I s'pose," she said, not because she agreed, but she did not want to prolong the conversation. She poured herself a cup of tea. The hot liquid might warm her up inside, and it would give her something to do other than stand and talk. Maybe Gwen would go and carry the water up soon. Then she could draw her own and take it up to Charlotte.

"You'll be all right," Gwen went on. "You're a sensible girl and you've got a good place."

Sensible girls could hurt just as much as silly ones, Gracie thought, but she did not say so.

"Yeah," she agreed absently, sipping at the tea. It was too hot. "Thank you," she added, in case Gwen thought she was sulking.

Gwen put down her cup and went out, patting Gracie quickly on the arm as she passed.

Gracie sipped her tea again, without really tasting it. It was time she ran the water for Charlotte. She would probably have to take up enough for Pitt too. Don't suppose Tellman would think of that.

Her tea was too hot to hurry. She was still only halfway through when the door opened and Tellman came in. He looked terrible, as if he had been up half the night, and had nightmares the little he had been in his bed. At another time she might have been sorry for him, now she was too consumed with her own hurt.

"D'yer want some tea?" she offered, indicating the pot. "It's fresh. And yer look like summink the cat brought in."

"I feel like it," Tellman replied, going to the teapot. "I was up until heaven knows when." He looked as if he had been about to add something more, than changed his mind abruptly.

"Wot for?" she asked, passing him the milk. "Yer ill?"

"No," he replied, looking away from her.

In spite of her own absorption in misery, she was aware that something must have happened. Perhaps it was to do with Finn. She had to ask.

"Why were yer up, then? Did summink 'appen?"

He looked at her closely, searching her face, then made his decision. "Mr. Pitt was up too. We were just trying to solve the case, that's all."

"And did yer?"

"No, not yet."

"Oh." She did not want to know any more about Finn. She was afraid of what it would be, so afraid her stomach knotted up in misery, but she also desperately wanted Pitt to win, he must! That was her first loyalty. That was the deciding thing which had driven her to tell him about the dynamite. She would rather not talk about it at all. She would rather not even have been there. But she had no choice; really, no one ever did have, unless they were going to run away altogether.

"I gotter get the water," she said, finishing the last of her tea. It was cool enough now. "Mrs. Pitt'll be gettin' up."

"I doubt it," he replied. "She was probably woken when Mr. Pitt went to bed. I expect she'll want to sleep in."

"P'r'aps, but I'd better see." She did not want to stay there with Tellman, of all people. She started towards the door.

"Gracie . . ."

She could not just ignore him. "Yeah?" she said without turning.

"Whoever killed Mr. Greville was the kind of person who's used to killing people. It wasn't done out of passion, or self-defense, or revenge or anything like that. I mean . . . I mean, if it had been Doll Evans, or Mrs. Greville, or someone like that, you could understand it. It'd still be wrong, of course, but you could understand it."

She turned around slowly. "It weren't Doll, I know that, 'cos I saw 'oo done it. She weren't as tall as Doll. It were Mrs. Greville or Mrs. McGinley, I reckon."

"No, it wasn't," he said, his face tight with emotion, his eyes steady on her. "The woman you saw tried to kill him, but he was already dead. She didn't know that, but his neck was broken. That's what we found out last night."

"Broken? How d'yer know that?"

"You don't want to hear that. And don't you go saying anything to anyone, do you understand? That's confidential police business. It's a secret. Maybe I shouldn't have told you."

"Why did yer?"

"I . . ." he hesitated, looking unhappy. "Gracie . . . I . . . I hate to see you hurt like this." He was acutely uncomfortable, there was a flush on his hollow cheeks, but he would not stop now he had begun. "But I thought it might help to know that whoever killed Mr. Greville was professional at it. You don't just kill someone that easily, with one blow, if you've had no practice." He was more wretched by the moment. "I daresay they think what they're doing is right, but it isn't right by any of the sort of things we believe in. You can't get freedom for people by murdering other people just because you think they stand in your way. What kind of a person does that make you?"

What he said was true. In her heart she already knew it. It had been a glimmer, like a door opening, the minute she saw the dynamite. It had been growing wider, more certain since then. She had not lost something real, she had only lost a dream. But dreams can matter very much, and it was too soon to feel anything but pain.

"Yeah, I know," she conceded, not looking at him. "I gotter take the water up all the same."

"Gracie!"

"What?"

"I wish . . . I wish I could make you feel better. . . ."

She looked at him standing by the table, awkward, so tired he looked hollow-eyed. He was lantern-jawed. No one could have called him handsome, or even charming, but there was a tenderness in him which startled her. Had it not been so obvious, she would not have believed it, but he cared for her, it was there, naked in his face.

"Yeah," she said quietly. "Yeah, I reckon you would. It's nice of you. I . . . I gotter take the water. She might be awake any'ow."

"I'll carry it," he offered. "It's heavy."

"Thank you." It was his job anyway, at least to carry the water for Pitt, but she did not feel like saying so, not this time.

He walked to the door and held it open for her while she went through, then filled the jugs and carried them upstairs for her, not speaking again. He did not know what else to say, and she knew that. It did not matter.

When she got upstairs, far from waiting for her, Charlotte was still sound asleep, as Tellman had said she might be, and looked so tired Gracie did not have the heart even to make a noise, let alone draw the curtains. She left the water and crept away again. If Pitt had to be up, that was another thing. Tellman put his water in the dressing room, and he could do everything he needed without disturbing Charlotte. She could always ring when she woke.

Gracie was downstairs again, passing the conservatory door, when she glanced sideways and saw Mr. Moynihan and Mrs. McGinley standing very close together, talking earnestly. She had no business to, but she stopped and listened.

". . . but, Iona, we can't just walk away from each other like this!" Fergal said wretchedly.

"Then how?" she asked, her face calm and sad, a stark contrast to his, which Gracie could see if she moved forward six inches. He was miserable and confused. There was almost a sulkiness about him, as though he felt not only profoundly unhappy but also aggrieved.

"Don't you care?" he demanded, the anger coming through in a sharp note. "Is this all it means to you? You can just say good-bye without fighting for what you want or weeping when you lose it? Perhaps I want it far more than you do?" That was said with challenge. He did not want her to agree, but if she did, then he was branding her cold, without fire or dreams, without the reality of love.

"What do you want, Fergal?" she asked. "Do you really know? Is it me you want, or is it a great romance, some desperate cause to suffer for, and perhaps to excuse you from having to fight for a Protestant Ireland you no longer totally believe in?"

"Oh, don't make that mistake," he said, shaking his head, his eyes dark and narrow. "Don't ever deceive yourself I don't know what I fight for in Ireland. I'll never change in that cause. I'll not bend the knee to Rome, whoever I love, or lose. I'll not sell my soul for a superstition, a set of beads and incantations, instead of the disciplines and virtues of God."

"That's what I thought," she answered wearily. "And I imagine you would know I would never give up the laughter and the love, the heart's faith of my people, in trade for the dark miseries of the north with all its anger and blame, its hellfire punishments and its vinegar-faced ministers. It is because I love you that I know it's best we part now, while we can still keep good memories and be sorry we hurt each other, not glad. I want to remember you with a smile."

He stood there motionless, still confounded. She had made the decision and taken it out of his hands, and that too annoyed him.

Iona looked at him for a moment longer, then turned and walked back towards the doorway to the hall.

Gracie was obliged to scuttle backwards in order to walk away with any kind of dignity, as if she had not seen them, and she heard no more. But she thought of it for the rest of the morning as she went about her duties. It was so easy to fall in love, sometimes, and so hard to give up the magic, the excitement, the color it lent to everything. But that kind of feeling did not always stand the test of honesty, of any kind of affliction except the momentary. Sometimes you stayed loyal for loyalty's sake, not because it was what you believed. Love of love was so easy to understand. It was what Mr. Moynihan had felt, and now he was angry and hurt because it had not transformed itself into something which would last.

Mrs. McGinley could see that. She was wise enough to leave it before it was broken too far even to remember.

Maybe it was best for Gracie herself to leave Finn Hennessey when she could still think of the cold glasshouse with its chrysanthemums and the smell of his skin and the touch of his lips. Better not to know too much about the rest, and the gulf between them. Some things could not be explained. The more you know, the worse it becomes. Their imaginations had met, and perhaps that was all.

Charlotte woke up with a start. The curtains were still drawn closed, but it was obviously mid-morning. Pitt was gone, and she could hear no servants on the landing. She sat up quickly. Her head was throbbing, her mouth dry. She had slept too heavily and too long. Where on earth was Gracie, and why had nobody called her?

Then she remembered the night, Pitt coming to tell her what they had discussed, and then Justine, and Piers, her own involvement, Pitt's anger and worry, and then his touch afterwards, the warmth of it.

But it was not only Piers's world which had crumbled around him; in a smaller way, Gracie's had also. Charlotte wished there was something she could do to help, but she knew there wasn't. There was no help for that kind of pain, except not to keep referring to it, or talking around it, trying to convince the person that it did not really hurt and was all for the best. Above all, never tell people you know how they feel. Even if you have had the same experience, you are not the same. Each person's pain is unique.

She climbed out of bed slowly, feeling as if her head would drop off if she were not careful. She must get dressed. They still did not know who had murdered Ainsley Greville or Lorcan McGinley, at least not officially. She had a sickening feeling there was little doubt left that it was Padraig Doyle, with all the grief that that would bring.

She would have to summon all the strength she had to deal with that. Eudora would be shattered. Pitt would be torn with compassion for her, aching to be able to help, and guilty because he was the one who would have to uncover the truth and prove it.

Charlotte would dearly like to tell Eudora it was her own distress and she would have to live with it. It was not Pitt's fault she had failed to grow close to her son, or that her husband was a callous user of people, or that her brother was an assassin.

But if she were honest, what she really meant was that Eudora had a grace about the way she suffered, and her need was consuming a part of Pitt that Charlotte thought should be hers. Not a very becoming sentiment.

The water in the jugs had gone almost cold. She could ring for more or use what was there. Cold water might wake her up anyway.

The door opened and Pitt came in. He stopped in surprise.

"You're awake." He frowned. "Are you all right?" He closed the door and came over towards her. "You look dreadful."

"Thank you," she replied waspishly, pushing her hair out of her eyes and reaching blindly for a towel.

He passed it to her. "Don't be sarcastic," he criticized. "You really do look poorly. I suppose I haven't realized how hard you've had to work to stop this from being a disaster, especially for Emily."

"She's terrified for Jack . . ." she responded.

"I know." He brushed her hair back off her face. "She has every cause to be."

There was a knock at the door, and reluctantly Pitt went to answer it, expecting Gracie, but it was Jack.

"Cornwallis is on the telephone to speak to you," he said.

Pitt let out his breath in a sigh.

"In the library," Jack added. He looked concerned. He glanced at Charlotte, smiled bleakly, then followed Pitt out.

Pitt went down the stairs feeling weary and apprehensive. He had nothing to tell Cornwallis that he would want to hear. And yet there was also something even more important, deeper into the core of himself, which had eased out. A knot which had been hurting him was unraveled and smooth. He would not ever completely understand Charlotte. He did not want to. In time that would become boring. There would always be occasions when he wished she were more obviously vulnerable, more dependent upon his strength or his judgment, or more predictable. But then she would also be less generous, less brave, and less honest to him, and that was too high a price to pay for a little emotional comfort. She could not give him every answer he wanted, any more than he could for her. But what they could give was far, far more than enough; it was full, heaped and running over. The few other things did not matter; they could be forgotten or done without.

He went into the library and picked up the telephone receiver.

"Good morning, sir."

He heard Cornwallis's distinctive voice on the other end. "Good morning, Pitt. How are you? What is happening there?"

Pitt made his decision about Justine without even being aware of it.

"We had a closer look at Greville's body, sir. He didn't drown. He was killed by a very skilled blow to the side of the neck. A professional assassin, or at the very least someone who knew precisely what to do and how."

"Hardly a surprise," Cornwallis replied with disappointment. "That only really tells us what we had already assumed. We can't keep those people there much longer—in fact, not more than tomorrow, or the next day at the very latest, and that may be more than I can manage. We can't keep this secret, Pitt. The conference report is due tomorrow. I can't delay beyond another twenty-four hours at the outside."

"Yes, I know," Pitt said slowly. "I do know more of what happened, but it doesn't yet prove who was responsible." He told Cornwallis about Finn Hennessey and the dynamite.

"Can't you get anything from him?" Cornwallis said, but with a downward inflection in his voice as though he took for granted a negative answer.

"Not yet," Pitt replied, but there was the faintest glimmer of hope in the back of his mind, too small to grasp.

"What are you going to do now?" Cornwallis pressed. "Surely from what you've told me it has to be Doyle or Moynihan. And Hennessey would hardly collaborate with Moynihan. Their views and aims are directly opposing! If they weren't, we wouldn't have an Irish Problem to begin with."

"I know all that," Pitt conceded. "But I can't prove it, even to myself, let alone to a court. But we'll go back to the bomb in Jack's study and see if we can't trace McGinley's movements better and see how he knew it was there. We may be able to deduce what he learned, and it might be enough."

"Please let me know this evening," Cornwallis instructed. "Even if you have nothing."

"Anything more on poor Denbigh?" Pitt asked him. He had not forgotten about the beginning of the case, or the anger and disgust he had felt then.

"A little, although I don't think it will help much." Cornwallis sounded very far away on the other end of the line, even as if his thoughts were distant. "We've been working on it with every man we could spare. We know a great deal more about the Fenians here in London than we did even a couple of weeks ago. But this man seen following Denbigh, and who we are sure is responsible for his death, is not among them."

"You mean he went back to Ireland?"

"No . . . that's the point. He infiltrated the Fenians as well. But he isn't one of them. He learned a few bits of information about their plans, membership and so on, and then went. I think they'd like to get him almost as much as we would."

Pitt was puzzled. "Then who is he, and why did he kill Denbigh?"

"I think that may be the point," Cornwallis answered. "Maybe Denbigh discovered who he was, and that's why he killed him, not to protect the Fenians at all. But it doesn't help you, because he certainly isn't at Ashworth Hall or you would have seen him. He's unmistakable in appearance. Your man is either Doyle or just possibly Moynihan."

"Yes," Pitt agreed. "Yes, I know. Thank you, sir."

Pitt bade him good-bye and replaced the receiver. He went to look for Tellman and found him in the servants' hall looking glum.

"Any tea?" Pitt asked.

"None that's fresh," Tellman answered dourly. After a moment's hesitation he straightened up from the table where he had been leaning. "I'll get some."

Pitt was about to stop him and to say they had important things to do, then he changed his mind. All they could do to begin with was think, and that could be done as well with a fresh, hot cup of tea as without.

Tellman returned ten minutes later with a teapot on a tray, with milk jug, cups, sugar and Suffolk rusks. He put down the tray with a grunt of satisfaction.

Pitt poured and stood with the steaming cup clasped in his hands, the saucer ignored.

"Go back over everything we know about what McGinley did the morning he died," he said thoughtfully. "How did he know the dynamite was there? Hennessey didn't tell him . . . which means Hennessey and his master were essentially on different sides . . . I suppose."

"Doyle," Tellman answered. "Hennessey was working for Doyle. He must have been."

"Denbigh wasn't killed by the Fenians," Pitt said slowly. "Cornwallis just told me."

Tellman's face lit instantly. "Have they got who did it?"

"No . . . no, I'm afraid not, they just know he wasn't one of the Fenians. He was an infiltrator, like Denbigh. The Fenians are just as keen to find him as we are."

"Why'd he kill Denbigh?"

"Possibly Denbigh found out who he was."

"How does that help us?" Tellman replied, and sipped at his tea. It was too hot and he took one of the rusks instead. "He isn't here. We'd have seen him. No one broke in, I'm sure of that. It was either Doyle or Moynihan who killed Greville. And somehow or other they also put the dynamite there, or else somebody is lying and Hennessey put it there after all."

Pitt said nothing. There was another idea in his mind, very vague, very uncertain indeed.

Tellman began his tea, drinking it gingerly, blowing on it now and then.

Pitt took a rusk, then another. They were excellent, crisp and very fresh, baked with a little butter. Then he drained his cup.

"I'm going to question Hennessey again," he said when he had finished. "I want you there, and possibly a couple of footmen. It could be unpleasant. And I'll ask Mr. Radley to be present, and Doyle, Moynihan and O'Day."

Tellman stared at him, his eyes widening. He was on the verge of asking what Pitt was going to do, then he changed his mind, put down his cup and obeyed.

The questioning took place in the library. They sat in a semicircle and Tellman brought Finn Hennessey into the room and took the manacles off his wrists. He stood, head high, defiant, staring at Pitt. He studiously ignored everyone else.

"We know you brought the dynamite into Ashworth Hall," Pitt began. "There is no point in your denying it, and to your credit, you have not tried. But you said you did not place it in Mr. Radley's study, and I believe you, because from other evidence, it does not seem as if you had the opportunity. Who did put it there?"

Finn smiled. "I'll never tell."

"We ought to be able to deduce it." Pitt looked around the room, first at Fergal Moynihan, sitting with his legs crossed, his fingers drumming on the leather arm of his chair. His fair skin was almost pasty, and he looked bored and in short temper. Beside him, Carson O'Day was eager, his eyes restless, flicking from Pitt to Doyle to Hennessey and back again. He was obviously impatient with Pitt's approach and irritated because he did not believe it would achieve anything. Padraig Doyle leaned right back in his chair, but his expression was guarded. Jack simply looked profoundly worried.

"This is wasting time!" O'Day broke in. "Surely you've questioned everyone as to exactly where they were, what they were doing, who saw them there and whom they saw? That seems elementary."

"Yes, of course we have," Pitt agreed. "And with what we have learned, it appears impossible anyone placed the dynamite where it was. So someone must be lying."

"There's one answer which seems to have escaped you," O'Day said with a touch of condescension. "McGinley put it there himself. He was not a hero trying to defuse it and save us all, as Hennessey would have us believe . . . he was an assassin placing it there to kill Radley. Only he was a clumsy assassin, and succeeded in blowing himself up instead. That solution would answer all your evidence, wouldn't it?"

"All the evidence of the explosion, yes," Pitt answered deliberately, a little tingle of excitement beginning in the center of the stomach. He must be very careful indeed. One slip and he would lose this. "But not the murder of Mr. Greville," he went on. "McGinley couldn't have done that because you yourself heard him talking to Hennessey at the relevant time."

O'Day stared at him, his eyes growing wider, his body motionless. No one else moved.

"Didn't you?" Pitt said quietly.

O'Day looked as if he had received an astonishing revelation.

"No . . ." he said almost under his breath. "No! I heard Hennessey talking to McGinley." He swung around to stare at Finn. "I heard you. I never heard McGinley's replies to you. I heard your voice. I heard you answer questions, I never heard McGinley's voice. I don't actually know if he was there . . . I assumed it. But you could be lying to cover for him, just as you did for the dynamite. He—" He stopped. There was no need to continue. The tide of color flooding up Finn's cheeks made it unnecessary. O'Day swung to face Pitt. "There's your murderer for you, Superintendent! Lorcan McGinley, acting for the Fenians, the saboteurs of Irish honor and dignity, prosperity and ultimate freedom to choose for themselves, not by bullet or dynamite, but by popular vote . . . the true voice of—"

"Liar!" Finn burst out. "You thieving, murdering liar! What freedom or honor is it to let women and children starve? To drive whole families off their land and steal it for yourselves? You hate the real people of Ireland. All you love is yourselves, your greed, your land and your dark, hypocritical, canting ways that deny the true Church of God! The Fenians are the fighters for Ireland!"

"Whether they are or not isn't the point in this, Hennessey," Pitt said clearly. "The Fenians weren't behind the murders here."

O'Day froze.

Doyle jerked around to stare at Pitt.

Finn Hennessey looked at him in total disbelief.

"Oh, it was someone who wanted to sabotage the conference all right," Pitt continued. "Because he feared the conclusions it might come to and what recommendations it would make to Parliament. But it was chaired by a liberal Irish Catholic. It wasn't only Fenians who had cause to be anxious over what the results might be."

"It was Fenians!" Hennessey said defiantly.

"No it wasn't," Pitt contradicted with increased vehemence. "Ask your Fenian friends in London. They were infiltrated by a man with light, staring eyes who had tried to run Greville off the road earlier on, and then in London killed our man in the Fenians—"

"Your man?" Doyle said sharply.

"A policeman named Denbigh. He was murdered just before the conference started. We thought it was because he knew of the Fenian plot to murder Greville, only we now know the man who did it was no Fenian." He looked back at Hennessey. "You were used, Finn, as you know you were . . . but not by your own side. You were used by the

Protestants. They put you up to this, for their own reasons, and let you and the Catholic Nationalists take the blame. They wanted this conference to fail because they cannot accept any compromise at all, or they'll lose the support of their own extremists."

"That's rubbish!" Moynihan exploded. "Absolute nonsense, and totally wicked and irresponsible! Of course it was the Fenians. It's exactly the sort of thing they would do. We were close to agreement, and they couldn't let that happen. It's Doyle!"

"We were close to agreement," Jack put in, his voice ringing with certainty. "It was a compromise . . . a real compromise, with both sides conceding something. But maybe one side never meant the conference to last? What could it matter what they gave away, to appear reasonable, if they knew it would never be implemented, in fact never be spoken of outside these walls?"

"The man with the light eyes . . ." Finn said, staring at Pitt. "He wasn't a Fenian?"

"No."

Finn turned to Doyle.

"No." Doyle shook his head. He smiled very faintly. "We want him as much as the police do." He glanced at Pitt. "Although if you repeat that outside Ashworth Hall, I'll call you a liar." He looked at Finn again. "You've been used, Hennessey, and not by your own."

Fergal swung around to O'Day, horror in his face.

Finn snatched himself free of Tellman and launched himself at O'Day, fists flying, and the chair collapsed backwards, throwing them both onto the floor.

Tellman started forward.

Doyle put his hand out and held him back.

"Let him be, lad," he said grimly. "If ever a man deserved beating, it's Carson O'Day." He looked at Pitt, his face filled with disgust. "You can't even get him for instigating the murder of Greville. And if he had not prompted McGinley to try to kill Jack, Lorcan wouldn't have blown himself up. God, it makes me sick!"

"No," Pitt agreed with ironic satisfaction. "But with Hennessey's help, we'll establish the chain of evidence and we'll hang him for conspiracy to murder Denbigh, and that will do." He looked down at O'Day struggling on the floor beneath the burning rage of Finn, a man used and betrayed and now condemned. "I think Mr. Hennessey will make very sure he succeeds in that."

"Oh, he will," Doyle agreed. "God help Ireland."

PHOTO: © JONATHAN HULME

Anne Perry is the bestselling author of two acclaimed series set in Victorian England: the William Monk novels, including *An Echo of Murder* and *Revenge in a Cold River*, and the Charlotte and Thomas Pitt novels, including *Murder on the Serpentine* and *Treachery at Lancaster Gate*. She is also the author of a series of five World War I novels, as well as fifteen holiday novels, most recently *A Christmas Return*, and a historical novel, *The Sheen on the Silk*, set in the Ottoman Empire. Anne Perry lives in Los Angeles and Scotland.

anneperry.co.uk

To inquire about booking Anne Perry for a speaking engagement, please contact the Penguin Random House Speakers Bureau at speakers@penguinrandomhouse.com.

Anne Perry is the bestselling author of two acclaimed series set in Victorian England: the William Monk novels, including *An Echo of Murder* and *Revenge in a Cold River*, and the Charlotte and Thomas Pitt novels, including *Murder on the Serpentine* and *Treachery at Lancaster Gate*. She is also the author of a series of five World War I novels, as well as fifteen holiday novels, most recently *A Christmas Return*, and a historical novel, *The Sheen on the Silk*, set in the Ottoman Empire. Anne Perry lives in Los Angeles and Scotland.

anneperry.co.uk

To inquire about booking Anne Perry for a speaking engagement, please contact the Penguin Random House Speakers Bureau at speakers@penguinrandomhouse.com.